MW00942084

LEGACY
of the ORBS

The AFTERLANDS CONVERGENCE

Book 3

Tim Fox

ISBN: 978-1-092-19295-8

To Galen, Gila and our Family,
Fox, Lehman, Diamond, Keating, Green, Biggs

CONTENTS

PART 1

LAWS OF ICE

CLIFF OF FACES

Cold darkness tunneled its way into Benethan Falka's heart. It grew colder with each uncertain stride he took. He gripped the hyperpulse pistol he'd snatched up from Cloud Commander Thaltra's corpse while dashing into the frozen passage on the heels of his comrades, led by an unknown rescuer. Benethan was dimly aware of the muted weapons fire bleeding through the ice from outside. Terrible temptation distracted him.

Brother Falka could, with one trigger squeeze, complete his original mission and earn redemption in the eyes of the Order. His target, Jaspen Ario, illegitimate daughter of the new Dictorian Consul, hastened forward in the dark not three paces ahead of him.

By killing her, he could secure the prominence of the Quill sect and forever prevent a scandal that would rock the Order to its core. None of the others could stop him, not even the marksman

Sand, whom Benethan would dispatch right before he dealt with treacherous Kemren Trince, the only one who knew his secret.

Yes, with one hyperpulse burst, Benethan could succeed where even the mighty Iron Cloud had failed.

The whole scenario repeated in Benethan's imagination. For the price of a small pile of corpses nobody would miss, the blue sash would be returned to him as well as his position in the Iron Robes. All he had to do—

A sudden explosion of shattered ice crystals rained down into the tunnel on his right. Lances of green flame ignited in the column of daylight now beaming through the new hole. In the same instant, the needle-stricken floor burst like a geyser, pelting him with grit. Out of instinct, Benethan leapt left, slipped on the frozen surface and lost his footing.

"Benethan!" Jaspen spun and reached for him with her only hand.

Beyond her, Kemren also wheeled about. "Hurry!" he said.

Benethan hesitated. He could finish it now. Finish *them* now, even if not quite in the sequence he'd envisioned.

Jaspen grabbed him by the collar, planted her thumbless mitten on the wall for purchase and hoisted him to his feet with surprising strength.

"Come on, Monk!" She whipped back around and almost collided with Kemren who was slower to resume his flight.

Benethan staggered forward behind them, his eyes fixed on Jaspen's stump, his mind replaying the last time he'd pulled the trigger on her. How he'd wished for a second chance. In a flood of understanding that froze him, he realized the Maker had now given it to him. But it was not the chance he had been imagining.

The gun suddenly felt very heavy in Benethan's hand. Too heavy to lift. Too heavy to hold.

More bursts of blasted ice resounded though the cavern behind him, the nearest loosing minor blizzards.

Benethan felt an almost overpowering urge to throw down the gun and it leave as he'd found it, but the folly of abandoning so powerful a weapon won out and he shoved it inside his parka instead. Then he ran.

He could see light ahead, around the next bend. When he turned the corner, he found the Pride stalled in front of him. The tunnel was wider here and they crouched, three on either side, pressed against the walls as if protected from the rain of death going on above.

At the head of the motionless team, their would-be rescuer clawed at the debris from a fresh collapse. The shaft of light pouring in through a ragged gap above the pile revealed a small figure dressed in a hooded parka, leggings, and boots unlike any Benethan had seen before.

Benethan's appraisal of their rescuer was cut short when, outside, the firing promptly ceased. He and the others waited with building unease as the silence stretched. Then came the rhythmic crunch of footfalls. Step by step, they grew louder.

Wolfe grabbed the figure and pulled him back deeper into the tunnel. An instant later, a shadow passed across the gap and stopped, cutting off most of the light. Next, the silhouette of a face descended to fill the small jagged frame.

The square outline of a hyperpulse pistol rose up at the man's chin. With a click, a thin beam of light shone into the tunnel. It emanated from front of the pistol and illuminated a small circle of cavern floor.

As the light began to pan their way, Benethan quietly slipped his hand into his parka to retrieve the pistol. At the same time, he could see the barrel of Sand's flintlock rising. Undoubtedly, this prospective assailant would be eliminated before he killed them, but it would be a short lived victory for it would reveal their position to his comrades who would reduce the cavern and all who hid within it to heaps of shredded flesh buried beneath a mound of powdered ice.

Not two arm-lengths from where Sable crouched, the light came to a sudden halt. Centered in its beam, Benethan could see a bootprint.

"Br—" the monk started to yell. A patter of sharp smacks coincided with the failure of his voice. Then the distant roar of a hyperpulse volley rolled in to fill the emptiness where his words should have been. His light wavered and he slumped sideways, his shadow sliding away from the hole as his body toppled out of sight.

Through the opening, startled cries rose, interspersed with renewed weapons fire, both loud and soft.

"Fall back!" roared a distant voice. "Find cover!"

Benethan and the others glanced at one another in bewilderment.

"The monks are under attack," said Sand.

"From who?" asked Sable.

"An equal in arms it would seem," said Wolfe. "But with the advantage of higher ground."

"Up on the ice?" asked Rawl.

Wolfe nodded, spun their rescuer around and shoved him back into the light.

Despite the drawn hood, the figure's face could be seen clearly: a boy's, made monstrous by a tattooed skull. His wide blue eyes looked out through ink-darkened sockets.

Benethan heard Geleb Rawl suck in a sharp breath. "Thrack," he growled and raised his musket to point it at the figure. Wolfe and Sand whipped up their weapons. A tiny red light appeared in the middle of the figure's chest.

"No!" Sable leapt between them, arms raised. "He saved us!"

"Trapped us more like," said Rawl, whose gun did not move.

Wolfe and Sand declined theirs just enough to remove Sable from their lines of sight. "Step aside," said Wolfe.

The scaler stood her ground.

Outside, a final hyperpulse discharge rent the bitter air. Then the world fell silent again. Two stand-offs commenced. Benethan felt the weight of the weapon pressed against his heart. No, he corrected himself, the stand-offs numbered three. And the Pride hung in the balance.

MOUNTAIN OF FACES

With forced calm, Jaio reaches up and lowers his hood. He hopes the Fane before him cannot hear the hammering of his heart. "I—" he begins, and gets no further.

The old one with the grizzled beard and tired, hate-filled eyes, surges toward him. "Silence, you murdering abomination!" he hisses and tries to push past the woman who stands between him and the subject of his loathing. In a flash, she slashes out with a dagger, forcing the man back.

"Sable," growls the huge figure with the triangular tiger fur hat and immense twin-barreled weapon. "He is a Thrack."

Sable merely settles into a defensive stance, dagger poised to strike.

Jaio has no idea why she has sprung to his aid, but he is sure if she hadn't he would already be dead. Now to seize this chance she has given him. "Kill me if you must," he hears himself say in the

Dead Tongue, "but please, first listen to the message I have to share."

Looks of startled surprise pass between the people before him.

"How is it that you speak our language?" The unexpected, almost casual, question comes from a non-descript man standing at the rear of the group.

"Quiet, Monk!" the old one growls. "We don't banter with Thracks, we just—"

The giant places a hand on the old one's shoulder. "Let him answer, Rawl."

Enraged, Rawl spins on the giant, "Let him— can't believe this. Have you all gone mad?" "That," he jabs the barrel of his gun toward Jaio, "is a monster."

"*He*," says another woman near the rear, "is a boy."

"Boy Thrack. Man Thrack. What's the difference? They are all savages who kill without mercy."

"If I'm not mistaken," says the monk. "We're still alive, thanks to him. And he is at *our* mercy."

"But…" Rawl splutters, though try as he might, additional words fail to come.

"But," finishes the monk, "he is unlike any Thrack I've ever heard of. Articulate and unarmed. Perhaps, we should not be so hasty in dispatching him. Perhaps, we might even benefit from what he has to say."

"Agreed," says the giant.

"Wolfe, no," Rawl moans, his final plea fading as the barrel of his weapon sinks.

In response, Sable's stance relaxes, but she remains where she is.

"Answer the question, boy," growls Wolfe, his voice deep and commanding.

"My name is Jaio."

Wolfe leans closer, all hard menace. "Answer the question."

"My mentor taught me the language of the Ancients, the language you also speak."

"We speak Anthemari," says Rawl. "More likely you tore the teaching from some helpless captive before you slit his throat."

The monk clears his own throat. "He speaks the truth, Rawl. The Order decided long ago to make the language of the late Antiquitic Age the common tongue of Anthemar. They saw it as one more way to help restore the glory of the times before the ice."

Wolfe holds Jaio's gaze. "Why are you here?" he asks.

"I bring a warning," says Jaio. "A…faction of the Oroken is planning the destruction of Anthemar."

"Pah!" blurts Rawl. "You lot still use bows and arrows."

"Those weren't bows and arrows that just drove back Acris and his Daggers," says a fourth man, who has to this point remained silent.

Wolfe nods. "I thought it was Thrack policy to reject the technologies of the past and destroy them at every chance," he says, though his words are intoned as a question.

A knot of discomfort cinches in Jaio's gut. He considers keeping the secret, but he knows the success of his mission depends on earning the trust of these people. And with this thought, a sudden dread awareness floods him. He now understands Lash's reluctance to deliver him to the Fane. Jaio's knowledge could be used to help them defeat the Ghosts thereby clearing the way for an invasion of the Homeland Steppe. Rather than stopping Taika's vision, Jaio could just as easily be the instrument of its unfolding. *What have I done?*

Wolfe simply watches, as if reading Jaio's inner struggle like a book. The big man will know a lie. *There is no turning back now,* thinks Jaio.

"We only destroy enough of what we find to make you believe that," he says. "Though," he hastens to add, "the attack on the monks surprised me as much as you. I did not know my companions possessed any teeth."

"Teeth?" asks Wolfe.

"It is our word for the ancient weaponry."

"Well, obviously they do," says the man with the long rifle and green scarf wrapped about his head to form a hat. "And they know how to bite."

"Even so, Sand" says Wolfe, "this faction would need more teeth than likely exist to affect the destruction of Anthemar. After all, I can think of no better way to unite the nine Protectorates than a Thrack invasion. And united, we would be a formidable force of opposition indeed."

"I do not know how Thorne plans to do it," says Jaio. "But he is confident he can. And I believe him."

"Thorne?" asks Wolfe. "Who is this Thorne?" Jaio can hear a new tension in the big man's voice and wonders if he has just made a grave mistake. *I will need to proceed with greater care.*

"He is a…" Jaio is not sure what to say. These Fane undoubtedly know nothing of Orols. "He is one of our leaders, a man with great technical skill and deep knowledge of the Fane."

"The Fane?"

The knot in Jaio's stomach cinches tighter. *So much for proceeding with greater care.* "In the way you call us Thracks, we call you Fane."

"What does that mean?" rumbles Rawl.

"It means those who profane all that is good, whole and sacred."

The leather of Rawl's mittens creaks as his grip tightens on his gun.

"How does Thorne have this deep knowledge of us?" asks Wolfe.

"He was Fane."

Wolfe nods a slow nod. It conveys no surprise, only confirmation of an opinion already held. "So, Eukon Thorne, that is what became of you," he says to nobody in particular.

"Yes," says Jaio. "Eukon. That's his first name. I heard his wife say it."

"His wife?" Wolfe's thick eyebrows rise. This does surprise him.

"Sorry," says the monk in back. "Who is Eukon Thorne?"

Wolfe pushes up the tip of his triangular hat. "Eukon Thorne is the mind behind Maxamantan power. That is, until about twenty years ago when his ambition put the fear of an overthrow into paranoid old Salazriole who banished him to the Snowsea and, in theory, to a quick death by Thrack, or ice."

"Oroken warriors did find him," says Jaio. "And they were going to kill him, but he proved valuable. So he was spared. By using his knowledge, he quickly rose to prominence and at the same time came to appreciate our ways."

"Appreciate living like a savage?" says Rawl. "He's gone mad more like."

"And now, mad, savage, or both, he wants revenge," says Wolfe.

"Perhaps, partly," says Jaio. "The way I heard it, he mostly wants to protect his new life. And he sees the threat the Fane represent. So he has made a weapon to destroy you."

"Why are you telling us this, boy?" growls Rawl. "Isn't that what you Thracks have always wanted, our destruction?"

"Some among us feel that way. But I am not one of them."

"Well, that's a comfort," says Rawl. "A crazy Thrack boy wants to help us poor helpless Fane."

"Enough Rawl," snaps Wolfe. "For reasons we have yet to understand, Jaio has brought us this dire news. I hear no deception in his words. Nor do I see it on his face. And, from my own experience, too much of what he says rings true."

Rawl grunts. "Even if some Maxamantan exile is living with the savages, how much of a threat could he be?"

"If he were anyone else, I'd say no threat at all. But Eukon Thorne…If he is intent on the destruction of Anthemar, he will stop at nothing until it is done."

"And you think he has the means?" asks green scarf Sand.

Wolfe turns to Jaio. "Did you yourself hear Thorne make this claim?"

"Not directly, but from a man whose word I trust."

"Then yes, Sand. I think Thorne has the means."

"I do know a part of his plan," says Jaio. "But it makes no sense."

"What is it?"

"He intends to reveal a large weapons cache to a lord called Maxamant in the northern Chamber Mountains."

"The Chamber Mountains?" asks the man whose name Jaio has not yet heard.

Jaio thinks back to a lesson with Gilinath, on the subject of Fane place names. "You call them the Vaultiten Mountains."

"I thought as much."

"Does that mean something to you, Kemren?" asks Wolfe.

"Before leaving Anchoresk, I learned of a massive cache thought to exist somewhere in the northern reaches of the Vaultitens. The Order fears it has already been found."

"By Salazriole Maxamant," says Wolfe.

"Or by the Oroken," says Kemren.

Wolfe's brow furrows. "Yet, somehow both scenarios favor Thorne. The question is how?"

Rawl grunts and winces at Wolfe. "You sound as if you expect us to figure it out."

Wolfe's cold steely gaze sets the old man back a step. "If not us, then who?"

Jaio can't quite believe he's heard correctly.

These people are supposed to take him into Anthemar. At least, that is how he has interpreted his dream until this moment. But now, he realizes the Mountain of Faces is as far into Anthemar as his dream took him. Maybe, he has come to guide these people up onto the Ice. To help stop Thorne. Jaio's certain about one thing. His words of peace will mean nothing until they do.

"Right," says Rawl. "Have you forgotten? We're trapped in a dead-end ice tunnel, pinned down by a band of homicidal monks wielding relic ordinance and bent on our annihilation. But let's just suppose we somehow avoid that fate, there's the present reality of our status as a Kestian Ice Watch team. We live at the margins of everything, hardly the place to gain the attention of those who might actually be able to stop this Thorne from wiping us all out."

"And who do you suppose might be better able than us to ascertain what Thorne plans to do and stop him?"

"I don't know," says Rawl. "The warrior monks of the Order."

"You mean, the ones out there trying to kill us," says Sand.

"The elite guards from one of the Protectorates then. Men with training for this sort of thing."

"How do we contact them, Rawl? How do we convince them? Even if we somehow do both, how long will it take them to mobilize and march to the Snowsea to begin their hunt for a man thought dead, a man nobody in Anthemar has seen for twenty years?" Wolfe pauses, but goes on before Rawl can answer. "Truly, Geleb, if you can think of anyone in a better position than us, I'm listening."

Jaio can almost see Rawl's mind struggling to come up with an alternative. Finally, his shoulders sag in defeat. "I can't. But we don't even know where Thorne is."

"I do," says Jaio.

"And I suppose you can take us to him?"

"With the help of my companions on the Ice, yes."

"Presuming we can get up there."

"Leave that to me," says Sable.

Wolfe nods. "Very good."

"Whoa!" rumbles Rawl. "I didn't sign up for this. Feeding a mob of scavengers picking at bygone bones is one thing. Venturing onto the Snowsea to help some prepubescent Thrack hunt a madman with the power to destroy Anthemar...that wasn't in the contract."

"You're free to go," says Wolfe.

"Free to...both ends of this tunnel have collapsed!"

"A problem we must deal with first." Wolfe sweeps his gaze over the rest of the group. "Once we do, the same applies to all of you. I am committed to helping Jaio find and stop Thorne. The rest of you must choose your own way."

Sable takes a step forward and nods. Sand shoulders his gun and does the same. Then, much to Jaio's surprise, another person also steps forward. Jaio can see her clearly for the first time. Something about her strikes him as familiar.

The man called Kemren falls in at her side. The monk is next, leaving only Rawl undecided. Dismay is written on his weathered face. Then his eyes narrow and cast about the group. "You lot'll starve without me."

A tiny smile tugs at the corners of Wolfe's mouth. "The Pride hunts on," he says.

"So," says Sand. "What's the plan?"

"Wait," says the woman near the rear. Her single word conveys a dozen emotions, anticipation foremost among them. She turns to the man beside her. "Please, Kem. My father..."

Jaio sees the man flash the sparest glance at the monk. In it, there is unmistakable fear. The monk's eyes are blank. No, somehow they are even more vacant than blank. Jaio sees a deep hollowness. Then the man looks back into the woman's eyes. Both his fear and the monk's hollowness are gone almost as quickly as they appeared.

"Jaspen," says the man. "Your father is Dalsen

Ario."

Everyone in the cavern except the monk and Jaio, to whom the name means nothing, shifts uneasily at this revelation.

Jaspen's face is a portrait of dismay. "The Tributan Consul?"

"Actually, he's the Dictorian Consul now. That is why you have been hunted. If word of your existence spread, the scandal could throw not just the Order but all of Anthemar into chaos."

"Holiness makes a hypocrite," rumbles Rawl.

"And you, Kem?" she says, her voice barely above a whisper. "Are you...?"

"A monk? Yes, I trained as an Iron Robe under your father. He sent me to Brink to watch over you. To protect you. I thought I'd failed when I was captured and heard you were dead. Then Ario came to me in the dungeon and told me that you lived. Again, he entrusted me with your protection and this time provided help, a trio of Mesoric warriors." He looks over to Sable.

"Gendut, Chetchut and Clungarto," she breathes.

Kemren nods. "I had no idea."

Sable lowers her head and Kemren returns his eyes to Jaspen's. "The rest of the story you know. And now I'm here, with you."

"A monk?"

"And not a very good one, I fear. For it seems,

I've fallen in love."

At this, the other monk does shift uneasily. Nobody but Jaio appears to notice. They are all too focused on the couple. The pair wraps their arms around each other and settles into a deep embrace.

Only then does Jaio see the mitten at the end of Jaspen's right arm, an arm that is clearly shorter than the left. The mitten has no thumb.

A sudden image of Orol Taika bursts into Jaio's mind. She is dying at the base of the Ghostway. He remembers it as if he were still there.

"Is the orb safe?" she asked as she pointed her stump at his chest.

Jaio remembers feeling the orb's weight pulling at his neck. "Yes, Orol," he said.

"Good," she replied. "You must safeguard it until you find me again."

"But how can I do that? I won't be coming back."

"Out there, Orol." She jabbed her stump toward the ice. "Look for me out there."

The vision fades and Jaio again finds himself in the ice tunnel with the seven people from his dream, one of whom he's sure is Taika. Only, she doesn't appear to remember him.

Kemren and Jaspen separate and turn to face the others. Jaio can't stop himself from staring at her.

"Welcome to the Pride, Kemren," says Wolfe.

"So, we're double-monked," says Sand with a grin.

"And Thracked," grumbles Rawl. "But we're none the freer for it."

"Freedom," says Wolfe. "Yes, that must be our primary focus now. Thanks to our...protectors up on the Ice, I think we should be safe here until nightfall, at which point we'll widen that gap," he nods up to the ceiling, "and slip out."

"I'm afraid darkness will not be our ally, Tactan," says the far monk.

"Why not, Benethan?"

"I believe the Iron Cloud possessed relic devices capable of allowing vision in the dark. If Acris's men searched the bodies before the Oroken attacked..." the monk leaves the rest unsaid.

Wolfe considers the monk for a moment then turns to Jaio. "Do your friends up top have such devices?"

"I don't know. But we would be unwise to assume they do."

"Then we'd better dig fast," says Wolfe. "We need to break through the blockage before the light fails and Acris resumes his hunt."

3

CLIFF OF FACES

Sable's arms ached from moving ice chunks. As the last person in the bucket line, she had the added toil of tossing the fragments of collapsed roof as far back as possible to make room for more. Between tosses, she watched the Thrack boy, Jaio, who worked side by side with Wolfe and Sand up front, digging their way forward bit by bit.

And what she noticed in those moments of observation aroused an unexpected emotion: jealousy. The boy cast frequent glances at Jaspen. The one-handed thawrunner didn't appear to notice. She seemed understandably lost in thought as she kept watch on the ceiling gap, her hand resting absently on the butt of the cap and ball pistol tucked in her belt.

Sable tried to ignore the feeling and instead attempted to imagine what the boy would look like without his tattoos. She would never know.

He would wear his skeletal visage for the rest of his life. Why did Thracks do it? To scare their enemies?

That was only a small part of why her clansmen wore the blue paint. And she suspected, like the paint, the tattoos also held deeper significance. What might it be? Maybe, if they survived this ordeal, she'd have the chance to ask.

Up at the front, Wolfe snapped a silencing fist into the air and everybody froze. Muted thumps and scrapes carried through the ice directly ahead.

"Somebody's digging our way," whispered Sand.

"Kem," said Wolfe. "Take Sand's place and Sand, cover our progress. Be ready for whoever's on the other side."

The spotter swapped places with Kemren and retrieved his long gun. He trained it on the jumble in front of Wolfe, Kem and the boy, Jaio. "Ready."

Digging resumed.

Soon, even the noise made by their work failed to drown out the sounds of excavation emanating from the ice before them. When breakthrough seemed imminent, Wolfe, Kem and Jaio stopped and stepped back. The tactan took up his gun as did Rawl and they joined Sand in covering the ice. Sand clicked on the red beam while Jaspen slipped off her mitten and slid the pistol from her belt.

Sable's hand went to her dagger.

Everyone stood frozen, watching, waiting. A tiny avalanche of crystals spilled down to the floor. A moment later, a mittened fist punched through sending a glassy spray into the cavern.

The fist withdrew and a woman called out, speaking an unfamiliar language. Sable recognized the final word. Jaio.

The boy responded in the same strange tongue and dashed to the hole to help open it wider. The Pride didn't move. Even Wolfe seemed uncertain about what to do. An unknown number of Thracks were digging toward them. Thracks who had stutterguns, and perhaps other unpleasant surprises. The tide seemed on the verge of turning.

Instead, when the passageway cleared, Sable and the others found themselves facing two young women, both bearing skeletal facial tattoos like Jaio's and clad in similar attire. Neither appeared to be armed except for bone-handled knives in leather sheathes lashed to their belts.

In the eyes of the more robust and chiseled woman, Sable saw defiance. The other's wide-eyed gaze conveyed an inexplicable eagerness as she faced the barrels aimed at her and her companion. The eager one cast an inquisitive, even anticipatory, glance at Jaio.

The boy spun and raised his hands before the Pride in a gesture of placation. "These are friends," he said. "Syree." He gestured to the fierce one then turned to the other. "And Galees."

"Girl Thracks?" said Rawl. "What's next?"

The one called Syree narrowed her eyes at the old provisioner. "Not Thracks. Oroken," she said in sharply accented Anthemari.

Galees took a tentative step forward. "We here to help you...to help you..." Her brow furrowed as she sought the right word. Finally, she shook her head and pointed at the opening behind her.

Syree nodded. "Escape. Then we lead way around enemies so you go with Jaio."

Jaio spoke a few words to her in Oroken. Her eyes widened with surprise. She shook her head and began to protest, but the boy merely slipped his hands free from his mittens and raised them before her, backs up. Sable tracked Syree's gaze down and, on the hand visible from her vantage, could see tattooed dots darkening the second knuckle of each finger. Syree fell silent and nodded. Then she looked up and swept her gaze over the Pride.

"We bring you with us."

Galees beamed and nodded.

Wolfe lowered his gun, which prompted Sable and the others to relax. Sand switched off the red beam.

Wolfe considered Syree then Galees and finally, Jaio. "This wasn't the original plan, was it?"

"No."

"You wanted us to take you into Anthemar."

Jaio nodded.

"Why?"

"To find a way for us to be at peace, without blood."

"Too late for that," said Rawl. "By, oh, a few centuries."

"Why now?" Wolfe continued. "Why you? And who did you suppose would listen?"

"The Ice is melting," said the boy. "Faster every round. And despite the…actions of our defenders who live atop it, the Ice has been our greatest protection against the Fane. So, the other Orols decided—"

"Orols?" asked Wolfe.

"Oroken elders. Wisdom keepers. We hold the knowledge of the Ancients."

"We? Does that mean you are one of these Orols?"

"Yes."

"You Thracks must not live very long," said Rawl.

"Most Orols are what you would expect," said Jaio. "Graying; informed by the experience of many years. I am…different."

"Why?"

"I'm actually not sure. I was only an

apprentice. But the eldest of the Orols appointed this task to me."

As Jaio spoke these words, Sable saw his gaze flit to Jaspen for an instant before returning to Wolfe.

"When I accepted," Jaio went on, "the elder elevated my status to full Orol despite my youth. It was the only way to give me enough standing among my people to secure their help getting me here."

"And no doubt," interjected Rawl, "sending a pup served to keep the vast knowledge of an old Orol from falling into our hands. Less to lose."

Sable felt her anger stir, and was surprised to see the boy smile. "That may be," he said. "They not only have vast knowledge. They have wisdom too."

Rawl harrumphed.

"That answers my first two questions," said Wolfe. "But not the third. Who in Anthemar did you think would listen to you?"

A stretched silence followed these words. Jaio wished he had the orb. He wished he had the *Companta*. But both were gone. He had only his words. He glanced from face to face then settled his gaze on Wolfe again. "You," he said. "Though I didn't know it until a few moments ago."

"When we learned of Thorne and committed to stopping him?"

"Yes," said Jaio. "Then I realized my mission was not to go into Anthemar, but to bring to the Ice those who would help defeat Thorne."

"Us," said Sand.

Jaio nodded.

"Suppose we succeed," said Benethan. "Suppose we stop Thorne from destroying Anthemar. Even then, I do not believe there is enough gratitude in the world sufficient to bring this peace you desire. Too deep and universal is Anthemari hatred of the Thracks."

"I believed the same about Oroken hatred of the Fane when I began my journey," said Jaio. "But now I think there may be incentives more potent than hatred. Incentives for peace."

"Sure," Rawl grunted. "And one day, old snowtip'll let us pet 'im like a lap cat."

"Are we not this very moment Thrack and Fane using words instead of weapons?" asked Jaio.

"Indeed, we are," said Wolfe, "thanks only to Sable who safeguarded you long enough for us to learn of our shared knowledge of Thorne and the threat he represents. However, the greater peace you imagine is something else entirely and will remain no more than supposition until Thorne has been dealt with. If we stay focused on the task at hand, we may have another chance to revisit the subject. But for now, escape must be our goal."

Wolfe shouldered his gun. "Gather your gear. We're leaving."

Sable and the others hastened to retrieve their packs, which they'd lined against the cavern wall while they worked. Sable hoisted hers on and turned to make her way toward the newly excavated hole only to find Wolfe standing before her, hard eyes looking into hers. She knew his question without him having to ask it.

"Killing our rescuer would have been wrong," she said, though, in honesty, she'd intervened for another reason. Deep inside, the residue of a memory nagged at her. She felt certain now it came from a forgotten dream about this boy. But she dared not use that as her excuse.

"Any other Thrack and we might all be dead. Remember that the next time you pull your blade on one of your own."

"But he sav—"

Wolfe cut her off with a slight shake of his head. "The team comes first, Scaler. Whatever lies ahead, we'll need each other if we're to have any hope of living through it."

"Understood, Tactan." Sable had to force herself not to look down. She didn't think she'd ever met a man so imposing. He belonged at the head of an army, not leading a handful of outcasts at the farthest edge of nowhere.

"Good." He glanced around.

Sable welcomed the break in eye contact and did the same. The others were still readying themselves and the Oroken were huddled by the exit immersed in an intense discussion. Then Wolfe turned back to her.

"I want you to follow the Oroken out," he said. "Read the tracks they left on their way here. Make sure the story they tell matches the story their tracks tell." He nodded to the three figures who now watched the Pride through skulls of ink. "And keep an eye out for anything else unusual."

Sable nodded and made her way to the Oroken. The boy, Jaio, saw her coming and smiled. What an odd smile it was, white teeth showing within a black maw of death. At once, his face struck her as both beautiful and terrible. Stepping up close and not looking away took all her will.

"Thank you...Sable. That is your name, right?" said Jaio.

She nodded.

"I'm in your debt for saving me." His voice conveyed genuine sincerity and inexplicable maturity. How, Sable wondered, could the savages of the Snowsea have produced a person such as this?

She nodded again and felt the gazes of the other two, one tight-lipped and cold, the other wary, but open and curious. The only teeth they showed were dyed into their skin.

"All right," said Wolfe. "We're ready." He looked at the boy. "Lead on, Jaio."

Jaio started toward the hole, but the fierce woman, Syree, blocked him with an arm and took the lead. Jaio started to protest, but a look silenced him and he relented. Galees followed him and Sable set off on Galees's heels. Sand fell in behind her.

The passage through the ice wove, climbed and dropped. In some places, they could stand and in others they had to remove their packs and crawl. At times, they encountered sections where daylight leaked, weak and blue, through thin ice. In the dim glow, Sable could see by the markings that the tunnel had been cleared by hand. The invisible monks must have been there some time, working on their trap and waiting for their prey like Sister Spider in her web.

Finally, daylight appeared ahead. To pass through the exit, Sable had to remove her pack yet again and shuffle out on all fours. By the time she emerged, Jaio stood waiting and offered her a hand up. Before she could think better of it, she took it and he hauled her to her feet. He was strong for his size and despite the mittens, she could have sworn she felt the heat of his grip. Her cheeks warmed and she quickly let go to get out of the way for Sand.

The two women, Syree and Galees, stood guard, facing opposite directions, looking down the narrow trench where the tunnel emerged at the base of the Cliff of Faces. The women both gripped elegant recurved bows carved of a rosy umber wood and now wore packs and quivers of arrows.

Sand emerged next and declined Jaio's offered hand. He readied his long gun as he stood and took up a covering position, back against the cliff face, eyes high to watch along the top of the trench.

Sable turned her attention downward and performed a quick reading of the signs as the others appeared from out of the darkness beneath the ice. She saw nothing to arouse concern: three sets of tracks, Jaio's overlaid by those of the two women all heading along the trench toward the ice cavern from the west. Beneath these prints, faint impressions remained of the boots worn by men who walked among the living no more.

Then she saw the drag marks, two pairs headed east. They gouged through a churn of many prints. The subtle differences in print size and tread pattern revealed at least six different people, maybe more. Her eyes followed their sign up the slight incline of the trench to the point where it dropped away out of sight.

"This way," said fierce Syree.

Sable glanced back. Everybody now stood assembled outside the hole and, except for Sand and Galees, faced west. Syree had already begun moving away, lithe like a cat.

"Wait," said Sable. "There's an unfinished story here."

All heads turned toward her.

"Six to ten walkers dragging two others, unconscious or dead, that way." She pointed east.

"How long ago?" asked Wolfe.

"Over a week."

"The other team?" said Sand. "The one whose tracks we saw on our way in."

"They dead by now," said Syree. "We must go so don't join them."

"I need to keep reading," said Sable.

Syree opened her mouth to protest, but Jaio spoke first. "Read on, Sable."

Syree clenched her teeth and relented with a terse nod.

Sable glanced at Wolfe, who also nodded. Before further objections could be raised, she spun and gave her attention back to the telling of the tale. The others followed in tense silence.

Sable ducked low as she approached the break and peeked over. The trench continued to run along the base of the cliff. It dropped at a slight angle to a trough some two hundred feet away. On the other side of the trough the trench continued about a hundred additional feet before being engulfed beneath the debris of a more recent ice fall.

Even from Sable's distant vantage, she could see that the drag marks did not continue beyond the trough. They veered south at the bottom and disappeared as if swallowed by solid stone.

For several moments, Sable waited and watched for movement. She felt one of the others slide into the cliff-side gap next to her.

"What do you see?" asked Sand.

"I'm not sure. The trail ends down there, but makes no sense. I will go take a look."

"I'll cover you from here. Signal when you're ready for us to follow."

Sable didn't reply. She simply slipped over the crest and began her descent. At first, the story unfolding before her offered no surprises. Not until she neared the trough did a new chapter open.

What, from a distance, had appeared as solid stone yielded a shadow. The darkness opened wider with each step she took until she found herself at the edge of a steep stone ramp angling down into a cavern carved out from beneath the base of the cliff. The black opening stood two heads high and four wide. Most of it was filled with the buckled remains of a massive door made of scorched, pitted metal. It had been bent inward by an explosive force of incredible power. Yet, the blast had only managed to create a gap at the bottom large enough for one person to crawl through at a time.

The drag marks led to the gap and vanished into the darkness beyond. They were, at the point of entry, almost totally obscured by knee-scuffs and boot-toe prints, all headed out.

Sable tore her gaze from the scene at the mangled door and analyzed every track on the ramp. None were fresh. Even so, she waited and listened for many long moments before venturing down. At the bottom, on the threshold of the unknown, she removed her pack and opened it to retrieve a grease lamp and flint striker.

The thudding of fast footfalls grew behind her as the others ran down from the west. In a moment, they were gathered on the ramp behind her.

"I was hoping for signal a little less disconcerting than your disappearance," said Sand.

Sable ignored him and lit her lamp. She didn't wait for the others to prepare theirs before crawling through.

On the other side, she stood while her eyes adjusted to the weak light. The sight nearly stopped her heart.

A massive gun barrel pointed straight at her

head.

She dropped the lamp, dove left into a roll and came up dagger in hand.

"Sable!" Sand yelled from outside.

From her new position, she now saw that the gun protruded from a massive vehicle nearly twice her height. It looked both boxy and sleek at the same time and rested on seven wheels encircled in metal tracks composed of many interconnected segments. Two additional wheels, one in front and one in back, floated in the air, the latter rimmed with frightening teeth. Crystalline frost and dust coated every surface.

The light from the opening suddenly dimmed as Sand surged through, rifle first. The little red light danced on the armored surface of the ancient, dead machine.

"Clear," he yelled and switched off the beam.

Sable took a steadying breath and sheathed her dagger. When she looked at Sand who was creeping toward the vehicle as if it might suddenly roar to life, her eyes caught the silhouettes of boot soles lined up in a row on the other side of the doorway.

"Sand," she whispered as she scooped up her lamp and relit it. She and the spotter moved toward the bodies as the rest of their party crawled into the chamber.

Soon, they all stood side by side looking down

at eight corpses clad in muddy, tattered parkas. Strips of filthy cloth, apparently torn from their undergarments, had been used as wraps to hold their mittens together. And only two of the bodies still wore the shredded remnants of their identifying shoulder sashes.

"Cortegrans," said Wolfe.

"What happened to them?" asked Jaspen.

Sable had seen her clansmen return from the Maxamantan mines wearing clothes in a similar state. "Who do you think dug the ice tunnels for the monks?" she said.

"The Cloud used them as workers?" asked Jaspen.

"Until they'd served their purpose," said Wolfe.

"Monsters," whispered Jaspen.

"Men," said Rawl. "Just men. Going where the arrogance of a higher calling too often leads."

"Where's that?" asked Benethan, his tone sharp-edged.

"Low." The old tiger hunter let the word seep into the cold, stale silence for a moment then turned away from the corpses and heaved off his pack with a grunt. "Now, we're going to need more light if we're to see what else we've found."

"Sand," said Wolfe. "Keep watch here while we try to determine the extent of this cache."

The tactan's words drew Sable's attention

away from the dead Ice Watch team and back to her surroundings. She had almost forgotten the main reason they were there. To find ancient relic caches.

Beside her, Jaio and the other two Oroken were, like the Pride, extracting grease lamps from their packs.

A low wet growl rose from somewhere in the darkness.

Weapons flew up and lamps were thrust high. At the farthest edge of the flickering flame's reach, Sable glimpsed a pair of glowing green dots.

"Out there," she said and pointed. An instant later, a jet of breath enveloped the dots. By the time the vapor cleared, they were gone.

Jaio stepped up beside her. She glanced over and saw his eyes lit by flame, dancing within their ink-darkened sockets. He smiled and whispered. "Taiga." The sight sent a chill through her.

"Sable," called Wolfe. "Did you by chance miss a set of prints?"

She tore her eyes away from the boy and looked instinctually to the floor. Nothing but boot prints. "No, Tactan. I saw no cat sign. There must be another way in."

"Sand," said Wolfe. "Change of plans. You're with us. We all stick close together from now on. Numbers are our best defense against this hunter."

MOUNTAIN OF FACES

Jaio strains to see deeper into the blackness, to confirm with his eyes what in his heart he already knows. Taiga, the tiger, is here.

"Circle tight," says Wolfe. "Once we're in formation, we move straight in. Sable, take point. Watch for tracks."

The small, quiet woman with the fur-lined cloak steps forward. Jaio falls in beside her. She casts him a wary glance, but says nothing.

"All right," says Wolfe. "Let's move."

Everyone but Wolfe, Sand and Rawl hold grease lamps. They hold their guns. All together, the ten of them advance as one.

"What is this thing?" whispers Sand with a nod to the massive armored vehicle to their right. "Some kind of steam carriage?"

"It is like one of the Order's steam carriages, yes," says the monk, Benethan. "But it used a volatile liquid for fuel instead coal or cordwood.

We've never discovered any to determine its exact composition, but all the other vehicles found from this era have reservoirs leading to their engines. So, we know—"

"Thank you, Benethan," says Wolfe.

The monk falls silent.

Jaio wants him to continue. What more does this representative from the knowledge keepers of Anthemar know? Or more precisely, what more doesn't he know? One thing is certain. At least in this instance, Jaio knows more. The question is does he risk sharing his knowledge? Why else would Taika have sent an Orol, if not for this?

"It was called a tank," he says. "And the fuel it used was called petroleum, a derivative of oil. The Ancients mined it from deep beneath the earth. By the time the Ice took hold, most of it was gone."

"How do you know this?" asked Benethan.

"My mentor taught me much about the Ancients."

"How then does your mentor know this?"

"We Oroken have been hunting the margins of the Ice since before the Fane even came into existence. And, like you, we too strive to learn from what we find."

"Then why do you not make use of what you learn?" A tone of exasperation colors the monk's words.

"Later, Benethan," says Wolfe. "We need to keep moving, quietly."

"Of course," says the monk.

The group continues forward past five more tanks lined up behind the first. On the other side of the frightening vehicles, massive buttressed support pillars stand at evenly-spaced intervals. Rays of girders spread from the top of each and interlock some fifteen feet overhead creating a metallic canopy above which spread the untold tonnage of the Mountain of Faces.

Beyond the pillars sits another row of six tanks facing another door, followed by more pillars and more tanks. At that distance, not enough light remains for Jaio to see, but in his mind's eye, the scene repeats forever. The same is true to his left, except for an area at the edge of vision where several pillars have failed and a massive heap of stone buries at least three tanks. Their flattened remains jut at odd angles from the beneath the mound. Against the mountain, they resisted with all the strength of a sparrow's egg underfoot.

The group passes the last adjacent tank and arrives at the first truck in an even longer line. The trucks all sit on wheels of metal. Small piles of black powder and rust flakes partially bury each wheel. And like the tanks, the frost build-up of fourteen thousand rounds sparkles in the lamplight.

Then come the skeletons of rectangular tents, set up in rows behind the trucks. Empty cot frames line what would once have been their interior walls. A few are overturned.

Solitary boxes, like the Orol's relic storage chests, sit at the foot of each cot frame. The lids of most are open.

"There was a whole army in here," whispers Sand.

"But no bones," adds Rawl.

"It's like they just vanished," says Jaspen.

"Look," says Sand. "Over there." He points with his long rifle.

Jaio and the others follow the aim of his barrel to a rack attached to the pillar. Standing side by side within it are dozens of hyperpulse rifles. A thick, riveted crossbar mounted to the rack locks the weapons in place. At one end of the crossbar, Jaio sees a keyhole.

"Jackpot," says Rawl.

"If we can unlock the bar and find ammunition and propellant," says Wolfe.

"This is what they were looking for," says Kemren in a tone of sudden understanding.

All eyes turn toward him.

"Explain," says Wolfe.

"Back in the Adminithedral, not only did I learn about the cache in the mountains, I learned about another one they were trying to locate along the Snowsea front. But they didn't have the coordinates, so its exact position remained a mystery."

Wolfe nods and looks toward Benethan. "Let me see our map." He slings his gun over his shoulder and sheds his mittens.

The monk reaches inside his parka and withdraws a worn, leather-bound book. He opens it and hands it to Wolfe.

The Tactan scans it for a second, slips some kind of marking stick from a sleeve in the spine and adds a few lines. Then he spins the book around and holds it out for everybody to see. Kemren and Jaspen lift their lamps closer.

"This band." Wolfe points the stick at a pair of parallel lines roughly contouring the line representing the edge of the Ice, but set apart from it in all but a few places. "This is the ancient front and we're here." He touches the tip of the stick to a bulge where the lines overlap. "My guess is that east of this lobe, the Snowsea and the ancient front part ways just like they do to the west. Any team keeping a similar record would know there is only one place left to search for fresh caches."

"Right where we are," says Jaspen.

"The Cloud didn't need to hunt for us. All they had to do was anticipate our move and set their trap."

"What about the calving that revealed the Cliff

of Faces? Was that just coincidence?"

From the back, Galees clears her throat. "No, not coincidence. After Jaio left, I saw tracks up on Ice. The monks. They set…" She looks at Jaio with imploring eyes and blows a puff of breath through clenched teeth imitating the sound of an explosion.

"Charges," says Jaio. "She told me back in the tunnel about finding footprints and blast points right after I'd left. The monks caused the calving. They appear to have been triggering fresh calvings every few days for quite some time."

"To lure in eager teams," says Sand.

"The Cortegran team bit first," says Rawl.

"And we bit second," says Wolfe.

"But weren't the monks after me?" asks Jaspen.

"Yes," says Wolfe. "I think they found this cache by accident. Probably noticed the door, or at least part of it, after a detonation and investigated further."

"Bonus for them," says Rawl.

"And it explains the Daggers," says Wolfe. "Until now, I thought Acris and the Cloud were working together to hunt down our thawrunner. But it didn't make sense. In all my years, I've never heard of Daggers and Iron Robes working together."

"They don't," both Kemren and Benethan say in unison.

"Then there was the liberal expenditure of relic ammunition. Neither the threat of scandal posed by Jaspen nor Acris's loathing for me could account for such flagrant use."

"Unless, they were counting on an even bigger payoff," says Sand.

Wolfe nods. "I'd wager, Acris and his Daggers know nothing of Jaspen. They came to find this cache in the only place it could be. No coordinates necessary." He taps the map.

"But that would violate the original pact between the Order and the Protectorates," says Sand.

"What pact?" asks Rawl.

Sand glances at the old man. "The one that says the Order will not field Ice Watch teams of their own, but will receive a proportion of the spoils obtained by the teams of the Protectorates."

"I think the rules have changed," says Wolfe. He taps the map again. "Those rules assume the existence of new caches to be found."

"But now that the well is running dry," says Rawl. "The Order wants the last of the water for itself."

Wolfe nods. "That's not the only reason. If, as Kemren said earlier, Salazriole or the Oroken have located the Vaultiten Mountain cache, the Order may find itself outmatched. Their only means of preserving the balance would then depend on securing this cache."

A low throaty rumble rises from out of the darkness.

"Kitty's still prowling," says Rawl.

"Let's keep moving." Wolfe sheaths the drawing stick, hands the book back to Benethan and returns his gun to hand.

CLIFF OF FACES

Benethan's mind had trouble with the magnitude of this find. As far as he knew, no cache to date even remotely compared. The chaos it could bring to Anthemar eclipsed any upheaval that might be caused by the scandalous indiscretion of a soon-to-be-overthrown Dictorian. And the danger only grew worse with every step.

True, without fuel, the tanks were worthless, but the pillar-mounted gun racks corresponding to the hundreds of tent frames filling the back half of the vast chamber were a different matter.

Taken together, those racks contained thousands of hyperpulse rifles.

A close inspection of the racks revealed locked drawers beneath each weapon. Ammunition and propellant no doubt awaited inside. If the keys to the drawers and binding bars could be found, Wolfe's Pride would become the most lethal Ice Watch team ever to roam the Parm. And the lowly Protectorate of Kest would control more ordinance than all the other Protectorates, and perhaps even the Order, combined.

No wonder the Daggers violated the pact.

At the edge of Benethan's vision, a glint of reflected lamplight wavered for an instant before vanishing.

Not glass. And not tiger eyes.

"Wolfe," he said. "Over there."

The Tactan turned the group in Benethan's direction and they proceeded toward the unidentified shimmer. As they neared, more glints erupted and a shape emerged into distinction. A tent, smaller than the others, and with its skin intact.

Benethan's mind resisted the dawning awareness revealed by his eyes.

At his side, Kemren sucked in a sharp breath. "Is that…?"

"Yes," said Benethan. "Kineticloth. A whole tent."

Wolfe reached out and touched it. "So, this is the stuff worn by the Cloud."

"Yes," said Benethan. "There's probably more here than exists throughout the rest of Anthemar. It's priceless."

"Which begs the question," said Rawl. "What's inside?"

Benethan moved to the flap before Wolfe could

appoint entry duty to someone else. The flap
hung loose, though stiff from the years and cold.

Slowly, gently, Benethan pushed it aside and
followed his lamp into the tent space.

The open-jawed remains of a seated soldier
greeted him. The frozen, partially mummified
skeleton slumped in a chair behind a desk facing
the flap. Shreds of an ancient uniform hung in icy
tatters from his bones. Wisps of colorless hair,
sprouted from his gray leathery skull around the
spot on top where a ragged hole gaped.

Benethan glanced through the legs of the table.
On the floor by the chair he saw many strewn
cylinders, cans of some kind and amidst them, a
pistol. It lay right where it had landed all those
thousands of years ago after the man had shot
himself.   It was not a hyperpulse weapon, but an
older firearm called a revolver.

Benethan stepped aside to let the others enter.
As they filed in, his Catalogian training kicked on
and he began mentally cataloging the scene. An
unidentified box sat in the center of the table.
Judging by the control pad on top, it was some
sort of mechanical device, but its purpose eluded
him. He'd never seen anything like it.

Next to it lay a small armored case, clasps
undone and opened a crack. Three of the
cylindrical cans stood beside the case. In faint
lettering running vertically along their lengths he

read the word *Lumosol*. Directly over the table, a broad dish like an inverted dinner plate hung from a cord. In the center, he saw an empty hole. The entire under surface was coated in some kind of pale powder.

Benethan then turned his attention to the tall free-standing cabinets behind the man. But his appraisal was interrupted when Jaio lunged past him and began an almost frantic survey of the box on the table.

"What is it?" asked Wolfe.

"I think," Jaio began. He rounded the table to look the side facing the corpse. "Yes, it is." He reached toward it.

"Stop!" said Wolfe who whipped up his gun. "That's far enough until you tell me what it is."

Jaio raised his hands. "There's no danger. It is a sound recorder."

"A sound recorder?"

"Yes, I was going to look inside for an orb."

"What's an orb?"

"It stands for Optical Recording Ball. It can store sounds for a very long time and plays them back when exposed to bright light." Jaio nods to the box. "May I?"

Wolfe lowered his gun and nodded.

With great care, the Oroken boy reached to the face of the box. Benethan heard a click then a moment later, Jaio lifted into view a perfectly round, glassy black ball about the size of a plum.

"I've seen those before," said Kemren.

"Those?" said Jaio, his excitement barely contained. "You've seen more of these?"

"Yes, at least, pieces of more."

"Pieces? Where? How many?"

Kemren opened his mouth to speak then closed it and shook his head. "I vowed not to speak of it. I've already said too much."

"To whom did you make this vow?" asked Wolfe.

"Dictorian Consul Ario."

"Please, Kemren," said Jaio. "You must tell me what you saw."

"I'm sorry."

"So, Brother," said Benethan. "Some vows you will keep."

A blood-chilling roar echoed through the cavern followed an instant later by the unmistakable reports of two hyperpulse weapons.

"Acris!" growled Wolfe.

"So much for being safe until nightfall," said Sand.

"We're trapped," said Jaspen.

"Maybe this guy," Sand nods to the corpse, "has the keys to the gun racks and we can even the odds a little."

"No time. We need to get out of here." said Wolfe.

"What?" said Sand. "Get out of here? We can't leave this find to them."

"We can and we will."

"But—"

"This is not a debate."

"What if we cause a diversion?" said Kemren. "Lure them away from the opening."

Wolfe shook his head. "Too risky. If even a single needle from one of their guns makes contact with flesh, that's it."

"The tiger," said Jaio.

"He'd just as soon eat us as help us," said Rawl.

"No, that's not what I mean. Sable, you said he must have come in a different way."

"Yes," said Sable. "That's right."

"So," said Wolfe. "If we can find his tracks in the frost, we can follow them back to where he entered the cavern."

Jaio nodded.

"Everyone but Sable, lamps dark,' said Wolfe. "Sable, you know what to do."

"Wait," said Jaio as he shoved the orb into his parka. "We can't leave the recorder." As he spoke, he flipped back the lid of the case next to it. Inside rested three orbs, each settled into one of a dozen form-fitting spaces. The rest were empty. Jaio snapped the lid shut. "This too," he said. Then he noticed the cylinders. "And these." He unshouldered his pack, shoved the cans inside and threw it back on.

Syree dashed forward and tucked the recorder under her arm and Galees snatched up the case by the handle.

"If these burdens slow us, they go," said Wolfe. "And remember, odds are that four of the Daggers are wearing kineticloth robes and can see in the dark, and one or two of them may be invisible."

"Great," said Rawl. "Just what we were trying to avoid."

"Okay, let's go."

Sand flicked on his red light and together with Wolfe, they shouldered out of the tent. For an eternal moment, complete silence engulfed Benethan and the others as they waited inside.

"Clear," whispered Sand.

Sable slipped out, lamp held low. It emitted just enough light for the rest of them to follow.

CLIFF OF FACES

Sable felt panic building as she crouched and
scanned the tiny sliding pool of lamplit floor for
tiger tracks. *This is hopeless*, she thought. Behind
her, the rest of the group trailed, slipping along as
quietly as possible.

Her eyes panned back and forth over the
frozen surface, looking, straining. Minute by futile
minute, time dragged and nothing appeared.
Then the leading edge of the light touched a sight
too impossible to be real: not a tiger print, but a
tiger paw. Next to it stood another. Sable's
widening eyes rose up the striped legs until they
found the faintest silhouette of an enormous head.
Two spots of green light glowed faintly on either
side of its center.

She needed to back away. She needed to shout
a warning. But she couldn't move or utter a
sound. Total was the lock of fear on her soul.

A blast of fetid warm breath hit her in the face.

Then the animal spun and bounded into the darkness to her left. Soft, but heavy thuds faded then stopped.

"What was that?" whispered Sand.

"The tiger," croaked Sable.

"Follow," whispered Jaio.

"What?"

"Do it!"

"Wolfe?"

From somewhere in the darkness not far behind them came a crunch, like a foot settling slowly on thin glass.

"Follow," whispered Wolfe.

Sable turned and began tracking. She could have sworn she heard the thudding of padded feet resume ahead of her. The sound then continued just at the edge of hearing. The tiger led her deeper into the chamber. Soon she came to an arched tunnel. The prints continued inside. Sable and her companions followed for some distance and nearly fell into the wide channel at the tunnel's heart.

Two beams made of heavy metal ran along the center of the channel. She hopped down inside and held the light for the others to follow.

"Railroad tracks," whispered Jaio.

Ahead, a grumble almost too deep to hear reverberated off stone. Somehow, Sable felt urgency in the guttural call.

"Quick," she whispered.

The last of her companions hopped down an instant before the dull thumps of bootsteps carried to them from the chamber beyond the arch.

Sable blew out her lamp. Around her she could feel the others huddled, breathless, still as statues.

"I know you're down there, Wolfe."

"Acris," said Wolfe.

"If you give yourself up, I'll let the rest of your team go. Oh, wait. Not the girl. You know who I mean, the little climber whose friends killed my charge."

"Let the girl go too, Acris."

"Or what?"

"You know I can only ask."

"That you can, Krugerhan. That you can. The answer is no," said Acris without even a pause to think.

"I'll come," said Sable.

"Stay where you are," whispered Wolfe. "That's an order. He has no intention of letting any of us out of here. We've seen too much."

"What can we do?" asked Sand.

"Give me your gun."

"What?"

"You all stay low and move down the channel as fast as you can. I'll stall for as long as possible then use the red eye to try for a shot."

"He's invisible, probably has night sight and kineticloth body armor," said Sand. "You're going to need help."

Sable heard rustling next to her, but couldn't tell who was moving.

"If you have a better idea," said Wolfe.

"I do," said Benethan.

Sable heard him stand an instant before the blinding green flash and roar of a stuttergun filled the tunnel. Despite her shock, she surged to her feet in time to see a figure flying backwards near the mouth of the tunnel. An instant later, a second figure appeared out of nowhere as the sweep of Benethan's sustained burst impacted him. He too went flying. But before he even hit the ground, the first was back up and raising his own gun. Sable grabbed Benethan and yanked him down just as the green fire sizzled through the air where he'd been standing. Another burst followed in short succession. It tore into the rim of the channel and showered them with grit.

"Kineticloth was designed specifically to counter hyperpulse," said Kemren in a tone Benethan recognized as the same tone he used in the novitiate training chamber when attempting to school a particularly thickheaded pupil.

"I know," said Benethan. "But pixelcloaks weren't."

"That's one advantage eliminated," said Wolfe.

"But at the price of our position."

"Fat lot of good it did us, too" growled Rawl. "The tunnel's black as midnight pitch."

"Hold on," said Jaio. Sable could hear him rummaging through his pack. Then came a sound unlike any she'd ever heard, reminiscent of a rattletail snake, but metallic and slower.

A sudden jet of bright, white light sprayed the rocky floor of the channel. It arced until it hit a cluster of hand-sized stones, where it lingered a moment before cutting off, leaving nearly two dozen radiant little suns lying on the ground.

"Grab a rock and toss it!" yelled Jaio as he scooped one up and lobbed it toward the chamber.

Awed as she was, Sable didn't hesitate. She snatched up a glowing rock and threw it as well. The others did the same and soon the tunnel shone. Sable stared in wonder at the palm of her mitten, shining bright as day.

"Great, now we can watch him come to kill us," said Rawl.

"They'll stay put," said Wolfe. "Acris knows what Sand can do."

With these words, the spotter grinned and clicked on the red beam of his rifle scope.

"Valiant effort," Acris yelled, though his words sounded pained. "But this only postpones the inevitable. For all of you!"

"He's got a point," said Sand. "Even though

there only appear to be two of them, they'll have no problem keeping us pinned here until nightfall when the rest of the monastic horde arrives."

"Maybe not," said Jaio. "Benethan, if you fire a sustained burst into the ceiling, you can collapse the tunnel mouth and make a big enough barrier to safeguard our escape. You won't even have to break cover."

Wolfe pushed back his tricorn and considered Jaio as if seeing him for the first time. "I like how you think," he said and nodded to Benethan. "Do it."

The monk aimed the stuttergun and squeezed the trigger. The high arch at the end of the tunnel exploded under the fiery green onslaught and rained down a torrent of rock and dust. Even when the blockage was complete, Benethan continued his barrage. It ended with an abrupt click.

"Out!" he shouted and shoved the empty weapon into his parka.

"Run!" yelled Jaio. "Unless you buried them, they'll start blasting through right away."

Sable spun, grabbed up a glowing rock and took off down the channel with her companions. Behind them, she could hear the faint roar of stutterguns above the pounding of their boots. Each long blast grew a little louder even as she and the others opened the distance between themselves and the chamber of tanks.

Despite their haste, Sable had no problem tracking the tiger. Paw-prints crushed into frost crystals formed over the course of millennia marked its path straight down the railroad channel. Judging by their spacing, the cat moved at a steady lope.

"Look," said Jaspen who ran at her side.

Sable took her eyes from the prints and scanned ahead. A massive cave-in filled the tunnel. But she saw no tiger.

"There must be a way through," said Sable. "Or the cat would be here."

"Right," said Jaspen.

Sable resumed tracking, found the spot where the tiger had leapt up onto the debris and begun bounding up to the far right. She followed as fast as she could. Jaspen and the others scrambled over the rubble behind her.

Sure enough, a narrow gap separated the summit of the cave-in from the jagged ceiling. To squeeze through, Sable had to shed her pack. She shoved it ahead of her and belly-crawled to the other side. Then she turned and helped pull Jaspen through.

Far to the rear, a sharp explosion echoed down the tunnel.

"Quick!" shouted Wolfe. "Acris is through!"

Sable peered past her companions as one by

one they hurried through the hole. Sand, Galees and Syree remained when a figure ducked through the far blockage and raised his gun. A tiny red dot settled on his chest an instant before Sand's rifle boomed. The man toppled back, but immediately struggled to right himself.

Galees dropped the case, tossed her bow through the gap then shed her pack. She held it before her and dove to the other side.

Sand's gun boomed again as Syree attempted to shove the recorder box through. It wouldn't fit.

"Leave it," shouted Wolfe.

"No!" Syree slammed on it with her fists. Her footing gave out and she slid on her hands and knees several feet back down the slope.

The slip saved her life. A line of green fire stuck the box, shredding it like paper. Everyone ducked as bits of hot metal and shattered circuits sprayed them.

Sand's gun roared a third time.

In a heartbeat, Syree scrambled back to the hole, slapped the remains of the box out of the way and slithered through behind her tossed pack.

"Come on, Sand!" Wolfe pointed his own gun back through the gap and cut loose the contents of both barrels without even aiming.

The blue smoke of the discharge swirled around Sand as he surged through to the gap. He jammed his pack across, but held his gun as he hauled himself beyond the threshold.

Green fire slammed into stone, throwing plumes of grit and dust.

Sand rolled through a hair's breadth ahead of a deadly lance of flame. The stock of his gun spun up into its path and disintegrated in a cloud of splinters.

"No!" he cried.

"Down!" roared Wolfe.

The hyperpulse stream blew the gap wider as Sable and the others ducked and slid down the slope as quickly as possible, dragging packs, trying not to fall. When they reached the bottom they retrieved their gear and glowing rocks and took off running again.

The ceiling overhead crackled from the impacts of hyperpulse needles slicing through the opening. Showers of shattered stone pattered down around them, punctuated by the occasional boom of a dropped boulder. One the size of a summer melon missed striking Sable by inches. She barely managed to side-step the bounce, stumbled and would have fallen had Jaio not helped right her. They pressed on.

A sudden rumble resounded at the cave-in and a large chunk of the ceiling collapsed, adding to the pile and sealing off the gap. Once the rockfall settled, the reports of the stutterguns could barely be heard.

"Serves…'em right," wheezed Rawl.

"Don't stop," said Wolfe.

"I knew…you'd say that."

Sable kept running.

"Wait!" yelled Jaspen from just behind and to the right.

Sable turned to see her standing by a waist-high hole in the wall. An ancient corroded grate hung open on a bent hinge. The one-handed thawrunner held her glowing rock low at its mouth. The tiger tracks disappeared inside.

Sable had forgotten all about watching for them.

"Well done," said Wolfe. "Everybody inside!"

Without waiting for another word, Syree ducked into the opening. Sand cursed and dashed through behind her.

"Go on, Jas," said Kemren. The thawrunner ducked in with her monk right behind.

"Sable," said Wolfe.

She shook her head. "I will rewrite our story in the frost."

"What about this opening? There's no way to hide it."

"There is another over there," she pointed to the opposite side of the tunnel where an identical circular grate could just be discerned in the weak light of the glowing rocks. "I will make them think we used that one."

"Be quick. We can't expect the rockfall to hold them for long."

"I will."

"She can't stay alone," grumbled Rawl. "I'll stay back and cover her."

"No," said Sable. "Too noisy. I will catch up." She didn't wait for a reply, but went to work.

"Too noisy! Well, I—"

"Go on, Rawl," Wolfe interrupted. "And Sable, don't be long."

"Understood," she said without looking up from the tiger track she was carefully smoothing away.

Soon the rest of her companions had disappeared into the hole and the only sounds within the railroad tunnel were her faint movements and the quiet, but building noise of Acris' assault on the cave-in.

7

MOUNTAIN OF FACES

Ahead of Jaio, everyone but Sable shuffles at a crouch along the tight dark passage. It is almost certainly a vent pipe for the railroad tunnel and rises at a slight incline, though not enough for the frost layer to compromise footing. And even though the Lumosol-doused rocks have begun to dim, they still put out sufficient light to guide the way. They also reveal disconcerting cracks and dents overhead as well as crumbling seams where pipe segments once joined, but now gape. The bits of broken rock that have leaked through over countless years form tiny mountain ranges on the pipe floor, some rising almost half the height of the pipe. Syree has to topple the largest to get by.

Jaio glances up from the next pile in time to see Galees's pack brush the ceiling as she steps over. This slight contact is enough to unleash a stream of grit and pebbles. Please stop, he implores and breathes a sigh of relief when the stream abates.

To take his mind off the claustrophobic and unstable confines, Jaio turns his thoughts to Sable. He knows Wolfe believes her capable of completing her task alone, but there are unforeseen risks no amount of capability can counter. And Wolfe is not Jaio's Fateholder.

He reaches forward and taps Galees. She pauses and glances back.

"Lend me your bow," he says. "I'm going back to cover Sable."

A mischievous grin grows on Galees's face as she hands over her weapon and quiver of arrows. "And here I thought the interest ran only one way."

"Interest? You think she…You think I…" He reminds himself who he is talking to and shakes his head.

Her grin simply spreads as she nods in a slow knowing way.

Jaio just turns and heads back down the passage. He moves as quietly as he can and when he reaches the mouth of the passage, he registers the quiet. The fighter monks no longer attack the rockfall. It has held, for now.

Jaio begins to step from the hole then pauses to watch Sable. She moves with slow meticulous grace as she creates, in essence, a set of markings that are the mirror opposite of events as they actually transpired. In the glow of the rock she holds, her face radiates confident focus. Maturity. Even wisdom, though Jaio doubts she is more than a couple years older than he.

No, she can't possibly find him of interest, a boy on the thin side of scrawny and tattooed with a mask of death. He slips off a mitten and touches the tips of his fingers to his cheek as if he might feel the rough bone of the skull he now wears as a permanent feature. But all he feels is the soft skin of a child.

"I know you're there," says Sable without looking up.

Jaio hastily shoves his hand back inside his mitten, steps from the hole and starts toward her. "Just wanted to make sure you're safe."

"Every print you make I have to erase," she says.

"Ah." Jaio draws back mid-stride and settles his airborne foot into a print he's just laid down. "Sorry."

She says nothing more.

If she likes me, she hides it well.

"You're…different from the others," he says.

"Everyone is different."

"Yes, I know, but what I mean is you're not Anthemari, are you?"

"I am Mesoric."

Jaio knows almost nothing of the lands beyond Anthemar. The specter of the Fane has loomed too large to afford much thought for anyone or anywhere else. However, a memory of some long-ago lesson with Gilinath conjures a most unlikely image, of a person sitting astride a great, galloping animal, as the Ancients once did.

"Your people tame horses?" he asks.

"Much more than that. We breed and raise the finest herds in the known lands. Horses are the heart and soul of Mesorica."

"And you ride them?"

Sable pauses and glances his way, a look of surprise on her face. "Of course. Everybody rides them."

Jaio hesitates, not wanting to acknowledge the sudden appearance of this divide between them. But worse would be to fall in. "We don't," he says.

Her look of surprise transforms into astonishment. "Are there no horses where you are from?"

"Oh, there are horses," he says. "But we don't ride them."

"Don't you know how?"

"We do."

"They why don't you ride them?"

"They don't want to be ridden." Jaio hopes this will be enough.

"I see," she says, her tone now soft and reflective. "I wonder what we would be without them. I wonder if my clan…" she trails off and returns her attention to her task.

"Your clan?"

"My clan was called the Blue Camels," says Sable, almost too softly to be heard.

"Was?" he asks.

She glances his way, sadness reflected in her eyes, then goes back to work.

"I too have a clan," he says, trying to change the subject and find some common ground. "The Oromola of the Homeland Steppe, a land far from here on the other side of the Ice."

"The ice does not go on forever?"

"No. And it is melting."

"So you said. Which explains how we found this place. And why the caches are running out…And why you have come here, not as an enemy, but as a friend."

"That's right."

"I see," she says. "The ice is not all that melts."

Jaio stands speechless. He can almost hear Orol Taika's voice carrying to him from the Ghostway: 'Laws of Ice now must thaw.'

"Why do you have two faces?" she asks. Her unusual question, and the uneasiness of her tone, snaps Jaio back from the Ghostway. He finds her looking at him, her work paused.

"Two faces? Oh, the tattoos." He thinks for a moment how to respond. "Those of us who choose the Ice are forbidden to go home. The skull marks us as dead in the eyes of our people and makes our return to the Steppe impossible. Any who try go back meet only the arrows of our hunters."

"Why?" Dismay has replaced Sable's unease.

"To fight the Fane, we must become too much like them; hard, merciless and willing to use the relics of the Ancients to defend the Steppe and those we love who hold true to the Oroken way."

"Ah," she whispers. "I understand." Her dismay has been replaced by sorrow.

"You do?"

She nods and resumes her work. "My clan went against Mesoric Law and established secret trading relations with the Maxamantans of Anthemar. We thought we could hide our activities. We thought we were in control of the technologies we obtained, but in truth, they controlled us and we were unwittingly changed, corrupted.

"The other clans realized our mistake before we did and called a Council of Consequences to decide our punishment. Not surprisingly, they chose banishment to Anthemar, where we went from a position of respect to one of near-slavery.

"So, yes, I understand the wisdom of your ways. I wish my clan had known such wisdom. If they had, my brother and I might not be the only ones left."

"Your brother? The blue-painted man who tried to kill you?"

"You were watching?"

"Yes."

"I am sorry you saw that."

"I also saw you spare his life despite what he did and what he said." Jaio wants to go on, yet nothing more comes to him that doesn't seem hollow, except for a question.

"Why did you risk yourself for me back there, in the ice tunnel?" he asks.

She pauses for half a breath then continues working. "To murder a man who has just saved you is dishonorable, no matter your animosity toward his people."

Jaio senses that there is more to it, but decides not to press her. He expects a return to silence, but she looks up at him again, inquiry in her eyes.

"The dots on your fingers, what do they signify?" she asks.

Jaio involuntarily glances at his mitten-covered hands then looks back up at her. "All Guardian Ghosts are marked with their clan of origin. Each finger represents a different clan."

"Guardian Ghosts?"

"It is our name for those of us who choose to go the Ice."

"But you have dots on more than one finger."

"I was marked as an All-clan Ghost and as an Orol—every finger; nine for the clans and one to indicate my status as an Orol in service to them all."

"How many other ten-dots are there?"

"None. I'm the only one. In the way that Ghosts are forbidden to return to the Steppe, Orols are forbidden to leave. Except me."

"Why can't they leave?"

"For the very reason Rawl supposed. We know things the Fane could use against the clans."

"So, you chose to break a tradition never before broken, give up your home and put yourself and your people at risk to come here offering a chance of peace thin as spider silk?"

"Thinner. I didn't fully understand my folly until it was too late to turn back."

Sable holds his gaze for a long moment. "I see no folly, only courage," she says. Then, without giving him a chance to reply, she returns to her work. Not that he can reply. The lump in his throat born of her words has stolen his voice. For the first time since leaving the Steppe, he feels his burden of self-doubt lighten, if only slightly, and in his heart, he feels a strange new warmth ignite.

Sable soon reaches the far hole and sets down her radiant rock so she can test the grate. Jaio can see her straining to open it. For the ruse to work, it has to be open.

"Should I make more work for you and come help?" he asks.

"No, wait." She removes her pack and pulls out a coil of rope. "I'm going to toss this over to you. Wrap it around that large boulder," she points to a long-fallen block of ceiling a few paces from Jaio. "And toss the rope back."

"Okay," says Jaio. "Ready."

She winds up and spins the coil his way. Amazingly, it unrolls in the air as it flies and he catches it by simply sticking his arm into the passing loop. Then, making as few new tracks as he can, he encircles the boulder and tosses the remainder back. He tries to mimic her spin, but it wobbles through the air and reaches her not as a coil, but a bunch. To her credit she says nothing and proceeds to feed it through the bars of the grate. She then cinches up the slack and ties a knot.

"How does this help us?" asks Jaio.

Without replying, she reaches into her pack and pulls out a climbing axe. A few paces from the grate, she slips the axe handle between the two parallel segments of rope then begins to twist the axe. The rope creaks as, turn by turn, it tightens. The strain builds and the turn-rate slows as twisting becomes more laborious.

When Sable looks like she won't be able to complete even one more revolution, a pop resounds from the grate, followed almost immediately by a staccato burst of shattering stone. Releasing puffs of dust and frost at the hinges and clasp, the grate rips from the rock and tips forward with a clatter.

"Impressive," says Jaio.

Without response, Sable withdraws her axe, puts it away and unknots the rope. Then she coils what she can and spins it back over to Jaio. Again, he catches the perfect loop over his outstretched arm. His return throw, after freeing the boulder, starts out better, but breaks apart midway and falls short in a tangle.

She glares at him as she retrieves it.

"Sorry," says Jaio.

She ignores him as she coils it back up before returning it to her pack and putting the pack on. Then she goes to work repairing the damage his shortfall has done to her false trail. She gives extra attention to the grate and continues the ruse some distance up the other pipe. Finally, she reemerges and works her way backward to Jaio, erasing her tracks as she draws near.

When she is just over half way across, the muted roar of stuttergun volleys resumes. Bits of ceiling rain down near the cave-in.

"Sounds like Acris found the keys," she says.

Jaio knocks an arrow and raises the bow toward the rockfall, ready to pull back and let fly.

The remaining distance Sable has to cross seems to take forever, but finally, she reaches the hole.

"Go," she says as she clears Jaio's tracks from around boulder.

Jaio nods, returns the arrow to the quiver and ducks in. He starts up while she backs in, pulls the grate into place and continues wiping away the evidence of their passage.

They've gone maybe fifty paces when a green flash lights the railroad tunnel. An instant later, an accompanying roar echoes up the pipe.

Sable spins forward. "Done," she says and shoves the glowing rock into her parka.

Jaio wheels and races up the tube as quickly and as quietly as he can. In a moment, the slight upward curvature blocks the view of the railroad tunnel, but he doesn't think Sable's decoy route will fool the fighter monks for long.

They hasten on for several anxious minutes. Then Jaio sees a faint glow ahead. It brightens with every shuffling stride until finally the source comes into view.

Sunlight pours down a shaft in the ceiling about twenty paces away, and hunkered at the bottom of the shaft are eight figures, armed and ready for battle.

"Jaio, Sable!" says Galees.

"Up front, Scaler," says Wolfe.

CLIFF OF FACES

Sable worked her way through the knot of crouched bodies to the base of the shaft. It shot straight up well over a fifty feet. A fat crescent of blue sky shone down from above.

To do this safely would take extra time. Sable didn't have any. She freed her hands from her mittens, slipped off her pack and pulled out her long rope and scaler's harness. Then she shed her cloak and handed it to Wolfe so she could put on the harness and drape the rope coil across her torso like a Catalogian sash.

Next she kicked off her boots, stood straight and offered a quick prayer to Sister Spider for sticky feet and fingers. She took several deep steadying breaths and felt the heat of her heart course along her limbs.

When it filled her digits with warmth, she pressed her back into the wall of the shaft. Then she kicked her feet up and planted them on the opposite wall. The first few halting inches skyward were not pretty. Back, feet, shoulders, back, feet, shoulders. But finally, she was high enough to slap her palms against the surface behind her. Then her inner spider took over. She swiveled until she faced down and started walking backward up the shaft. The evenly-spaced seams as well as numerous cracks and crumples offered adequate points of purchase and helped speed her on her way.

The ascent took only a few moments. Near the top, she swiveled face up again then introduced a rotation into the remaining climb so her feet came up under the partial blockage, a vented lid, half-askew. When she reached it, she placed the toes of one foot against the under surface and shoved. The cold, thick, metal cover barely moved. She tried again and almost broke the bond of friction holding her in place.

New strategy.

She scurried down a few feet and rotated again to bring her legs up beneath the opening. This time, she shoved her legs into the sky and hooked them both over the edge of the shaft. When she felt secure, she released her hands and let herself hang by her knees. Then she began to work her way around the lip of the shaft until her legs bumped up against the lid.

From there, she reached up and across while

twisting her torso. She was just flexible enough to gain a grip on the far rim with one hand. She then pulled her feet back in one at a time and settled her knees against the far side of the shaft. In one fluid motion, she pushed off with her legs and reached with the other hand. Her body swung and untwisted. She planted her toes on the wall just as her fingers found their grip.

The final pull up and out of the shaft left her on her back panting and looking into the dome of a clear blue sky. A stiff, cold wind streamed over the gentle slope where she lay. She wanted to rest a moment and breathe in the air, but had no time.

Sable rolled over on the pebbly earth and struggled to her feet. Her aching arms resisted her efforts to reach up and slip off the coil of rope, but she managed it. Then she searched for a secure tie point. Except for the mouth of the shaft and a tiny encircling island of naked, windblown stones, the largest no bigger than a fingertip, ice stretched away in every direction.

"Ice it is." She slipped her hammer free and unfastened three long, barbed pitons made of a lightweight, but supremely hard relic metal. She ran to the interface of ice and earth where the ground was frozen solid. There, she drove the pitons in then she ran the rope through all three eyes before tying the securing knot.

After a few sharp tugs to test the set, she

dashed to the shaft, heaved the lid aside and threw the rope into the darkness. It slapped the wall as it uncoiled and, when finished, immediately began to vibrate as the others started working their way up.

"Only two at a time!" she yelled down.

"Two on the way," yelled Wolfe.

9

CLIFF OF FACES

Jaspen stood with Kemren and Benethan at the bottom of the shaft. She had all she could do to keep from shaking. As much as she feared the homicidal monks who chased them, she feared this climb more. Above her, Jaio and Wolfe hoisted themselves aloft hand over hand while they kicked and scrambled up the wall.

"I can't do it," she said.

"Yes, you can," said Kem.

"Hand over hand takes *two* hands." She held up her stump.

"I told you, we're going to tie you in and, once Benethan and I are up, all of us will hoist you to the top."

A distant clang resounded through the passage from behind.

Okay, she didn't fear the climb more.

"Quick, tie me in," she said.

Kemren started to loop the rope around

Jaspen's waist, but Benethan intervened. "Not like that. You need to construct a harness."

"And how do you know about that?"

"When you've spent weeks at the Wall with Sable, you'll know about it too. Now go, Brother. I'll be right behind you."

Kemren hesitated but nodded and held Jaspen's gaze. "See you on top." He started for the rope, but she grabbed him, drew him close and kissed him hard on the lips.

"See you on top," she said.

He gave a quick uncharacteristically nervous nod with another glance at Benethan and then he was gone.

Benethan created the harness with the remaining loose rope and Jaspen stepped into it. He tightened it, did a tug test and nodded. "You're all set."

Without another word or glance, he shot up the rope at a surprising speed.

And then she was alone.

As the sounds of climbing faded from above, new sounds—clanks and thuds—grew louder from behind. Against her better judgment, she looked back down the passage.

A movement in the far depths caught her eye just as she lurched upward. The jerky, halting ride she had expected did not happen. Instead, she practically flew up the shaft, so fast her ears popped.

In moments, she reached the top where multiple pairs of hands grabbed her and hauled her out. Kem helped undo the harness and Sable disconnected the rope from a small roller clamped to the edge of the shaft. Then she unclamped the roller and reattached it to her belt. The others stood with hands on knees trying to catch their breath. All but Wolfe, that is.

He went to the heavy metal lid and picked it up without so much as a grunt. He then slammed it down over the shaft.

Muffled shouts carried up from below.

"Get back!" yelled Jaio.

Wolfe merely executed an unhurried turn while wiping his hands. He didn't even flinch when the lid blew skyward on a lance of green flame. And he strode casually away as the now-mutilated hunk of metal crashed to earth behind him amid the faint curses of Acris.

Wolfe paid the ranting Dagger no heed as he turned his attention to Jaio, who, like Jaspen and all the others, simply stared at him. "Sable needs her cloak and boots back."

10

THE ICE

What?" says Jaio, whose mind is still on Wolfe's nonchalant dismissal of the deadly monk. "Oh, right." He quickly unshoulders his pack and withdraws Sable's gear. As he walks over to hand it to her, he can't help noticing her bare feet. They are wider than he expects and strong in appearance the way a woodworker's hands appear strong in comparison to the hands of a scribe.

Behind him, he hears Galees suppress a giggle. He feels his face flush and hopes his tattoos hide it. The upturned corners of Sable's mouth give him his answer.

"Here you are," he says just as a boot slips from his grip. He reaches to grab it and loses the other. It bumps a few feet down the gentle slope.

Sable lifts the cloak from his arms and dons it while he retrieves her fallen footwear. In the longest moment of his life, he snatches up the boots and hands them to her.

"Thank you," she says.

He spins and hurries back to his shed pack. Never has he felt such embarrassment, not even when Syree called him out on the frequent occasions he shadowed her a little too closely. When, he wonders, did he lose the shield of naïve childhood infatuation that had protected him? All he knows is, it's gone.

He can't bring himself to look up. He's not even sure if it's possible when Wolfe comes to his rescue. "All right, Jaio. We're on the ice."

Jaio grabs the new subject like a lifeline, puts on his pack and surveys their surroundings in an attempt to find his bearings. The ice-free hillslope offers the best clue. It almost certainly faces northeast where the heat of the sun is most intense. Otherwise, it would be buried beneath tons of ice, incessant wind or no.

He rotates and walks a few paces north, further up the hillslope toward a snowy summit perhaps three or four hundred paces distant. Behind him, Jaio hears the sudden rhythmic crunch of pebbles shifting under moving feet.

"Where are they?" says Jaspen.

"Where are what?" asks Wolfe.

Jaio turns to face the group.

"The tiger tracks."

The others begin to glance around.

"Nowhere," says Sable, her tone bewildered. "And, thinking back, I saw no paw marks in the pipe either."

"Must 'a doubled back," says Rawl.

"There were no tracks leading down the pipe," says Jaspen. "Only tracks leading up."

Jaio can feel his panic building. He knows the very idea of Taiga will strike their Fane sensibilities as superstitious nonsense. They are trained to flatly reject the inexplicable, even when their own senses confirm it. And the inexplicable is all he has to offer.

Wolfe will know a lie and so, Jaio braces himself to lose what credibility he has earned.

Sable turns to face him. He can see her mouth beginning to form a question, but when their eyes meet, she pauses. Can she see his panic?

"We must have missed something," she says. "But it doesn't matter. We're out...So, Jaio, where do we go?"

Again, she saves him. Can she now see his gratitude?

Wolfe eyes them both, just long enough for discomfort to stir. Then he settles his gaze on Jaio and reiterates Sable's question with a raised eyebrow.

Jaio turns back to face the hill. "This way."

THE SNOWSEA

As had become his custom, Benethan fell in at the rear of the group for the climb up the snow hill. Thankfully, the spring sun lacked sufficient heat to soften more than the top couple of inches, so he didn't sink in much during their ascent. Benethan's eyes quickly settled on Kemren. The others might not have noticed Jaspen's noble protector falling back, but Benethan did.

Soon, the soft-hearted monk strode next to Benethan. "What's your game, Falka?"

"You're welcome," said Benethan.

"What?"

"It was my pleasure to help save your dearest Jaspen back there."

"Don't toy with me. I saw the stuttergun in your hand when we first ran into the ice cavern. You had the perfect chance to use it, to earn back your sash, to serve the Order."

"So, why didn't I?"

Kemren let the silence answer for him.

"Because, the situation has changed."
Benethan decided to leave it at that. He didn't
really know how to speak of it anyway, and even
if he could put his inner turmoil into words,
Trince wouldn't believe him.

"Changed? How? The training of an Iron
Robe assassin leaves no room for change, no real
change at least."

Benethan spun on Kemren before he could
stop himself. "I am not an assassin," he hissed,
then, just as quickly, recovered his composure,
turned back and kept climbing. "I was not given a
choice."

"You always have a choice."

"No, not always, not when you don't know
enough to make a different one."

"But now you do? Know enough, that is?"

"You have seen what I've chosen." Benethan
said and then, without missing a beat, changed the
subject. "But what about your choices, Kemren? I
don't understand why you haven't called me out,
why you haven't told Jaspen who I am."

A slight smile appeared on Kemren's face.
"Because of what you've chosen, Brother. Because
who you are strikes me as someone other than
who you were. I just wish I understood the
reason. A touch of healthy disillusionment,

perhaps?"

"No, not disillusionment. Reprioritization. My team comes first." Benethan surprised himself with that one. He'd never admitted it before, let alone uttered it aloud. And of all the people to hear it, why did it have to be Kemren Trince? "It's a simple matter of survival," he added, though without conviction.

"You care about them," said Kemren through his growing smile. "Maybe, there's hope yet."

These words drew forth the memory of one of Benethan's early lessons as a Catalogian novitiate. 'Hope,' his instructor had said, 'means nothing by itself. Whenever you hear it invoked in isolation, always ask, hope *for what*? The meaning of any hope can only be found in these two additional words.'

Hope for what? thought Benethan as he watched Kemren put distance between them, trudging back up to walk with Jaspen. Benethan still didn't know an answer, but he felt a little closer to finding one than he had even before starting up the hill.

He turned his attention to the nine people who ascended ahead of him. Fane and Thrack, side by side. Bound by a deeper commonality he'd almost forgotten about. Their shared humanity.

Hope for what? he asked himself again.

Hope for us.

At the front of the group, Jaio came to a halt on the hilltop. Syree and Galees stepped up beside him.

Then, one by one, the view beyond the hill opened to each member of the Pride. Whatever they saw stopped them in their tracks a few steps shy of the summit, even the implacable Wolfe. His hand rose seemingly on its own and pushed up the tip of his tricorn.

Benethan told himself that no matter how startling the sight, he would not draw up short. But he did.

There, some two hundred yards away sat a great wooden sailing ship, elevated on six stout legs attached to massive skis. The finely carved likeness of a snarling tiger's head adorned the bow. And a single mast stood tall, sails bound to its double rank of spars.

A lone figure stood on the deck, hands on the opposite railing, facing away from the hill, out toward a drop off, the drop above the Cliff of Faces. Three more figures lay on their bellies at the edge of the drop off. Long ropes bound them to the ice boat as they looked down over the valley below.

Galees put her mittens to her mouth and whooped. The figure on the ship started and whirled around. Galees waved and whooped again.

The figure waved back then turned and began jerking one of the ropes. In response, the prone figures rolled to look then slithered backwards a few yards before standing and hastening toward the vessel.

"Come on," said Jaio. "*Tigress* awaits." He set off down the hill with Syree and Galees.

Benethan and the other members of Wolfe's Pride waited for word from their namesake.

"I think we may have underestimated the Thracks," said Rawl.

"Indeed," said Wolfe. He tipped his tricorn back down. "Indeed." He adjusted his pack and the huge gun slung over his shoulder. Then he started the descent. Benethan simply stood and watched as the rest of the Pride followed.

Where were they going? When he tried to imagine possibilities, he could see no further than this ice boat. If he wanted answers beyond that, he'd have to go find them.

In the face of this unknown, an unknown more total than any he'd ever before encountered, one thought comforted him. At least, he would not go alone.

PART 2

GHOST'S CHANCE

FROSTBITE

All around the gathered skateships, mountains rise like sharp black teeth, biting into the blue-gray light of a predawn sky. Keethu dangles from the chipper's cable beneath the belly of *Frostbite*, taking in the stunning view while overhead Teeg struggles to straighten a kink in the line.

Frostbite sits between the Orokota skateship, *Farfire*, and the Oronish skateship *Waketorrent*, in a circle of eight vessels arrayed like flower petals around Orol Thorne's spider-like monstrosity, *Invincible Dawn*. Keethu glances southward through *Waketorrent's* six legs, to look back along the mountain glacier they've followed north for over a week to reach this point: the ninth node, called the All-clan Node.

Try as she might to spot the ice-filled gap through which they traveled from the Open-hand Node, she cannot make it out. In every direction, all she sees are peaks, in rank upon rank to the farthest edges of vision.

"Okay," says Teeg from the braking chamber porthole above. "You're free. Let's get this over with."

"I can see why Galees…I mean Lupin likes this job," says Keethu. She silently chides herself for once again using bone-name instead of skin-name. She hopes it will be easier when she earns a skin-name of her own.

Teeg doesn't seem to care. "Well, you two can have it when she gets back."

The thought of Lupin's return reminds Keethu of the reason she and Teeg were given de-icing duty: so Lupin could help convey Jaio to Anthemar. Keethu doubts she'll ever see the boy Orol again, which stirs only a slight twinge of remorse, but she prays to all the clan spirits that the others with him are safe and on their way back to *Frostbite*.

"Do you think Jaio is still alive?" she asks as she grabs the first access rung and starts to pull herself, one by one, outward toward the first frozen braking claw. The winch clicks as Teeg gives the cable slack.

"If he's made contact with the Fane, no," says Teeg. "His mission is hopeless. Orol Thorne has the only realistic option."

"Destroy the Fane."

"With the Ice melting, there's no other way to

truly insure the safety of the clans. And who knows, we might even be able to go home. Can you imagine it, the first Ghosts ever to return to the Steppe without jeopardizing their families and facing *real* death?"

"I hope you're right." Keethu clips herself into place beneath the forward left claw-port and hefts the axe to start chipping away the build-up from a fierce, if brief, blizzard that struck and fled in the deep hours of the night. She's about to go to work when a movement to the west catches her attention.

In the weak morning light, she sees a figure stagger up into view from where a glacial arm drops out of sight over the edge of the flat where the skateships are anchored. The figure offers a feeble wave, takes two unsteady steps then topples.

"Quick, Teeg! Lower me down!"

"What?"

"To the Ice. Somebody just collapsed out there by the edge." She points then unfastens her clasp and swings free.

"We'll call for help," says Teeg.

"No time! He looks injured!"

"All right." The gears chatter as Teeg unwinds line. In a moment, Keethu's boots settle onto the Ice. Thankfully, the blizzard has blown away the powder leaving a solid surface still hard enough from the night freeze to support her weight. She hastens out of her harness.

"Be careful," yells Teeg. "Could be a Fane trick!"

Keethu pats the knife at her hip as she takes off running toward the fallen figure.

The run is longer than she expects. Distances on the Ice are always hard to judge. But she finally arrives and finds a man folded on his side, his left parka sleeve darkened with blood around a thumb sized hole in the shoulder. She gently rolls him onto his back. He lets out a pained groan.

His wincing face bears the tattoos of a Ghost, but she doesn't recognize him.

His eyes crack open. When they find hers, he tries to focus and reaches up with his good hand to grab her sleeve. His lips tremble and he wheezes something in a tongue she doesn't know. He seems to sense her confusion and repeats the statement, this time more emphatically. It is short and after a few repetitions in her mind, she has it memorized. She repeats it back. He relaxes, smiles, and repeats it once more, this time as a faint fading whisper. "Maxamant" and "cache" are the only two familiar words. Then his smile fades, his eyes roll back and his body goes limp.

Keethu presses hard against his wound to stop the bleeding and cranes her neck to call for help.

But she cuts off short when she sees half a dozen figures racing toward her across the Ice.

One she recognizes: the Oronish fateholder, Cappen Leegon. The wiry man pins her with his over-sized green eyes while his companions aid the fallen Ghost.

The fateholder taps the back of his hand with his other mitten; a kensign request to display her clan dot.

She slips off her mitten to reveal the tattoo on her right pinky finger.

"Oromola," he says.

She nods. "I'm Keethu."

"Did Sidray speak?" he asks in halting Molatongue.

"Yes," says Keethu. She repeats what she heard.

Leegon nods. "Ah." He gazes west and says something in Nishtongue, his voice heavy with both determination and anxiety.

"What does that mean?"

He looks her in the eyes with a gaze colder than the Ice. "It means nothing to you." He leans close until his nose is almost touching hers. "Keep what he you heard to yourself. Understand? If you don't, I will know. And you don't what to find out what *that* will mean."

13

TIGRESS

A light snow fell as *Tigress* raced east toward a place Jaio called the Open-hand Node. Whatever that meant? Jaspen didn't much care. Too oppressive was her exhaustion, both from the ordeal of the previous days and also from an almost-sleepless night of jolting and bouncing as the windsled sped away from Acris and the Cliff of Faces, first by the light of the waning day, then by the light of the setting moon. Not until the predawn disappearance of the waxing crescent beyond the northeastern horizon did the windsled finally pause to wait out the darkness.

The pause seemed to last only a few short moments. Then at first blush of day, the were off again. Rawl snored through it all.

Jaspen peered out from within several enveloping layers of 'bou fur and looked at the ceiling of the hide tent the Ghosts had erected on the deck for her and her companions. Early morning light glowed beyond the smoke hole where snowflakes danced in the weak column of smoky heat rising from the pile of glowing embers in the brazier at the heart of the shelter. Around her, the rest of the Pride slept, except for Sand who sat by the entrance flap, keeping watch.

"Did you get any sleep?" she whispered.

"Some," he said, which Jaspen suspected meant, none.

"I can take a turn."

"New day's already here."

"What will it bring, I wonder?"

A long, high, bird-like note sounded from outside. Jaspen and Sand exchanged puzzled looks. The note then faded almost to silence before breaking into a familiar trill, quick and watery. Jaspen recalled waking to this very tune on countless spring mornings throughout her childhood. This song had often turned out to be the best part of her day.

"Scrub sparrow," she said.

The thud, thud of footfalls on the deck rose above the music. They came to a halt just outside the tent.

"Good today, no…ah, good morn…ing," said the giant Bengus in choppy Anthemari.

Sand tossed the tent flap back. The big hairy man stood there smiling out from behind the tattooed skull dyed into the skin of his thick-bearded face.

"Warm tea and food." He spun before anyone even had a chance to respond and headed aft.

Jaspen focused on the idea of tea, wriggled from the furs, found her boots and followed Sand into the frozen dawn. Outside, the morning sun struggled to break through the thinning haze of flakes that swirled within racing bands of low, cold ground-fog. All around, the desolate expanse of the frozen world spread as if it went on forever. Try as she might, Jaspen couldn't imagine living atop the Snowsea with nothing but a windsled to call home.

Inside the tent, Rawl's rhythmic rasping finally ceased and she could hear the rest of the Pride beginning to stir.

Jaspen glanced forward and saw the spirit boy, Jaio, standing alone at the bow, playing a flute, sending sparrow song out over the tiger's head. Jaspen didn't know why she thought of him as a spirit. Maybe, because of his facial tattoos. But then, why not Ghost? She couldn't say. Somehow, spirit just fit, especially now as he played. Tea all but forgotten, her feet carried her his way.

"Am I interrupting?" she asked as she stepped up beside him.

He lowered the flute from his mouth mid-trill. "Oh," he didn't exactly seem startled by her appearance, but she did notice a sudden uneasiness. "No, please, join me." He slid sideways to make more room for her. And she caught him snatching a glance at her stump. Now, his discomfort made more sense. She knew from long experience, the best way to normalize the situation.

She raised her arm and tugged off her mitten. "Don't let this bother you. It stopped bothering me years ago."

"It's not that," said Jaio as he slipped his flute into his parka. "I'm just wondering...I'm not sure how to ask without sounding too forward."

"How did it happen?" she guessed.

He nodded.

"Most folks don't ask. They just assume a tiger made a grab for me while I was out gathering yak dung."

"You were born with it, weren't you?"

Jaspen found her voice momentarily stolen by surprise. Nobody guessed that. She nodded.

Before words returned to her, he continued, but with his voice lowered almost to the point of inaudibility. "Does the name...Taika mean anything to you?"

This caused her surprise to give way to curiosity. "Taika? No, but why do you ask?"

"She was the Orol who sent me. Very old. Very wise. She sacrificed herself to help me on my way. And as she was dying, she told me she would be with me. She told me to look for her out here." He gestured to the Ice.

Jaspen waited for him to explain how this related to her. But he said nothing more.

"And?" she said.

"Oh, of course. And she had only one hand, the left, just like you."

"So," said Jaspen as the pieces fell into place. "You think I'm this Taika."

"Our meeting seems too uncanny to be chance."

"Sorry, Jaio. Even if I believed in such things, as far as I know, I'm just Jaspen."

She could see the disappointment in his eyes. "I thought so," he said. "But I had to ask."

"She must have been very important to you," said Jaspen.

"In truth, I hardly knew her, but suffice it to say, she had more impact on my life than even my mentor, Orol Gilinath. And when she said she'd be here, I think I believed too much."

"Maybe, she is here, just not the way you think." Jaspen gently tapped her stump on Jaio's chest.

"That sounds like something my mentor might say."

The fondness and familiarity conveyed in Jaio's tone prompted Jaspen to offer a guess of her own. "Orol Gilinath raised you, didn't he?"

"Yes. How did you know?"

"I think you would have mentioned your parents otherwise."

"All I know of my parents is my mother's name: Annequoia."

Jaspen considered asking what had happened to her, but seeing the sad, distant look on Jaio's face, decided against it. "What a beautiful name," she said.

Jaio offered an appreciative nod, reached into his parka and pulled the flute out again. He held it out to Jaspen. She took it gently and admired its simple elegance.

"Gilinath said my mother left it for me. I think of that every time I play. It's like a part of her is with me."

Jaspen nodded, at a loss for a response that wouldn't sound trite, and handed the flute back.

Jaio returned it to his parka. "Come," he said. His melancholy seemed to evaporate. "Let us join the others for tea and peminca. Once we're all settled around the fire, I have something else to show you." He glanced up into the thin morning mist. "The sky should be bright enough."

14

TIGRESS

Despite the chewy toughness of the Oroken food-strips called peminca, Benethan found their subtle, spicy blend of flavors much to his liking. Every bite tasted a little different, and after even a small portion, he felt revitalized, his hunger not exactly sated, but reduced. The Order's dry-tack traveling bread paled by contrast, with its unsatisfying gritty texture and singular saltiness.

Benethan glanced around at the others. Everyone ripped and chewed or sipped tea from plain wooden bowls. Everyone, that is, except Sable, who sat examining a strip of peminca as if it might be poisoned.

Benethan considered his own half-eaten strip. For a monk dedicated to learning the ways of things, he'd let his stomach get the better of him. He glanced toward Jaio. "What is in the peminca?"

Jaio only met Benethan's gaze for a second

before looking over to Sable, who now stared at him awaiting his answer.

"A mix of berries, herbs, meats and bone meal bound with tallow."

"What kinds of meats?" asked Benethan.

"Hard to say," said Jaio. "It all depends on what the hunters brought down when the time came to prepare their food offering for the Ghosts."

"What are the most likely possibilities, then?"

"Yak, caribou, elk, deer, pronghorn, paka...or as you call them, woolephants."

"Anything else?" asked Sable.

"Perhaps."

Benethan did not miss the unspoken exchange of meaning known only to Jaio and the Mesoric.

"Perhaps what?" he asked.

"It does not matter," said Sable. She never took her eyes from Jaio as she grasped the peminca strip in both hands and raised it almost reverently before her. "We best honor the lives that feed our lives by giving them thanks." She closed her eyes, offered the peminca what Benethan could only assume was a silent bow of gratitude then lifted the strip to her mouth and tore off a generous chunk.

He said his own silent prayer to the Maker and did the same. Everyone else seemed equally moved by her display and repeated some personal variant. Then general eating resumed.

The unlikely gathering sat before a large brazier in two groups, Thrack and Fane, facing one another across the crackling yak-dung fire. Not surprisingly, Jaio sat equidistant between the groups with his back against the mast. Only the ancient steersman, Segray, remained at his post, tiller in hand holding *Tigress* on course.

What would Benethan's superiors think if they could see this? Mortal enemies for as long as time recalled, sharing a meal.

One by one, the chewing stopped and thirteen drained bowls found their way into a single stack. Benethan tried not to see any symbolism in this, but of course, the effort itself meant he'd failed.

"Thank you all for this fire," said Jaio, sounding very formal. "We are finally fed and rested enough to consider what comes next. But first, I have something to show you. It may have bearing on the course we choose."

Jaio slipped off a mitten and reached inside his parka. Benethan had to suppress his Iron Robe training. The boy is not reaching for a weapon, he told himself without conviction.

"This may be a little startling. And I don't know what will be revealed, if anything. I will do my best to help you understand what we hear, if I can. And should any of you need a pause, say so."

Benethan shifted uneasily as did several of the

others.

Jaio withdrew his hand. In his tattoo-dotted fingers, he gripped the black glass ball he'd taken from the metal box in the chamber beneath the Cliff of Faces.

With great care, he cupped it in his other mittened hand. It immediately began to hiss like softly falling rain. Benethan watched it as if it might explode.

Time stretched and tension built. A sharp clatter broke loose and everyone jumped as if expecting the ball to shatter. But it sat unmoving and intact within its nest of leather.

"Dammit," muttered a man's deep, tired voice.

"It does speak," whispered Sable as if, up to this point, she had not believed Jaio's claim.

"Okay," said the voice. "Here goes. This is Major Preston Keith Anchor. I am now the Northern Provincial Army Field Commander, Fort Rushmore Operations. Today is September 12th in the year of...yesterday's lord two-thousand-eighty-two. As the new senior officer on site, I inherit the orders of my former commanding officer, the late Lt. Colonel Lionel LeBlanc. These orders are to use this recording device to document the progress of our invasion into MA-held territory so as to preserve a record for posterity. However—"

Jaio covered the orb with his hand, causing it

to fall silent. "Who needs an explanation?" he asked.

Everyone nodded their head, even Benethan. As extensive as his schooling in the Late Antequitic Age had been, he lacked sufficient historical context to make sense of most of what he'd just heard.

Jaio began to explain. As the necessary stories within stories unfolded, so did Benethan's amazement at the depth of the boy's knowledge. Benethan also admired the boy's ability to make the ancient reality comprehensible not only to the Pride, but to his fellow Ghosts as well, despite the fact that their grasp of Anthemari barely exceeded that of your average six-year-old.

Once everyone felt comfortable in the basic knowledge of their world as it had existed fourteen thousand years ago, Jaio started to lift his hand from the orb.

"Wait," said Benethan. "How do you know all of this?"

"I've been learning it all my life from my mentor and the other Orols, who did the same, going back for generations beyond count, perhaps all the way back to the time of Major Anchor and Lt. Colonel LeBlanc."

"Throughout all those years, the Orols kept the memories alive?"

Jaio nodded. "In stories they passed on mouth

to ear, mind to mind."

"They didn't have any orbs to help them?" asked Kemren.

"Actually," said Jaio. "They had one. It's called the Founding Orb. The whole Oroken way of life was inspired by the story it contained. Until recently, the Orols kept it safe and only brought it out when they needed a fresh telling."

"They don't keep it safe now?" asked Sable.

Jaio looked down and shook his head. "The eldest of the Orols gave it to me right before I left for Anthemar. She thought it might help me fulfill my mission, but before I arrived, I lost it."

"The story still lives in your mind, does it not?" asked Sable.

Jaio looked up and met her gaze. "Yes, it does."

"Maybe, when we've finished hearing what this orb has to say, you will share the story from the other, in your own words."

Jaio nodded and gave her a smile filled with gratitude and, if Benethan was not mistaken, something more. Great, he thought.

Jaio lifted his hand from the orb.

"—as there will be no invasion, I hereby authorize myself to use this orb for a different purpose. The other three are yours. I won't be needing them; there's really not much left to say.

"I'll begin with a briefing of my situation. Four

days ago, Lt. Colonel LeBlanc…relieved himself of command with the help of his Colt .45. Since then, I have exercised…actually, I've exceeded, my authority as his successor to discharge all the troops from duty with full honors thereby freeing them to go wherever they will, present location excepted, of course. Consequently, I now find myself alone.

"Do not think my choice to disband the Northern Army was made lightly. We waited almost two weeks beyond the Omega date for the promised supply train to arrive with food, fuel and the 105-shells and coaxial hyperpulse cannon upgrades necessary to turn our Mothball Division of century-old Abrams into something more than a collection of big door-stops. Oh, and let's not forget the most important cargo: Field Marshall Beckett, and her staff.

But the train didn't show and we burned up what little petrol we had left maintaining power to the sat-net terminal. In the end, all our attempts to contact Beckett, Provincial Command and even Colonel Pratt with the Southern Army failed.

"Yet, we still held out three days beyond the exhaustion of our rations. And for the record, the troops faced this ordeal with as much valor as any soldier might display in combat. They deserve to be remembered for their loyalty, courage and sacrifice. But I doubt they will be, at least not by history.

"After all, history is a chronicle of the age-old chess game world powers have been playing since the dawn of civilization. It records only moves and countermoves that leave both sides ravaged and the board all but emptied. But what about the far greater challenge of preserving the balance of the unbloodied board? What about acknowledging the fact that the people symbolized by every piece, no matter their skin tone, sex or creed, have hearts hued not black or white, but many colors? And what about the truth of the playing surface itself, a surface that represents the land we all share? This land has no squares. We paint those on ourselves to create a false sense of gain in the face of the violence and loss born of each advance. These advances are what make history.

"Well, my troops—my people—deserve to be part of a better story than that. And who knows, maybe this orb will help them find their way into such a story.

"No, I haven't always held this heretical view. I trained for decades in the art of playing the game and I believed history to be the only narrative capable of conveying any meaningful legacy.

"Coming to my...unorthodox perspective took prolonged entrapment in a state of helplessness; it took feeling like an armless man sitting before the board, looking at all the pieces in place, but lacking the means to move even a single pawn. Only then did I see through the fallacy of sides and squares. Only then did I realize a truth beyond winning or losing: to play at all is to suffer a deeper defeat and miss the chance at a kind of legacy written not in history books, but in a life simply lived.

"So, when command fell to me, I chose to look through the paint. I chose to embrace the human heart above the Provincial heart or the Mesoamerican heart. I chose to reject the game."

"But that didn't mean I was going to follow LeBlanc's example. His way out is not mine. So, here I am, talking to this box, setting the record straight, as the early snow falls and the men and women of my command, now freed from the shackles of history, disperse into the folds of the world. Alive at least, and with a chance for better.

"Yes, I ordered them to lock down their weapons before they left. I couldn't have the creation of a rogue army on my conscience along with everything else. And when the last of them crossed the threshold beneath the gazes of stone Presidents who outlasted one nation and are about to outlast another, I closed and sealed the doors without hesitation.

"Then I joined the Lt. Colonel in his tent and began this recording. To whoever finds it, don't bother looking for me. I know another exit and plan to head out as soon as the sun breaks the eastern horizon, which will be in… ten minutes.

"And since sunrise is about the only thing I can be sure of anymore, it seems like a good time to start my new life.

"Oh, and if you've come to claim the orb archive, sorry. LeBlanc sent it south a week ago with Corporal Hayes's infiltration squad under orders to deliver it to our allies in Texassippi. A fool's errand if there ever was one. Their APC only had a hundred and twenty miles of fuel left, at best. Then what were they supposed to do? Walk the rest of the way, past the MA border garrison and through the emptiness of the Central Ebbland, all the while carrying hundreds of talking glass balls full of follies best forgotten?

"Had it been up to me, they never would have left. Instead, LeBlanc made me sign the order.

"Well, I won't be signing any more orders. I'm getting out of here. I'd blow this place if I could, but the timer-charges are on the train. So, the best I can do is lock the door behind me.

"Go ahead, call me a deserter if you want, but I'm not deserting anything that's not worth leaving behind. The truth is, the time is well past, not just for me, but for all of us, to find our way back to what's left of the world humanity deserted in order to follow Gilgamesh down the long, disastrous road of warfare, conquest and planetary plunder we paint up pretty and call history.

"Recording that history for all time in shiny billiard balls strikes me as just another disaster, which is, I suppose, why I'm recording a different story into this one. I have no illusions that a single orb holding the naked words of a broken army major stands a ghost's chance in Hell of countering hundreds of orbs filled with the painted words of civilization's most revered minds who've been passing those words down since the first scribe put chisel to stone.

"But those scribes and all the generations who followed them save those who are alive today didn't know how it was all going to play out. And I'm pretty sure I do. So, I'll take my ghost's chance.

"Now, I'm late for that new life. Somewhere out there I have a family to find, and I've delayed the search long enough."

The orb emitted the sounds of shifting cloth and a few muffled thumps. Then came a sharp click followed by silence.

Everybody sat and stared. Benethan's mind reeled. He didn't need Jaio's help to know that the words of Major Anchor contradicted the deepest truths of the *Companta*. He also knew it did so with an authenticity beyond question.

A part of Benethan wished he had never heard it, but he had. The damage was done. There would be no way for him or the others to unhear it, even if he smashed the orb to powder.

Into the building silence, the rain-like hiss commenced again, followed by the clatter.

"Dammit," said Major Anchor as a second replay began.   Only then did Jaio cover the orb.

For a moment, nobody spoke then the quiet young Ghost named Brye cleared his throat. "The sun rises in the west," he said.

"During Major Anchor's time, it didn't," said Jaio. "It rose in the east."

"How can that be?"

"The oldest stories of the Orols say that sometime during the long forgetting between his age and ours, the world turned upside down."

Brye shook his head. "When I hear his words, I think the end of the Ancients turned the world right side up. And we are here to make sure it doesn't turn upside down again."

Across the fire from Benethan, the Ghosts all nodded. Benethan, by contrast, felt his mind cast up a wall of resistance even though he could not draw clear enough meaning from the statement to say why. He could only say with certainty that he would have rejected it outright if not for the resonation he felt in his gut.

"What is a…chess game?" asked the fierce

woman, Syree.

All eyes turned to Jaio. And much to Benethan's surprise, the boy Orol knew far less about the game than he did, thanks in large part to many a humiliating defeat at the hands of Laureate Consul Noyova.

Once Jaio finished his short description, Benethan leaned forward. "Actually," he said, trying not to sound too smug. "There's more to it than that. Allow me to explain." As he proceeded, he struggled to convince himself his wish to enlighten the Thracks did not stem from a sense of intellectual rivalry with a tattooed teenager. Yet, try as he might, he could think of no other reason. And it was too late to stop now.

He focused on the game and soldiered on.

By the end of the lesson, the Thracks sat scratching their heads. Benethan thought he'd been clear, but from their looks, he knew he had been defeated as surely as if he'd faced Noyova across the board. Too many details. He needed to keep it simpler, to hit only the most important points, like Jaio did in his explanations. The boy made it seem so easy.

"Maybe if we build a set, it will make more sense," said Kemren.

Benethan nodded.

Wolfe leaned forward and gave his attention to Jaio. "I think it's time you told us the story of the other orb; what did you call it? The Founding Orb?"

Jaio opened his mouth to speak, but before he could Sable raised her hand. "Wait," she said. "First, your story."

"Good idea," said Wolfe. "Then you can tell us of the orb."

Jaio cleared his throat. "Really, they're both parts of the same story, a bigger story."

"Then let's hear that story,' said Wolfe.

Jaio nodded, drew a long breath and began. Benethan and the others soon found themselves transported to a minor hill in an ice-free land Benethan did not even know existed. On top of the hill, a naked boy awaited a vision and tried to stay warm as a new day dawned...

THE ADMINITHEDRAL

Guide cables clanged against ancient beams and oily gears chattered as their great metal teeth rolled together, meshed and separated. Slowly, the massive telescoptic magnifier at the heart of the Adminthedral slid along its arched track. A team of deaf-hands at the eastern end of the arch grunted with each turn of the rope-bound crank-wheel as they labored to heave the apparatus into position.

Since the hour was still early, they did not have to hoist it far before it was in place. Fine focus would commence once with the removal of the cover.

Dictorian Consul Dalsen Ario stood below, at the center of the soaring glass tower where he watched and tried to care what, if any, new offerings of ancient wisdom the sun might draw forth from today's target orb fragment. A small part of him hoped the hot focused light would reveal more than it had throughout the last fortnight, if for no other reason than to serve as a distraction from his unending anguish about Jaspen. Had Kemren and the Mesoric mercenaries done the impossible and saved his daughter from the Iron Cloud? Ario knew better than to cling to hope. But cling he did.

He forced his attention back to the task at hand and tried to busy his mind with a silent recitation of the results from the sun's previous fourteen long slow arcs across the sky: a paltry three hundred fifteen individual words, fewer than ten complete sentences and only two unbroken expositions of more than fifteen seconds in length. And none of these aural strings had contained so much as a syllable worthy of inclusion in the next edition of the ever-growing *Companta*.

So far, Ario had contributed less than half as much new material as his predecessor, the arrogant Dagger, Xathier Hawkenesse, despite having held the Order's highest seat for over twice as long. Yet not even this fact managed to stoke his competitive fire. In truth, the ember of ambition had gone cold within him. Not even a spark remained.

"The first fragment is almost in place, Brother Ario," said a smooth baritone voice from behind.

Ario turned to face the speaker, Tributan Consul Sigmos Bomechor, head of the Dagger sect and Ario's recent rival for the high seat of the Order. Ario wished he could make himself dislike the man as he had disliked Hawkenesse, but between the thoughtful eyes and easy smile, Bomechor exuded an air of open sincerity Ario appreciated. And now, with the Cloud afield and Maxamant threatening, Ario wished Bomechor had won the seat.

Bomechor leaned over his work in the targeting alcove. Early morning light danced on the surface of his silver sash as he made final, minute adjustments to the position of the orb fragment within the spider-like grip of the suspension arms.

"This one looks to be a fifth if not a sixth order," said Bomechor.

Over half complete, thought Ario. The most intact orb he'd seen thus far had been a fourth order. "Perhaps the Maker will favor us with an equatorial break as well," said Ario.

"Such fortune is long overdue, to be sure," said Bomechor. Ario almost believed the Dagger cared more for the well-being of the Order than his own reputation.

"That it is." Ario stepped over to the simple chair set up behind the dictation table facing the alcove. He sat and looked down at the blank page of the leather-bound journal lying open before him.

Bomechor strode from the alcove and took up his position, standing behind Ario's right shoulder, where he would witness and assist with interpretation and validation of whatever they heard, if anything.

"Ready, Brother?" asked Bomechor.

Ario nodded, took up the quill and opened the ink pot beside the book.

Bomechor signaled to Brother Felsis, the deaf-hand in charge of the telescoptic cover as well as final targeting. The unhearing monk pulled the cover away and in that instant a blinding point of light struck the burnt back wall of the stone alcove behind the orb. A thread of smoke immediately began to rise from the blackened stone. Then the hot point of lens-focused sunlight tracked toward the orb fragment as the sharp scent of scorched earth hit Ario's nose.

Ario marveled again at the fine dexterity displayed by Brother Felsis who deftly guided thousands of pounds of glass and metal with a skill unmatched by even the best marksmen. In a moment, the beam reached its target. The orb absorbed the light the way a parched sponge soaks up water.

Now, they would find out if the invisible spiral of sounds recorded within the orb remained intact or if the spiral had been shattered by a polar break, thereby rendering Ario's first fifth-order orb no more talkative than a common river stone. He and Bomechor waited while Felsis made fine beam adjustments, seeking the hidden point where the concentrated spear of sunlight would trigger playback.

A burst of static resounded from the alcove and Ario heard the quick snap of Bomechor's robe sleeve as the Dagger thrust his fist skyward to signal Felsis to cover the lens.

Ario dipped the quill and readied himself. He would have one chance at this. An orb could only be forced to speak a single time; the stab of light that made it work also melted the point of entry into the aural spiral. Whatever it contained would play out from the burn to the end, or to next break in the spiral, and never be heard again.

"—ototype Optical Recording Ball mark three has double the playing time of the mark two but costs half as much to produce," said a woman, her tone excited. "And as you will hear in a moment, the sound quality is noticeably improved."

"You have exceeded our expectations, Doctor. And ahead of schedule no less," said another woman, though with far less enthusiasm. "But conditions throughout the Northern Provinces are worsening far more quickly than even our most pessimistic models predicted. As much as I want orb research and development to continue, the present must take precedence over the future. I'm sorry. Now, if you will please turn that off."

"Wait. The happenings in the world out there at present are exactly why the orbs are needed now more than ever."

"I'm sorry, Doct—"

"Minister, please, think about this. Every human who will ever live is alive at this very moment as genetic potential within us. But unlike other forms of life, we humans don't enjoy the same instinctual sanity. Those who will follow in our footsteps will need to inherit more than our genes. They will need to inherit our stories if they are to learn how to live well in the far more fragile world we are leaving to them, a world we *made* fragile as a direct result of our actions. They need us to—"

"Thank you, Doctor. But I'm sorry. As much as I admire your intentions, our job now is to figure out how to leave descendants. Period.

"Don't get me wrong. We will use the orbs we already have to record what we can. So rest assured, our children will have something to work with. It may not be enough for you, but it will have to be enough for them."

"But the orbs are not being used to tell the kinds of stories they will need."

The minister huffed. "How do you know what kinds of stories they will need?"

A lengthy pause followed this question, giving

Ario time to catch up in his dictation.

"You're right, Minister," said the Doctor. "I may not know what kinds of stories they *will* need, but I do know what kinds of stories they *won't* need; they won't need stories about how to advance today's technological frontiers into a future where the infrastructure to do so will not exist, nor ever be possible again. They won't need stories promoting the conquest of other countries or the colonization of other planets. And they won't need stories that compel them to see this planet as little more than a pool of resources for their exclusive short-term benefit. Yet, those are the kinds of stories the orbs have thus far been used to preserve."

"Correct me if I'm wrong," said the minister. "But the orb itself is a product of today's advancing technological frontiers, is it not? So, doesn't that mean cutting off funding is exactly what I ought to do for the sake of the future? Wouldn't that be the best way to make sure our descendants aren't subjected to any more worthless stories?"

Ario hears a clear sigh, followed by another stretched silence. Then the doctor speaks, her voice quiet, reflective. "How about using the unique potential of this particular technology to help our children understand why they live on a tired and angry planet? How about using the orbs to record an admission of our mistakes and, if nothing else, to offer an apology? How about passing on a story that frees our descendants from our legacy so they can pursue their own?"

"Doctor Oroken," said the minister.

Hearing the doctor's name caused Dalsen Ario's quill to stall as if by its own will. He glanced back to see Sigmos Bomechor staring wide-eyed at the orb.

"Your idealism is perhaps commendable," the minister went on.

With great effort, Ario continued to write.

"But we've spent too many millennia and too many lives building this legacy of progress and industry to simply let it die. Civilization must live on and it will, thanks to you.

"Now, we are done here. This has been a very enlightening discussion. I think it will make an excellent addition to the archive under the subject heading of naïveté."

"No, please Minister. Don't use my invention to—"

"To what? Record a story? That's what you created it for, isn't it? And that's what we've been using it for. To record the story of this grand global society we've built so that our children will have a blueprint to follow when the snow melts and the time to rebuild finally arrives.

"Thanks to your invention, we'll be ready.

Now, the guards will escort you back to your cell. Good day, Doctor Oroken.

Ario heard the sound of scraping; chair legs sliding on a hard floor.

"Oh," said the minister. "You might be interested to learn, we just received intel as to the whereabouts of your accomplice in last week's...what are they calling it on the newsfeeds? Oh yes, the Zookeeper's Revolt. Hernán Lopez and the stolen orb should be in our custody within the week. And all the animals that were released across the Provinces as a result of his unauthorized Arknet broadcast using your Netcell are being rounded up as we speak. Or should I say, all the animals that haven't yet succumbed to the elements.

"So much for your little act of civil disobedience. Pointless. Now, where is that off switch? Ah, here we are."

A sharp click followed this last word. Then silence. The quill fell still in Ario's hand, but he couldn't quite bring himself to lift it from the page. He wanted more. Needed more. But no other sounds emanated from the alcove.

"We must convene the Tributan Council," he heard himself say.

"Why?" said Bomechor. "There is nothing here suitable for inclusion in the *Companta*."

"What?" Ario couldn't believe his ears. "This

is the first reference to the inventor of the orbs we've ever found."

"And she was a criminal who somehow became the namesake of Anthemar's bane!"

"Hers was clearly a crime of conscience. And as for her name, coincidence." Even as Ario said it, he knew better. But he couldn't betray his most cherished memories, no matter the risk.

"Coincidence! Hardly. She stands in opposition to everything we stand *for*, just like the Thracks."

"But the minister explicitly voiced our sacred mission. Surely, her words belong in the *Companta*."

"Taken out of context as they would need to be, her words raise too many questions: why did she feel compelled to state the obvious? What was the counterview to which she was responding? And who possessed sufficient merit to warrant such a response from a figure as prominent as the minister?

"No, Dictorian, the *Companta* would not gain enough from her words to cancel out the damage that would be caused by the answers to these questions, questions which would almost certainly be asked. And I, for one, am not willing to break my oath to truth in order to fabricate nonthreatening answers."

"How is complete omission any less a

violation?" Ario understood the danger in this question, but could not hold his tongue.

To his surprise, Bomechor simply smiled. "What does not exist requires no omission."

"What are you suggesting, Brother?"

"The orb and your dictation must be destroyed, for the good of the Order," said Bomechor.

Throughout Ario's many years as a Tributan assisting prior Dictorians with their work in this chamber, not once had utter destruction of an orb and its content been contemplated, no matter how unsavory the subject. Material deemed unworthy of the *Companta* simply went into the vault. And there were many volumes of such material. To recommend annihilation was unheard of. Maybe, Ario had misjudged this Dagger after all.

"Surely, they belong in the vault."

In response, Bomechor raised his fist again. Up at the telescoptic controls, Brother Felsis uncovered the lens and aimed the beam into the orb.

"What are you doing?"

Bomechor said nothing. He simply stood there with his fist in the air as the orb absorbed the light.

"Stop, Brother."

The orb began to glow red like the dawn sun on a smoky morning and still Bomechor maintained the signal.

Ario turned and yelled for Felsis to cover the lens, forgetting for a moment the monk's deafness. He raised his own hand and gave the counter-sigh to override Bomechor's order.

Felsis kept his gaze fixed on Bomechor.

Then Ario remembered. Felsis is a Dagger.

Ario ran toward the ladder leading up to the telescoptic control platform. Behind him, he heard the rustle of paper followed by footfalls. He spun in time to see Bomechor striding toward the alcove with the dictation journal in his hands.

"Sigmos, don't!"

Bomechor simply laid the journal atop the radiant orb. A white-hot point of light struck the page, instantly igniting the paper.

Ario stood in shocked silence as flames blossomed and spread. Bomechor held onto a corner until the flickering heat threatened his fingers then tossed the burning mass into the back of the alcove, where it completed its combustion.

As soon as the last of the book-fire dwindled to a few lines of smoke, Bomechor turned and offered Ario a broad smile.

At that moment, the radiant half-orb slumped and fell from the grip of the spidery mechanism that held it. Partially liquefied, it oozed between two fingers like thick syrup and dropped to the alcove floor where struck the stone with a sound more like a splat than a bang.

Its inner light faded quickly as it cooled and soon it lay there shiny and black like an overturned finger-bowl made of midnight darkness itself.

Bomechor started back to the dictation desk, but paused to kneel by the fallen orb. He considered it for a moment then drew a dagger from his robe. With the metal ball at the end of its hilt, he smashed the rapidly-cooling orb into countless smoking shards.

He then stood, tucked the dagger away and pulled another orb fragment from his pocket. "Looks like a third order," he said. "I'll have it ready to go in a moment. Maybe, this one will have an equatorial break, and contents worthy of your ink."

Ario stood in stunned silence at the base of the ladder. His mind struggled to accept what had just happened. Bomechor might be able to unhear the words of Doctor Oroken, but Ario didn't think he could.

The memory would do him no good, however. Bomechor would deny any reference to it, and all other potential sources of evidence had, in a mere handful of moments, been completely erased from existence.

He numbly returned to his chair and was drawing a new journal out of a drawer when the triple-chime sounded.

Bomechor paused from his placement of the new orb fragment in the suspension mechanism. "I will see what urgency interrupts our work," he said and headed around the alcove.

Ario stood and followed. Now that he'd seen Bomechor's true colors, he had no intention of letting the Dagger hear the message unaccompanied.

Bomechor swung the massive door open as Ario strode to a halt at his side. Beyond the threshold stood Laureate Consul Selas Noyova accompanied by two Tributan Consuls — Brother Omombis Pendletree, Administrator of the Kiddyon Protectorate and Brother Galowyn Turue, Administrator of the Kestian Protectorate.

All three monks wore masks of extreme anxiety. Ario felt a knot of dread form in his gut.

"Apologies for the disturbance, Brothers," said Noyova with a slight bow. "But we bring grave news."

"Go on," said Bomechor.

"Maxamant has invaded Kest."

16

TIGRESS

In the aftermath of yet another squall—this one more sleet than snow—Jaio and his companions have spent the better part of the morning working to break *Tigress's* skids free from the resultant crust. Jaio can no longer say for certain how many such mornings they have endured since leaving the Mountain of Faces almost three weeks earlier. Too many, especially now that they are deep in the mountains well beyond the Open-hand Node and headed north, following the faint signs of the skateships.

Jaio has told the Pride about the great vessels, but he knows their appreciation will remain only partial and abstract until they see the sight with their own eyes. Rawl simply refuses to believe the vessels could be anything more than glorified windsleds. After a lifetime of deep prejudice, his mind only seems capable of stretching so far without the help of his senses. That stretch won't be long in coming. Segray puts their arrival at the final node and the rendezvous with the skateships at three to six days depending on wind and weather. At this point, Jaio suspects six is more likely, even with everyone working as efficiently as possible.

He is impressed at the speed with which the Pride has learned from Bengus how to help run the windsled. Despite the effort involved in training, the big tooler simply refused to let seven able bodies pass the journey as little more than dead-weight. So, he folded them into the crew. Shortly afterward, the Anthemari word for snowflakes resounded often across the deck.

"Claws clear!" shouts Galees from almost directly over Jaio's head. She dangles by a rope beneath the belly of the windsled, her chipper's axe gripped in her hand. Jaio and Sable work with larger pickaxes to free the forward port skid from the ice crust in which it is imbedded. Other pairs work on the rest of the skids.

All around them, the radiance of the rising sun has been surging then ebbing then surging again as fast-flowing streamers of ground fog wash by. They sparkle with suspended flakes.

Despite the beauty, Jaio only half-notices. His thinking mind, his Orol's mind, is too busy replaying the lengthy conversations he has had with Wolfe and the others. The most memorable aspect is the imposing tactan's frustration. The leader of the Pride wants a plan, but the simple fact is, they don't have enough information to form one much beyond the base goal of stopping Thorne. No amount of thinking will change that.

Jaio pauses and removes a water skin from its pocket in his parka. He offers it to Sable. She smiles and accepts. Simply watching her drink fills him with deep joy of a kind he's never felt before. And the way she watches him suggests that she feels it too. Even though she speaks little, Jaio can sense a bond between them growing by the day.

"Smoke!" comes a faint cry from high above.

Sable hands the skin back and Jaio tucks it away as he and the others step out into the open to look up at the mast. There in the lofty rigging Syree is pointing northwest.

Jaio and the others look that way. Just ahead of the summits of the farthest peaks and visible through the thinning haze is a spreading black pall fed by multiple columns of thick sooty smoke.

Wolfe is the first to move. He heads for the rope ladder leading up to *Tigress's* deck. Jaio starts to follow.

"Come on, snowflakes, keep working," booms Bengus. "We can't move fast if we're stuck fast."

Jaio hesitates, torn between helping Sable finish freeing the skid or going with Wolfe.

Galees lowers herself down to the Ice and waves him off with her hand. "Go on." She unclips her harness and takes Jaio's place at the skid. He offers a grateful smile and heads for the ladder.

By the time he reaches the top, Wolfe is already deep in conversation with Segray at the tiller. Jaio hurries to hear what they're discussing.

"You're sure," says Wolfe. "Those peaks are the Dividing Ridge?" He nods to the far summits just visible beyond the smoke.

"Without Ticker, I can't be absolutely sure, but all the landmarks seem right, yes."

"So, Gray Horn burns."

"Gray Horn?" asks Jaio.

"The stronghold of the Kiddyon Protectorate." Wolfe enunciates every syllable slowly, deliberately, as if each one takes all his will to force out through his clenched teeth.

Segray retreats a step.

Jaio feels the same inclination, but holds his place. Wolfe's agitation seems excessive. "But you are Kestian?"

"If Kiddyon has fallen, it can only mean Kest fell first."

"To whom?"

"Maxamant. The question is why now? What has changed?"

"As soon has we're free, we'll be heading that

way," says Segray. "Perhaps, the situation will become clearer."

Wolfe surges toward the side rail. "How close are we to break out?" he calls down.

Before anyone has a chance to answer, Syree whistles from above. "Skateships dead ahead! Approaching fast!"

Jaio, Wolfe and Segray run to *Tigress's* bow. They gaze north across the Ice. At first, the only movement comes from the last westward weaving snakes of sparkling ground fog. Then the first set of swollen sails rises above the haze. A moment later, the second lifts into view followed in close succession by six more. The whole Guardian fleet.

Jaio expects Wolfe to shout warning, but the big tactan seems frozen by the sight.

Jaio runs amidships and leans over the railing. "Everybody, up top now!"

This snaps Wolfe awake and he runs to the ladder as the sounds of sudden activity down below fill the quiet morning air. He grabs tools and piles them on the deck as one by one, everybody clambers up the ladder.

"Pride, duck low!" calls Jaio. "They may have telescoptics. We mustn't let them see you."

"Or you, Ghost Orol!" shouts Kahala.

Jaio realizes he's not supposed to be there either. He crouches and sidles to take cover behind the starboard gunwale. That's when he notices Sable is not among them.

"Where's Sable?" he shouts. He hopes he doesn't sound as desperate as he feels.

"Here," she calls from the ladder.

"Hurry!" rumbles Bengus as he opens the hatch to one of the aft cargo holds. "All of you, inside."

Sable slips aboard and dashes with the others toward the opening in the floor of the deck.

"What were you doing?" asks Jaio as they shuffle aft at a crouch.

"Erasing our prints."

From behind, Jaio hears a gasp. "They're monsters!"

Jaio turns to see Rawl gaping at the eight looming skateships. Even though they are still quite some distance away, their immensity is now beyond doubt, especially the one in the center; Thorne's triple-masted, eight-legged behemoth.

Much to Jaio's dismay, the rest of the Pride— with the exception of Wolfe—have also responded to Rawl's exclamation and are similarly immobilized by the view.

"Keep moving!" orders Wolfe.

Sable grabs Rawl as the others tear their stunned gazes from the approaching fleet and drop down into the cargo hold. Jaio hops in last and manages to duck low just before the hatch slams down. The smell of partially digested plant matter assaults his nose. They're in the fuel hold, surrounded by sacks of dried yak dung.

Then darkness engulfs them. Only a few narrow slivers of light filter in around the hatch seams and between a couple deck boards. Jaio glances at the forms huddled with him in the dimly-lit space. Weeks of brazier fires have cleared more than enough room for the eight of them to fit, though far from comfortably.

"I'm thinking this whole 'stop Thorne' plan may need a little revision," says Rawl.

"We'll find out soon enough if we still enjoy the element of surprise," says Wolfe. "Until then, quiet."

Jaio listens to the noises from above; rapid footfalls, clattering and other assorted bangs and thuds accompanied by the occasional curse from Bengus. "Get those extra tools stowed!" Eventually, the sounds subside. Jaio imagines his fellow Ghosts gathered at the bow to await the arrival of the skateships.

For an incalculable span no doubt shorter than it feels, nothing changes. Then Jaio begins to feel a tremor. At first, he believes it to be a figment of his imagination, but as it builds and his companions begin shifting uncomfortably around him, he realizes the skateships are close enough for their immense weight to shudder the Ice. Soon the crackling hiss of skates cutting through ice and snow becomes discernible, then grows until it is almost deafening.

"Cover your ears," calls Jaio.

The words have barely left his mouth when a pair of heart-stopping booms resound from outside, one to starboard, one to port. They cause the windsled to jolt. A bag of dry dung discs tumbles into Jaio from behind making him jump.

Then comes a horrible metallic rending sound. It starts at a volume loud enough to make Jaio's ears ring, then rapidly fades to silence.

"What in the name of snow-tips fangs?" Rawl huffs.

"Close guess," whispers Jaio.

"What?"

"They're not fangs, they're braking claws. Two skateships have stopped."

"Quiet," orders Wolfe.

The tremors subside as six of the eight skateships continue on their way. Soon, the noise of huge metal blades cutting across the Ice has faded enough for Jaio to hear the clang of rigging amid metallic groans and the shouts of Ghosts.

"Cappen!" calls Bengus. "You needn't have come to fetch us. We were on our way."

"Good to see you too, Clank!" calls Cappen Aiomida. "Mission accomplished?"

From the sound of her voice, Jaio believes *Frostbite* to be on their port side. But what ship sits to starboard?

"Aye. We're ready for whatever comes next."

"Good to hear it. But I'm afraid you'll need to stay aboard *Tigress* since her sister skateship is not with us. However, I do have some volunteers who are eager to help fill out your crew."

"Keethu, Teeg!" calls Kahala.

"That's not necessary," says Bengus. "We'll be just fine withou—"

"Clank!" Kahala and Brye protest in unison.

The big tooler chortles. "All right. All right. No need for mutiny. Send 'em over."

"Please allow me to offer you some assistance as well," calls a new voice, this one coming from starboard.

"Kind of you to offer, Cappen Leegon," yells Bengus. "Two extra hands are more than enough."

So, thinks Jaio, the other skateship is *Waketorrent*, the vessel of the Oronish Ghosts.

"I insist," says Leegon. "Sothio, Ghen," he shouts. "Transfer over to *Tigress*. Help them however you can."

"Fateholder?" asks Bengus, his tone thick with disapproval.

"We will not turn down aid freely offered," says Cappen Aiomida. "Thank you, Cappen Leegon."

A long pause commences. Jaio imagines

Leegon offering one of his legendary condescending nods.

"Find them a task, Clank," says Cappen Aiomida.

"Aye. I'll put 'em to work," he calls. Then under his breath, he grumbles. "With the bluntest picks I have."

"As soon as they're aboard, prepare to move," yells Cappen Aiomida for all to hear. "We still have some distance to travel today. And we don't want the other ships to get too far ahead."

"Understood…Okay, snowflakes! You heard her. Let's finish digging out so we can be on our way…Kahala, Brye, take *those* pickaxes down for certain new members of our crew."

Jaio hears the sounds of heavy footfalls coming closer. They stop on top of the hatch. "You hear all that?" Bengus whispers.

"Every word," says Jaio.

"Can we trust the four who are coming aboard?" asks Wolfe.

"The two from *Frostbite*, aye. But we'll have to be careful how we make the introductions. As for the two from *Waketorrent*, I strongly doubt it. They're Oronish, after all. Way above our lowly station, as far as they're concerned, at least. I'm not even sure why they stopped. I would've expected—"

"Okay," Wolfe interrupts. "We'll avoid them.

Can you arrange for a breakdown to stall our rendezvous with the other ships?"

"Sure, but why?"

"So we can learn as much as possible here before we plunge into the hornet's nest."

"Right, one cracked skid-mount coming up." The tooler moves away.

Wolfe waits until he's gone then casts Jaio a puzzled look. "Tell us more about the fleet."

Jaio proceeds to fill the Pride in on what he knows of the skateships and their Ghost clan crews.

17

TIGRESS

Keethu and thick-necked Sothio strike alternating blows at the ice crust embedding *Tigress's* rear port skid. Only a few dozen paces away, Keethu's best friend Kahala, with whom she has not spoken in weeks, works to free the front port skid with Sothio's sticklike counterpart, Ghen. Keethu knows the pairings are no accident.

Aboard *Frostbite*, Cappen Leegon no doubt has many ears. But aboard *Tigress*, the Oronish fateholder is deaf. And for reasons Keethu cannot understand, he is determined to make sure she keeps Sidray's secret to herself.

Of course, all this has done is make her want to share it the first chance she gets. And, best friend or no, Kahala is not the person she has in mind as the recipient of what she knows. She needs someone who can speak Oronish, someone who is probably even closer to her in space than Kahala, and, at the same time, much farther away. She glances up at the looming hull of the windsled, wishing she could see through it, wishing she could somehow make contact with the old man at the tiller.

Her eyes settle on one of the steering rods leading straight from the tiller to the skid where she and Sothio work. She tries to subdue the smile on her face as an idea arises. With all the casual subtlety she can muster, she adjusts position ever so slightly. Once she is in place, she raises her pickaxe as if to strike another blow to the Ice then executes her slip. As she goes down, the pickaxe swings high and impacts the connecting bolt on the rod-pivot. She lands hard on her rear for effect.

If Map has his hand on the tiller, he most certainly felt the blow. And nothing is more likely to grab his attention than possible damage to *Tigress's* steering mechanism.

"What was that?" shouts a scratchy voice from above.

"Sorry, Map," she says as Sothio offers her a hand up. "I slipped and hit the tiller rod." She accepts the offered hand and even feigns a smile of gratitude.

"With a pickaxe?"

"It was a glancing blow." She brushes ice crystals from her parka as she pretends to examine the bolt. "Everything looks fine."

"To the untrained eye, perhaps…I'm coming down."

"I'll check it out," says Clank from where he works at the central port skid.

"You're blind to anything that can't be fixed with a hammer," says Map. "Nobody touch anything until I get there."

Clank lumbers over, nudges Sothio out of the way none-too-gently and proceeds with a close examination of the pivot bolt. Sothio's jaw clenches, but he says nothing, being outnumbered eight Oromola to two Oronish.

"Oh," moans Clank. "This doesn't look good." He pulls a hammer from his parka and begins banging on the locking pin holding the bolt in place. Keethu can see nothing wrong with either pin or bolt.

"Didn't Map tell you to wait."

"I think I can have this fixed before he gets here," says Clank. He lands another blow, which sends the pin flying into the snow.

"Ah, now look what I've done." He surges to the spot where the pin disappeared under the surface and begins fishing around. "Well, don't just stand there you two, give me a hand."

Both Keethu and Sothio hurry to his side, drop to their knees and start sifting through the crystalline heap of ice shavings.

The crunch of uneven, but hurried footfalls

draws to a halt behind them. "What have you done?" Map's voice shakes with rage. "I told you not to touch anything."

"It was a minor fix. Not a bother. I just…hit the pin a bit hard. We'll find it."

Keethu shuffles backward until she's behind Sothio then she stands and sidles up next to Map. On the Ice in front of her, the Oronish brute continues to hunt for the lost pin. She thinks about trying to set up a meeting with Map for later, but doesn't imagine when later might come. So, she just leans close to the livid wayfinder and whispers in his ear.

"Map, just listen," she says, then asks, "What does this mean?" She recites Sidray's words.

Whatever it is, the words cause Map's eyes to go wide and his temper to evaporate. She glances at Sothio with exaggerated intensity and touches her mitten to her lips.

Map's brows rise in understanding. "You great oaf, Clank!" He sinks to his knees with effort and joins the search. Keethu quietly resumes as well.

When Sothio has strayed several paces away, Map whispers something to Clank.

After a few more minutes of futile effort, they give up.

"Not to worry, Map," says Clank. "I can hammer out a replacement in no time."

"No time?" Map glares at him.

"Okay, not exactly no time, but soon. Then we'll be underway." Clank sets off for the ladder before Map or anyone else has a chance to reply.

"You and your hammer," mutters Map.

About half-way to the ladder, Clank pauses and looks back over his shoulder at Sothio. "I could use your help…" He squints as if the effort to dredge up the man's name causes him physical pain. Then he shrugs and finishes with, "my Oronish friend."

Sothio looks confused. "Me?"

"I need muscle and you appear to have more than anyone else here. Come on."

Sothio casts Keethu a quick concerned glance then hurries to catch up to Clank.

"We'll keep looking," calls Map, making a show of flinging crystals. As soon as Clank and Sothio are out of sight, Map stops and turns to Keethu. "Where did you hear those words?" he asks.

"From an Oronish Ghost named Sidray. What do they mean?"

"If you heard correctly, Sidray said, 'Tell Thorne, we led Maxamant's men to the cache. They have secured all the weapons.'"

"Why would Orol Thorne want to reveal a weapons cache to the Fane?" Keethu asks.

"Are you sure you're remembering correctly?"

Keethu thinks back, pictures the moment in her mind. She can see Sidray's lips moving, hear the words replay as they have thousands of times in her daily effort to preserve them in her memory. She nods.

"Then this is very disturbing news indeed. We must inform Cappen Aiomida."

"Wait," says Keethu. "We have to be discreet. If the Oronish fateholder, Cappen Leegon, finds out I told you…" she leaves the rest unsaid.

"Leegon is in on this too?"

Keethu nods.

"Then we must be very careful indeed. The idea of Thorne and a few misguided Ghosts conspiring with the Fane is one thing, but a fateholder? I would never have thought it possible."

"There may be more to it than we know," says Keethu.

"No doubt there is," says Map as he continues searching for the pin. "Okay, back to breaking ice. I'll go resume my derision of Clank, and send that Oronish snowbear down to assist you so he doesn't get suspicious." He struggles to his feet, offers a conspiratorial wink and hobbles off toward the ladder.

Keethu hefts her pickaxe and resumes her attack on the ice, her heart lighter than it has been for weeks…until she happens to look toward the

Kahala and sees Ghen watching her. She averts her gaze without haste and tells herself there's no way he heard her conversation with Map above the cacophony of falling pickaxes. But the glint she saw in his eyes suggests otherwise. She focuses her attention on the skid and strikes another blow.

18

TIGRESS

Kemren's body felt solid and warm at Jaspen's side. And despite being trapped in *Tigress's* cramped, dark, dung hold, she enjoyed the chance to simply be close to him, to feel his arm around shoulder, his chin resting gently on the top of her head. She closed her eyes and tried not to let anything else invade her mind.

The noise from outside certainly made that difficult. Her breath caught every time a shadow broke through one of the threads of incoming sunlight or footfalls thudded across the hatch overhead. Each instance caused her to wonder if this would be the time they were found out. But so far, every disturbance had passed by.

Somewhere not too far away, Bengus cursed.

Another set of footfalls approached, quicker with an uneven gait. The old man, Segray, she thought.

They came to a halt on top of the hatch.

"Can you hear me, Orol," the old man whispered.

"Yes," whispered Jaio.

"Keethu has just conveyed some rather disturbing news. If she heard correctly, Orol Thorne appears to be in league with the Fane."

"What?" Jaio sat up with such a start he banged his head on the hatch.

"Keep quiet," grumbled Wolfe.

"What did she say?" asked Jaio.

"She heard a message she was not supposed to hear, a message intended for Thorne about the successful revelation of a weapons cache to one of the Fane Protectorates."

"Maxamant?" asked Wolfe.

"Indeed. I can't imagine how this might have bearing on your plans, but thought you should know. Now, I have already lingered too long." Without further comment, the old man limped away.

"Does it have bearing?" asked Jaspen.

Before Jaio could respond, Wolfe leaned forward. "It is the piece that finishes the puzzle," he said, his tone low, almost inaudible.

"You think Keethu heard correctly?" asked Jaio.

"I am certain of it."

"So, Thorne is conspiring with the Fane?" asked Benethan.

"No, that was Segray's supposition, not the message. The message made no mention of secret treachery."

"What else could it mean?" asked Kemren.

"It means we are too late to stop Thorne outright. His plan to destroy Anthemar is already under way."

A shocked silence followed these words.

"But he just deliberately revealed a cache of weapons to them," said Kemren. "How does bolstering their arsenal aid in their own destruction?"

"He revealed the cache to Salazriole Maxamant."

"Is Maxamant not Fane?" asked Kemren.

"Yes, but so are those against whom he has already unleashed his new-found power."

"Kest and Kiddyon," said Jaio.

Wolfe nodded. "The Protectorate of Cortegras would be next, but I suspect their Liege, Lord Entyne, has decided to ally with Maxamant rather than suffer the same fate as his northern neighbors. Together he and Salazriole will try to pressure Vantling into doing the same."

"Lenowen Vantling will never join with Maxamant," said Sand.

"Agreed. Which means more smoke will soon foul the sky, thereby clearing the way to Anchoresk."

"What about the western Protectorates, Adrucat, Prees, Froynen and Satcha?" asked Benethan. "Surely, they won't sit idle."

"No, by now word has undoubtedly reached them and they are, at this moment, choosing sides, if they have not done so already."

"Satcha, Prees and Adrucat will likely side with Maxamant, but Froynen is as stubborn as Vantling," said Sand.

Wolfe nodded. "Lady Casayle will resist, but at best, she can only hope to slow the others as she retreats."

"The pieces are in play," said Benethan.

"So," said Jaio. "Thorne revealed the cache knowing the Fane would use it to destroy themselves."

Wolfe shook his head. "If Thorne were playing a game of chess, this might seem the case, but he has created a situation in which both sides serve his interests. So, to see what is really going on we must look deeper."

"I don't understand," said Benethan.

"The coming battle will not deliver the total annihilation Thorne desires. Bloody as it will no doubt be, one side—black or white—will surely win and gain the spoils in ordinance obtained from the losers."

"Which means, the threat Thorne hopes to eliminate will still exist," said Jaio.

"Exactly," said Wolfe. "So we must ask ourselves how might Thorne's actions make it possible for him to eliminate the threat to his family and the life he has come to hold dear?"

A heavy silence followed as everyone considered Wolfe's question. Jaspen tried to make all the pieces fit. She envisioned great armies locked in combat, all coming together at the fabled citadel of the Catalogians. She recalled what Jaio had said about Thorne's plan to destroy Anthemar with a weapon. A single weapon.

Powerful as such a weapon might be, Anthemar was vast. Perhaps Thorne was speaking figuratively, exaggerating for effect.

Jaspen tried to put herself in his position. What, above all else, made Anthemar a threat to his family and homeland? The answer suddenly seemed obvious: the relic weapons, which, until now, have been scattered throughout the nine protectorates and Anchoresk, spreading them too far apart to be eliminated in a single blow. And with this thought, the pieces suddenly came together, quite literally.

"He's found a way to gather the dangers in one place, where his weapon will be able to destroy them all," she said.

Wolfe nodded. "Well done. As soon as the armies converge on Anchoresk, he will make his move."

"What will his move be?" asked Jaspen.

"That, I cannot say. Most likely, he has managed to activate a relic nuke-bomb from the late Antiquitic. Yet, if this is the case, we have yet to determine how he intends to use it from here. Figuring that out will be one of our tasks. At the same time, we must warn the forces below of the trap into which they are marching."

"You honestly think they will listen," blurts Benethan.

"Not all of them, but enough, perhaps."

The monk shook his head. "Enough for what?"

"Enough to give Jaio a chance to complete his mission. It's the only chance for Anthemar and the Oroken."

"The Oroken? How is peace the only chance for the Oroken. If Jaio is right, they have the means to wipe us out uncontested. And, as cold as this will sound, isn't the outright elimination of an enemy preferable to making a peace that will surely break once enough generations have gone by for the motivating memory to fade into irrelevant legend and the human hunger for more to reassert itself?"

"Human hunger is at issue here," said Wolfe. "But not for more."

"What do you mean?"

"Don't you see, Benethan? Thorne's plan is not

about eliminating an enemy. It's about eliminating weaponry. But what he overlooks are all the people holding those weapons who will also be eliminated. These people hail from every corner of Anthemar. And when they die by his hand in the service of the Oroken, the mothers, fathers, brothers, children…the families of everyone he kills will remember, and their memories, rather than fading will only fester over the generations like an open wound waiting for the ointment of vengeance to be applied.

"This memory will unite all of Anthemar…in a hatred far more terrible and lasting than the animosity that exists right now. And once the survivors have multiplied and their children have grown up in this hatred, they will be hungry for retribution.

"This is the true hunger Thorne will bring. Insatiable and all-consuming. And eventually this hunger will lead them where?"

"Across the Ice," said Jaio, his voice almost inaudible and thick with fear.

Wolfe nodded. "Ice that is melting, opening the way a little more every day for vengeance to come with new weapons and the simmering will to use them. No, Brother, Thorne's solution is no solution at all. And even at the cost of our lives, we must do everything in our power to help Jaio succeed."

Benethan raised his chin the way he did when he was about to argue his point. But before he could open his mouth, Sable leaned forward, glared at him and shook her head. "No more 'can't' words, Monk. You listen now to what we *can* do." She waited until his chin sank, then settled back and nodded to Wolfe.

He tipped up his tricorn and considered her as if seeing her for the first time.

"Okay" said Benethan. "What can we do?"

Wolfe let out a long breath. "The convergence of Protectorate forces on Anchoresk will likely take several weeks, more than enough time for us to thwart Thorne's plan. But we'll have to split up," he said.

Jaspen didn't like the sound of that and reached for Kemren's hand.

Wolfe turned his attention to Jaio. "You must go to the one person in Anthemar who might be able to help your words reach enough ears to matter."

"Who is that?" asked Jaio.

"Dalsen Ario."

Another stunned silence filled the cargo hold.

Wolfe then shifted his gaze to Jaspen. "And you, thawrunner, are the one person who might be able to gain our Ghost Orol an audience," he said.

These words caused Jaspen's heart to skip a

beat as a hundred different emotions welled into her throat from the pit of her stomach.

"What?" said Kemren. "No way. She—"

Jaspen squeezed Kemren's hand. "I'll do it."

"Jaspen, no. It's too dangerous."

"If Jaio goes, so do I, Kem." She cast Jaio a questioning look.

The boy hardly hesitated before nodding. She nodded back then turned to face Kemren. "Please come with us."

Kem simply stared at her for a moment then offered a grim smile. "Of course."

"I'm with you too," said Sable.

"As am I," said Benethan.

Kemren's eyes narrowed. "Why?"

"You lost your pixelcloak, remember. Without me, you'll never get into the compound, let alone reach the Adminithedral."

"And without me, you'll starve," grumbled Rawl.

Wolfe grunted approval and turned his attention to Sand. "I'm afraid we must part ways, my friend," he said. "If the Red Strand still exists, it will need its captain."

Sand seemed unsurprised by this and nodded, but for once had nothing to say.

"And when you see Lady Kest, tell her what is happening. Ask her to trust her general one last time."

"And what will her general be doing?" asked Rawl.

"Dealing with Thorne."

"If," said Benethan, "We can figure out how to escape from this hold without been seen."

"I have an idea about that," said Jaio.

TIGRESS

Jaio and his companions don't have to wait long for Bengus to do another walk-by. He pauses on the hatch and yells at Syree to do a better job securing a spar sail. Then, through his beard he quietly asks, "Was that enough time?"

"Actually, Bengus. *Tigress* needs to be abandoned, with everyone but Wolfe left on board."

"Oh, now that'll take a real breakdown to pull off. You sure you want me to cripple our trusty windsled?"

"I'm sure."

"And supposing you want us to sneak the tactan aboard *Frostbite*, do you by chance have a suggestion as to how we might go about it?"

"You wouldn't want to leave any of the food bundles behind."

"One of 'em is going to be a mighty heavy bundle."

"Can you do it?"

"Aye, I'll manage, but it may take a bit. I'm going to have to deal with our Oronish guests first."

"Bengus?"

"Don't worry, I'll leave their skulls intact, much as I'd like to knock 'em together."

"Good."

"I'll let you know when we're ready. Oh, and you'll want to hold on to something." Then he is off, tromping aft.

At first, Jaio counts breaths while he waits, but somewhere around two hundred, his mind wanders to the sounds leaking in from outside. He tries to paint a mental picture of the scene based on what he hears. It's not very challenging and he finds himself nodding off. At his side, Sable appears to have fallen asleep already, curled beneath her scaler's cloak. He delights in her closeness even if the cloak shields him from feeling even a hint of her warmth. He closes his eyes and continues listening.

The abrupt cessation of pickaxe blows startles him awake. Something feels amiss. The cause eludes him a moment, until he considers the slim odds of freeing all six skids from the grip of the Ice at the exact same moment.

And shouldn't the silence below be followed by increased foot traffic on the deck as the chippers climb back aboard? Instead, the deck falls silent as well.

Across from Jaio, Sand shifts uneasily. "Something's wrong," he whispers.

Jaio turns to nudge Sable, but finds only a sack of dung discs in the spot where she'd been sleeping.

He glances around in the darkness searching for her and is about to ask the others where she is when a deck-board overhead lets out a long, slow creak.

Jaio freezes. Across from him, Sand and Wolfe bring their guns up.

Outside, someone clears his throat. "Ah, it's me," says Bengus. "Just me, going to open up the hatch now, nice and slow. Just me."

Wolfe lowers his gun and motions Sand to do the same.

Wood squeaks as the big tooler twists the catch and lifts the hatch. The pure white light of a mid-day sun pours in, momentarily blinding Jaio. When his vision recovers, he finds Bengus looking down at him with frightened, sorrowful eyes.

"Sorry, Orol," he mumbles.

"Stay down," Jaio tells Wolfe and the others. He stands before they can protest. There before him, Keethu, Teeg and the crew of *Tigress* are lined up like a human shield in front of Cappen Aiomida and a wiry, large-eyed man who can only be Leegon, fateholder of the Oronish skateship *Waketorrent*.

Arrayed in a circle around the whole group are at least two dozen Ghosts, half of them familiar and half not. Lash and Eyeshine hold hyperpulse pistols, as do two of the Oronish Ghosts. However, Cappen's second and the night-singer keep theirs trained at the deck while the Oronish have theirs raised. All the rest hold bows, arrows nocked, fingers on strings.

Jaio's appearance brings a broad smile to Leegon's face. He places a hand on Kahala's shoulder.

"And to think," Leegon says in halting Oromola. "I almost did not believe your tale."

"I'm sorry, Jaio," Kahala blurts out. "Ghen threatened to—"

"Tell your Fane friends to leave their weapons and come out, hands high."

Jaio starts to translate, but Wolfe and the others have already disarmed and are climbing up onto the deck. Their emergence causes the tension in the air to spike. Most of the Ghosts, both Oromola and Oronish, shift uneasily. Lash and Eyeshine raise their guns.

"I don't need to know the words to understand what he wants," says Wolfe.

Jaio watches for Sable to follow Jaspen from the hold, but Jaspen is the last one out. She stands beside Kem and the others, facing the two Cappens.

Aiomida locks her eyes onto Jaio's. They blaze with anger so hot he can almost feel it, but even so, he refuses to look away. "You were supposed to be going to them, not bringing them here," she says. "What were you thinking?"

"Ah, ah," Leegon raises a finger to his lips. "Remember Thorne's orders. No talking with the Ghost Orol."

"Thorne be damned," says Aiomida as she wheels on her Oronish counterpart. "I will have answers."

Leegon's cheery facade evaporates. "You will do as Thorne commands."

"Or what?"

Leegon raises a hand and most of his hyperpulse-armed Ghosts shift their aim from Jaio and the Pride to Aiomida and her Ghosts. "Is a boy Orol and this…this pack of Fane really worth risking your crew?"

"You tell me." Aiomida raises her own hand, but the response is quite different. Every gunport on the flank of *Frostbite* snaps open and from each a thick barrel juts forward. Even at Jaio's distance, he can see they are noticeably larger in diameter than pistol barrels. At the same time, a line of Ghost archers surges to the side rail. They draw back and aim their weapons across at *Waketorrent*.

"Stand down, Leegon. Let's find another way."

"Thorne will not tolerate—"

"Thorne is Fane!"

"Thorne *was* Fane. Now he is our Orol! And he has pledged to destroy the Fane!"

"Jaio is our true Orol, sent to the Ice by the council not to destroy the Fane, but to treat with them. And if Orol Jaio has deemed it necessary to bring these six Anthemari to us, I would at least hear why before blindly delivering them into the hands of Thorne."

Leegon's eyes narrow. "Thorne will hear about this."

"I don't think so." Aiomida pumps her fist once toward *Waketorrent* and a lance of green flame erupts with a roar from one of the upper gunports. In the same instant, the antenna array atop *Waketorrent's* mast explodes in a spray of sparks and metal fragments.

"I'm not going to give you time to bring your cannons out of storage, Cappen Leegon. Stand down now or I will signal my crew to delimb your ship and drop her masts."

"I could kill you before you have the chance," he hisses.

"My crew will recognize that as a signal too, though," she pauses, "it will convey a slightly different message."

"Which is?"

"To target more than just the skates and masts.

"You treacherous—"

"I have betrayed no one! I merely want answers. If you force this, the cause will be impatience and weakness on your part not treachery on mine. And everyone here will know it. Now choose."

Leegon's chin sinks and his shoulders slump. "You're right. Very well, I shall—" In a sudden burst of motion, he shoves past Kahala and before Jaio even realizes what is happening, Leegon is behind him, arm across his neck and something cold pressed into his temple.

"Thorne thought you might try something like this!" the Oronish fateholder as he glares at Aiomida.

A clatter from *Waketorrent* resounds across the Ice. Jaio strains against Leegon's arm to look up. Out of the corner of his eye, he sees gunports open and barrels emerging. Oronish archers rush to the side rails.

"Now," sneers Leegon. "The Ghost Orol and I will be leaving. Do with the Fane what you will. As you pointed out, Thorne already knows how they think. He has no interest in them."

"Leegon, don't—"

"Silence!"

Jaio's mind races, but everything is happening

too fast. He can barely keep his footing as Leegon all but drags him toward the rope ladder. The Oronish Ghosts have formed a line of protection and shuffle back in step with Leegon to cover the escape.

Jaio's companions can do nothing but watch.

When Jaio and his captors reach the rope ladder, Leegon whirls around. "Climb down, boy, slow and steady," he says. The fateholder's grip loosens and Jaio glances over the rail. Two can play the surprise-move game.

Jaio shoves Leegon's arm away and launches himself over the rail. Shouts go up while he's in the air, flailing to control his fall—

Whoomph! His feet hit the ground at an awkward angle, but instead of fighting his momentum, he uses it to energize a sideways roll. He hears a sharp snap and feels his hip press into something hard. He fears he's broken a bone, but when he finds his feet and takes off running toward *Frostbite*, everything seems to be working without pain, at least, without as much pain as he would expect from a broken bone.

That's when *Waketorrent* unleashes a full broadside cannon barrage and arrow volley against *Frostbite*. Jaio ducks out of instinct and covers his head as the hyper-pulse cannon bursts explode against *Frostbite's* hull. The Oromola skateship groans and sways from the impact.

Then the arrows strike with sharp thwacks, clangs, thuds and a few cries pain. Deflected, broken shafts spin down amid chunks of glass, wood and metal. They crash onto the snow all around Jaio. A jagged knot of glowing-hot iron the size of his fist misses him by less than a hands-width. It hisses at the bottom of the blackened crater it made, jetting steam into the air.

Jaio resumes his flight. Ahead, he sees *Frostbite's* lowered ramp. Ghosts are huddled around it, firing bows across at the Ghost archers who are returning fire from *Waketorrent's* ramp. Jaio focuses on reaching the safety of the Oromola skateship. The fast thuds of running feet grow louder behind him. To his right, he hears a heavy thump.

Something trips him from behind just as *Frostbite* returns fire. Inchoate images flash across his vision as he tumbles: a skeletal face with furious eyes, plumes of smoke bursting against *Waketorrent's* skin, her central leg crumpling with a terrible metallic scream, Leegon and his circle of protectors racing up the Oronish skatship's open ramp, a sling-strap bursting sending the bow of *Frostbite's* windsled, *Owl*, crashing to the Ice with a thunderous boom and a crack like lightning, Wolfe shouting at Sand and pointing, a shadow-figure climbing up a piece of *Waketorrent's* broken leg and disappearing through the narrow gap between the skateship and the windsled strapped to its belly.

Jaio struggles to find his feet again as more cannonfire resounds amid desperate cries and howls of pain. Acrid smoke singes his nose. Green flashes rip the air.

"Jaio!" someone calls. "Look out!"

What? He spins just in time to see the incoming fist. A sharp jolt of pain bursts in his skull followed by sudden, total darkness.

20

TIGRESS

The moment Jaio jumped, Wolfe lunged to the railing and tried to do the same. But a pair of Ghosts clamped onto his arms and held him back. He strained against them as he watched the boy hit and roll. Then he saw the orb tumble out. He shouted to Jaio, but the boy leapt to his feet and ran for the Oromola skateship without so much as a sidelong glance.

At that moment, the two Ghosts hauled Wolfe away from the siderail and tried to shove toward the ladder with the rest of the Pride.

"No," he growled, spun and tore into them using moves he hadn't attempted since his cadet days. The melee that followed didn't last long then he was leaping over the rail.

He hit hard, forgot to roll and felt something give in his left ankle. He ignored it and searched for Jaio.

Wolfe spotted him just as *Frostbite* absorbed

Waketorrent's first cannon and arrow volley. All Wolfe could do was watch in horror as whirling stone-tipped shafts and smoking debris crashed down around the boy. Somehow, amazingly, he survived it unscathed, but his pause had given his pursuer time to close the gap.

A thud resounded from behind Wolfe and he spun to see Sand spring out of a roll to his feet.

"Jaio dropped the orb!" Wolfe shouted above the cacophony of the battle. He pointed toward the dark spot in the snow at the base of the windsled's ladder. "Go get it while I help Jaio!"

Sand nodded and bolted away.

Someone on *Tigress's* deck yelled Jaio's name.

Wolfe spun in time to see a huge Ghost drape the unconscious boy over his shoulder and set off without apparent effort toward the Oronish skateship. Wolfe lumbered in pursuit, but his will could not overcome the stab of pain brought by each step. The resultant limp slowed him too much to catch up. But even so, he would not give up.

The Ghost who bore Jaio's limp form dashed inside the monstrous ship. On his heels, the last of the Oronish warriors fell back behind him and the ramp started up.

Wolfe fought through the pain to run faster.

A few paces ahead, a fallen Ghost—one of Thorne's personal protectors—lay sprawled on the ice, two arrows protruding from her back. In her hand, she still clutched the stuttergun. Wolfe veered for the weapon. He estimated he had time to retrieve it, clear the ramp of defenders and secure the entry long enough for help to arrive. Then, they could board the ship and rescue Jaio.

He bent for the gun then hesitated. This skateship was going to take Jaio to Thorne, the very person Wolfe needed to reach. It was a risk, but he could get there without killing.

Wolfe stood, raised his hands and resumed course straight for the skateship. The last two of the Oronish archers guarding the ramp drew back their bows and aimed for him. But they didn't fire.

"I surrender," he called. "I'm Kestian General Krugerhan Wolfe. Thorne knows me. I have information."

The Ghosts hesitated. One looked into the ship and spoke. The ramp stopped moving.

Wolfe pressed on, feeling hopeful.

Then Leegon appeared behind the archers. He glared and yelled something in a language Wolfe could not understand, except for one hope-crushing word. Fane.

Leegon raised a stuttergun and cut loose a quick burst.

Wolfe felt a thousand simultaneous hornet stings slam into his right shoulder followed almost instantly by complete numbness. His arm then seemed to turn to water. He saw it flop to hang senseless at his side. Despite this, he could think of only one course of action. Keep moving. But his head began to spin and his legs suddenly felt leaden. Before he could even attempt another step, they gave out and he crumpled to the Ice.

"Wolfe!"

Was that Sand?

Wolfe thought so, but couldn't tear his eyes from the skateship. He watched Leegon and the two Ghosts retreat inside as the ramp continued to rise. It had not even fully closed when a resounding boom rent the air and the massive vessel lurched forward.

The overlapping chatter from multiple sets of gears accompanied its slow acceleration. The crippled central leg rose into the air shedding its skate, a damaged strut and many other pieces as it did so. At the same time, the fore and aft legs rotated closer together to compensate.

Wolfe glanced back to see if *Frostbite* would pursue, but the Oromola skateship just sat there bleeding smoke from numerous wounds, the rear mast canted at a sharp angle. And though there was ample opportunity to fire more shots at *Waketorrent*, *Frostbite's* guns remained silent.

A building fatigue emanating from his shoulder made Wolfe's skull too heavy to hold up.

His head fell back onto the snow. Where was his tricorn? Must have fallen off somewhere. He didn't need it now anyway.

Wolfe clenched his teeth hard less from the pain of his injuries than from his failure to protect the one person who needed his protection more than all the others. Once, he might have wept, but too many years spent walling away the soft parts of his spirit had long ago left his eyes dry, no matter the anguish. Instead, he simply stared at the emptiness left in the skateship's wake. The aptness of the vessel's name drew forth an unexpected chuckle. Its departure would unleash a torrent to be sure. But he would not see it. Nor would he have any more chances to stop it.

Eventually, he became aware of Sand kneeling next to him and Ghosts hurrying about tending to the injured and dead. His gaze found Sand and to his surprise the spotter's eyes could still shed tears. Sand was holding his tricorn.

Then the rest of them came into view—Rawl, Syree, Benethan, Bengus, Segray, Galees, Brye, Kahala, Kemren and Jaspen.

"Oh, no," grumbled Rawl as they knelt around him.

Kahala let out a grief-stricken moan. In it, Wolfe heard the pain of terrible guilt. That would not do.

With his good hand, he reached for hers. Her

whole body trembled as she slipped off her mitten and grabbed hold. How cold he must be that she could feel so warm? He fought for focus. "Leegon did this, not you," he said.

She lowered her head.

"I took a chance," he added. "My choice… Understand?"

She nodded.

Wolfe's eyes then sought Jaspen's. She needed… something.

The orb.

He turned his gaze on his spotter.

"Did you get the orb, Sand?"

Sand withdrew the glassy ball, but kept it covered and silent.

"Good. Give…" Wolfe never remembered the act of simple speech requiring so much energy. "Give it to Jaspen."

Sand handed it over to her.

"Take it to your father."

Jaspen nodded and squeezed her wet eyes tight unleashing a fresh stream of tears.

Almost time.

Wolfe looked from face to face. One was missing. Why couldn't he remember which one? He strained to raise his head to find…her. Her.

"Where is Sable?"

The Pride exchanged uncertain glances.

"Gone," said Jaspen, with a sniff.

"Dead?" Wolfe could barely force the word from his mouth.

"No, just gone, without a trace."

Wolfe rolled his head south. In the gap between the kneeling forms of Syree and Benethan, he could just make out *Waketorrent's* silhouette, growing smaller in the far distance. Or were the mountains growing larger?

No matter.

There's still a chance, he thought. A ghost's chance.

His lips struggled to form a smile. "I think Jaio does not go alone," he said. Then he gave his attention back to the ten people encircling him, Anthemari and Oroken, his beloved Pride all. "And neither do I."

With his final breath, General Krugerhan Wolfe gave one last command. "Stick…to the…plan."

21

WAKETORRENT

In the lonely, rattling darkness, Sable fought to suppress her sobs. She sat, head down, hugging her knees, her back against the starboard gunwale of the Oronish windsled. Inches above her, the metal belly of *Waketorrent* formed a low ceiling. It seemed to radiate pure, lifeless coldness; a coldness to match the chill in her spirit.

Sable squeezed her eyes tight, but even so the scene kept repeating again and again in her mind: Wolfe limping toward *Waketorrent*, hands up, choosing surrender over combat.

Had he been facing an honorable enemy, it would have ended there, with the rejection of his offer or with his capture.

But then the green flash puckered the right shoulder of his parka. And he went down. She knew he would never get up, not from that.

With all her will, she had wanted to go to him, to be there with him, to say goodbye.

But she could only watch from her hiding place.

Now, still hiding, she rocked with grief.

At first, she only heard the voice singing "Kradut's Mourning for the Fallen Friend." Then she recognized the voice as her own.

No, she thought, Wolfe will have a different song. Despite the slim danger of being overheard, she transitioned into "Kradut's Mourning for Fallen Kin."

She hoped the growing distance between herself and Wolfe—as *Waketorrent* bore her away—would not be too great for the song to release his spirit from the shell of his body. She sang it over and over until she reached a moment when a wave of inexplicable peace washed over her. She could not distinguish this moment from any other, but somehow she knew the song had done its work. He was free.

"Goodbye, Tactan," she whispered and looked up from her knees.

Time to focus on the living, on the one person for whom she would never sing any of Kradut's songs, because her heart could not survive losing him. Jaio.

The riveted metal underside of the skateship vibrated and jolted above her. She slipped off a mitten and reached up to press her palm against the cold, hard surface.

Somewhere on the other side, he was a prisoner. Sable had to give all her attention to him now. He needed her help. Nothing else mattered.

PART 3

STORMRACE

INVINCIBLE DAWN

Eukon Thorne climbed up through the ceiling porthole and stepped off the pilot house ladder onto the encircling balcony to look down over the Ice below. There, six other skateships arranged themselves in Morningstar Formation around his vessel, *Invincible Dawn*, the flagship of the Ghost Fleet.

Actually, he considered every skateship his. After all, had he not designed them? And had his Breakborn family not built them using his knowledge of the vast deposit of relic materiel stored in the old military depot at Vanquisher's Break? Without Thorne, the Ghosts of the nine Oroken clans would still be relegated to a miserable existence on the Ice aboard their archaic wooden windsleds.

Thorne strode to the northern railing shadowed by his two silent Breakborn guards, Braukis and Kharkin. He gripped the shiny metal crossbar and appraised the proceedings. As usual, *Mantis*, the skateship of the Oroshone, dropped claws too near the Orokota skateship *Farfire*, leaving an overlarge gap between it and the Orochin skateship, *Mirage*. If Thorne had been thinking, he would have ordered *Mantis* and *Farfire* to leave space for the as-yet-absent *Waketorrent* and *Frostbite*, thereby solving two problems at once.

Instead, Thorne had ordered the opening on the eastern quadrant between the Oroyenne skateship, *Resulote* and the Oroklam skateship, *Winter Leaf*. Strategically safer perhaps, if there were any real possibilities of danger. But all reports from the Anthemar Plain indicated that the Fane were too preoccupied fighting each other to worry about a threat they likely didn't even know existed. Or if they knew—thanks to that misguided boy, Jaio—they almost certainly did not believe.

The thought of Jaio and his absurd mission aroused something almost like pity. Then Thorne reminded himself of the damage this so-called Ghost Orol had already done: two fateholders duped and a skateship crippled.

How Jaio had managed these feats, Thorne could not imagine, but he knew better than to underestimate his real opponent. Consequently, he kept the remaining fateholders close at hand with orders to gag Jaio should they encounter him. As paranoid as these measures might seem, a part of Thorne worried that they would not be enough.

Several weeks of waiting still remained before the completion of his plan, and every idle moment offered another opportunity for some mishap, a mishap that might delay his return home. Already, he'd been gone too long. His mind drifted again to Mayrel and Aleekio, who were waiting for him at Vanquisher's Break.

Thorne spun and strode to the southern railing where he looked out beyond the Orotenin skateship, *Aurora*. A seemingly endless sea of frozen peaks filled his vision. Yet, he knew his beloved wife and their unruly son were out there, beyond sight, safe at the Break.

A single contact whistle sounded from the crow's nest overhead. Thorne waited for a second call, but none came. He wheeled and strode with haste back to the northern railing, pulling a relic telescoptic magnifier from his parka pocket as he went.

Belly pressed against the rail for stability, he raised the eyepiece and scanned the distant Ice. He didn't have to wait long before a single pair of masts rose into view. They ran full sail, more or less, with a hard lean to starboard. In a moment, he recognized the silhouette.

Waketorrent.

"Where is *Frostbite*?" he growled, feeling a hot anger kindle in his gut.

It blossomed into full flame as the Oronish skateship drew nearer and he could discern scorch marks and ragged holes marring the sails. Then he saw the skateship's mangled central port leg drawn up against the hull like the desiccated limb of an injured locust. Thorne's fury reached incendiary intensity.

"What did you do to my ship?" he hissed through clenched jaws. He surged to the ladder. "Call Leegon!" he yelled down into the pilot house.

"Yes, Orol!" replied an appropriately frightened voice.

Thorne stood by the ladder and watched the approaching skateship while he waited. The radio operator made the call. When, after a few silent seconds no response came, he repeated it.

Then Thorne saw the tangled mess of metal and wires hanging from the masthead. "Stop calling!" he shouted. "Sound the alarm!"

He hurried back to the railing and gazed down on the fleet as bells chimed and crews scurried to stations.

No *Stormdancer*. No *Frostbite*. And *Waketorrent* in a sorry state: almost a third of Thorne's fleet. This had to stop, or he wouldn't have any teeth left to do what needed to be done after the Fane were finished; if he was going bring a new order into being throughout the land, from Anthemar to the Steppe and perhaps beyond, he would need all his ships.

He hurried to the ladder and started down, on his way find out why he'd lost another one.

"Leegon had better have something to show for this," he said.

Braukis and Kharkin had the good sense to remain silent.

23

INVINCIBLE DAWN

Wake up, Jaio," says an age-roughened, but commanding voice. The speaker sounds unnaturally subdued and very far away. "Ah, good. Good to see you finally coming around." Each of these words seems to draw nearer and rise in volume until the last one originates less than a pace distant.

The pain draws nearer as well, but doesn't stop at any distance. Rather, it bores into Jaio as his senses return. He winces from a building throb in his left cheekbone. And when he tries to open his eyes, only the right complies. The other lets him know in no uncertain terms not to try again. He takes a deep breath and considers what the snatch of sight revealed: the smooth, metal ceiling of a small chamber, dim and torchlit.

"The last time we met," says the speaker. "You left in such a hurry I didn't have the chance to bid you a proper farewell. Or to persuade you to stay."

Jaio struggles to sit up. A firm hand grasps his shoulder and helps. He carefully opens his right eye again and finds himself looking into the warm grandfatherly face of Eukon Thorne.

"You?" breathes Jaio, nearly muted by surprise.

"Me," Thorne replies with far too broad a smile. He sits on a leather stool with caribou antler legs. It is positioned beside the fur-covered cot where Jaio has been sleeping. Thorne shifts the stool closer and offers Jaio a waterskin.

Jaio hesitantly accepts it. The possibility of poison crosses his mind, but he suspects he wouldn't have awakened at all if Thorne wanted him dead. He takes a long, deep draw then hands back the skin. "Where am I?" he asks.

"Welcome aboard *Invincible Dawn*." Thorne gestures around the small, chill room as if he expects the sight to elicit awe.

"*Invincible Dawn*?"

"My masterpiece," says Thorne. "Three masts, four gun decks, eight skates and more than a few surprises. Later, I'll give you a tour?"

"How long have I been out?" asks Jaio.

"Half a day."

"What happened to *Frostbite*? *Waketorrent*? My friends?"

"Your friends, yes. I have been told about your

Fane friends. Most unexpected. And intriguing. Tell me about them."

Jaio simply meets Thorne's inquisitive gaze and says nothing.

Thorne smiles. "Leegon says they wore the sashes of a Kestian Ice Watch team and that one of them was a woman."

Woman, singular, thinks Jaio. Either Jaspen or Sable has eluded detection. Jaio has a pretty good idea which one and sees a chance to help reinforce the oversight. He offers a simple nod of affirmation.

"The Snowsea front is a dangerous place for a woman."

"It's a dangerous place for everybody."

"Indeed." Thorne leans forward and his smile dims. "Even for a Kestian Cavalry Commander who apparently fell out of favor with his lady liege and found himself cast to the Ice."

Cavalry Commander? Jaio furrows his brow in confusion then catches himself and shifts to a look of blank indifference.

"Surely, you know who I mean, the great wall of a man with the tiger fur tricorn?"

Jaio struggles to remain unreadable.

"I see," says Thorne. "Well, I suppose it doesn't matter, since knowing his identity is no longer of any real consequence other than the satisfaction of my curiosity."

A foreboding chill washes over Jaio. His own curiosity overrides his silence. "What do you mean?"

"The man is dead."

"Wolfe? No, he can't be." Jaio's mind reels. It can't be true.

"Wolfe, you say. Commander Krugerhan Wolfe?"

"General Wolfe," says Jaio.

"General? General. Too bad Leegon didn't make a trophy of his hat. I should love to hang it from my cabin wall."

"He's coming to stop you!" Jaio can barely speak through the growing lump in his throat.

"Not this time, unless he comes back as a…ghost."

Jaio fights to contain his tears, and fails. He can hear the truth in Thorne's words.

"Why do you weep for your enemy, Jaio? The Fane are corrupted beyond redemption. As an Orol, you of all people should be able to see that. The nine clans will never be safe so long as the Fane remain a threat. They are the ones who must be stopped."

In Jaio's mind, he hears the voice of Belara Oroken reciting Felicia Concora's poem, "Invincible." He wipes his tears and levels his one-eyed gaze on Thorne. "I will not join with a foe, even one who would fight for all I hold dear."

Now, Thorne looks confused. "Me, a foe? We are not foes. We are more like family, Jaio. Despite your tattoos, you are Breakborn. You have simply been misled by your so-called friends. They are your real foes."

Jaio fights to steady himself. "You will not succeed."

Thorne narrows his eyes. "Who will stop me? Your other Fane friends? Treacherous Aiomida?"

Jaio has a more obvious answer, but Thorne appears to have overlooked it, so he decides to keep it too himself. Instead, he offers Thorne a hard, defiant silence.

Thorne smiles again. "I didn't think you had anyone else in mind. And I don't intend to wait long enough for the unholy alliance you've created to cause me any further difficulties. I've already sent four of my skateships back to finish this."

Jaio can only stare at him in shock.

"Oh, and I almost forgot." Thorne reaches into his parka pocket and pulls out a pair of slender pale objects Jaio does not at first recognize. "I'm sorry," he says as he offers the objects to Jaio.

With trepidation, Jaio reaches out to accept them. Thorne lays the snapped remains of a bird-bone flute in Jaio's palm. Jaio feels his grief deepen and more tears rim his eyes. He remembers the snap he heard when he jumped from the windsled. He mistook it for one of his own bones. A part of him wishes it had been.

Will I lose everything? This thought reminds him of Anchor's orb. He almost feels for it, but catches himself just as his free hand starts to move. He transforms the movement into a double-fisted grip on his flute, which he then holds tight to his chest.

Thorne eyes him with a look of curious suspicion. This look tells Jaio Thorne doesn't have the orb. But then where is it?

In the long uncomfortable silence that follows, neither of them moves nor speaks. Then Thorne stands, turns and pushes open the small room's porthole door revealing a torchlit corridor beyond. Jaio can see the torsos of two guards, one on either side of the porthole.

Thorne steps through then looks back at Jaio. "It's not too late for you to secure a place at my side after all this is over. The choice is yours. You have until I return to make it." He sets off without telling Jaio when he will be back.

One of the guards turns and slams the hatch shut as Thorne strides away. The click of a lock punctuates the old man's departure.

Jaio feels for the orb, though he doesn't need to. Thorne would have taken it when he took the flute fragments.

In the dim light, Jaio holds the two pieces of his

flute together. The break is clean, but as perfectly as the pieces mesh, they will never again make music.

24

TIGRESS

Jaspen and the other four remaining members of
Wolfe's Pride stood on the ice facing the looming
specter of *Frostbite* where dozens of Ghosts busied
themselves working on repairs.

Two guards with stutterguns flanked the five
of them while they awaited the arrival of the
Thrack leader, Cappen Aiomida, to determine
their fate. This Cappen, Segray and the tall,
forbidding Lash, worked their way from body to
body, offering some unintelligible ceremonial
words before others wrapped the deceased—both
Oromola and Oronish—in furs and bore them
away into the skateship.

When the procession at last reached Wolfe's
body, Aiomida, Segray and Lash simply paused
while two attendants began wrapping him in a
woolen blanket. Though they moved him with
fluid care, Wolfe himself had already frozen and
more resembled a stone statue than a person.

Jaspen had all she could do not to look away.

Once the attendants had finished and, with obvious effort, lifted Wolfe from the ice, the Cappen and her companions followed them to the Pride. The body of the tactan was placed gently, and with surprising solemnity, at their feet. Then, without looking up, the bearers turned and headed to the skateship. Aiomida, Lash and Segray stepped forward and came to a halt facing the Pride.

Sand knelt and placed the worn tiger fur tricorn on Wolfe's chest.

Aiomida waited for him to stand then spoke in the tongue of the Oromola. Segray translated.

"Why did Jaio bring you here?"

Jaspen and her companions glanced at each other. She had assumed Sand would lead the team now, and maybe eventually he would, but one look told her, he would need more time to reach that place.

"We came to stop Thorne," she said.

Segray translated.

Aiomida spoke again. Segray nodded and turned back to Jaspen. "How did you plan to do that?"

"Wolfe," she began then had to pause. Using his name somehow felt wrong. "Our tactan didn't have a clear plan—"

"He was clear on the first step," Sand

interjected. "Acquire the target."

Jaspen nodded, happy to see Sand regaining his focus. "Then," she added. "We reached this place and learned of the weapons cache Thorne revealed to Lord Maxamant."

Segray's translation transformed into an increasingly tense conversation in which the old man went from a mere interpreter to an animated participant. Jaspen heard the names Leegon and Keethu and, more than once, Fane. Finally, Aiomida raised a hand for silence. The three of them turned back to the Pride and she spoke again, her voice now hard, her speech sharp as a blade.

Segray, red in the face, cleared his throat and conveyed her question. "Cappen wants to know why Thorne would do such a thing? And I must say," he added under his breath. "So do I."

Jaspen and Sand alternatively conveyed Wolfe's theory as simply and succinctly as they could. As they spoke, Segray's eyes widened with understanding. Then, when they'd finished, he began relaying their words.

Almost immediately, Lash shook his head and tried to interrupt, but Segray held his ground and would not be silenced. By the end, the tall frightening Ghost merely simmered while Aiomida turned back to the Pride and asked her next question.

"Why would you want to stop him?"

Oh, how Jaspen wished Wolfe were with them, alive. His response would be so much better. She tried to remember his words, but realized she would have to use far fewer. And she would have to use her own. Sand too seemed at a loss.

Finally, she took a deep breath and proceeded. "Thorne's course can lead only to an endless cycle of vengeance. And now that the barrier of the Ice is melting, that cycle will go on until both the Plain and the Steppe have been utterly devoured and there is nothing left to feed the hatred."

At the conclusion of Segray's translation, Lash huffed and spoke. Segray's ears flushed with apparent anger. But Aiomida simply nodded.

"Lash says your tactan is dead because he was an idealist and a fool. So long as the Fane possess relic weapons, there can be no hope for the Oroken. To think otherwise is naïve."

Jaspen felt her own anger spike. She pointed at the skateship. "And as long as you possess your relic weapons, there will be no hope for the people of Anthemar. Which leads us right back to where we are now; in need of another option."

Segray smiled and translated. Lash ground his teeth. Aiomida held Jaspen's gaze for a long moment then spoke.

"So, how do you propose to stop Thorne?"

Jaspen hesitated. This task Wolfe had

appointed to himself. And whatever he'd had in store had died with him. But she didn't dare say that. Her mind raced. "Jaio," she blurted out then hastened on. "That was his part of the mission. Only he and Wolfe knew the details. The five of us had different parts to play." She turned to the spotter and nodded.

He cleared his throat. "I was the captain of the Red Strand; the Kestian cavalry scouts," he said. "I am to return to that duty and seek the support of my Liege and her allies."

"And I," said Jaspen, "was to go to Anchoresk with the others to seek aid from the head of the Catalogian Order."

"And why would Dalsen Ario listen to a pair of Watch monks, an old tiger hunter and a former bathhouse dung collector?" asked Segray without first translating Jaspen's words to Aiomida and Lash.

"Dalsen Ario is my father." Much to Jaspen's surprise, she did not feel the fear she expected to feel in the face of this revelation. She felt pride.

"Your…" Segray's words failed him.

Lash snapped at the old man to translate.

Segray steadied himself then passed on the new information. With the final words, both Aiomida and Lash turned their wide eyes on Jaspen.

"He loves me," she said. "He will listen." She

hoped with all her heart that this was true.

25

FROSTBITE

Put your backs into it, snowflakes!" Bengus roars as he and over half the remaining members of *Frostbite's* crew haul back on ten heavy ropes bound to the skateship's lopsided mast. Metal groans as the mast straightens. At the same time, three winch crews crank as fast as they can to tighten the tension cables that will provide permanent mast support. If, that is, the port cable-splice holds where the stuttercannon volley sliced through the line like a dagger through thread. Bengus offers a silent prayer to whatever spirits might be listening.

As soon as the winches release their last strained clicks, Bengus drops the rope and dashes back to the rear railing to examine the mast. "All right, gentle now, ease up. Give some slack."

Slowly the ten lines sag and go limp. The mast holds steady.

"Great work! We're half way there!" With the

cables holding the mast in place, Bengus turns his thoughts to the job of repairing the damaged counterbracing below-deck.

He takes off for the stairs, leading his team of toolers toward their next project. But at the mouth of the stairwell, Cappen Aiomida stops him. "A word, Clank," she says while casting furtive glances about the deck.

Bengus hesitates as his team squeezes past and continues down. "No time, Cappen. I've work to do."

"How is *Tigress*?"

Cappen's odd question draws Bengus up short. He casts her a puzzled look. "Sound enough, all in all. Why?"

"Iceworthy?"

"Cannonfire knocked out half an arm of the topmast, but she should still run all right. Most of the mayhem took place above her head."

"What about *Owl*?"

"Not so lucky, I'm afraid. Main hull beam cracked when it fell. All we can do is mend the strap, lash it back on and take it to the Break for repairs."

"Good."

Bengus's confusion mounts. "Good?"

Aiomida ignores him. "You have a new mission now," she says.

"What might that be?"

"Help the Pride reach Anthemar."

With these words, Bengus's confusion lifts and he leans closer. "I knew you wouldn't forsake them," he whispers.

"But it has to look like an escape. Do you think they can crew *Tigress*?"

Bengus grimaces. "They learned the basics well enough, but there's only five of 'em now. I don't think…"

"They only need to reach the drop off." She nods to the west. "Then it's just a matter of steering. Gravity will do the rest."

"Down the glacier?"

"Quiet…Yes, down the glacier. It's just like the Ramp…Well, maybe a little bigger."

"Without me?"

Cappen glares at him. "It's a one-way trip, Clank. And we don't have much time. The rest of the crew blames the Pride for the nine Ghosts we lost. They want blood. And I have to look like I want it too. Which is why Lash's interrogation can't last much longer. The Pride must be gone before it ends." She nods to *Tigress*.

"How do we get 'em over there," asks Bengus.

"That should be easy, thanks to Lash."

"Lash is in on this?"

"Let's just say, Jaio is not the only one gifted with the power of persuasion. And for Lash's part, he made a big show of revulsion at the very idea of the Fane defiling *Frostbite* by setting even one foot aboard. Consequently, the interrogation is taking place down on the Ice, underneath *Tigress*."

Bengus scratches his head. "So, if I'm not going, why are you telling me all this?"

"If you and your team finish mast repairs too quickly, we'll be forced to give chase."

"Even if we can't pursue, what about the guns? We've a full broadside facing west. *Frostbite* could blast *Tigress* to splinters."

"Not if they have prisoners."

"Prisoners? Who?"

At that moment, a shout resounds across the deck, followed by several more. Ghosts abandon repair duties and rush to the port rail.

Mingled in the general din of dismayed and angry cries, Bengus hears several repeated words, Lash, Map and Fane.

"It's started. Get below, Clank," says Cappen Aiomida. Then she dashes out onto the deck. "What's happening!" she yells.

Bengus spins and races down the stairs. Other Ghosts dash past him, headed up. He sees bows in many hands and more than a few stutterguns.

26

TIGRESS

Benethan pretended to hold Segray hostage at the braking claw lever while Kemren hid behind Lash en route to the tiller. The rest of the Pride crouched amidships, taking cover behind the port gunwale. They hastened to strap down the wrapped body of Wolfe, whom they had successfully carried aboard before the alarm call sounded.

As soon as Kemren and Lash reached the steering arm, Kemren yelled, "Go!"

Benethan hauled back on the lever with his free hand and the claws retracted with a boom. Then he and Segray moved to the masts where Segray quietly suggested Benethan order him to release the lines so the mainsail would unfurl.

Benethan barked the command and tried not to look up as he and the old man shuffled from one tie down to the next. Dozens of enraged Ghosts lined *Frostbite's* high rail, all of them aiming weapons at the windsled. But none fired.

At the center of the onlookers stood Aiomida, a stuttergun gripped in her own steady hand. She remained silent, playing the part she had to play; with the Fane, there would be no deals.

A sudden shout from high in *Frostbite's* rigging broke the brittle silence. "Contact! Fore-port quarter!"

Benethan was still working out which direction to look when Segray gasped. The old man was looking the wrong way—aft-starboard. Then Benethan realized *Frostbite's* lookout spoke from the reverse frame of reference: the skateship faced south while *Tigress* faced north. He whipped his head around.

Four skateships bounded toward them and had obviously been in view for some time before being spotted. They seemed just minutes away.

"Quick," whispered Segray.

Benethan felt the old man yank his sleeve. He fought for focus and dragged his captive to the primary release line. Segray gave the slip knot a tug and the mainsail unrolled down the mast. It immediately began to swell. And even before snapping full, *Tigress* lurched forward. The Ghosts at *Frostbite's* rail roared with fury and waved their weapons. But now the mood seemed to have changed. They weren't so much hurling venom at the windsled as cheering on the approaching quartet of skateships.

"No time to gawk," grumbled Segray. "We need to spin the spars to quarter port or we'll never outrun them."

Like an overbearing dancing partner, Segray led the way while trying to make it look like he was following. Benethan prodded him to make the appropriate adjustments, which proved quite a challenge for both of them with one of Benethan's arms wrapped around the old man's neck. But, despite the difficulty, they managed to swing the sail.

And *Tigress* responded.

The distance between the windsled and *Frostbite* opened quickly after that. Soon, Lash deemed the gap sufficient to abandon the ruse and the prisoners were released.

Everyone but Kemren darted to the aft railing. The four skateships were opening formation, spreading to pass *Frostbite*, two on each side.

"They're too close," said Lash. "We'll never make the turn west without being cut off."

"I know another way down," said Segray.

"Where?" asked Lash.

"Stay the course. North." Segray ran to the tiller and took over for Kemren. A great toothy smile spread over his face. "All right, snowflakes," he yelled, doing a surprisingly good imitation of his burly friend. "Take positions, like

Bengus taught you. Speed's the one thing Thorne gave up when he decided to make those skateships so big. And it's the one thing we need right now."

Benethan and the rest of the Pride scrambled to their posts. And the race was on.

THE ADMINITHEDRAL

Dalsen Ario followed Brother Selas Noyova and two full squads of Iron Robes through the rear door leading into the Dictorian Consul's private audience chamber deep within the Second Tier of the Adminithedral. Once inside, Noyova began to strategically position the warrior monks around the chamber while Ario strode to the austere stool at the head of the room and sat down, his back to the small fire being laid in the chamber's great hearth.

Ario tugged the slack from the golden shoulder sash he wore over his kineticloth robe and settled into the proper pose, at once relaxed and commanding. His two personal guards stationed themselves at each shoulder. They held their hyperpulse pistols in plain sight, a rare show of force in this sacred space.

As Ario waited for the crackle of flames to steady and for everybody to take their positions behind ancient stone roof-support columns and at the far double-doors, he marveled at the timing of Brother Edmaril Acris's return from the southern Snowsea bearing the contents of one of the two greatest relic weapons caches ever found. The other was, at that very moment, in the hands of Lord Salazriole Maxamant who now used it to make his long-anticipated bid for empire.

Ario couldn't quite believe the turn of events. Not ten minutes earlier, he had been helping organize for the influx of refugees from the sacked strongholds of Kest, Kiddyon, Vantling and Froynen, all the while wondering how long the Order and the ragtag remnants of the four beaten armies might hold out against Maxamant and his allies.

Now, Ario thought the defenders of Anchoresk might not only hang out, but have a real chance at victory. He might even survive it if he could somehow keep from being overthrown in the *next* ten minutes. After all, Acris was a Dagger. And the Daggers controlled the new weapons.

Noyova, looking more skeletal and gray than usual, hastened back to stand at Ario's right elbow.

"I still believe we should wait until a third squad has taken up position in the rear corridor," the old man wheezed.

"Why?" asked Ario. "Are we not all members

of the same Brotherhood?"

"Indeed we are, but with enough incentive, even brothers will turn on one another."

"I believe there is greater incentive to remain united." Ario turned his attention forward. "Admit them," he said.

The two Iron Robes at the front of the chamber levered up the locking bars and heaved the double doors open. On the other side stood Sigmos Bomechor. Just behind him and to his right stood the man of the hour: Edmaril Acris, gaunt, unshaven and still clad in the filth of hard travel. His eyes, however, sparkled.

The two Daggers strode into the chamber followed by a retinue of twelve guards. Each of them held a hyperpulse rifle of a style unfamiliar to Ario. The weapons resembled the pistols, but with longer barrels, fixed shoulder stocks and larger ammunition clips.

Bomechor and Acris came to a halt before Ario and bowed, though neither as deeply as protocol demanded nor for the customary duration. Not a good sign.

"Welcome, Brothers," said Ario.

"Thank you, Dictorian, for agreeing to meet with us on such short notice," said Bomechor.

"If the rumors are true, how could I refuse?"

"Oh, they are true," said Bomechor. He glanced to Acris. "As you can see for yourself."

Acris turned and took the rifle from the guard behind him, then stepped forward and hefted it with pride. "We found over ten thousand of these, plus ample ammunition and many other relics, including…" He let the word hang as he handed the weapon back to the guard and then unshouldered a bulging pack.

Ario leaned forward for a better look as Acris sat the pack on the floor, knelt and opened it. The monk then reached inside. As he stood, he lifted out a scalloped gray robe, stained with blood and mud.

Seeing this caused Ario's heart to leap. *Kemren succeeded. Jaspen is safe!* It took all of Ario's will to remain passive. At his side, he heard Noyova's robe rustle ever so slightly. The sight of the Iron Cloud robe no doubt had a very different effect on the old monk.

"This, as you well know, was not part of the cache," said Bomechor. "Nor were the other three, all of which were worn by…corpses."

"What?" Noyova hissed. "Impossible!" He stabbed a bony arthritic finger at the Daggers. "You've been waiting years for an opportunity to eliminate the Cloud, and when the chance finally presented itself, you couldn't resist."

"I assure you, Brother," said Acris, his tone even and sympathetic. "I would have offered them aid against their attackers had I arrived early enough to do so, but when I found them, they had already been slain."

"It seems," Bomechor added. "The four of them took it upon themselves to secure the cache alone. Their downfall came not at the hands of any Daggers, but resulted from overconfidence and a surprisingly cunning foe."

"You lie!"

Acris reached deep into his pack again. The nearest Iron Robes tensed and their hands started for the weapons hidden in their robes. But the disheveled monk pulled out not a gun, but a thick crossbow bolt with a hexagonal shaft. He held it up in an open palm and offered it to Ario. Noyova stepped forward and took it.

"What is this?" growled Noyova.

"This is the weapon that bested the Cloud," said Bomechor. "It divides into six pieces while in flight. And if fired from sufficient distance, the pieces will pass through kineticloth."

Acris pulled another from his pack and demonstrated the separation process.

"Magnetics," said Ario. Ingenious, he thought. His agents would be well rewarded.

"Yes," said Acris. "It's the ideal weapon if you want to increase your odds against an invisible enemy."

"But who wields such a weapon?" asked Noyova.

"Mesorics. At least two, and likely more, but if there were others, they escaped," said Acris.

"Mesorics?" Noyova shook his head, clearly trying to make sense of it all.

"Quite a coincidence, wouldn't you say?" asked Bomechor. "The Cloud confronted by the only enemy capable of defeating them? And a most inexplicable enemy, to be sure."

"Inexplicable indeed," breathed Noyova with the sparest glance at Ario.

Ario's instinct screamed a warning. The Daggers obviously suspected treachery and now Noyova suspected as well. And Noyova knew the one person with clearest motivation to eliminate the Cloud. But the Daggers didn't, which was Ario's only advantage. His next words would very likely be the most important of his life. He needed to divert any suspicion away from himself. This, he realized would require him to take a great risk. He turned to Noyova, the commander of the now-fallen Iron Cloud.

"So, Brother, why did you dispatch the Iron Cloud to the Snowsea in the first place?"

Noyova suffered only the slightest hesitation then smiled his yellow-toothed smile.

Ario's insides turned to ice. He knew he'd miscalculated and his secret was about to be revealed.

"I sent them to assist in the hunt for the pincer

cache, of course."

Ario fought to suppress his surprise and relief as well as to find his next words. "Without telling me?" he asked.

"Yes, Brother," said Noyova. "My apologies. I thought the chances of success too slim to be worthy of mention. Had I known—"

"We shall discuss this more at a later time, Brother. At present, the question of the Mesorics is the more pressing concern. It suggests a traitor in our midst, so we must ask ourselves who would gain by eliminating the Cloud." Ario turned his gaze on Acris as he said this. A feeling of pity for the luckless Dagger stirred in his chest, but he forced it down. The good of the Order sometimes required the sacrifice of innocents.

Noyova didn't miss a beat. "Yes, someone well-placed, if not now, in the past and hungry to reclaim lost prestige. Such a person might be unwilling to share in the discovery of so great a prize as the pincer cache."

Acris bristled. "How dare you?"

Noyova shrugged. "Name someone else with motive and means?

Bomechor turned his wary gaze on Acris.

Acris's eyes widened with fury. "This is outrageous! If what you say were true, why wouldn't I have covered my tracks? Why didn't I simply make the Cloud disappear without a trace?"

"You knew their fate could not long remain hidden and a suspect would be sought," said Noyova. "What better way to shift blame away from yourself than by revealing your own crime?"

"I can't believe I'm hearing this!" Acris wheeled on Bomechor. "You have to believe me, I—" Two of the Dagger guards surged forward and grabbed Acris by the arms.

Acris struggled to break free. "I had nothing to do with the death of the Cloud!"

"We shall discuss this more at a later time, Brother," said Bomechor. The senior Dagger nodded to the guards, who hauled the raging Acris away.

Before they'd even left the Chamber, Ario cast Bomechor a grave look. "As disturbing as this turn of events is, we must focus *all* our energies on the Maxamantan threat."

"Agreed, Brother. Agreed."

INVINCIBLE DAWN

The ache in Jaio's jaw throbs and he rolls it in
slow circles in an attempt to keep it loose. At the
same time, he tries to open his swollen eye beyond
a mere slit. And he listens for Thorne.

As Jaio lies on the cot, he is no longer sure how
long he's been awaiting the old man's promised
return. Too long on the one hand and not long
enough on the other.

A part of him hopes Thorne never returns. The
self-proclaimed Orol scares him. Never before has
Jaio met someone so thoroughly incapable of
seeing beyond himself. The Ancients had a name
for Thorne's disease. Megalomania.

Jaio remembers the day he learned the term
from his mentor, Orol Gilinath. It was early
summer. The first clear day after a week of rain.
Gilinath took him to a place where a small
mountain stream spilled into the Flowing River.
The water racing down the main channel ran clear.

The stream water ran brown with silt.

Jaio and Gilinath stood in silence at the confluence for some time then Gilinath headed downstream. Jaio knew better than to speak. Gilinath would say what he had to say in good time. Perhaps, even on another day.

Jaio watched the water dance and tumble as the two of them walked along beside it. He was surprised at how long the two columns—clear and brown—remained distinct. But finally, by mid-day, the silt had tainted the whole river.

That was when Gilinath stopped and told the story of a terrible world-wide war waged about a hundred and fifty rounds before the Ice. Though many who fought and died in this war believed in their opposing causes, the catalyst was a single man who stoked the conflict into an inferno with his hatred, hatred disguised as its opposite within a cloak of shiny words. Gilinath did not know the man's name. True to Oroken tradition, the first Orols had let it die. But they did preserve the name of his self-absorbed affliction: megalomania. They also preserved his story as a cautionary warning.

Gilinath finished sharing the warning then turned to face the river and spoke again. One small stream, he said, a stream far away beyond sight can color the waters of a whole great river from bank to bank all the way to the ocean.

Without the memory of the higher reaches, the color might seem normal. The Orol's job is to keep the memory of genuine normalcy so the return to clarity comes as a welcomed event rather than a source of fear and further clouding.

That, thinks Jaio, is why Thorne is not an Orol. Thorne is a stream clouded by a raging inner storm. And he's headed for the river.

Jaio glances around the dim interior of his tiny cell. *And I'm right in his path. If I fail to bring clarity, I risk becoming clouded myself. Or worse. A storm.*

The sound of grating hinges stirs Jaio from his thoughts. He sits up on the edge of the cot and watches the door. Muffled footfalls come to a halt just outside. The lock clicks and it swings open. "Wait here," Thorne tells the two guards as he ducks inside.

Jaio stands to face him. His heart pounds. As much as he wants to maximize the distance between himself and Thorne, he knows, with the death of Wolfe, the task of stopping the old man has fallen to him. To do that, Jaio must stay close.

"So," says Thorne. "What is your choice? Are you going to cling to your naïve delusions about forging a peace with the Fane or are you going to join me in building a world of true peace after I stop the Fane in the only way that has a chance?"

Jaio pretends to consider these words. Then,

with what he hopes appears as a look of surrender, he says, "I see now that we want the same world. And you've convinced me there is only one way it might be realized."

"Good," says Thorne. "I had hoped you would come to your senses. I have no doubt, the world to come will be a far better place if we work together to build it." He steps forward and places a hand on Jaio's shoulder. "Now, let me show my masterpiece."

Thorne gently, but firmly, guides Jaio ahead of him through the hatch, past the two Breakborn guards and into the cold, metal reality of the skateship beyond.

29

TIGRESS

Tigress seemed to skim the ice rather than ride upon it. In fact, Jaspen thought the windsled spent more time airborne than in contact with the frozen surface beneath them. She leaned against the rope-spool holding the emergency anchor and gripped the forward rail while watching for dangers ahead as she and her companions flew along.

Without Sable high atop the mast on lookout, Jaspen alone held the fate of the vessel in her hand. And she enjoyed a far poorer vantage. But there was no other choice. There were already far too few of them to man all essential posts. Lash's face shimmered with sweat from the exertion of racing around the deck trying to fill the holes in the crew.

And worse, even though three of the pursuing skateships had fallen far astern, the fourth slowly closed the gap. Segray said it was called *Mantis*.

As it drew nearer, the resemblance to its namesake became all the more apparent—six legs, both longer and thinner than the other skateships, supported a much narrower hull with taller masts and sharp triangular sails, all taut with wind.

"Are there by chance any cannons stashed below that we might use to slow them down?" yelled Sand above the noise of their breakneck flight.

"Windsleds don't come with cannons," replied Segray.

Jaspen glanced at the spool of anchor rope and an idea unrolled in her mind. "What about tangling their legs with this?" she yelled and pounded the spool with her stump.

Sand glanced her way and a smile tugged the corners of his mouth.

"Brilliant idea!" yelled Segray, who then translated her suggestion to Lash.

The tall, intense Ghost nodded and raced to the spool. He unfastened the clamp binding the anchor to the outer hull then, together with Jaspen, heaved the dangling iron V up onto the deck. When she started to help unspool the rope, he glared at her, pointed to her eyes then pointed forward. She resumed her vigil, but in her peripheral vision, watched him let out all the rope and sever it with his dagger. Then he dragged rope and anchor astern.

Despite the risk, Jaspen glanced back periodically as Lash proceeded to retrieve other ropes, which he bound at even intervals along the anchor rope. He then threw open a deck hatch and extracted a roll of canvas: a spare sail, Jaspen guessed. This he spread out along the rear gunwale and bound to the secondary ropes.

When he'd finished, he turned to Segray and spoke.

Segray nodded. "When *Mantis* is almost on us, I'll give the signal. Everybody but Jaspen run aft and help me lift the drag.   On my mark, we shove it overboard, with as much width as possible. Understand?"

Segray translated.

Everyone sounded the affirmative and maintained their positions.

Soon, *Mantis* loomed close enough to necessitate resuming the ruse of forced compliance. Segray and Lash again became prisoners of Sand and Benethan respectively.

And the skateship edged closer.

When the first grappling rope sailed their way and fell short by only a few yards, Segray gave the signal and banked to starboard.

Benethan mock-shoved Lash astern as Kem and Rawl hurried to take positions at either end of the sail roll. Together, they all lifted.

"Tiger's teeth!" shouted Rawl. "A woolephant

weighs less than this!"

A warning cry went up on *Mantis* just as the rope-bound sail dropped over the railing and unrolled to the ice.

Then Benethan and Lash muscled the anchor from the deck and dumped overboard. Even from her place at the bow, Jaspen heard it boom on impact. A split second later came the rip as *Mantis's* starboard skate tore through the partially-opened sail. The ripping gave way to groaning as the drag of sail against leg increased and the skateship's masts tipped forward in response to the sudden loss of momentum.

Jaspen didn't have words suitable to describe the tortured sounds *Mantis* made when the last of the slack in the anchor rope played out. The whole skateship heaved hard to starboard with a thunderous jolt. The fore-starboard leg buckled and the middle leg sagged, sending the bulk of the skateship plunging to the ice. The wooden hull of the windsled strapped to its belly burst like an egg shell under *Mantis's* weight and then the skateship struck hard throwing up a massive fan of shattered crystals. The crippled vessel swung nearly ninety degrees before it ground to halt in a field of glacial debris, splintered wood and strewn yak dung discs.

In the silence that followed, cries of pain and fury rose into the air. They quickly grew faint as

Tigress opened the distance, leaving the immobilized *Mantis* behind.

"Well done!" shouted Segray. "And none too soon. We have reached our turn."

Jaspen finally resumed her duty. Luck alone had kept them from plunging into a crevasse during the last few breathless moments.

As Jaspen watched for dangers, Segray eased the windsled to port. Lash and the others adjusted the sails to keep hold of the wind. Soon, they headed due west toward a mountain-free gap where the ice just seemed to drop off into open blue sky.

When it looked as if they were about to fly off the edge of the world into oblivion, Segray shouted to bank the sails and ready the braking claws.

The windsled slowed and then, on Segray's signal, Benethan released the claws.

Tigress came to rest at the head of a glacial arm that dropped down from the ice sheet all the way to the distant Anthemar Plain. Several miles beyond the terminus of the glacier, many columns of smoke rose from the smoldering ruins of a Protectorate stronghold.

Everybody joined Jaspen at the bow to gaze down upon the ominous scene.

"Gray Horn," said Sand. "There's a good chance we'll find mounts down there that fared better than their riders. We'll need them if we're to reach Anchoresk ahead of Maxamant's army."

Lash glanced back and spoke. Segray translated.

"You had better hurry."

Jaspen followed Lash's gaze. The wreck of *Mantis* appeared as little more than dot in the distance. And three more dots could be seen near it. Two of the three raced past, headed toward *Tigress*.

Lash turned his attention back to the Pride and spoke again. Segray nodded.

"They are only minutes away. Bind us and leave us here," said Segray. "Then take *Tigress* all the way down the glacier, but be sure to brake before you think it necessary or you'll find yourself running on stones."

"I'm guessing that wouldn't be good," grumbled Rawl.

"No, it wouldn't."

"Are you sure Thorne and the others won't suspect you of helping us?" she asked.

"If it were just me, they undoubtedly would," said Segray. "But Lash has a certain reputation. We will play it to our full advantage. Don't worry about us."

"Thank you," said Kem.

"Just don't fail," said Segray.

"Go," said Lash, not needing a translator this

time. He grabbed binding ropes and headed forward to throw down the ladder. Segray followed.

Sand clambered down to the ice after them and bound their wrists. As Sand climbed back aboard, Jaspen and the rest of the Pride watched their two Oroken rescuers stride away from the windsled, headed toward the growing silhouettes of the approaching skateships.

She wondered if she'd ever see the old man, the tall warrior or, for that matter, any of the Ghosts again. The idea that she might not stirred a most unexpected emotion. Sorrow.

Sand clambered back up the ladder, hauled it in and bound it in its bracket on the gunwale.

"Positions everyone," he called as he ran to the tiller.

Jaspen dashed to the bow while the others took up their places. An anticipatory wave of vertigo rose from her gut when she noticed the forward skid tips jutting over the break into open air. Beyond them, the glacier dropped away from the mountain ice sheet at a sharp angle. The idea of riding the windsled down to the Plain far below conjured images Jaspen couldn't afford to conjure. She squeezed her eyes shut and fought to clear her mind in preparation for the task before her: watch for crevasses and other dangers that might make her imagined horrors come true.

One by one, the rest of her companions called ready. Yet, they waited.

"Jaspen?" called Benethan from the braking claw.

"Oh, right. Ready!" she yelled.

Rawl and Kemren unfurled the sails and Jaspen felt the strain build as the fabric began scooping wind. *Tigress's* forward legs creaked and groaned as the vessel tried to tilt forward.

"Now!" shouted Sand.

Benethan heaved back on the lever and the claws retracted with a boom. *Tigress* leapt forward and tipped over the edge.

"Bank the sails!" shouted Sand.

Jaspen glanced back to see Benethan clambering from the claw lever up the sloped deck to help Kem and Rawl return the sails to their bundled state.

How any of them could keep their footing as the windsled rattled and bucked down the glacial slope she could not imagine. She could barely keep her own footing even with a firm grip on the forward rail. Yet, somehow they did it. Then they scrambled to the claw lever and worked to ready the spring for braking.

Jaspen gave her full attention to the glacier. Their descent now depended on her and Sand.

She squinted into the wind and scanned beyond the blur of the near distance to the discernible features beyond. Minor crevasses and dips came into view and whipped beneath them almost too quickly for her to register. With each one she thought the windsled would come apart. But somehow *Tigress* held together.

"Claw ready!" shouted Benethan above the roar of the wind and the screams, rattles and bangs of tortured wood.

Jaspen more felt than saw Kem and Rawl stumble to the rail at her side. Now she did not watch alone.

Nobody spoke as the windsled careened toward the Anthemar Plain. The remaining distance would likely take the better part of a day by foot. Jaspen estimated minutes at their current rate.   Faster than she'd ever gone before. It stirred a feeling beyond terror. Only her singular focus forward kept her from cracking and ducking down to hide behind the gunwale like a child caught in the open during one of the frequent thunderstorms spawned by the Snowsea and cast upon the Parm and anyone unfortunate enough to find themselves beyond the safety of Brink.

As the end drew nearer, she felt her fear begin to ebb. Then she saw the shadow-line, like a bolt of aqua-blue lightning crackling across the ice. It spanned the width of the glacier. They could not avoid it.

"Brake, Monk!" she screamed.

Benethan let out a yelp and released the claws. Too late.

The springloaded blades bit the snowy surface for only an instant before the vessel soared out over the crevasse and the grind of recurved metal against snow fell silent.

Without support, the forward skid tips shot upward as the legs dropped. She watched in silent terror as the far rim of the crevasse rose before them. She thought for sure they were going in. Then, somehow the skid tips caught the other side and turned their momentum into a jarring upward surge.

The middle skids kept the surge going and the rear skids finished it with a deafening whump!

Then came the timeless instant of total, smooth, soundlessness as *Tigress* went airborne.

The landing on the far side of the crevasse broke like the wave-front of an avalanche roaring in from behind.

The rear skids hit first. Their earsplitting slap preceded the thunderous explosion of wood as the legs blew apart. At the same moment, the nose of the windsled plunged back toward the ice with a force so great the middle and forward legs suffered the same fate as the rear.

The ragged screech of the braking claws rose above the general grind for only a heartbeat before being cut off with a jolt as they tore free. They chattered and scraped along the bottom of the hull as *Tigress* left them behind.

Then the windsled was sliding on her belly down the remaining expanse of the glacier. Jaspen clutched at the rail and peered forward past the masthead. She wished she hadn't. They were racing toward the glacial terminus. And as much as she again wanted to hide, she couldn't tear her eyes from the sight.

The final distance to a drop of unknown height played out as if in slow motion. And at the end, she did close her eyes.

But the plunge didn't happen. The sense of deceleration hadn't been a product of her mind, but an actual event.

The cacophony quieted and then with a final decisive, though anticlimactic, thump gave way to the whispers of cold glacial breezes.

Jaspen opened her eyes.

What remained of *Tigress* had come to rest not ten paces from the edge. Jaspen tried to stand, but the deck sloped hard to port and she found it difficult to keep her footing.

"Is everybody okay?" yelled Sand from the rear, his voice shaky but loud.

One by one, everybody but Rawl responded in the affirmative. The old provisioner sat against the gunwale holding his right arm tight to his body.

Sand and the others worked their way to him.

"Just strained, I should think," said Rawl.

"What happened?" asked Sand.

"Holding on for dear life is what happened. And if I hadn't been, I'd be a smear on the snow somewhere back up there." He jerked his head aft.

"Can you move?" asked Sand.

"In a moment or three."

"All right, you take it easy while the rest of us start unloading."

Sand, Benethan, Kem and Jaspen clambered up to the storage hold containing their gear. Prying the hatch open proved a challenge, but working together, they managed it.

The first thing Jaspen saw was Wolfe's twin-barreled rifle lying atop a pile of dung discs. The sight caused a swell of emotion to ball up in her throat. At her side, the others fell still as well, looking at it.

Benethan moved first. He hopped down into the chaos, picked up the gun and handed it up to Sand. The spotter eyed it for a second then took hold and lifted it clear.

Kem jumped in next and began helping Benethan dig out packs, Sand's and Rawl's guns and Sable's scaler's belt. The dangling carved-bone wedges rattled as Benethan lifted the belt from the jumble.

"I'll take it," said Jaspen.

Benethan handed it to her. She straightened the wedges, rolled the belt carefully and pushed it deep into her pack.

"Load as much cooking fuel as you can," said Rawl from where he sat at the gunwale.

Soon, everyone shouldered bulging packs and skidded back down to Rawl who was gently rolling his shoulder. He offered a pained nod. "Good to go," he said.

But nobody moved. Before they could be on their way, one last task remained, a task of grief. Jaspen and the others looked across toward the opposite gunwale. At its base rested the wrapped body of Wolfe. The ropes binding him to the deck rings had held.

Jaspen knew they couldn't risk taking the time to lower the tactan from the glacier to the ground so they could entomb him in a rock grave. The Thracks above might attack at any moment. But he couldn't just be left as he was either.

The immobility of her companions suggested they too were at a loss. Sable wasn't even there to sing one of her mourning songs.

Then Jaspen saw the open storage compartment with its load of dung discs.

She felt a twinge of remorse for *Tigress*. The windsled had become a kind of home over the past few weeks. But clearly, the shattered vessel would embark on no more journeys, save one.

"Sand," she said. "Bring your flint." Before he could respond, she began clambering back up to the storage hold.

"We'll meet the rest of you on the ice," said Sand.

Nobody spoke as the sound of boots moving along the deck punctuated the quiet whispers of the chill breezes. Sand clambered up to join Jaspen at the edge of the hold. He shed his mittens and pulled a tinder bundle from his pack. Then he produced a flint.

Jaspen shed her mittens and held out her hand for the flint. "You shield the wind," she said.

Sand nodded and handed her the flint. Then he held the tinder to the deck and cupped his hands around it. Jaspen pressed the flint to the wooden surface with her stump and unsheathed her dagger.

"Ready?" she asked.

Sand nodded.

She leaned low and struck the first sparks.

On the fifth try, the flash drew a thread of smoke from a tiny glowing pinpoint deep inside the bundle. Jaspen added the slightest hint of breath causing the pinpoint to swell and touch off a few more around it. In the instant before her lungs had no more air to give, the bundle birthed a flame.

Jaspen sucked in a quick breath and gave it to the hungry newborn flame. It flourished and begat offspring of its own until the bundle popped and smoked.

Sand scooped it up from beneath and hopped down into the hold where he placed it amid the dung fuel. Fire engulfed the bundle as he laid on the shredded remains of a woven-grass fuel-storage bag. The flames devoured the dry fibers almost too fast for Sand to pull his hand away.

He tossed a whole bag on then broke discs and added the fragments to the growing fire. Finally, he threw a few whole discs atop the blaze and scrambled out of the hold.

He and Jaspen put their mittens back on and stood side by side looking through the rising column of smoke at the wrapped form beyond. Then the heat drove them back and they scurried for the ladder.

By the time they'd reached the surface of the glacier and joined the others, a swirling maelstrom of flames licked up the mast into the bundled sails. Jaspen sensed Sand's movement at her side and glanced over to see the spotter withdraw Wolfe's tiger-fur tricorn from his parka. He considered the worn hat for a long moment, then threw it spinning into the flames.

"Goodbye, General," he said and wiped his eyes. Then he turned and headed for the edge of the glacier.

The rest of the Pride followed. Kem fell in beside Jaspen and brushed her mitten with his. She reached out and took hold. She never wanted to let go, but in only a few steps had to do so to make the climb down to the ground.

To her relief, the terminus of the glacier stood only about thirty feet in height and fell away in uneven terraces, offering a descent almost like a staircase. Easy enough to traverse on foot, but Jaspen didn't care to imagine what would have happened had the windsled gone over.

At the bottom, the frozen, rocky earth stretched away into the visible distance. Jaspen stepped onto the stony surface without giving it much thought, but as soon as her boots settled with a quiet, familiar, but long-unheard crunch, the sensation froze her in place. She could feel the pulse of the land, a living, vital pulse she'd not felt in all the weeks when her every footfall fell either on wood or ice.

How the Ghosts could spend years living an icebound life seemed suddenly unimaginable.

"I never thought I'd miss this place," said Rawl. "Actually, I never thought there was anything here to miss. But solid ground is certainly something."

Kemren and Benethan too had paused to test their footing as if trying on a new pair of boots.

Only Sand seemed indifferent to the touch of the land. He stood staring back up at the glacier, watching the black billow of smoke ascend from the burning windsled.

"We'd better get moving," he said, though, without moving. His rifle and Wolfe's made a X across his back.

"To Gray Horn?" asked Benethan.

Sand spun to face the group and nodded. "It will be our best chance of finding—"

The sharp call of a wolf cut the air. It resounded from the north, very close by.

Several more calls followed in quick succession. Then came a chorus of terrified whinnies.

Sand and Rawl whipped their guns off their shoulders. "—horses." Sand finished his statement and took off toward the noise.

Jaspen and the others followed. Snarls and yips rose in volume as they rounded a lobe in the glacier. Ahead, Sand drew to a halt facing a scene Jaspen could not yet see.

In a moment, it came into view. A pack of five wolves stood with hackles up and teeth bared facing a herd of six horses, all riderless, but wearing saddles and dragging reins. The horses stood looking out from a narrow dead end crevasse that emptied a small stream onto the Plain. The lead animal, a massive black stallion, swung his head side to side and snorted in defiance.

The wolves dashed from side to side looking for a weak point to press the attack. They had not yet seen the Pride.

Sand quietly slipped Wolfe's gun from his shoulder and handed it to Benethan. Then the two of them plus Rawl readied their weapons as Jaspen and Kem drew their daggers.

"Wait until I give the word," whispered Sand.

He flicked on his sight's red beam and aimed it at the ground in front of the largest of the wolves. At first the great slate gray alpha didn't notice, but when Sand began to dance the beam over the stones at the wolf's feet, the animal caught the movement, hopped back with a start and eyed it.

The other wolves immediately detected the change in their leader. They paused and watched him, more than one head canted sideways in apparent confusion. And just like that, the hunt seemed forgotten.

Sand pressed the dot closer to the alpha who stumbled back.

Sand then fired.

The ground at the alpha's feet exploded, causing it to yelp, spin and nip at the flying stones all at once, which ended with the wolf going down in a tangle of flailing legs, tail and teeth. Then the wolf was up and bolting north.

The rest of the pack tracked with the report of the gun and spun to face Sand. A fierce green fire burned in their eyes as they bared their fangs, laid back their ears and considered the new threat.

Rawl cocked the hammer on his musket.

"Wait," hissed Sand.

First one wolf, then another glanced at the fleeing alpha. When, after several long, silent, motionless seconds, nobody moved, the farthest wolf broke and raced to catch up to the alpha. The rest didn't wait another breath before following.

The pack soon disappeared over a distant rise. Sand shouldered his gun and turned to face the horses. He held his hand out, palm up and approached slowly. The stallion's black coat quivered and it snorted as the spotter drew near.

"Be careful," said Rawl.

Sand ignored him and kept moving. "Onyx?" he said. "Is that you, old boy?"

"You know that horse?" asked Benethan.

"I think so. The question is does he remember me?"

Sand drew to within a pace. The horse's nostrils flared, blowing a cloud of vapor across Sand's palm. Twice more it tested the scent of the outstretched hand then it stepped forward, touched snout to fingertips and gave a soft whinny.

Sand stepped forward and hugged the horse's

muzzle. "I have some sad news, my friend," he said. "As do you, it would seem. But our sorrows will have to wait." He turned back to the Pride. "This is Onyx. He and the others will help us. Come on, we need to hurry. The most dangerous wolf of all is the alpha whose pride has been injured."

"Wolf's pride," chuckled Rawl.

Sand smiled and led the black horse out of the crevasse. The other five followed.

Onyx's acceptance of Sand had a calming effect on all of them, horse and human alike. The animals almost seemed relieved as Jaspen and the others secured packs and mounted. Sand helped with fine adjustments then went to Onyx.

"I guess it's you and me now," he said. "Though I wish it were under different circumstances." With the fluid smoothness of long practice, Sand swung up into Onyx's saddle. Then he set off southwest, on a course to avoid the burning ruins of Gray Horn and head toward their ultimate destination, Anchoresk.

Somewhere between here and there, they would have to sneak past an army. Then they would face the real challenge: infiltrate the Adminithedral at the heart of great Catalogian monastery and make contact with Jaspen's father. "He loves me," she had said.

But a deep and growing doubt settled like a

lump of cold lead in her chest. What if he didn't?

There was only one way she would find out. She kicked her mount forward. Behind her, the extra horse followed, untethered, yet bound to the others by a force far stronger than any rope. This thought brought her a small measure of comfort. She clung to it as she left the glacier and the smoldering remains of the windsled behind.

30

SNOWSEA FRONT

The clatter of repair work on *Waketorrent* proceeded without pause until the final hint of daylight bled from the cloudless sky. Even then, Sable waited for night to deepen before risking a peek out through the gap between the gunwale of the windsled and the belly of the skateship. The ice below reflected starlight and the warm orange glow emanating from many small round windows on the side of a second skateship parked some distance away.

At least one sentry stood watch by the lowered rear ramp of the other ship. And a second sentry circled the top deck. She could only assume equivalent eyes surveyed the ice from *Waketorrent* as well as the ship on the opposite side.

The frigid night air lacked the will to stir even a single flake of powder snow. In such pure stillness and silence, the slightest sound would carry far. She'd have to move with great care.

Sable shouldered the knotty coil of rope she'd constructed using small portions of the many ropes binding various windsled components to the deck. She hoped the segments would be small enough for their theft to go unnoticed. By her estimate, she had a total length of roughly twice the distance to the ground. Just enough.

As quietly as possible, she crept forward until she crouched behind the windsled's masthead, some kind of bird judging by the carved feathers on the back of its neck. At her side, the anchor hung from its winding spool. Sable checked for the far sentries, saw none and leaned over the rail to work her rope around one of the anchor's stout recurved limbs. She froze half-way through the process when the deck guard on the other skateship strode into view.

As soon as he rounded back into the shadows, she resumed her work until she had guided half the rope around the limb. She coiled both halves on the deck, one by each foot. Then she waited.

The sentry made another pass in and out of sight. The moment he disappeared, Sable unrolled each coil to the snow then slipped over the rail and took both lengths in her hands. Quick as Sister Spider, she lowered herself hand over hand down the doubled rope. At the bottom she released one of the halves and pulled the other, slowly, deliberately, so the thump, thump of each knot barely sounded as it bumped over the anchor limb.

Finally, the last knot slipped free and the rope fell. She couldn't help the slithering hiss as it settled on the ice, but she did manage to catch the end before it slapped down. Then she coiled the whole length as fast as she could and dashed behind one of the forward skate legs, where she buried the coil beneath a mound of skate-shattered ice.

The guard stepped into view just as she finished. He paused and scanned *Waketorrent*, perhaps having heard the rope. But he didn't linger long before continuing on his way.

Sable breathed a calming breath and turned her attention to the enormous eight-legged skateship parked in front of *Waketorrent*. Jaio was somewhere inside. She'd seen Thorne's men carry his unconscious form aboard as soon as they'd arrived. Somehow, she had to get over there and make her way aboard as well.

She watched the two neighboring skateships for many long minutes to find a window when both deck sentries were out of sight at the same time. As for the sentries she couldn't see, she'd have to put her trust in the Windstar. She looked up and found it in the night sky. When it emitted a particularly strong pulse, she ran.

Reaching the nearest leg of the huge spider-ship seemed to take forever and as soon as she arrived she crouched down in the deepest shadow and did a frantic search for sentries. Much to her relief none appeared and no alarm sounded.

The passage of a few more quiet moments gave her heart a chance to settle. Then she shifted her attention to the skateship. Unlike the smaller versions, this one lacked a rear ramp. Instead, a bulbous compartment like the abdomen of a massive arachnid protruded aft from the main body. Small round windows dotted the underside and flanks of the compartment, but, in contrast to the rest of the vessel, no light shone from them. And best of all, the compartment appeared to lack an upper deck, which meant no circling sentries.

Sable shifted her gaze to the rear leg behind which she hid. It appeared to pass within jumping distance of the compartment's riveted skin. Between the rivets and the seams, she thought she'd be able to find enough hand and footholds to gain secure purchase.

"Let there be enough," she prayed to Sister Spider. "Or show me another option."

The sentries made another pass and Sable saw no other way so she knelt to remove her boots for the climb. A soft crunch, crunch in the snowy surface from behind froze her and sent her heart racing again. Slowly, her hand went to her dagger as the steady cadence of footfalls grew louder. A vision of the blade's former owner, Regimon Cathra, flashed in her mind. Seeing his spirit, knowing he was with her, helped calm her nerves.

When the walker seemed only a pace away, Sable sprang to her feet, spun and planted herself in a defensive stance.

There before her stood a tiger, mouth slightly agape, puffing crystalline breath into the night air. Sable staggered back. The tiger matched each retreating step she took, but did not close the distance. As terror built, Sable clung to the memory of Regimon as she clung to the dagger. That alone held panic at bay long enough for her to see a complete lack of hunger in the great striped cat's starlit eyes. She stopped backing away. The tiger fell still less than an arms-length in front of her.

A soft grating resounded overhead, from the belly of the dark compartment. Then she heard the unmistakable whine of uncoiling line. The end smacked the ice not three paces to her left. She angled toward it, and groped to snag it without looking. There was no way she would take her eyes off the tiger.

After a moment of flailing, her arm snagged the rope. In one motion, she sheathed the dagger, grabbed hold of the rope in both hands and began hauling her skyward faster than she had ever climbed before.

The cat let out a low, wet grumble and strode up to the end of the line where it turned its massive head skyward to watch her ascend. Then it padded a few casual circles around the end of the rope before loping back toward *Waketorrent* following the line of its own tracks.

That was when Sable saw her tracks on the same line. And one by one, the tiger was replacing them with paw prints until none of her tracks remained. In her mind, the memory arose of the tiger she had saved from Sand's shot when they had first reached the Parm. *Could it be?* she wondered.

The building fatigue in her arms drew her back to the present. She glanced up to see how far she had left to go—too far—then turned her gaze back to the tiger and kept climbing.

The great cat had just walked into the starshadow beneath *Waketorrent* when Sable felt a hand grab her wrist. She looked up with such a start she almost let go of the rope.

"It's okay," whispered a voice from out of an open porthole. "I'll help you."

INVINCIBLE DAWN

Jaio stands beside Thorne at the forward railing of *Invincible Dawn's* pilot house balcony. Frigid swirling winds creep inside his drawn hood and bite at his nose and cheeks. Yet, despite the cold of the exposed deck and the potential for warmth in the compartment just below their feet, Thorne prefers the open air. The ability to keep an eye on the fleet no doubt plays a large part in his decision to stay topside throughout most of the daylight hours.

Jaio has to admit the sight is impressive: seven fast moving skateships running at full sail and arrayed in a wedge formation before *Invincible Dawn*. Ahead of them stretches the seemingly endless expanse of the Ice. The fleet has been traversing it for several days, ever since leaving the mountains. How much longer they will do so, Jaio has no idea, and Thorne, when asked, responded with a quick, sharp glance and nothing more.

Jaio knows better than to ask again. The cracks in the old man's façade of paternal kindness have been growing and spreading like fissures in hammered basalt. The escape of the Pride and the forced abandonment of the irreparable skateship *Mantis*, struck the initial blows against the stone of Thorne's resolve.

Enough days have passed for Jaio to see the toll this is taking. The old man obsesses over every detail, issuing immediate radio reprimands every time a skateship slips out of position by even a few paces and calling on the Ghost Cappens to submit vessel and crew status reports four times a day. Keeping up with it all has turned the skin beneath his eyes dark and baggy. The eyes themselves, sunken and haunted.

The muffled sound of boots on metal rungs draws Jaio's attention to the hatch. He turns and looks past Thorne's ever-present pair of guards in time to see the weathered, blocky face of *Invincible Dawn's* Breakborn Cappen, Ladashi, emerge into view. To Jaio, the man seems less Cappen than messenger. In every way, Thorne runs the ship. Yet, even so, Ladashi maintains a stoic, commanding presence.

"Orol Thorne," he says.

"Yes," Thorne replies without moving.

"The slipsong is nearly complete."

This news elicits a straightening of stooped shoulders followed by a slow turn to face the messenger. "Thank you, Ladashi. Inform the fleet. Upon our arrival at the Sunrise Node, initiate the Morningstar."

Jaio silently recites the mnemonic he used to remember the names of all the nodes. Sunrise was not one of them.

"Yes, Orol," said Ladashi.

"Oh, and have Leegon take his windsled to pick up the scouts."

"Yes, Orol." Ladashi descends back into the pilot house.

Thorne gives his attention to Jaio. "To answer your question of four days past, we are within a few breaths of our destination." He turns back to the rail and resumes his vigil.

Jaio settles in by his side again and gazes from the fleet to the wavering horizon. Nothing but a featureless white expanse stretches for as far as he can see. He can just hear the voice of the radio operator rising up through the open hatch.

A moment later, the outermost ships in the formation begin to veer away, followed by the next pair and then the last. At the same time, they reduce sails and begin to slow. The *Dawn* quickly overtakes them.

Once the flagship has passed all but the lead ship, it begins a gentle bank to the north. The other skateships maintain relative positions and bank as well. Soon, they are all headed due north and every sail on every ship is withdrawn from the wind.

"Hold on tight," says Thorne.

Jaio tightens his grip on the rail.

Boom!

Invincible Dawn lurches with a groan as the braking claws slam down and Jaio is pressed into the railing. The other skateships then use the last of their momentum to arrange themselves around the flagship. Their journeys end one by one with the thunder of springloaded blades impacting the Ice.

Frostbite is the last of the skateships to stop. It comes to rest on the *Dawn's* far side. In the aftermath of its brake explosion, the long play of thumpers and hissing skates gives way to a startling silence. Other than the random clatter of rigging and faint shouted commands emanating from the skateships as their crews secure positions, a cold wind barely whispers.

Thorne spins from the rail and walks with guards in tow all the way around the edge of the balcony surveying the deployment of the fleet. "Very good," he says. "Very good." He concludes his circuit where it began, at Jaio's side.

"What is the Sunrise Node?" asks Jaio. He wonders if the Mountain of Faces is anywhere nearby. They passed several rises in the last few days that might have been the Swell, but at the distance the fleet maintained from the edge, he couldn't be sure.

"This is the Sunrise Node." Thorne indicates their location on the Ice with a sweep of an arm. "A new age will dawn here."

Jaio tries to follow the gesture, but the sweep of his eyes reveals nothing but flat white ice.

Thorne appears to sense Jaio's confusion and pats him on the shoulder. "Everything will make sense soon enough." He starts for the hatch. "Come, there is no more need for us to risk frostbite up here. Let's find some warmth and wait for the scouts to return."

One of the guards, Braukis, precedes Jaio and Thorne down the ladder and the second, Kharkin, follows. At the bottom, Thorne guides them not to the hatch opening onto the upper deck, but to another ladder leading deeper into the skateship. The four of them descend in the same order to the *Dawn's* upper gathering chamber. As aboard *Frostbite*, a replica riverside lodge fills most of the chamber.

Thorne and Jaio walk side by side around the outer wall to the round lodge entrance. Braukis throws open the flap and steps inside onto the sandy floor.

"Clear," he says.

Thorne motions for Jaio to follow. Jaio ducks inside with Thorne right behind him. Then, much to Jaio's surprise, Braukis leaves and closes the flap on his way out.

Jaio glances around. A low dung fire crackles within the ring of river stones bordering the central brazier. A few burning sconces fastened to the cedar plank wall add their wavering warm glow to the light of the fire.

Thorne sheds his parka and heads for the stone ring. As he sits, Jaio notices a rolled 'bou skin and a small rough hewn box on the floor at his side. "Have a seat, Jaio. We've earned a rest."

Jaio, already beginning to overheat in the relatively warm space, slips out of his parka. The thin buckskins underneath even feel a bit much, but he leaves them on and pads across the sand to sit beside Thorne.

They both simply warm their hands for a while and watch the flames. Jaio has to admit, even though he knows the sense of familiarity he feels here is born of an illusion, it nonetheless gives him a certain contentment he has not felt in a very long time.

Overhead, a roof beam creaks.

Finally, Thorne reaches to his side, picks up the hide and the box then rotates to face Jaio. "Back up a little," he says, his tone almost gentle.

Jaio rotates to face him and complies.

Thorne unrolls the hide to reveal a painted image. At first Jaio thinks it is a depiction of the Catalogian banner with its black and white diamonds. But then Thorne rotates the hide so the flat edges, rather than the points, face them.

A chess board.

Thorne opens the box. Inside are two sets of finely carved pieces, one of a pale wood, perhaps birch or maple and the other of a grainy wood darker than any wood Jaio has seen. Stained perhaps.

"Do you know chess?"

Jaio finds himself nodding even as the words of Major Anchor flood his mind.

"Excellent!"

Jaio struggles to calm his thoughts. After weeks of waiting, he now has only a moment to take this opportunity before it passes. "Allow me to set the board," he says and holds his hand out for the box.

"By all means." Thorne smiles and passes it over.

But instead of placing the pieces, Jaio sets the box down at his side. This draws a puzzled look from Thorne. Jaio doesn't know the wisdom of what he plans next, but one thing is certain, he will not play the game. The deeper lesson chess has to share can only be learned by not playing. It is a lesson Jaio must somehow make clear before the man before him unleashes a nightmare upon Plain and Steppe alike.

With slow, deliberate movements, Jaio takes hold of the near edge of the painted hide and rolls it back up before setting it aside. He then lifts the box and begins placing the pieces in the sand. He is careful to intermingle colors and shapes so that they are evenly mixed and in close proximity to one another. The whole time, Thorne says nothing.

When Jaio is done, he looks up to find the old man scowling at him. "You mock me?" Thorne asks through clenched teeth.

"I challenge you," says Jaio. "I challenge you to see beyond the painted squares to the common ground on which all the pieces stand. I challenge you to recognize the wood at the heart of each piece whether Pawn or King, white or black. I challenge you to discover the laws of kinship that run deeper than the rules of division."

Thorne glares at Jaio. "You naïve little boy," he growls. "There are no such laws. But even if there were, the refusal of just one of these pieces," Thorne snatches up a pale rook and shakes it in Jaio's face, "to recognize those laws will make the blood flow." He slams the piece back into the sand and sweeps it around toppling all the rest.

Jaio nods to the solitary rook. "And what becomes of that one? Sure, the risk of attack has been eliminated, but look at the cost: condemned to a brief, miserable and solitary existence in a ruined land. And it comes about not as a consequence of fighting back against an attacker, but in order to preclude the possibility of attack before the need even arises and may never arise, especially if everyone is committed to preventing it."

"Be silent!" Thorne surges to his feet.

Jaio remains seated. "Don't you see? Such an act makes you that one piece. It makes you the attacker. It makes you the bringer of ruin... Please, let me go. Give me a chance."

"Guards!"

The flap whips back and the two Breakborn warriors duck through, stutterguns in hand.

"Take this boy below and lock him up."

Without a word, the guards march over to Jaio and, none to gently, haul him to his feet.

"Please, Orol." Jaio struggles against the iron fists clamped around his arms. "Don't do this."

"It's the only way, Jaio. You will see. When the time comes, you will see."

The sudden clatter of an opening hatch resounds through the lodge chamber, followed by fast moving footfalls headed toward the flap-entrance.

"Orol," says Ladashi from outside.

"I told you not to disturb me," growls Thorne.

"I know," says the Cappen as he partially lifts the flap and peers in, "but I thought you would want to be informed right away. Leegon just signaled from the edge. He found the scouts already there, awaiting pick-up. They report that all armies have converged on Anchoresk."

"So, Lord Salazriole is ahead of schedule. Excellent!" Thorne turns his attention back to Jaio. "It looks as though the time has just come." He strides past and motions with a sharp wave of his hand for the guards to follow along with Jaio.

Ladashi opens the flap all the way and steps aside to make room for Thorne. The old man ducks through the lodge opening. The guards shove Jaio after him.

Thorne pauses to face Ladashi. "Assemble the gondola crew and have them report for duty immediately."

"Yes, Orol." Ladashi hastens away, around the side of the lodge and out of sight.

Thorne, Jaio and his captors all head for the winding staircase at the rear of the chamber, where they descend to next lower level. There, the stairway empties onto a long corridor and Thorne sweeps aft, almost at a run, with the guards on his heels, dragging Jaio along.

Ahead of them, Jaio sees a round door, closed and with a heavy-looking hand-wheel at its center. Thorne grabs the wheel, cranks it until it thuds to a stop then heaves the door back. This reveals a second such door not a pace beyond. Again, Thorne turns the wheel, only when it stops, he shoves outward. Beyond the open door stretches a dimly lit corridor ending in a steep stairway, going up.

Braukis takes over restraining Jaio as Kharkin retrieves a torch from a wall sconce behind them and dashes forward to lead the way. The flames reveal an unadorned passage with recessed lectric bulbs lining a low curved ceiling, riveted metal walls and a gratework floor. Evenly spaced along the passage are six round doorways, three to a side. Each has a wheel-handle at the center.

No sooner has Thorne started down the passage behind the torchbearer when the arrhythmic pounding of several sets of fast moving feet grows louder from behind. Jaio strains to peer back and sees six figures running their way. The figures are clad in puffy, full-body suits of heavy, russet leather. Dark goggles cling to their foreheads atop skull-hugging hoods. Only their faces show, faces without tattoos. Breakborn.

Braukis spins Jaio forward and drives him on behind Thorne. Kharkin hands the torch to the old man and ascends the stairway. At the top, he cranks another circular door-handle in the ceiling and shoves the hatch open. Then he reaches back for the torch and climbs through with Thorne right behind.

Firm prodding prompts Jaio to climb up after them. From behind, the thudding footfalls give way to clanging, as the six leather-clad Breakborn enter the passage. A hatch slams and a wheel spins with a drawn shriek. Then a new round of iron shrieking commences as the handle on one of the six side doors begins to turn.

The sound grows faint as Jaio's head passes up through the hatch. The sight at the head of the stairway gives him pause. Torchlight reflects off the many square glass panels set in interlocking riveted frames that all together compose an oblong dome. The glare of flames on glass prevents him from seeing into the darkness beyond.

Jaio completes the climb and steps onto the gratework floor. Then he gives his attention to rest of the dome. Just forward of center, a great wooden wheel with many spokes and handles stands on a stout pedestal. Behind the wheel and to the right he sees a simple stool mounted behind a console similar to the one on *Frostbite*. Jaio recognizes it as a relic radio.

Opposite the radio console is another mounted stool behind a console Jaio does not recognize. Kharkin goes to this console and flips a switch. In that instant, a cold blue light bursts from the tops of eight self-standing lectric lamps that encircle the rear half of the dome. Dozens of smaller lights—

green, red, white and yellow—ignite on the two consoles.

A huge smile spreads across Thorne's face. He hurries forward to stand beside Kharkin who flips a hinged cap over the torch flame, smothering it.

Thorne glances down at the console then turns to Jaio. "Come up here, boy," he orders and Braukis pushes Jaio toward the old man.

As soon as they stand side by side, Thorne points to a line of six green lights, all dark. "Watch," he says. His wide-eyed enthusiasm reminds Jaio of a child at the Oromola fishing camp awaiting the first piece of salmon following the three-day ceremonial fast.

One light blinks on, followed in short order by the rest. As soon as they are all illuminated, Thorne reaches up and flips another switch. A deep mechanical rumble rises in volume and the floor begins to shudder. Then seams of light knife through the darkness beyond the dome. The seams widen as great metal panels unfold to reveal the open sky. In a moment, the panels drop out of sight beyond the rim of the glass dome.

He and his captors are then gazing through a rectangular framework of thick girders at the blue, cloud-streaked, expanse beyond.

Jaio is taking in the sight when the six goggled Breakborn scurry into view outside. They set to work adding angular supports to the structure, mounting winches and attaching ropes to some unseen object hidden in a compartment behind the dome.

Once all the components are in place, they start to crank. A massive cylinder, the size of a four family lodge, begins to emerge. It slides on its side upward along tracks headed for the top of the rectangular frame centered above the dome. The drag is slow with frequent pauses to make adjustments, but after many breathless moments a jarring boom sounds as the cylinder drops into place within the rectangle. Then four of the red-clad Breakborn go to work bolting it down with thumb-thick bolts.

The other two run toward the rear of the dome and begin heaving out a pair of black lines made of some smooth, flexible material Jaio cannot identify. They pull the lines forward and fasten them to the end of the cylinder.

Once the bolts and lines are in place, one of the Breakborn turns to face Thorne and thrusts his arms high in the air three times in quick succession. Thorne nods and all the Breakborn head for a hatch behind the dome, where they drop out of sight. A hand pulls the hatch shut on the way down.

"We are ready," says Thorne.

Jaio can make no sense of what has just transpired. "Ready for what?"

"This." Thorne flips open a recessed panel in the console and grabs the handle underneath. Then he pulls the handle up and twists.

Boom!

Jaio jumps with fright as the top half of the cylinder bursts skyward, arcs away and drops out of sight. A loud hissing then follows. At first, nothing appears to happen, but soon, a shiny silver bulge rises into view at the top of the cylinder. The bulge grows and grows. In moments, it is the size of the dome. And it keeps growing.

It swells into the shape of a giant fat fish, held in place above the dome by a meshwork of thin lines covering it like a down-swept hand-net scooping for a salmon. All the while the fish fattens until its silvery skin strains against the net. Finally, when Jaio thinks it will surely break the lines, the hissing stops.

The six Breakborn reappear outside. They are wearing pack frames now with broad, thin panels fasted to them. The Breakborn scramble up the lines onto the fish. And Jaio watches in astonishment as they mount the panels at the rear end like fins. Lines are then attached and another signal is given.

Thorne steps to the wheel and turns it, left then right. Flaps on the two vertical fins mirror his turns. He then pulls back on the wheel causing the whole column to tilt aft and the flaps on the horizontal fins go up. A push forward causes the fins to tilt down.

The Breakborn give another signal and clamber down the lines. Once they are inside again and the hatch is closed, Thorne flips open another panel on the console to reveal a large red button. He places his thumb on it then hesitates.

Slowly he removes his thumb and turns to Jaio. "Why don't you do the honors?" he says.

Jaio shakes his head. Whatever the honors might be, if Thorne wishes it, Jaio doesn't.

"I insist." Thorne nods to Braukis, who forces Jaio forward.

Jaio tries to resist, but the muscular man holding his arm probably outweighs him by three times or more. His efforts to plant his feet and stay put do not even slow his approach to the console. Then Braukis is forcing his balled fist down toward the red button.

"No," he groans as his knuckles touch the smooth round surface.

"Yes," says Thorne and the button depresses with a click.

A quick-fire series of four sharp pops resound from below and aft and suddenly, the floor begins to gently sway as the world outside the dome falls away.

"Open the viewport!" Thorne cries out in

delight.

Braukis pulls Jaio away from the console so Kharkin can sit down on the stool. Once seated, Kharkin pulls back on a protruding handle. At the front of the dome, gears begin to clatter and the floor at the head of the chamber begins to roll back beneath the gratework.

Jaio's captor pushes him forward until he's standing several paces in front of the spoked wheel. A sense of vertigo builds as the retracting panel slides open beneath his feet. Through the gratework, he can see the Ghost Fleet growing smaller on the Ice below. Only then does he see the sheen of glass beneath the grate. He peers down past his feet as the skateships recede to dots.

"We're flying," he whispers. Even though he sees it and feels it, he can't quite believe it.

"Welcome aboard my cloudship, *Daybreak*."

The retracting panel finally clanks to a halt. By then, the front quarter of the dome—everything forward of the wheel and two consoles—has an open view of the snowy mountainous landscape below. And Jaio stands in the middle of it.

"Lower the engines," says Thorne.

Kharkin presses two more buttons, which initiate a series of thuds, whirs and rattles followed by two sharp decisive clanks. A moment later, a pair of oscillating whines reverberate for a few strained breaths before producing almost simultaneous roars that settle into a steady unified grumble.

"Engines running," says the control operator.

Thorne turns the great wheel and points the cloudship due north. "To Anchoresk! In mere hours, we shall arrive at our target and complete our mission."

"What are you going to do?" ask Jaio. He can hear the dread in his own voice.

"Down below, in a special hold, *Daybreak* carries a nukebomb with the power to erase Anchoresk and the surrounding armies from the face of Anthemar."

Jaio remembers the Orol's stories of such weapons. When detonated, they erupted like volcanoes, throwing up great mushroom-like clouds made of smoke, fire and the ashen remains of everything caught in the blast. "If you drop it, you'll be destroyed too."

"Oh, this is not a typical nukebomb. In order to minimize damage to a fragile atmosphe, the Ancients designed this one to release its energy along a lateral plane. They called it a sweeper. Which means, the safest place to be is directly overhead. We'll be watching from there. You might think of it as watching from the eye of the storm."

Jaio's mind races. How can he stop Thorne? He turns to Braukis. "Listen to me, Braukis, this is mass murder. Do you want to be part of—" The arm across Jaio's throat clamps tighter cutting off his air. He gasps and claws for release.

"No more words, Jaio." Thorne nods to the guard.

Braukis releases his grip, but before Jaio can utter a sound, a thick strand of cloth drops over his face and cinches tight across his mouth. Then his arms are yanked behind his back and bound.

"From now on," says Thorne, "you just watch. And while you're watching, maybe you'll think about what this means; a way for you and the rest of the Ghosts to finally go home to the Steppe."

There are other ways, Jaio tries to say, but it comes out an incoherent mumble.

"In the end," says Thorne. "I think you'll thank me."

Jaio gives his head a vehement shake and strains to pull free from the bindings. They don't budge. Fighting down panic takes all of Jaio's will, but he forces himself to breathe and turns his gaze forward. Whatever chance he might have will become no chance if he loses his head.

Only then does he notice the falling snow. Fat flakes patter against the glass. The last faint impressions of the Ice and mountains soon disappear within a swirling haze. A storm is overtaking them. And maybe, it will do what he cannot. If the cost is his life, he'll gladly pay it. He

.ɔres the storm to hurl the cloudship
ɔund.

_ursed weather," growls Thorne as he pulls
.ɪck on the wheel. "Drop more ballast," he orders
Kharkin. "We'll climb above it and wait it out."

"Yes, Orol."

Thorne glances at Jaio. "Don't worry, boy. This is only a minor setback. The break of our new day might be delayed, but it cannot be stopped any more than tomorrow's sunrise."

Jaio feels the last of his hope drain away. And with its passing another dread feeling he never thought he'd feel begins to take root in his heart. Resignation.

All he can do is watch.

So deep is his despair, he almost misses the faint shuffling coming from the wall vent to his left. By the time he glances over, it's gone leaving him uncertain he heard anything at all.

ANTHEMAR PLAIN

Sand, Benethan, Kemren and Jaspen belly-crawled the last few feet to the top a minor rise overlooking the broad valley of the Catalogians. Behind them, in a shallow, dry gully, Geleb Rawl stood with the horses.

The telescoptic tube slung across Jaspen's back jostled side to side as she shuffled along. At the summit of the hill, she spun the tube forward and raised it. A blurry, circular smudge filled her vision. She lowered the tube and held it to her chest with her stump while she fished her filthy Kestian sash from the parka pocket to which it had been relegated since she and her companions had ridden away from the glacier...how many days ago? She could not be certain. Twenty, perhaps.

Throughout that time, they'd trailed in the wake of devastation left by the advancing army of the Maxamantan Alliance. It had been almost unbearable. Carnal horrors flashed in her mind every time she blinked and no amount of tears would wash them away; snarling, bloody-faced wolves straddling pink rib cages that poked up through the sticky remains of shredded parkas.

She only hoped the food, fuel and equipment scavenged from the abandoned packs of the dead could be used to save lives not yet lost

With her teeth, Jaspen held a corner of the soot-and-sweat-stained sash and tried to pull it open with her fingers. It resisted her efforts, the damp fabric having begun to harden in the frigid air. But she managed. Then, she proceeded to wipe the blot of grit from the lens.

As she rubbed, she glanced at Sand who was already scanning the scene below with the other salvaged magnifying tube. "Not good," he whispered. "Maxamant's forces have encircled the Citadel and trenched in."

"Let me see," said Benethan.

Sand handed over the tube. At the same time, Jaspen raised her relic image magnifier and looked down into the valley. But she ignored the gathered army in favor of the only thing of any real interest to her.

After a moment of searching, the shimmering tower at the heart of the Adminithedral filled the magnifier's circular frame and, in that instant, the building transformed from an impressive, though flat and distant, generality into a truly awe-inspiring wonder with depth and immediacy. If she reached out, she thought she might touch it.

"How are we supposed to get through to the citadel?" asked Kem.

"There must be a way," said Sand. "Look for Kestian banners."

A part of Jaspen knew she should shift her gaze to the army arrayed around the monastery, but she couldn't tear her gaze from the immense glass spire. Her father was in there. And if by fortune's favor the Pride made it through Maxamantan lines, she would soon join him.

"What good will that do?" asked Benethan.

"Maybe, I can create enough of a diversion on my way to meet Lady Kest for you to slip in. And who knows? I might even make it in too."

"Unlikely, but…" The gravel let out a soft crunch as Benethan made a slight shift. "…Yes, the Squells have not yet been overrun."

"The Squells?"

"The shanties to the southwest, between the crop fields and the main gate. Irrigation canals run straight through the current Maxamantan position right up to the edge of the outlying hovels. If you can hold their attention long enough, we can use the canals to cross their lines and reach the cover of one of the hovels. Then it will just be a matter of working our way to the gate without getting shot. I know the entry password. They'll let us in."

Jaspen finally adjusted her gaze to look at the abandoned collection of ramshackle shelters and the fields beyond, cut now with the dark scars of trenches dug by the forces of Maxamant and his allies.

"You sure the distance isn't too great?" she asked.

"No, but—"

From down in the gully, Onyx let out a loud whinny and chomped down hard on his bit. The clank of teeth against metal sent a chill up Jaspen's neck. She glanced back to see Rawl trying to calm the great black beast.

"Keep him quiet," hissed Sand.

"Tryin'" grumbled Rawl as he stroked the warhorse's withers.

Jaspen started to shift her attention back toward Anchoresk when a faint stain in the morning-gray sky gave her pause. Beyond the rim of the next hill, on the other side of the gully, rose a distant column of smoke. "Look," she said to the others and pointed.

Sand, Benethan and Kem followed the aim of her stump. Before any of them responded, she heard, or more accurately felt, a deep vibration emanating from the same direction.

She and Sand looked at one another. "Feel that?" she asked.

He nodded, snatched the telescoptic tube from

Benethan and sprang to his feet. "Come on, quick!"

Jaspen, Benethan and Kem leapt up and chased after the spotter as he raced down the slope, crossed the gully in front of a bewildered Rawl and surged up to the top of the opposite hill.

By the time Jaspen and the two monks had crawled up beside the spotter, he was looking through the telescoptic tube, his face grim. Jaspen lifted her own tube and panned it about until she hit the smoke plume. Then she followed it down to the source.

What she saw kindled a new kind of terror deep in her core. The smoke poured from twin stacks at the rear of a massive box of riveted armor plates. The squat, rectangular box rolled toward them on wide chattering tracks that looped around a dozen wheels. From the hub of each giant forward wheel, a gun barrel protruded. A third, larger barrel jutted forward from the right face of the main hull. The purple and red barred banner of the Maxamantan Protectorate flew from the end of a wobbling pole just behind the top hatch where the commander's head could be seen in silhouette.

"Tank," she whispered.

"Let me see," said Benethan.

She gladly handed him her telescoptic tube.

"Steamcrawler, actually," he said. "Modeled

on the Late Antiquitic tanks like those we saw at the Cliff of Faces, but more akin to the Catalogian steam carriage. The Order has been playing with a similar design, but clearly Lord Salazriole is much farther along in—"

Jaspen couldn't believe her ears. "No time for technical admiration, Monk," she said. "It's coming right for us. We need to get out of here!"

"She's right," said Sand, "And we have other problems." Jaspen glanced at Sand who now aimed his tube not at the steamtank, but farther left. Her eyes tracked with the tube and there, in the far distance, a second ominous armored vehicle lumbered forward. She whipped her gaze right and, at roughly the same distance she saw a third.

"Can we slip between them?" she asked.

"On foot, maybe, but with the horses, I don't see how."

"And we can't fall back toward Anchoresk or Maxamant's rearguard will see us," said Kem.

"Let's follow the wash downstream," said Sand. "With luck, we'll find a narrow slot we can hide in until they pass."

"Then we'll have an army and a line of steamcrawlers between ourselves and where we need to go," said Benethan.

"I'll just need to make a better diversion," said Sand.

A feathery snowflake dropped to the ground in front of Jaspen. She looked up to see several more drifting silently down. They fell from a building mountain of clouds rolling in from the south.

She'd lived at the edge of the Snowsea long enough to know what clouds like that meant.

"A storm is coming," she said. "We need to find cover from that too."

Sand cast his gaze skyward then hurriedly shuffled back down the slope until he could stand without risk of observation by the steamtank. "Come on," he said and ran back in the direction of Anchoresk.

Jaspen, Kemren, and Benethan shared a look of uncertainty and followed. Again, they joined Sand at the summit of the hill overlooking the Catalogian stronghold. Only this time when they gazed out across the broad valley, the Adminithedral tower, the Squells and all hints of the encircling Maxamantan Alliance forces were gone, obscured by the impenetrable curtain of falling snow that swept toward Jaspen and her companions.

Behind them, the chugging of the steamtank grew louder as it continued its approach.

"We don't need to find cover," said Sand. "Cover is just about to find us." He raised a hand and caught a snowflake in an upturned palm.

"That's not what I meant," said Jaspen. "If we

don't take shelter soon, we will be completely covered, as in buried alive and frozen."

"Then we'd better hurry so we can use the veil of snow to help us get into Anchoresk before that happens," said Sand. "Mount up. We need to exit this wash before the crawler crests the hill." He nodded to the summit on the far side above which the rising column of coal smoke could now be clearly seen.

The four of them ran for the horses.

"What's happening?" asked Rawl.

"We'll tell you all about it later," said Sand. "For now, we ride." He swung up into Onyx's saddle without apparent effort. The others displayed almost as much finesse. Jaspen however, still struggled. She glanced at Kem and saw in his eyes the unspoken offer of help. He knew better than to speak it aloud.

Jaspen sprang like a pouncing tiger and heaved with her one hand. This time, she successful mounted on the first try and Sand nodded as he kicked Onyx to a run. The other horses followed without need of prompting. Jaspen rode at the rear.

When she crested the hill, she glanced back over her shoulder one last time. Through the thickening haze of falling flakes she saw the belching stacks and swaying Maxamantan banner rise into view above the peak of the far hill. Then her mount carried below the line of sight and she gave her attention to what lay ahead. At the moment, all she could see were the faint snow-spattered forms of her companions.

At the head of the line, Sand appeared as little more than a gray smudge in the almost uniform wall of white that now enveloped them.

Just like the foreseeable future, she thought, *drawing ever closer, coming to a point.* Who could see beyond that point? She certainly couldn't, but she wanted to. Her father might be there, and a long life with Kem.

As white blindness fast stole her vision, first swallowing Sand, then Rawl, then Benethan, and finally, all but the faint swaying tail of Kem's mount, these thoughts helped her maintain focus.

She held onto to them like lifelines as she peered out through the tunnel of her hood and pushed on.

PART 4

DAYBREAK

ANTHEMAR PLAIN

Coal smoke spews from the stacks of the
Harkener ironcreeper as it struggles to advance
through deepening drifts a few short paces ahead
of Oan. The young Mediant's Escort cautiously
follows in a compacted track and watches through
the opening of his drawn hood as the foul-
smelling pall grays the swirling snow. His eyes
sting every time he and his two companions walk
through an acrid gyre.

If not for the cover of the blizzard, they would
never have risked such close proximity to the
menacing vehicle. Nor would they be venturing
this near to a Harkener hold-out. Even with the
protection of the storm, Oan and Pren both
advised against this action, but their charge
insisted. And as Mediant Moon's Escorts, bound
by a solemn oath, they deferred to her judgment.

So, here they are, snow-whipped and
following a heavily armed war machine manned

by potential hostiles and headed toward an uncertain destination. The chances of the trio remaining unseen seem slim at best. Years of Escort training can only hope to offset the odds so much.

Oan glances over his shoulder. "I'd feel better, Mediant, if we backed off a little." He cringes at the need to almost shout in order to be heard over the chug and clatter of the lumbering vehicle as well as the bluster of the icy wind.

The shadow-circle of Mediant Moon's hood-opening turns his way. Even though she is only about two paces behind Oan, her pure white snow-hare fur cloak renders her otherwise invisible. The same is true for Oan's fellow Escort, Pren, who walks at the rear of the line.

"I don't want to risk losing our way in this storm," says the Mediant. Oan can hear the anxiousness in her voice. It's not something he's heard on any of their previous journeys and it makes him uneasy.

"The snow is deep enough now," he says. "We'll know we've veered from the path if we sink in up to our knees."

"Very well." The Mediant halts and crouches to reduce the impact of the wind. Behind her, Pren does the same.

Oan turns to face the Mediant and kneels. He pulls his hood back enough for her to see his face.

"Is everything all right?" he asks.

The Mediant pulls her hood back as well. For all the years Oan has known her, the sight still gives him pause. Her entire face is tattooed like a starry night with a crescent moon in the middle of her forehead. The pattern of the Tiger constellation hovers above her left brow. Above her right, the Wolf. Even though the two celestial beings live as opposites in the sky, they live as neighbors on her flesh.

Throughout Oan's many journeys with Mediant Moon, he has learned much about her, but the markings, like her past, remain a mystery. He discovered early on, she will not speak of them. So, for the sake of the peace, he long ago stopped asking.

Mediant Moon meets his gaze, the whites of her eyes appearing unnaturally bright within the dark starscape of her visage. "No," she says. "Everything is not all right. I fear we may lose this one."

"But we've lost Harkeners before. When they weren't ready. When their faith in the false promises of the past remained too strong. And I've never known you to fear the loss. We've always just withdrawn to wait until they are ready."

The crow's feet at the corners of the Mediant's eyes deepen as she offers something resembling a smile, but filled with sadness, and something else. Determination. "There are reasons, Oan, reasons I can't lose this one," she says. Oan waits for her to offer more, but she doesn't. Instead, she stands. "The machine is far enough away now. Let's go."

Oan rises with Pren and considers pressing the Mediant again, but the time is not right. So, he nods, turns and resumes walking along the channel of crushed snow. The ironcreeper appears now as a faint smudge in the distance ahead.

As they trudge on, the wind eases and finally goes still. Yet, if anything the snowfall thickens. Its consistency has also changed. The original light dry powder typical of the deep inlands has been replaced by wet, heavy flakes more akin to coastal snow. It creaks like old boards beneath their feet. In the silent moments between their steps, Oan can hear the creeper laboring harder to move forward against the building pack.

From behind him, Pren lets out a quick warning click. Oan wheels to find her facing back along the compressed track, her banded staff in hand, its wooden shaft and metal deflection rings concealed within a white linen cover. The Mediant has also spun around and stands still and alert gazing past Pren.

Oan removes his staff from its tension clasp on his back and slips around the Mediant to join

Pren. "What is it?"

"Listen," whispers Pren.

At first, Oan hears nothing other than the rumble of the creeper and the incessant gusts of wind. Then a rhythmic thudding becomes discernible through the wintery haze.

"Soldiers," says Pren. "Marching this way along the trough."

"Will they see our footprints?" asks the Mediant.

Oan glances down to check. The fur coverings over the soles of their boots appear to have done their jobs. Only a master tracker could hope to see the faint impressions they've left in the compacted path. "I don't think so."

"We need to find cover," says Pren.

Oan scans for options. The ragged wall of the trough rises almost to mid-thigh. All the cover they need is on the other side, only a few steps away.

"Jump over the edge," he says. "And be careful not to break through. Then hunker low. With luck they won't notice us at all. But if they do, they'll think we're just a trio of snow covered rocks."

Pren goes first and hurdles the margin easily. Oan jumps next and joins Pren in reaching out to offer assistance to the Mediant. She declines and makes her leap just as the faint outlines of marching men begin to coalesce in the distance. All but the fringe of her cloak makes it, causing a partial collapse which leaves their hiding place exposed.

Oan doesn't hesitate. He hands the Mediant his staff, helps her burrow in behind him then edges forward to the break where he quickly scoops up fallen chunks and uses them to start rebuilding the wall.

All too quickly, he realizes he doesn't have enough time. The column of musketeers is quite visible now. In seconds, they'll see the gap. And him.

Oan can think of only one option. He settles into the hole and fills it with his own body. He wonders if this is how snow hares feel when a wolf is padding by while they sit in plain view, frozen, waiting.

His downturned hood is not quite closed, leaving a slit through which he can see into the trough. In moments, the first sets of boots appear less than an arm's length away. Then come the next. And the next. Line after line, the musketeers thud past for what feels like hours.

Finally, the last of them move out of sight and the drumbeat of stomping feet gives way to the quiet whisper of falling flakes. Through it, the rumble of the armored vehicle can barely be heard. Soon, it too disappears.

Only after the singular hush of snowfall returns, does Oan risk a look up and then down the channel. "All clear."

He feels the Mediant and Pren stir behind him. He turns to face the Mediant, who returns his staff.

"We're too close," he says. "We need to retreat to a safer vantage and let this play out."

"Normally, I would agree with you, Oan. But not this time. If a window of opportunity opens at all, it will be fleeting. We will need to be very close so we don't miss it. I'm sorry if that makes your job harder."

"Mediant," says Pren. "I agree with Oan. We are vulnerable. And against their guns, our staffs will be of no use."

To help emphasize her words, Oan arcs his staff over his shoulder and clicks it back into its tension-clasp.

"I'm sorry," repeats the Mediant. Then she steps into the channel and continues walking.

Oan and Pren hurry to join her, one on either side.

"What is going on?" asks Oan. "You haven't been yourself since we left Cindermist Hall."

"You will learn soon enough. For now, I must ask you to trust me. We must see this through."

"Mediant," says Oan. "I swore an oath to honor your will. And I intend to keep it."

"As do I," says Pren.

"But to honor it fully, we need your trust as well."

The Mediant stops. Her two Escorts step around to face her. She lowers her hood with her thumbless right mitten and considers them both in silence for a moment as the snow settles in her graying, sandy hair. Oan notices for the first time how much she seems to have aged, even since their departure from Cindermist less than three moons earlier.

"You are right," she says. "I too swore an oath, but if your trust is lost in keeping it, the price is too great." She pauses to look them both in the eyes. "These Harkeners are more dangerous than any we've ever encountered. They are quite possibly more dangerous than any in the world."

"How? We've seen powderguns and ironcreepers before. The users of these will outstrip their means of support just as fast as did the others," says Oan.

"The Harkeners down there have an arsenal of ancient weaponry far more deadly than powderguns and creepers. If they came to understand the extent of their advantage over, well, everyone, they could be invincible."

"If that is true, why do they use powderguns?" asks Pren.

"Because, they can build powderguns and

replace the ammunition they expend. But they can only find the relics. And with every find, and every use, the supply shrinks. All the ancient caches may have even been emptied by now."

"So, they hold these relic weapons in reserve?" asks Oan.

"Yes. And not just that. The whole social order of Anthemar has been built around them."

"So, what has changed to bring us here now?"

"The same thing that always attracts the attention of the Keeper's Council. These Harkeners stand on the threshold of a reckoning. In this instance however, we have to make sure their crossing does not unleash upon the world an unstoppable plague of violence, oppression and exploitation."

Oan and Pren exchange glances.

"The risk is that great?" asks Pren.

Mediant Moon nods. "Forgive me for not telling you sooner."

"There is nothing to forgive, Mediant," says Oan.

Pren nods. "You may be our charge, Annequoia. But you're also our friend. We're with you, oath or not."

Oan nods agreement.

Annequoia Moon, esteemed Mediant of the Keeper's Council, offers them a grateful smile. She then she shifts her gaze to look along the channel toward the soldiers, the ironcreeper and the great Harkener monastery in the valley beyond. "There is one more thing," she says.

"What, Mediant?" asks Oan.

"I think the man I love is down there."

34

DAYBREAK

To wish for a never-ending storm is to wish for the impossible. Jaio knows this as he gazes down through *Daybreak's* observation window at the expanse of roiling clouds below the cloudship. But he wishes for it anyway. Nothing else seems capable of stopping Eukon Thorne from annihilating Anchoresk and everyone gathered there. This very likely includes his friends, unless they've been waylaid in their efforts to infiltrate the Adminithedral and contact Jaspen's father.

Jaio can envision countless possible reasons for their failure to reach the Catalogian stronghold. None of the scenarios bring any more comfort than the one in which the Pride succeeds. Either way, they meet their end.

Helplessness threatens to consume him as time slowly passes. Eventually, the building ache in his jaw and shoulders claims his attention. He longs to have the gag removed from his mouth and his wrists unlashed, but he knows Thorne will not take the risk. Every time Jaio tries to stretch his neck or otherwise shift position to gain some measure of relief, Braukis, the guard behind him, responds with a sharp shake to straighten him up.

Meanwhile, Thorne remains silent. Jaio supposes the old man is simply standing at the wheel, enjoying the view, contemplating the annihilation of thousands of people. What hope there might be for another chance to talk, to plead, to beg, dies a little more with each passing moment.

Jaio's legs grow increasingly leaden as the evening wears on. Then dusk arrives, bringing a distraction: a sky painted in colors without names. The first is a yellow to which the brightest meadow bee might only aspire. This then transforms into a russet glow more vibrant than the hottest campfire coal. Finally, a purple several shades richer than a larkspur blossom covers the world. Only as the glow gives way to gray does Jaio realize that his discomfort has, if only for a few moments, surrendered to awe.

The pain reasserts itself as the last of the atmospheric pigment drains away. At the same time, a new torment begins when someone brings Thorne a meal. The scent of savory spices stirs Jaio's appetite. His stomach grumbles as he listens to noisy chewing. But the old man offers him nothing.

When at last the chewing stops and the attendant returns to take away the leavings, night is well under way. Stars ignite in the wake of the sun's receding afterglow. Jaio has never seen so many. They fill the sky in such abundance, their combined light silvers the cloud-tops and, in the haze of sparkles overhead, he has trouble discerning even the most familiar constellations.

Once again, Jaio finds himself in awe.

Then Thorne clears his throat, breaking the celestial spell. "Even if the clouds lift in the night, I suppose I'll have to wait until daybreak to begin the new age." Thorne lets the words hang for a moment then adds, "Turn him."

Braukis spins Jaio around to face Thorne, who grips the pommels of the great wooden wheel and looks past them into the darkness.

"I wouldn't want to spoil the poetry of it, after all," he concludes through a cold smile.

Jaio tries to speak again and finishes his incoherent mumble with an upward turn, hoping Thorne will hear it as a question. Maybe, the old man's curiosity and vanity will move him to risk removing the gag.

In response, Thorne's smile simple grows colder. "I will happily answer any question you have, tomorrow afternoon. Once you've come to your senses."

Jaio shakes his head and strains against his bindings. He can feel the cordage cutting into his wrists, bringing pain and the stickiness of blood, but he doesn't care. Braukis tightens his grip on Jaio's shoulders, squeezing, crushing until finally Jaio gives up and goes still.

"Save your strength, Jaio. The night promises to be long. And as I'm sure sleep will elude us both on the eve of so momentous an event, we might as well pass the dark hours together, side by side. Think of it perhaps, as a taste of what a mutually prosperous future might look like; me, in control of Anthemar and you, my governing Orol on the Steppe. We could do great things."

Jaio can feel the heat of anger rising in his ears even as the temperature in the gondola drops. Despite the weak flow of warm air entering through the wall vents, he realizes he can see everyone's breath. Thorne doesn't appear to notice.

Outside, gaps of darkness widen between the rolling swells of silver clouds. Soon, the openings grow broad enough to see snow-covered mountains far below, illuminated by slowly shifting bands of starlight. The bands are moving northeast. The cloudship appears to be moving with them, riding the incoming cold front as it pushes out the weakening storm surge.

"We appear to have been blown off course,"

says Thorne. "No matter." He turns to Kharkin, the control operator seated at the adjacent console. "What direction to Anchoresk?"

Kharkin consults some instruments than examines a map. "Ten degrees to port, Orol."

Thorne turns the wheel. "Engines full ahead. We don't want to be late for sunrise."

The cloudship vibrates as the motors accelerate. They fill the gondola with a muffled roar. At the same time, the air coming in through the wall vents grows warmer. Breath soon becomes invisible again.

"We should be there soon, Jaio. Then we'll just have to hold position and wait."

What follows is the most agonizing night of Jaio's life. At once, he thinks it will never end and also feels it flying by. All the while, he struggles to stay on his feet as the weight of everything seems to bear down on him. Braukis frequently heaves him up none-too-gently every time he begins to sag under the growing load of frustration, guilt and helplessness. He has failed.

By the time the cloudship reaches the valley of the Catalogians, the sky is clear. Dawn is still some time off, yet the stars now silver the snow-covered land as they had the cloud tops. In the far distance, a tremendous spire of glass stands at the center of two concentric rings of firelight; the bonfires of the two armies. Reflected flames make the tower look as if it too is burning. Jaio has no doubt, at dawn, it will be.

"You may be wondering why we don't go closer," says Thorne.

Before Jaio can nod, grunt, or otherwise respond, not that he has any intention of doing so, the old man goes on. "We don't need to. From here, the blast wave will reach the target at almost full force. Yet, we will be out of range of even the most powerful hyperpulse cannons, if they have any, which, as of the last report I received, they don't." He chuckles.

"Not that they will even see us. Their sights are set on each other, like a pair of quarrelling dogs unaware of the wolves closing in on them both." Jaio feels a hand other than Braukis's squeeze his shoulder. "We are the wolves."

Jaio recoils, only to be jerked back into position by Braukis.

"You would prefer that they rip and tear each other apart? You would have them endure terrible suffering to reach a far more desolate end than we will bring quickly, almost without pain? Make no mistake. The world as we have known it will not live beyond the dawn.

"The question is will the manner of its ending make way for a better world to begin? Without our help, I fear the slow grind of this conflict will devour Anthemar and the Steppe, leaving nothing but an uninhabitable wasteland in its wake."

Jaio barely hears anything past the word "help." "Hllff?" he puffs through his gag with as much incredulity has he can muster.

"Yes, help. You have to take the long view to understand. Those people down there, whether fief-lord or Monk, are like dogs faced with a shrinking pile of table scraps. The desperation and violence of these dogs will only worsen as the pile becomes smaller. And there can be no doubt no new scraps will be tossed. The table has long been cleared and the masters retired to their final sleep. The pile can only shrink.

"And so, blood will flow in ever greater amounts until the scraps are gone. To believe otherwise is to suffer from the same delusion as believing the dogs will recognize the ultimate futility of their efforts and abandon the scrap pile by choice prior to its exhaustion. They simply lack the vision to see how abandonment could prevent years of long and pointless carnage.

"So we must do what they cannot. Destroy the scrap pile and all who covet it. As brutal as this act may seem, in the long run, it will save many more lives than it will cost. It will be hailed as mercy. And our legacy will inspire gratitude and admiration, for making the hard choice in our time to insure a better life for our descendants."

Jaio shakes his head and tries to turn away. He

doesn't want to hear any more. Not because he finds Thorne's perspective repulsive, but because he can hear the sense in it. Of the two of them, Jaio holds onto a hope as thin as a frayed thread, whereas Thorne clings firmly to the time-tested rope of historical precedent. When have the scrap piles ever been abandoned by choice? The vision of snarling mongrels snapping at each other for some remnant shred of meat nearly consumes Jaio's mind. But in the periphery, another vision lingers: his friends risking everything to give him the chance to realize his delusion. Seeing them in his mind's eye, he knows, even if they all fail, they are not dogs.

Thorne is not wholly right. And no matter what happens when the new day begins, he never will be.

35

THE SQUELLS

Hidden in the snowy silence of the Squells and wrapped in te darkness of a moonless night, Jaspen Ario almost convinced herself that she and her four companions were not trapped in no-man's land, holed up in a sagging shanty between two armies mere hours away from trying to destroy each other. If only the five of them had been able to infiltrate the great monastery of Anchoresk before the storm had cleared. But they had only made it as far as the abandoned hovels well outside the gate.

At least the horses were safe. The image of Sand gently removing all their gear, thanking them for their company, and setting them free prior to reaching the Maxamantan lines still raised a lump in Jaspen's throat. How full of life they'd seemed as the great black stallion Onyx led them thundering away into the veil of fast-falling snow.

After that, Jaspen and her companions had found a secluded rock overhang where they'd waited out the worst of the storm before sneaking through the Maxamantan lines. It seemed so long ago; days, not hours.

Kemren stirred beside her and leaned forward to part the ragged hide flap and peer into the waning night. Frigid air poured in through the gap triggering a full-body shiver despite her parka. It felt like deep winter, not the cusp of summer. Despite the tiny flame burning in a grease lamp on the floor, their crystalline breath coated every surface in a fine layer of frost and made all their movements crackle.

"Not a cloud in the sky," said Kemren. "I don't think we can count on one last squall to cover our final approach."

"How deep is the snow?" asked Sand.

"Looks to be well above the knee."

"If we have to peg-hole all the way to the front door through that," said Rawl, "we'll make it maybe by supper-time tomorrow, if, that is, one side or the other doesn't pick us off just to put us out of our misery."

"What choice do we have?" asked Benethan. "We need to get inside."

"Then what?" asked Rawl. "Ask to see the most powerful man in Anthemar—excuse me,

Dictorian Ario's illegitimate daughter is here to see him. Might we have an audience?"

"Once we're through the gate," said Kemren. "I can take care of that."

"Which leads us back to our immediate problem," said Rawl. "The gate."

"I have an idea," said Jaspen. She turned her attention to Benethan. "Do you still have your robe?"

The monk nodded, a puzzled look on his face.

"Put it on while the rest of us find some rags." She turned her attention to the back wall and the pile of shreds mounded there that may once have been clothing. "We need to make ourselves look like stragglers."

"Rescued by the good Brother," said Rawl. "Brilliant!" He joined Jaspen at the mound, as did Kemren and Sand while Benethan rummaged through his pack. After a moment, he pulled out his Catalogian robe and slipped it on. Then he belted it and draped the shoulder sash across his chest.

Soon, everyone was ready. Jaspen extinguished the lamp and stowed it. Benethan pushed back the flap and stepped up onto the snow. Jaspen anticipated his plunge through the crust, but much to her surprise, the surface held. Slowly, he transferred his full weight. Not even a crack. He took a tentative step forward. Then another. And stayed on top.

Jaspen and the others clambered up out of the shanty to join him. When they were all huddled on the snow, Benethan gave them a nod and dashed at a crouch to the nearest cover behind the next shanty between themselves and the gate. One by one, the rest of them followed with Sand bringing up the rear.

They repeated the dash and pause again and again until at last, nothing but open ground stood between themselves and the entrance arch leading into the Catalogian stronghold of Anchoresk. Stockade walls had been erected around the perimeter linking the forbidding cannon mounds. And a pair of massive steam carriages blocked all but a bodies-width of the entryway. A thick, long gun -barrel jutted from the riveted iron nose of each immense machine.

Wavering torchlight backlit the whole scene. Within the fiery glow, no other movement could be seen. Catalogian and Protectorate banners hung limp from countless poles. And except for an occasional clank or cough, silence filled the unmoving air

"Now what?" whispered Kemren.

Jaspen heard Benethan let out a shuddering breath. "I make a run for it."

"*You*?" asked Jaspen. "I thought *we* were going to make a run for it."

"You just need to be visible when I tell them where to look. Then they'll provide cover so you can make it inside."

"I'm going with you," said Kemren.

Benethan shook his head. "Maxamantan sharp shooters will be watching. I might be able to cover most of the distance unseen if I go alone. More than one will be much more obvious. Besides, I'm a lot quicker than you are."

Even though Kemren acquiesced with a nod, the look on his face sent a chill through Jaspen.

"Trust me," said Benethan. "I'll have you inside in a few minutes." He took a deep breath and turned to face the entrance.

A sudden memory flashed through Jaspen's mind, of the night long ago when the assassin monk tried to kill her. Kemren's parka, the parka she now wore, had saved her. Without heed to the cold, she unshouldered her pack. "Wait, Benethan," she said.

He paused and cast her an uncertain look as she wriggled out of her parka.

"What are you doing?" asked Kem.

"Increasing the odds," she said as she handed the parka to Benethan. "Wear this."

Strangely, he didn't ask her why. He just removed his robe and parka and put hers on. Then he covered it with the robe again. "Thanks," he said.

As Benethan readied himself, Jaspen donned his parka, slung on her pack and re-bedraggled herself with rags.

"See you shortly," said the monk. And without pause, he sprinted out toward the gate. Several cries went up from the wall, but then almost as quickly came the call to stand down for a Brother.

The boom of a musket retort echoed out from somewhere nearby in the Squells. An instant later, a plume of snow erupted just ahead and to the right of Benethan.

The monk then began to duck and dodge with a speed Jaspen couldn't quite believe. More booms resounded. And around him more geysers of impacted snow burst into the air. Someone on the wall shouted a command and a whole musket volley unloaded on the sharp shooter positions. But it made no difference.

The closer Benethan got to the gate, the greater the Maxamantan effort to stop him. By the time he'd closed to within five paces of the gap between the steam carriages and the wall, musket balls were pattering all around him, clanging off the carriages, punching splintery holes in the wall, bringing the snow around his feet to a crystalline boil. Yet Benethan ran on.

The Catalogian defenders unleashed another blind volley, again to no avail.

Even so, when Benethan grabbed a steam carriage wheel spoke and began pulling himself toward the gap, Jaspen thought he might make it. Then a lance of green flame seared out from the far Maxamantan lines, caught him in the middle of the back and threw him through the opening. His splayed body crashed to the snow and slid, limp arms dragging at his sides, out of sight. In the next moment, the world fell silent again.

Jaspen and the others huddled together, eyes wide in horror. How long they remained frozen, she had no idea.

Suddenly, a beam of lectric light shot out from the top of the wall in their direction and began to pan closer. Her companions scrambled for cover and Jaspen nearly followed, but from somewhere in depths of her numb mind she remembered Benethan's final instruction. Be visible.

So, as the others hid she crawled toward the beam.

"What are...?" Sand began then nodded and moved to join her.

A moment later, the beam found them and steadied. It held just long enough for Kemren and Rawl to appear. Then it went dark.

Nobody moved.

From the other side of the wall, Jaspen heard a series of dull thunks followed by hisses. A half dozen smoking canisters arced overhead and dropped into the shanties behind them. Great plumes of smoke erupted in a rough semi-circle and soon the air was filled with a thickening haze. The Catalogian stronghold soon disappeared from view. That's when a voice yelled, "Run!"

Jaspen and the others did not need to be told twice. All together, they took off for the entrance.

Musket shots resounded from behind and plumes burst around them, but none too close.

Jaspen fought to ignore them and focused on following Benethan's tracks until the steam carriages emerged into view. Something whistled by her left ear as she dashed through with the others right behind her. Then they were all in and safe.

A cheer went up from the wall. But Jaspen barely noticed it.

Standing in front of her, face bloody, but wearing a pained smile was Benethan.

"You're alive," she breathed.

"Thanks to you." His words came out more as a groan than as regular speech. "Come, I'll show you to the camp." He winced as he turned and headed toward a mass of ragged tents in the distance. Kem hurried to offer a hand, but Benethan waved him off. "No special attention. Now hurry."

Jaspen understood the need for caution and haste. Already, they'd drawn too much attention to themselves. The best they could do now was disappear before their rescuers recovered from the shock of recent events and started asking questions.

Even so, when Jaspen began to follow, the sight of Benethan's back caused her pace to momentarily falter. His sash was gone and the entire middle torso of his robe and the surface layer of the 'bou hide parka underneath hung in burnt shreds, yet the underlying shell of kineticloth showed no signs of damage. It shimmered shiny and silver as if brand new. She shuddered to imagine what would have happened has she not traded parkas with him.

Benethan led them quickly into the mass of squalid humanity taking refuge in the makeshift tent camp that had been built to replace the Squells. Only after they'd found a noisy knot near a provision cart did he stop. With hands on knees he tried to speak while at the same time gasping and wheezing. "We need…to hurry. After that entrance…they'll be looking for us."

Jaspen shook her head. "We need to rest."

Much to her surprise, Benethan offered no protest. He simple sank to the ground where he sat cringing with every breath.

Rawl unshouldered his pack. "I think I might have something to help with the pain," he said.

While the provisioner dug around in his sack,

Sand put a hand on Benethan's shoulder. "I owe you, monk," he said. "With luck, I'll get the chance to repay the debt. But now I need to find Lady Kest." He looked at each of them, farewell in his eyes.

Jaspen knew the spotter needed to go, but the thought of parting struck her like a physical blow. She had to suppress a surge of emotion as she met his gaze and nodded. "Be careful, Sand."

"You as well." Without another word, he strode into the crowd and headed away.

As she watched him go, her sixth sense drew her attention to the provision cart. A young monk—barely more than a child—serving bowls of gruel to hungry refugees appeared to be staring at Benethan. He noticed her watching him and immediately gave his full attention to filling the next bowl.

Jaspen turned back to face the others. "We need to keep moving," she said.

"Why?" asked Kem.

"That serving boy was watching us."

Benethan looked up and gazed past her toward the provision cart. "What boy?"

Jaspen glanced back that way to find a gray-bearded old monk ladling slop into wooden bowls. The boy was nowhere to be seen.

"He's gone," she said.

"Not good," said Benethan.

With the help of both Kemren and Rawl, the battered monk struggled to his feet. He twisted to look at Kem. "Lead on, Brother," he said.

Kem nodded. "This way." He began pushing through the hungry masses, heading away from the Adminithedral.

"Uh, Kem, the tower's over there," said Rawl with a nod to the soaring glass tower.

"I know." Kem guided them out of the tent Squells and onto an open field where neat rows of snowbound lean-tos had been erected around a central pavilion tent with the banner of the Vantling Protectorate flying from its peak. Kemren kept his distance from the seemingly empty camp.

When they finally reached the far side, he drew up short facing a low broad building surrounded with spiked barricades. Dozens of sentries walked slow circuits on the other side of the barricades and dozens more made their rounds along the rooftop battlements.

"Oh no," he groaned. "Those defenses weren't there before."

"We're headed toward the Iron Robe chambers?" said Benethan.

"The Iron Robe dungeon, actually."

"Have you lost your—" blurted Rawl.

"Sshhh," hissed Jaspen.

"It's our only way in," said Kem. "But we have

to get past the guards."

"Great," moaned Rawl. "And just how are supposed to do that, as anything other than prisoners, that is."

Rawl's words took a moment to register in Jaspen's mind, so often did she simply tune him out. But this time, they made it in. And from them, an idea germinated. "Yes, as prisoners," she whispered.

"What?" Rawl wheeled on her. "Are you insane—"

This time she did tune him out. "Benethan, how about leading a trio of thieving Squell rats to the lock up?"

The monk eyed her, then the others, all of whom still wore the filthy rags they'd taken from the Shanty. "At any other time, there would be no way. But under present circumstances, if we can convince them the pauper cells are full, it just might work."

"We'll have to leave our packs," said Jaspen.

"I'll wear one of them," said Benethan. "So they don't see my back."

"We can dump the rest in a lean-to with our guns," said Kem.

"Good chance we'll be able to pick it all up later," added Rawl. "After tomorrow morning, the occupants won't likely be coming back."

Jaspen wished she'd been able to discount this

comment, but it too broke through. She glared at the old provisioner. "Unless we succeed," she retorted. For emphasis, she made a show of shedding her pack. As it was the lightest, Benethan chose it as the one to wear.

Both she and Kemren had to help him put it on. Tears leaked from his eyes and unintentional moans escaped his gritted teeth as they gently lowered it in place. He let out a sharp gasp when they finally released their grip and the full weight settled against his back, covering most of the hyperpulse damage. Seeing his agony, Jaspen suspected cracked if not broken ribs and wished they'd found another way. But at this point, getting the pack back off would probably be worse than leaving it in place.

Benethan took a few long controlled breaths and slowly adjusted his shoulders. Then he nodded. "I need to bind your wrists behind your backs."

Kemren opened his mouth as if about to speak then shut it and unwrapped one of the rags bound around his waist like a belt. They tore the rag into strips and Benethan lashed all their wrists firmly, but with enough slack that, with a little effort, they'd be able to wrestle free. Then he lined them up with Rawl in the lead followed by Jaspen and finally Kemren.

Jaspen expected Rawl to complain about being

first, but much to her surprise, he said nothing.

Benethan then reached into the lean-to and extracted Rawl's stubby hunting musket from their pile of belongings. Jaspen could see him strain to heft it, but once it was leveled on them, his tension seemed to ease. He fell in at the end of the line.

In Jaspen's mind, she envisioned the gun barrel jammed into Kem's back. The image frightened her more than she thought it should and she found herself wishing she could switch places with the man she loved. But Kem would never go for it. And so, with all her will, she drove the thought from her mind.

"Okay," said Benethan. "Let's move."

DAYBREAK

Dawn arrives almost imperceptibly with the death of a star. One moment, the faint point of radiance hangs suspended just above the northwestern horizon. The next, pale blue-gray light swallows it.

After that, Jaio watches with building panic as star after star vanishes within the surging tide of the approaching sunrise. Against all hope, he renews his efforts to pull free from the bindings and, no surprise, feels Braukis's grip tighten on his arms. Not caring, he kicks back with his boot, hoping to crack a kneecap. His blow glances off the huge man's shin. Pain shoots along Jaio's arms as Braukis forces him to his knees.

"You would do well, Jaio, to understand, you are not here to stop this. You are here to bear witness, to understand and to grieve what we must do as I will grieve. Knowing that the chance for a better life has come to this is the worst kind of knowledge, but it offers the most powerful lesson when we face it, eyes open, heart exposed. Only from this experience might we gain sufficient commitment to make sure it never comes to this again."

Too fast, the light is building. A few strands of far clouds have already begun to blush.

Jaio shakes his head and tries to rotate on his knees to face Thorne. But Braukis holds him fast.

"Take him all the way forward," orders Thorne.

Braukis hauls Jaio to his feet and shoves him onto the grate. Jaio plants his feet, but they merely slide along the metal gridwork as he is forced to the forward rail. There, he is surrounded by glass, his field of vision filled with open sky above a vast snowy horizon.

Time crawls as the sun nears. Jaio actually jerks with a start when the rim of fiery brilliance breaks the far edge of the world. He watches the sun swell and soon it hovers in full view, bathing the cloudship in blazing light. Features on the land below then ignite along their margins.

"Daybreak is here," says Thorne. "Open the bay doors," he orders.

"Yes, Orol," replies Kharkin.

Jaio hears a sharp click. A metallic chattering sound fills the gondola. It lasts for only a few heartbeats before falling silent.

"Begin the arming sequence."

Jaio hears a series of clicks ending with a quiet, repeating beep, beep, beep. "All systems, check. Sweeper armed," says Kharkin.

"I do this without fanfare," says Thorne, his tone solemn. "I do this for the people of Anthemar, the Homeland Steppe and Vanquisher's Break. I do this for the future."

Jaio tries to writhe free, putting everything he has into breaking the grip of his captor. The result, more crushing pain. Even so, he doesn't relent. Tears of anger, frustration and sorrow spill from his eyes and his wrists again grow slick with fresh blood as he thrashes and lurches. Braukis clamps his arms harder.

Beep, beep, beep.

Jaio lifts a boot and slams it down hard on the man's toes. Braukis grunts and presses Jaio into the rail. Jaio can barely suck in breath against the pressure of the metal bar across his stomach. But he continues to fight, kicking up a heel between the guard's legs, not quite high enough.

Beep, beep, beep.

He can't take the sound any longer and raises his head to release his hard earned breath as shriek. It arrives as little more than a moan and soon dies in his raw throat.

"Enough, Jaio."

A sharp slap resounds through the gondola

and the beeping stops. An endless instant later, a jolt rocks the ship. It is accompanied by a muffled bang. Jaio's legs almost give out as the cloudship lurches straight upward. He struggles to straighten. A movement below draws his eyes to the floor glass. On the other side, a massive, fast-spinning, ring-shaped object falls away.

Paralyzed, Jaio can only watch as the ring's rotations accelerate to a blur and it appears to shrink. Then its elongated shadow appears on the snowy ground below. The two race toward each other.

An instant before bomb and shadow collide, Jaio anticipates the blinding flash, the roar, the blast wave unleashed. Instead, their meeting raises nothing more than a silent plume of snow.

The most complete silence Jaio has ever known consumes the gondola. It remains unbroken as the plume sprinkles back down leaving a modest crater filled with debris and shattered earth. Only when stillness reclaims the white plain below does the silence shatter.

"No!" bellows Thorne. "This can't be! Not with my triple failsafe redundancies! The odds are beyond calculation!" Jaio hears frantic slapping and attempts to turn. Rather than try to stop him, Braukis turns with him. They are met with the sight of the old man smacking the drop button over and over again. "Now! Engage!"

An utterly novel sound, at once a sob of relief and a guffaw bursts out of Jaio, barely pausing to bypass the gag.

Thorne wheels to face him. The old man's eyes are wild with rage. "You find this funny?" he roars.

Jaio can't help himself. He nods.

Thorne stalks toward him. Jaio tries to retreat, but Braukis holds him in place.

Instead of halting to face Jaio, however, Thorne storms past to the forward railing. "Come here," he growls. Braukis spins Jaio and pushes him up beside Thorne. The old man is gazing out into the distance.

For a few moments, Thorne says nothing. As Jaio listens to the old man's breathing calm, he looks down at the crater again. A movement at the center grabs his eye. And somehow, despite the distance, he clearly sees the source of the movement.

A tiger bounds up out of the bomb debris and lopes north. Jaio can only stare, until, at his side, Thorne adjusts position.

Slowly, deliberately Thorne raises a hand and points toward the horizon. Jaio follows along the invisible finger-line with his eyes and sees the far off tower of glass. Yet, as impressive as the sight is, it only holds his gaze for a moment. He quickly looks back down toward the crater. Despite the fact that an open plain stretches out unbroken in every direction, the tiger is nowhere to be seen.

"In the end," Thorne goes on. "This changes nothing. The dogs will still tear each other apart. It will only take longer and cause more suffering. I tried to bring a quick end, a merciful end, but fate has chosen otherwise. We now have no choice but to wait it out. When they again turn their attention to the Ice, they will be all the weaker and we will be ready.

"If only…" his words trail off and his eyes grow wide again, except this time not in fury, but with the excitement of sudden awareness.

"If only!" Thorne turns to face Kharkin. "Mount the telescoptic!"

As the console operator hastens to comply, Thorne spins and lunges to the voicecaster. He flips a toggle switch and holds up the hand transmitter like a weapon. "I'm not finished yet!"

Jaio's mind reels. What does the old man have in mind? As soon as Thorne begins to speak, Jaio finds out. What he hears makes his insides go cold, as cold as the snow-covered world below.

FROSTBITE

Up on the Ice, a bitter south wind whistles through *Frostbite's* rigging. High on the main mast, a loose rope bangs against a spar. The monotonous tempo reminds Cappen Aiomida of a thumper. But her skateship sits unmoving on the Ice and nobody sings a slipsong.

Aiomida glances over at Ticker who stands gripping the rail nearby. *Frostbite's* slipsinger is as silent and tense as the rest of the crew, staring north, awaiting the promised flash that will signal the end of the Fane and the end of the threat they have for so long posed.

The same vigil commences on the other seven skateships in the Ghost Fleet as well. Every hand watches and waits.

Aiomida considered passing the vigil in the command dome with Lash and Map, but decided her place was with her crew. She can feel their anxiety building as the sun rises higher, and the flash doesn't come.

The bang of the dome hatch flying open causes her, and most everyone around her, to jump with a start. Lash leans out.

"Cappen! Thorne is calling!"

A spike of worry pierces Aiomida's gut. She shoves back from the rail and races to the dome.

By the time she ducks through the port hatch, she can hear Thorne's voice, scratchy, commanding and gushing impatience. "...all Cappens respond!"

Map hands the transmitter to her, "You're the last one, Cappen," he says.

She keys the button and holds the transmitter to her mouth. "Cappen Aiomida here, Orol."

"Good. Listen carefully! Circumstance has forced a change in plans. We must use the fleet to accomplish the mission."

Aiomida and Lash exchange a shocked look.

"Please repeat," asks another Cappen. Aiomida is not sure which one.

"Take the fleet into Anthemar! As soon as the tower comes into view, hold and wait for my signal to attack. I say again, do not attack until I give the order! The Fane must not be distracted from their self-inflicted destruction. Only after they have done most of your work for you and are at their weakest will you fall on them like wolves and wipe them out!"

"He's lost his mind," says Map. "Skateships can't skate over rocks."

Aiomida waits for one of her fellow commanders to incur Thorne's wrath by pointing this out. Instead, the silence stretches. With an exasperated exhalation, she keys the voicecaster again. "We'll ground out," she says.

"After yesterday's storm? I think not! Now, do as I say!"

Aiomida looks out at *Frostbite's* deck. In the few areas not yet cleared, the fresh snowfall is nearly waist deep and almost has hard as the Ice. "Could enough have fallen to support us?" she asks her companions.

"If we plane the skates, perhaps," says Lash.

"The added surface area will slow us down," says Map.

"That's better than cutting all the way through," says Aiomida. "We won't move at all if our skates strike stone."

The speaker pops. "We're preparing to descend now," says Cappen Leegon. Aiomida spins to look over at *Waketorrent*. The forestarboard leg is already elevating, and Ghosts are racing across the solid, fresh crust to rotate the skate from edge to plane.

Aiomida turns back to Lash. "Plane the skates," she orders.

Lash nods and races out the porthole.

"But, Orol," Leegon goes on, using his most submissive tone, "If we *all* go down there, we won't be able to get back up to the Ice."

"You won't have to. In the new world that will have dawned, skateships will no longer be needed."

"But if something unanticipated happens, the Steppe and the Break will be left defenseless."

Thorne's response to this is slower in coming.

"Right you are, Cappen Leegon," says Thorne. "If the *Dawn* remains on the Ice, it will not only safeguard the Break and the Steppe. It will also be able winch the other ships back up once they've completed the mission."

"Understood," says Ladashi, Cappen of the *Invincible Dawn*.

"Is it wise to leave only one ship?" asks Leegon. He adds just enough emphasis to the word 'one' for Aiomida to suspect some hidden meaning.

"Right you are again, Cappen Leegon."

With these words, Aiomida realizes what's coming.

"Cappen Aiomida, you will hold with the *Dawn*."

And just like that, Thorne not only removes *Frostbite* from play, but insures her compliance by leaving her ship in the company of a far more powerful and obedient vessel. Aiomida's frustration simmers. Yet, with every other Cappen listening, she knows better than to even hesitate in her response. "Yes, Orol."

"Very good," Thorne replies.

She slaps the wall. "Curse him."

"Should I tell Lash to stop planing the skates?" asks Map.

Aiomida shakes her head. "Just in case circumstances change," she says.

She watches the fleet of six skateships prepare for their invasion of Anthemar. What had, only moments earlier, been a scene of almost total stillness is now one of frantic movement. Clan banners ascend to mast tips. Heaps of snow drop from sail covers as scrambling riggers remove the covers for storage. And under the bellies of the skateships, chippers, dangling like spiders, ready breaking claws for retraction.

Lash returns as the first of the ships drops sails, releases claws and begins maneuvering into a north facing position. A part of Aiomida hopes they will shake apart during their slide down the massive glacial ramp to the Plain. But with a grade no more perilous than the ramp at the Break and a layer of fresh snow to smooth the ride, she is almost certain they will make it.

What puzzles her is why even a part of her wants the mission to fail. Clearly, the nukebomb didn't work, so Thorne's new plan makes sound sense. Yet for some reason, she wants it to fail. She doesn't have to think long to recognize the reason.

Jaio.

Another part of her still holds out hope, foolish though it is. Especially now, when her chance of being in a position to offer him aid has just been reduced to zero.

With practiced efficiency, the fleet is soon arrayed in offset chevron formation at the head of the ramp, with *Waketorrent* taking the point position. Then the radio pops.

"The fleet is ready, Orol," says Leegon.

"Proceed," says Thorne.

The skateships stagger their advance to give each other plenty of maneuvering room. Aiomida hates the feelings of helplessness and irrelevance that build within her as she listens to the distant releases of breaking claws and watches the vessels drop away.

"Cappen," says Map. "The *Dawn*."

She tears her eyes from the final departing ship and glances toward *Frostbite's* massive eight-legged neighbor in time to see the last of the visible gunports slide open.

ANCHORESK

Somewhere nearby water dripped, its slow rhythm adding to the chill melancholy of the dank Iron Robe dungeon. Weak flames fluttered in neglected wall sconces as Jaspen followed Kem past door after barred door set into the stone walls on both sides of the claustrophobic tunnel. Behind her, Rawl trudged, his footfalls striking the cobble floor with all the subtlety of falling trees. Benethan, by contrast, crept along at the rear without making a sound.

Kem had led them to the lowest level and now appeared to be set on reaching the point farthest from the entrance.

"We headed for Ario's summer retreat?" whispered Rawl.

"Quiet," snapped Benethan.

"What for? Haven't heard a sound but for the first two cells on the top level and haven't seen even a single sentry. I wager they've more important matters to matter than sloggin' round down here guarding nothing."

Jaspen rounded on him. "Another word and I'll give them something to guard," she hissed.

Rawl growled, but kept his mouth shut.

"I think we're almost there," whispered Kem. "One more bend."

Just as he was about to round the corner, two figures emerged from the shadows ahead. They wore monk's robes and held stutterguns. The weapons were both trained on Kem. Seeing this nearly caused Jaspen's heart to stop.

Kem jolted to a halt and, spreading his arms to block her, he began backing up.

Then, from behind, rusty hinges screamed for an instant before being cut off by a loud bang. Jaspen whirled and saw another four figures emerge from a cell. The first pair surged into the hall to block their escape. They too held stutterguns at the level.

The last two slowly positioned themselves behind the warrior monks. One, tall and bony, appeared to be ancient beyond old. He gripped a cane in one hand and in the other, the shoulder of his shorter companion. Jaspen recognized the companion. The serving boy.

"Well, what do you know, Andern? You were right," said the wizened monk as he smiled a huge yellow-toothed smile and looked right at

Benethan.

Despite Jaspen's fear, this aroused confusion. She watched Benethan's shoulders slump. And the barrel of the musket he held slowly sank toward the floor.

"Did you forget your mission, Brother Falka?" the old man asked, still looking at Benethan.

Falka? Where had Jaspen heard that name before?

"All you had to do was kill her, not bring her back here."

With these words, the mountain of pieces Jaspen had been trying for months to ignore all fell into place at once. She staggered back into Kemren, who caught her and held her up. If he hadn't, the shock would have felled her.

Benethan didn't move.

But Rawl did. He grabbed Benethan and spun him around. "You two-faced wretch!" The provisioner hauled back to smash a fist into Benethan's face.

Instead, with the speed of a striking rattletail, Benethan snapped up the musket and popped Rawl in the forehead with the butt. The old tiger hunter dropped.

"No," shouted Jaspen. Anger welled in her chest and she lunged at Benethan, but Kem grabbed her and held her back. "Let me...go!" she snarled as she struggled to break free. Then she made the mistake of looking into Benethan's face. Seeing his blank eyes froze her. His slow, almost imperceptible, shake of the head shattered the last of her courage. A sob burst from her chest, "Why?" She sank to her knees. "I trusted you."

"Your new sash awaits, Brother Falka," said the skeletal monk.

Benethan trained the musket on her and cocked the hammer. Then his face inexplicably softened and in a whisper almost too quiet for her to hear, he spoke. "I've tried to be a better monk than the first one you met, Jaspen Stillwind."

As before, hearing this name provoked a deep urge to run. But shock froze her. She could only stare at him in dismay.

Benethan looked up and past her. "Down, Kem!"

In a blur of motion, Benethan spun and pulled the trigger. The explosion seemed to go off inside Jaspen's head. At the same time Kem pulled her to the cobblestone floor.

Ears ringing, she looked up through the expanding plume of powdersmoke in time to see the old monk tip over backwards, a hole in his robe right over his heart. At his feet, the boy crouched low and pressed his hands to his ears.

Benethan surged toward the nearest monk who backed away as he hastened to bring the stuttergun around. The flying barrel of the musket hammered down on his hand first, breaking his grip and knocking the stuttergun away. Before the stricken monk could recover, Benethan lowered his shoulder and rammed into his chest, folding him and driving him toward his neighbor.

The second monk fell back and cut loose. The impact from the roaring green flash appeared to reverse Benethan's advance, but as the body of the first monk soared away, Benethan emerged from behind and leapt for the gunman. The brief melee that followed happened too fast for Jaspen to fully grasp. One moment, Benethan and the monk were engaged in what looked more like a dance than a fight. Then it abruptly ended, with the monk raising his hands and backing away.

Benethan stood before him, aiming the stuttergun at his face.

A sudden thump resounded from behind Jaspen and she felt Kemren's embrace liquefy. She glanced over in terror as he seemed to melt to the floor. Then a burst of pain erupted on the top of her head. She gasped as someone hauled her to her feet by her hair.

She'd completely forgotten about the two monks behind them.

"Drop the weapon, Falka," said a voice from behind her. An arm encircled her throat wrenched back hard, forcing her to gasp for breath. She could feel the cold touch of the stuttergun barrel against her temple.

Benethan hesitated.

"Now!" The gun pressed harder, pushing her head to the side, forcing her to wince.

Benethan started to lower the gun then Jaspen heard another thump. In response, the arm around her neck fell away and the pressure on her temple stopped. Then her assailant crumpled. She expected to see Kemren standing there, but he still lay unmoving on the floor.

Instead, she saw the fourth monk, stuttergun still held aloft following the blow he'd delivered to the back of his comrade's head.

Jaspen whipped around to stare at him in shock.

He smiled.

"Traitor!" screamed a high pitched voice. The accompanying stuttergun volley slammed into the chest of Jaspen's rescuer, throwing him back down the corridor. She spun to see the boy, Andern, unleash another volley at Benethan. It blew the stuttergun from his hand and hammered him to the wall.

Without thought, Jaspen found herself scooping up the gun her assailant had dropped. She raised it in time to see the last monk diving for Benethan's lost weapon. The burst she fired actually surprised her, as if her finger had its own will.

The monk flew past Benethan, hit the wall with his head and went down.

Jaspen spun toward Andern who was spinning toward her. They leveled their guns on each other in the same instant, but neither of them fired. Andern gripped his weapon with both hands.

The ensuing standoff unfolded as if in slow motion. Andern's wide eyes held hers as fast breaths of vapor burst from his mouth to mix with the lingering powdersmoke. Did her face wear the same mask of fear? Is that why neither could act?

"Andern," said a weak voice from the adjacent wall.

Benethan.

"The last time we met, I gave you a most terrible and difficult order. And you obeyed. Now, I'm asking you to do something even harder, listen and decide for yourself what to do.

"No. I won't listen to a traitor."

"I acted not out of treachery, but out of a commitment to an opposing loyalty."

"What loyalty?"

"Peace."

The boy shifted uncomfortably, but his aim didn't waver. "The Order exists to keep the peace."

"If that's the case," said Benethan. "Why are there Daggers? Why are there Iron Robes? Why does the Order demand weapons from the Protectorates and threaten violence if they don't comply?"

"So we can defend the peace!"

"Weapons cannot defend a true peace."

Andern shook his head, but said nothing.

"Open your eyes, Andern. Look at what's happening outside. Look at what just happened here. Look at what I have done. Look at what you're about to do. None of it serves true peace.

"Please, serve true peace. Put down the gun."

The boy didn't move. Jaspen could see the sheen of sweat on his brow, the clenched muscles in his jaw. Soon he would surrender to the easy solution. The trigger.

She needed to do something to help him make the other choice. And hearing Benethan's words helped her decide what that something needed to be.

Slowly, she lowered her gun. Andern stiffened, thrust his weapon farther forward and licked a drop of sweat from his upper lip. Jaspen placed the stuttergun on the cobbles and lifted her hand.

"Go, Brother Tega," whispered Benethan. "No more blood. Please, just go." Benethan's head lolled, his eyes closed and he seemed to slowly deflate like a punctured water skin.

Jaspen felt a surge of panic and couldn't stop

herself from starting his way.

Andern tracked her just long enough to see that she was no more threat to him, then he whirled and sprinted down the corridor.

Jaspen barely registered the boy's hasty departure as she knelt by the monk. She felt his neck for a pulse and found a weak rhythm. "Hold on, Benethan," she growled and began looking for tiny holes in his flesh. She found them on the back of his right hand. His arm all the way to the elbow had swollen to over twice its normal size and turned purple.

Jaspen quickly untied the rope belt and bound it as tightly as she could around his arm just above the elbow.

"You're the best monk I've ever met," she whispered. "I'll get you some help."

Though she couldn't quite believe her priority, she glanced at Kem's prone form then dashed to Rawl. "Wake up!" she shook him. When he didn't stir, she slapped his swollen face.

That drew an angry growl. "Treacherous monk," he mumbled. "I'll kill him."

"Rawl, get up! Benethan's hurt. You have to help him."

"Help him!" This inspired the grizzled grubber-doc to sit up. "Help that—"

"He saved us, Rawl. Now shut up and get over there."

"Saved us?" Rawl slapped himself in the face then settled his slightly unfocused gaze on Jaspen. "What happened?"

"He took a stuttergun volley in the hand."

"Oh, no!" Rawl struggled to his feet with Jaspen's help and staggered over to the fallen monk. Jaspen stayed just long enough to show Rawl the injured limb then ran to Kem. She tried to ignore Rawl's exasperated stream of profanity as she knelt by the man who'd used himself as a shield to protect her.

"Kem," she leaned down and kissed him. He let out a soft groan. She kissed him harder and felt him respond. Then she withdrew and helped pull him into the sitting position.

"Jas," he groaned. "You all right?"

She nodded. "Thanks to Benethan and one of the other monks." She glanced over to where their mysterious rescuer had fallen and saw him struggling to his feet.

Jaspen helped Kem to his feet while the monk, stooped and stiff, shuffled to them. He clutched his gut and winced with every short step. "Broken ribs for sure," he wheezed as he came to a halt facing them. Before they could speak, he cast Kem a knowing look. "I see the Mesorics worked out," he said. "Good. Though, this is the last place I'd expect you to be. It's not exactly an out of the way hamlet suited to the long anonymous life Dalsen said he wanted you to live."

Jaspen had no idea what this meant and that made her uneasy. "Who are you?" she asked.

The monk offered a pained smile. "A friend of your father."

The casual way he spoke the words startled Jaspen. She heard no judgment, no surprise, nothing unusual at all, as if she were the daughter of a common smithy or tanner.

"Uh," rumbled Rawl. "I hate to spoil the reunion, or whatever it is you're doing, but our monk here needs treatment beyond my means. And it sounds as if we're about to have company."

Jaspen, Kem, and the monk turned to listen. Sure enough, fast, heavy footfalls could be heard coming closer.

Kem drew a battered dagger and faced the monk.

Jaspen almost gasped, but Kem made no threatening moves and the monk seemed totally unfazed.

"You don't by chance have something better than this for picking locks?" Kem asked.

The monk broke into a huge smile. Using the hand not devoted to cradling his injured ribs, the reached into his parka. A moment later he pulled out a small hide pouch and gave it to Kem.

Kem opened it with trepidation and fished out two keys.

"I thought you said this was the last place you'd expect to see us," said Kem.

"I did," he looked at Jaspen. "But your father appears to have thought otherwise. And as usual, he was right."

Kem clutched the keys to his chest. "Thank you."

The monk looked over to Rawl. "Go with your friends. I'll make sure Benethan is cared for."

"Aw no, I'm not leaving him to a bunch of—"

"If you don't go," said the monk. "The three of us will likely wind up in a cell instead of the infirmary."

"Oh, I see. Well, when you put it that way." Rawl stood and hurried over to join Jaspen and Kem.

"Quickly," said the monk. "They're almost in view."

Without another word, Kem turned down the side corridor and strode into the darkness. Jaspen started to follow, but when, out of long-ingrained habit, she pressed her hand to her parka to feel for the bulge of the orb, she felt nothing. She padded around and fought to stifle a rising panic. Then she remembered, she wore Benethan's parka.

Jaspen spun on her heel and sprinted back to the unconscious monk.

"What are you doing?" asked Rawl. "They're almost on us!"

Jaspen reached carefully into the parka he wore and found the orb. She grabbed it, pulled it out and ran. On her way toward the side corridor, she jumped over a stuttergun. For a moment, she considered picking it up. For a moment.

She dashed past Rawl and entered the corridor, glancing back one last time at Benethan and their rescuer. Then she pocketed the orb and turned all of her attention to the hope she held above all others, a hope that seemed almost close enough now to touch.

Her father.

DAYBREAK

Early morning sunshine floods *Daybreak's* gondola with warm brilliant light. Jaio feels the building heat on his face, a sensation he always enjoyed in the past. But now, it only reminds him of time slipping away.

Eukon Thorne stands in front of Jaio at the forward railing of the observation grate. The old man peers at Anchoresk through a relic telescoptic with two parallel lens tubes, each nearly as long as a child's arm.

"What are they waiting for?" he growls. "Let the fight begin."

Both Braukis, who is still restraining Jaio, and Kharkin, who now holds the wheel, remain silent.

The sound of footfalls on the stairs rises above the ubiquitous creaks and groans of the wind-buffeted gondola. Without taking his eyes from the telescoptic, Thorne calls out, "Yes, what is it?"

The lack of an immediate response elicits a

huge sigh. "Speak!"

"Daddy?" says a high quavering voice.

In the same instant Thorne whips around, Jaio's head snaps to the side as his world spins. The flash of pain across his vision takes a moment to clear. When it does, the sight steals his breath.

Before him stands Thorne's son, Aleekio, with Sable half-crouched behind holding a dagger to the boy's throat.

Kharkin already has his stuttergun out and aimed.

"No!" Thorne gasps.

Braukis hauls Jaio close, wraps a thick arm around his throat and draws his weapon as well. Jaio strains to breathe as the two Breakborn cover Sable. Thorne surges into view, hands up, placating. "Please," he moans, "don't hurt my son."

"Stop!" says Sable. She lifts the elbow of her knife arm for emphasis.

Thorne freezes a pace in front of Jaio.

"Drop the guns and kick them over here," she says, her voice like ice.

The Breakborn don't move.

"Do it!" shouts Thorne.

Braukis and Kharkin exchange hesitant glances.

"Now!" Thorne reaches over, rips the stuttergun from Braukis's hand and tosses it toward Sable. It clatters to the gratework floor and slides her way. As it's about to pass her by, she slams a foot down on it, and pulls it closer with the sole of her boot.

"Kharkin!"

The second Breakborn winces, gives his head a frustrated shake then does the same. His gun comes to rest a pace in front of Aleekio.

Sable shuffles forward, pushing the boy ahead of her until she can hook it with a boot heel and pull it back. Then she opens the distance again.

"Don't hurt him," pleads Thorne.

Sable ducks lower and picks up a weapon without taking her eyes from Thorne and his guards for even an instant. She shoves it in her belt and picks up the other. This one, she aims at Thorne, all the while holding the dagger less than an inch from Aleekio's skin.

"Release Jaio."

Thorne shoots Braukis a panicked look accompanied by a vigorous nod.

The pressure around Jaio's throat abates and he feels the bindings on his wrists loosen, then slip away. Finally, the gag departs his mouth. His unconscious impulse to close his jaw causes a burst of pain to burst in his ears. He sets his firm gaze on Sable.

"Don't hurt Aleekio," he says.

"Just get over here, Jaio," says Sable. "Behind

me."

Jaio shakes his head. Despite everything, he will not let her harm the boy.

"Dammit, you noble idiot, move your ass!"

The slight mismatch between her exasperated tone and her words gives Jaio pause. Is this her way of asking for his trust? He hopes so and does as she says.

As soon as he's with her, she starts moving toward the port wall.

"All of you, down the stairs."

The two guards glance at Thorne, who nods. Yet, when they start for the exit, Thorne holds in place.

"Unless you know how to fly this ship, you are going to need me here."

"He's right," whispers Jaio.

Sable gives her head a frustrated shake.

Now, thinks Jaio, it's your turn to trust me. He picks up the binding rope and damp gag from the floor. "To the rail," he orders Thorne. "Right in the middle."

Thorne complies and Jaio sets to work lashing him in place. In a few moments, the old man is bound tight, midway between the wheel and the telescoptic station, out of reach of everything.

Jaio considers leaving the gag off since Thorne will need to be able to speak if he is to tell them how to fly the ship. But he decides it can be removed later and ties it on.

"Now, you meat slabs," Sable says to the two guards. "Down the stairs. Slowly."

As Braukis and Kharkin stride past, Sable backs up to maintain some distance and walks into Jaio. He is suddenly aware of their closeness and quickly steps aside.

He hurries to the wheel and holds it steady while Sable and Aleekio escort the two guards below.

As soon as she is out of sight, Thorne slides as close to Jaio as his bindings will allow and tries to speak. The gag kills the words, but not the imploring tone.

Jaio starts to respond, but realizes his intention is to gloat and so offers nothing but a single, final shake of his head.

Thorne's face turns red and he tries to pull free. But the futility quickly becomes apparent and he settles.

Then the thump of footsteps again carries up the steps. They sound quicker than before, and, if possible, lighter.

Aleekio appears, all by himself, looking serious. Behind him, Sable climbs into view, dagger sheathed and gun held at ease, aimed upward.

Jaio casts her a puzzled look to which she responds with a sly grin.

"Daddy," says Aleekio as he storms up to Thorne. "You've been bad."

Thorne stares at him with a look of uncomprehending shock.

"You hurt my brother." He tips his head toward Jaio. "And you were going to hurt the world!" The boy reaches into his parka and pulls out a fist-sized rectangular device with a bundle of wires protruding from one end.

The gag barely contains Thorne's startled cry. He seems to forget he's bound as he tries to reach for the device and almost yanks himself off his feet. Only a mad scramble to regain his balance keeps him upright. Aleekio takes a step back and pockets the device.

A smile grows on Jaio's face. "You took that out of the bomb," he says.

Aleekio glances over. "Of course, silly. I couldn't let Daddy hurt the world."

Jaio looks at Sable. "You two have been allies all along."

They both nod and Aleekio walks to him, looking sheepish. From his other pocket he withdraws a battered leather pouch. "I'm sorry," he says and holds it up for Jaio. Recognition takes nearly a full breath as he reaches out with trepidation to take it.

"The orb!"

Aleekio offers an apologetic nod.

"Thank you for returning it," says Jaio as he takes the pouch and hangs it from his neck by its cord. The weight feels at once strange and familiar. He gives Aleekio a grateful smile.

Aleekio beams. "No scolding?"

Jaio shakes his head.

Aleekio's happy eyes suddenly narrow and he spins to face Thorne. "You need a scolding." He stalks over and plunges his little hand into his father's parka pocket. The old man watches frozen and dumbfounded as his son rummages around. Then Aleekio pulls his hand out holding the *Companta*. He glares at his paralyzed father for a moment then turns to Jaio.

The break in eye contact awakens Thorne. He strains at the bindings and tries to yell. By his tone, his command is clear, though the gag renders his words incomprehensible. Aleekio ignores him and hands the book to Jaio.

"Thank you," he says again and tucks the Catalogian tome in his own parka pocket. He glances back to Thorne. The look on the old man's red face causes Jaio worry that the gag might burst into flames.

Aleekio nudges Jaio none too gently and pushes his way between Jaio and the wheel.

Jaio steps back. "You know how to fly this thing?" he asks.

"Of course, silly." The boy's small hands

barely encircle the pommels.

"The question is," says Sable. "Where to?"

Jaio releases the wheel and nods. He needs time to think. Of all the scenarios he's anticipated, this is not one of them. Where to start? In his mind, he hears the voice of his mentor, Orol Gilinath. 'When faced with a challenge, no matter how daunting, start with what you know. And, if possible, don't seek the solution alone.'

"Thorne's fleet is on the way to Anthemar to do what the bomb didn't. They are waiting for the Fane to bloody themselves in battle. Once the fight is over, the skateships are to sail in, wipe out the survivors and destroy everything."

"We have to stop them," says Sable.

"Yes, but what can we do from up here?"

Sable turns toward Thorne. "Call them off!"

Thorne's eyes narrow to furious slits.

"I'm afraid we've lost our leverage with him," says Jaio.

"Then how about you? Aren't you also an Orol?"

"It's just a word, Sable. I'm nobody."

"That is not true. Cappen Aiomida, Lash, Bengus, Segray...the whole crew of *Frostbite* has risked everything for you."

"And I failed." He looks her deep in the eyes. "You and Aleekio stopped Thorne while I stood here gagged, bound and helpless."

"Not helpless, Jaio. We were your help. We still are. And I believe *Frostbite* still is too. They'll know the bomb didn't go off. And they'll believe you did it."

"But I didn't."

"That doesn't matter. The only thing that matters is that it didn't go off. Which means we still have a chance. Aiomida and the crew know it as surely as I do. But you have to know it too."

Jaio finds himself nodding. Some part of him other than his mind has latched onto her words and begun working with them. That same part also sets him in motion before his mind can stop it.

His lips touch hers. And she responds, not by pulling away as he expects, but by leaning into him and placing a warm palm on his cheek.

"Eeewww!" says Aleekio.

Jaio can't stop himself from laughing. Neither can Sable and all too soon their first kiss ends. Yet, Jaio can think of no better way. He glances over at the boy whose face wears a look of revulsion as he watches from behind the wheel, where he stands with arms stretched high to reach the topmost pommels.

The sight causes Jaio to laugh again.

Aleekio, still wincing, turns to face forward and tilts his head to one side so as to see through the wheel spokes and past central column.

"Maybe, we can find something for you to

stand on," says Sable.

"No need. I'm good," says the boy.

"All right." Sable turns her attention back to Jaio. Her look is serious except for the smile in the corner of each eye. His smile is a little less subtle.

"We need to focus on a plan," she says.

He nods. "If only we could contact *Frostbite* without everyone else hearing."

"Oh," says Aleekio. "That's easy."

At the railing, Thorne yells into the gag and tugs at the bindings.

Aleekio points to the voicecaster console. Jaio and Sable hurry to it. Jaio sits on the stool. He feels Sable place her hand on his shoulder. The touch warms him inside the way the rising sun warms his skin.

"See that top line of switches?" asks Aleekio.

"Yes," Jaio and Sable say in unison. They're looking at eleven toggles, all of them down except for the one on the far right.

"Switch the up-one down and the nine-one up."

Thorne rages into his gag again. This alone confirms that Aleekio knows what he's talking about. Jaio flips down the eleventh switch and lifts the ninth.

"Now, just *Frostbite* can hear."

Thorne's rant amplifies.

"It's okay, Daddy," says the boy. "Jaio and

Sable are good people. You'll see."

Jaio picks up the transmitter then sets it down on the console. "I need to check something." He stands and passes Thorne, giving the old man a wide birth as he heads to the forward rail to look through the telescoptics. Finding Anchoresk takes him a moment, but when he does, the sight exceeds his wildest imaginings.

Looking through the relic lenses, he feels as if he can reach out and touch the spire of glass. Morning light sparkles from its many panes like sunbursts glinting on the surface of a giant inverted icecycle. Taller than even the tallest tree Jaio has ever seen, the tower rises from the biggest, most ornate building he has even seen. He has a hard time tearing his eyes away to assess the surrounding scene.

Despite the magnification, the distance is too great to make out any specifics. The two opposing forces appear as little more the dots and blobs. There is, however, a clear, white space separating them. And the visible columns of rising smoke are few and small.

Jaio feels fairly certain the battle has not yet begun. "All's quiet."

"Good," says Sable.

Jaio returns to the stool and picks up the transmitter again. Yet, he still cannot make himself use it. The desire for his mind to have more time to work through all the variables holds his hand.

"What's wrong?" asks Sable.

"I need to think about this some more."

"Tell me what you have in mind."

He nods. "Okay. So, the skateships are waiting for Thorne's signal which means they are either still on their way to Anchoresk or are waiting just out of sight."

"Yes," says Sable. "And?"

"In both cases, the Fane don't yet know the wolves are watching them." He risks a glance at Thorne and sees he has the old man's full attention. There is fear in his eyes. Strangely, it gives Jaio strength.

"What if they saw the wolves before they started to fight among themselves? Do you think they'd still fight among themselves?"

"No, they'd turn to face the wolves."

"Exactly. They'd unite."

"Against us," says Sable. "Won't that just make the battle bloodier."

"Only if they choose to fight it."

"What would stop them?"

"Another enemy, common to all of us. The enemy Fane and Ghost alike have enlisted for centuries to fight for them, but must now confront. Together."

Sable's face transforms into a mask of

bewilderment. And the creases in Thorne's brow deepen.

"Who is this common enemy?" asks Sable.

"The Ancients." He picks up the transmitter and keys it. "Cappen Aiomida, this is Jaio. Can you hear me?"

A moment later, he hears a pop. "Jaio?" says a man's scratchy, tired voice. "Orol Jaio?"

"Hi Segray. Is Cappen there?"

Jaio hears a clatter and a whoop. "Uh, sorry. I'll go find her." Another pop, followed by silence.

Jaio and Sable look into each other's faces as they wait. Then the voicecaster pops again. "Jaio, this is Cappen." She is breathing hard.

"Good to hear your voice, Cappen," he says.

"Yours too. How did you stop Thorne?"

"That's why I'm calling. His plan for destruction has not been stopped only postponed. To stop it, I need your help."

"Anything."

The immediacy and conviction of her reply momentarily stuns Jaio to silence. The feel of Sable's hand squeezing his shoulder and the memory of her words brings him back.

"I need you to race for Anchoresk as fast as you can."

Heartbeats pass. No reply.

Off to Jaio's side, Thorne begins to chuckle.

And the empty air grows heavier.

Finally, the pop arrives. "We're on our way."

Thorne's chuckle transforms into strained laughter.

Jaio glares at him and picks up the transmitter again. "Cappen,"

"Yes, Jaio." He can hear the resignation in her voice. She does not think they will be able to get past the *Dawn*, but is going to try anyway.

"A little change of plans," says Jaio. "Have everything in place to move, but wait for my signal before heading out."

"Understood."

Thorne continues to chuckle and shake his head as if in sympathy.

Jaio turns to Aleekio. "Can you tell me why *Daybreak* is so shiny?"

Thorne falls silent and his eyes grow wide.

"Of course, silly. It's covered in kineticloth. Even the airbag is kineticloth. That's a fun word to say. Kineticloth."

"Yes it is," says Jaio. "And you can really fly this cloudship?"

The boy grins. "Of course, silly. I helped build it."

"Okay, then. Full speed back to the Sunrise Node!"

"All right!" shouts Aleekio. He turns to Jaio. "Here, take the wheel!"

Startled, Jaio grabs the pommels and Aleekio hops to the control console where he flips some switches then turns a large round dial positioned beneath two small twist knobs, each labeled 'off' in the vertical position and 'on' in the horizontal. Both are on. As Aleekio rotates the large dial, the roar of the running motors builds until its nearly deafening. Even so, Thorne's enraged howls can still be heard.

Aleekio then returns to the wheel. Jaio happily relinquishes control and the boy gives it a mighty spin. Jaio and Sable almost topple as the cloudship heaves into a tight starboard rotation.

Aleekio looks at Jaio. "What's the plan, Cappen," he says.

"We go spider hunting."

40

THE ADMINIITHEDRAL

Jaspen clung to the worn wooden ladder just below Kemren who craned his neck to hold his ear against the closed, round hatch overhead. A few rungs below Jaspen, Geleb Rawl kept surprisingly quiet, particularly in light of the lengthy duration the three of them had been hanging there in the silent chute. At least Jaspen suspected it was silent. The hammering of her heart beat a deafening tempo in her ears. The thought of her father only a few paces away drove every other thought into the recesses of her mind.

"Still quiet," whispered Kem.

The faint sounds of movement and heated conversation when they'd first ascended had ended some time ago, but Kem had wanted to play it safe. So, they'd waited. When Jaspen's hand had grown tired, she'd looped her right elbow over a rung. Now, she switched to her left elbow.

In the faint torchlight rising up from the sconce far below, she saw Kem look down at her. "I think we should try it," he said.

Jaspen nodded.

"We should have tried it last week," grumbled Rawl, apparently unable to contain himself any longer.

Kem reached up and banged softly on the metal hatch then pressed his ear against it again.

"Anything?" breathed Jaspen.

"Nothing." He used his knuckles this time producing a slightly sharper, louder rap.

A moment later, a single quiet thud resounded from above. As time stretched and nothing else happened, Jaspen began to doubt her ears. Then a sharp click resounded and the hatch began to rise. The blinding brilliance of sunshine burst through the widening seam.

Jaspen squinted and shielded her eyes with her stump. The hatch swung completely aside and a robed figure seemed to materialize as Jaspen acclimated to the glare. The figure offered a hand. Kem grabbed hold and clambered out. The two of them stepped out of view.

Jaspen didn't move. Couldn't move. She just hung there more than a body-length down in the chute and stared up through the opening.

Then someone stepped close again and kneeled. His face peered down at her with eyes so familiar, though not as bright, and a beard just as full, but graying, and a smile she never thought she'd see again, yet here it was, unchanged and perfect.

A sob rocked her.

In response, her father offered his hand.

She felt her good hand and legs propelling her up as if by their own will. The distance closed. She could reach him now.

Jaspen hooked her stump over the top rung and extended her open palm to his. Their hands touched, gripped, held. She felt his heat and strength, so real. Not a dream.

Then he pulled her out and she found herself standing before him.

How long they just stood and looked at each other, Jaspen could not say. Long enough for Rawl to extract himself from the chute and fall in beside the peripheral blur of Kem, who stood a couple paces behind her father.

"Oh, Jas," her father finally breathed. "How I've missed you."

These words reminded Jaspen of the many years spent longing for him. Of wondering about his sudden and final departure. And suffering the torture of not knowing what she had done that had made him never come back.

Through the swirl of emotions these memories unleashed, she tried to ask, but all she could manage was. "Why didn't…?" Then her throat closed on another sob.

Her father looked down and gave the gentlest of nods. "I'm so sorry, Jas. I meant to return, but the suspicion of the Order caught up with me that final night. Two agents missed seeing you by a breath. Nothing ever terrified me more. And for your safety, I vowed to stay away, but I never stopped thinking about you. I never stopped loving you."

A part of her wanted to be angry. To ask how hard it would have been to send her just one message. But another part of her knew the answer. It was why he'd sent Kem instead.

"I never stopped loving you either," she said in a rush and threw her arms around him. He drew her close and surrounded her in his oh, so familiar embrace. The scent of him hit her hardest, bringing back a flood of nights when he'd stayed too late to tell her one more story, or played chase outside even though they risked being seen.

When at last they broke apart, tears were streaming down both their faces. He gave her another nod and a smile then stepped back and turned to admit Kem and Rawl into the circle. Much to Jaspen's surprise, Kem stood there dry faced, but Rawl was blubbering like a baby.

The crusty old tiger hunter hastily wiped his eyes and muttered something about the harsh light, then cleared his throat and stood facing her father. Rawl seemed to be leaning back on his heels as far as possible. One snap and Jaspen thought he might flee. Never had she seen him so edgy. Then she remembered who her father was to everyone but her: Dictorian Consul, Dalsen Ario, head of the Catalogian Order and possibly the most powerful man in Anthemar.

"Father," she said with a nod to Rawl. "This is Geleb Rawl, celebrated tiger hunter and master provisioner." She glanced over to Rawl. "I owe him my life many times over."

"Aw," grumbled Rawl. "Meals don't count. Just doing my job."

"I'm not talking about all the meals you made," she said.

"Right," said Kem. "That was how you tried to kill us."

Rawl cast a venomous glare at Kem, who responded with a shrug and a grin.

Her father laughed and extended a hand. "Thank you, Geleb Rawl. I am in your debt many times over."

Rawl actually blushed.

Then Jaspen's father turned to Kem. "Your choice of a safe haven surprises me, Brother Trince."

Kem held up the pouch with the keys. "Apparently, our arrival is not completely unexpected."

"A father's foolish hope; emphasis on foolish. What are you three doing here?"

Kem looked at Jaspen. "It's a long story," he said.

"I'm afraid I need the abridged version. I don't have much time, as you might well imagine. I need to get back to helping plan Anchoresk's defense."

Jaspen heard the weariness in his voice for the first time. How could she make him see the futility of those efforts. She could think of only one way. The truth.

"Father," she said. "This is a trap."

He cast her a puzzled look. "What is a trap?"

"Everything going on outside. The coming battle. All of it."

"We may seem trapped, Jas. But the Order and our allies have a few surprises in store for Lord Maxamant."

"No, that's not what I mean." She shook her head. How to explain?

"Then what do you mean?" he asked.

She could hear the condescension in his voice. Daughter or not, she was a bathhouse fuel-dung gatherer and he was the head of the Catalogian Order. Unless she could shock him, he would not hear her, not really. It might require stretching a few truths and omitting a few details.

"The Oroken plan to destroy us."

His eyes widened. This he did not expect. "How do you know this?"

She gestured toward Kem and Rawl. "We've been living with a group of them for the past few weeks."

"Living with Oroken?" He glanced over to Kem and Rawl who confirmed her claim with nods. Now she had his full attention.

"They're friends. But their—"

"What clan?" asked Jaspen's father. Now it was her turn to be surprised.

"Oromola."

His eyes seemed to lose their focus, to look through her. "Oromola," he whispered.

"Do you know of them?" she asked.

"Hmm? Oh, a little. As I'm sure you're aware, they hold tight to their secret life on the Ice. Please, tell me what you learned from them."

"One of their leaders, a man named Thorne—"

"Eukon Thorne?"

Again, he surprised her. "Yes, how do you know of him?"

"By reputation only. But I thought he was dead."

"No, Maxamant exiled him to the Snowsea where the Ghosts…" she interrupted herself to explain the Ghosts. "The Ghosts are what they call—"

"I also know of the Guardian Ghosts," he said.

Before Jaspen could ask how, he went on. "So, they didn't kill him."

"No, he proved useful."

"I'm sure he did," said her Father.

"They adopted him and proclaimed him an Orol. You know about Orols too, don't you?"

Her father nodded. "Yes, but I thought they were forbidden from venturing onto the Ice."

"Normally they are. But Thorne's knowledge inspired the Ghosts to make an exception. For twenty years he lived with them in a hidden oasis called Vanquisher's Break where the Ancients had a supply station. He used the relics from the station to help make weapons for the Ghosts. And one of those weapons is called a nukebomb."

Jaspen's father sucked in a startled breath. "Nukebombs are real?"

Jaspen nodded. "Thorne plans to use his on Anchoresk."

"Anchoresk? Not Cannonguard?"

"Why would he want to destroy Cannonguard?" asked Kemren.

"To avenge his exile."

"He'll get his revenge if Maxamant comes here. And he'll also achieve his larger goal, to wipe out all the armies of the Fane so they will never become a threat to Vanquisher's Break or to the Oroken homeland. He's already completed the first step of his plan."

"Which was?" asked her father.

"To lure all Fane forces here."

"Lure? Nobody lured Salazriole Maxamant here. He found a massive weapons cache. That is what enticed his allies and gave him the courage to attack."

"He didn't find it. Some of Thorne's loyal Ghosts revealed it to him."

Jaspen's father stared at her in stunned silence as her words soaked in. She just stood there and let the full weight settle. Finally, her father blinked. "But the armies have all been gathered here for days and nothing has happened?"

"I don't know why Thorne hasn't acted yet. Maybe, the blizzard slowed him down."

"As it has slowed us," her father reflected.

"Maybe…" The image of Jaio flitted through her mind. Could he have succeeded in stopping Thorne? It seemed too much to hope. "All I know is," she continued. "As long as the armies of Anthemar remain here, we're all in terrible danger."

Her father squeezed his eyes shut and pinched the bridge of his nose. When he once again opened them and met her gaze, he looked somehow even older, grayer. "If you thought my station might give this message a voice that would be heeded, I fear you overestimate what even a

Dictorian is capable of."

"What are you saying?" asked Jaspen.

"I doubt my own advisors will believe this story. As for our Protectorate allies, they are itching to confront Maxamant, and as of late, have good reason to feel confident in their chances of victory."

"You've secured the weapons cache from beneath the Cliff of Faces," said Kem.

"How do you know of that cache?" asked Jaspen's father.

"We were there when the Daggers arrived," said Jaspen.

"It only stands to reason what they would do next; bring it here," said Kem.

"Then you know how the odds have evened." Jaspen's father sighed. "I fear nothing but the bomb itself will dissuade our allies from pressing the fight. Which, of course, will mean it's too late."

"There must be something we can do?" said Kem.

"I'm sorry, Brother Trince. If Thorne doesn't destroy us, we're going to do it ourselves. Either way, fate holds us one move away from checkmate. The best you can do is get out of here as fast as you can."

"No," said Jaspen. "We've come too far to just give up. All along the way impossible odds rose before us, but we prevailed. Jaio might even have stopped Thorne. To quit now would be to the greatest betrayal—"

"Wait," said Jaspen's father. "Who?"

"Ghost Orol Jaio. His people sent him to Anthemar on a peacemaking mission, but Thorne captured him before he made it."

Jaspen's father didn't seem to be listening. He had that far off look again. "Is this Jaio…is he Oromola?"

"Yes, but how did you—"

"And younger than you?"

Jaspen nodded.

"Did he tell you his mother's name?"

"I think so. Anne-something. It was very beautiful."

"Annequoia," Jaspen's father said, his voice soft and whistful.

"You knew—" Sudden realization stole not just Jaspen's words, but her capacity for speech as well as her very breath.

A long shocked silence consumed the chamber.

"If you had been a boy," Jaspen's father said at last. "Your name would have been Jaio. Your mother must have chosen it for your brother."

Jaspen felt Kem step up and wrap his arms around her.

Tears threatened to spill from her eyes again. "You didn't know about him?" she asked her father.

He shook his head. "She left too soon. Without a word. Just like I did."

Rawl cleared his throat. "Well, the way I see it, this is your chance to be here for him. Because you can bet, if he did stop Thorne, he's on his way. But you'll never meet him if all hell breaks loose before he arrives."

Jaspen's father stood motionless for a moment, deep in thought. Finally, he shook his head again. "There's nothing I can do. The only course is to get you out of here."

"Now hold on holiness, you believe her, don't you?" asked Rawl. "You know the story your daughter risked everything to bring to you is true?"

"Yes, but convincing me is one thing. Convincing the Tributans and the Liege-lords… It's too much to hope."

Jaspen heard the truth of these words and felt her hope crack. Much to her surprise, a new possibility appeared in the gap. "There's only one other person who needs to be convinced," she said.

Her father and Rawl stared at her. From behind, Kem whispered, "Lord Maxamant."

Jaspen nodded.

Kem released her and stepped around to face her.

"He'll never back down," said her father.

"He might if we lay everything out in the open," said Jaspen.

"What do you mean?"

"Tell him about Thorne and the cache the Daggers brought back from the Cliff of Faces," said Jaspen.

Kem nodded. "If Maxamant knows he's in a madman's crosshairs and that his advantage has been erased, he might welcome the chance to fall back without a fight."

"But he loathes the Order. He'll never listen to me," said Jaspen's father.

"Maybe, he'll listen to me," said Jaspen.

"You?" Her father's unintentional condescension laced the word like poison.

How it hurt.

"She made short work of a Dictorian's misgivings," grumbled Rawl. "I'd wager old Salazriole doesn't stand a chance."

Jaspen latched onto the tiger hunter's words and took a step closer to her father. "If you tried to arrange a meeting, would he accept?"

"This is madness," said her father. "Any such meeting would be a trap."

"But is it something you could do?" she asked again.

He let out an exasperated sigh. "Yes, a personal request to negotiate, issued from me is one thing I have no doubt he'll accept. But hear me, Jaspen. He is the embodiment of treachery. Even with a full contingent of Iron Robe escorts, we will be in grave peril."

"No Iron Robes. We show no fear. It will make him doubt his advantage."

"Or he'll simply exploit our vulnerability and kill us."

"He'll at least want to hear what we have to say first, right?"

Jaspen's father considered her, the condescention now gone from his face. "You're willing to make that sacrifice, for this?"

She nods. "Are you?"

"No," he said. "Not for this." He gestured to the glass tower around them and by extension the whole of the world beyond. "But for you, yes. And for Jaio."

She lunged forward and hugged him again.

Their embrace ended all too soon and Jaspen's father turned to Kem and Rawl. "I won't be able to talk you into staying behind, will I?" he asked.

Kem shook his head while Rawl just raised a bristly eyebrow and set his jaw.

"Very well. If you dress as Kestian Ice Watch survivors, he may accept the four of us. Your costume will also help lend credence to your story."

"But aren't Kest and Maxamant mortal

enemies?" asked Rawl.

"All the better," said Jaspen's father. "It will affirm the magnitude of the threat. If nothing else, he will at least know we believe the threat is real. I just hope he will believe it to be real as well."

Rawl hrumphed, but said nothing more.

"Now," said Jaspen's father. "I need to go make arrangements. You will be safe here. On the cart over there," he pointed to an ornate carafe and covered platter perched atop a simple wheeled cart parked beside a small wooden desk in the center of the room, "is some food and water. Help yourselves. I'll be back soon." He started to turn.

Jaspen grabbed his sleeve. "Thank you, father," she said.

"For what? Agreeing to lead us to almost certain death?"

"For honoring your son."

DAYBREAK

Jaio holds *Daybreak's* wheel steady while Aleekio helps Sable into one of the puffy red airsuits. Outside the windows, wisps of occasional clouds whip by. Their rapid passing reveals just how fast the cloudship is moving. *Frostbite* at full sail with a tailwind would have been left behind almost as quickly.

At the forward rail, Thorne watches in quiet, simmering fury. Once again, Jaio regrets turning down Sable's offer to take the old man below. But Jaio wanted the imposter Orol to see everything that is about to happen, whatever it may be. He supposes he still does, though as they near their destination, he has to fight ever harder to suppress a building sense of doom. They're going to take on the *Invincible Dawn* in a half-glass box hanging from a gas bag. He reminds himself, their aim is to cause a diversion, not to defeat the monstrous skateship.

On the white plain down below, six elongated dots come into view, heading north, driving for Anchoresk. Each is kicking up a wide fan of ripped snow.

"Ready," says Sable. In each hand she brandishes a stuttergun. They both drape from shoulder straps slung in opposite directions across her chest.

Aleekio runs to look out the window. "You better get outside, we're almost there." He dashes to a round porthole hatch in the rear wall and tries to spin the wheel with his tiny arms. It won't budge. Sable steps up behind him to assist and together they open the hatch. A ladder ascends on the other side.

Sable turns and casts Jaio one last glance. The meeting of their eyes adds the most unbearable layer yet to the building sense of doom. But he knows why someone has to go out there. And she is by far the most qualified.

"Tie in right away!" he calls to her. "And watch out for—"

"I'll be careful," she says, cutting him off. Then she pats Aleekio on the head, pulls her goggles down over her eyes and steps into the ladder chute. Aleekio closes the hatch behind her and runs for the wheel. He too is now wearing a pair of goggles.

On his way past the control console, he slaps a

button without even pausing. A metallic chatter joins the engine noise and the lower armor panel slides forward from the belly of the cloudship to cover the underside glass.

"Outta the way," Aleekio barks as he shoves Jaio away from the wheel.

Jaio jumps aside.

"Over there," Aleekio points back to the control console. "See the lever in the middle."

Jaio hops to the panel and finds the likely candidate. "This one?"

"Yeh, pull it gently when I say."

"What is it?"

"The Vent/Inflate control." He fixes his slipping, lopsided goggle-gaze on Jaio. "Remember, pull gently, when I say." Then he's back to flying.

"Got it."

Jaio sits on the stool, grabs the handle and turns to peer through the forward glass. Soon, the frozen world seems to be rising before them and Jaio realizes, the cloudship is passing over the ramp.

Far ahead two dark dots emerge into distinction. They sit side by side near the head of the ramp, one far larger than the other.

"Okay, Jaio. Now!"

Jaio pulls back gently on the lever at the same time Aleekio shoves the steering column forward.

It doesn't budge. Jaio starts up to offer help.

"No, hold the lever!"

Jaio sits back down while Aleekio grunts and tries again, straining with all his might. With his boots slipping back by jerks, the wheel arm finally tips.

"Pull more!"

Jaio pulls the lever a little farther. He's almost convinced himself something is wrong, until he glances over and sees the landscape filling the window, rushing up at them. And dead center is a growing dot with eight legs. Next to it sits the second, smaller dot with six.

"Okay, wait. Wait."

"Wait for what?"

"To push the lever the other way, silly."

"How hard?"

Aleekio heaves back on the pommels in an effort to right the column and again, it doesn't budge until his little legs are pumping as if he's running backwards on ice.

"Uh, hard. Really hard. Now!" The column slowly swings aft.

Jaio shoves the lever away. Nothing seems to happen. *Invincible Dawn* continues to grow at an alarming rate.

"Kill the engines!" shouts Aleekio.

Jaio's eyes dart across the console and find the controls Aleekio used to start them. He flips the switches and, after a couple of sharp bangs, the roar outside falls silent. This appears to have no influence on their plunge.

Jaio can now see other dots racing around on the *Dawn's* deck, looking up, pointing. Even at so great a distance, they clearly appear confused.

The radio pops. "*Daybreak*, come in! Orol Thorne!"

Why isn't Sable firing? If she doesn't take out the voicecaster now, the *Dawn* will be able to warn the whole fleet about the new danger from above.

"Orol!"

The cloudship continues to fall. Jaio grips the edge of the console with his free hand and braces for the collision. At the last moment, the gondola begins to level and the *Dawn* disappears from view beneath the lower armor plate. Then the world seems to explode.

In a deafening cacophony of scraping metal and shattering wood, Jaio's grip tears free. He flies forward, past Aleekio and the wheel and crashes into the railing. The impact knocks the wind from his lungs and he collapses. As he fights for breath, he hears grunting. Across from him, Thorne is struggling to his feet. Beyond the old man, the top of the *Dawn's* rear mast is visible outside. It slowly drops away as *Daybreak* climbs.

A sudden jolt rocks the cloudship, bringing the ascent to an abrupt end.

"We're caught on something!" shouts Aleekio from the console. How the boy managed to keep from being tossed into the glass during the impact, Jaio cannot imagine, yet, he's leaning over the controls, shoving the inflate lever forward with all his might.

Jaio attempts to stand so he can go help, but the effort sets the gondola to spinning. He sinks back down and sucks a few more breaths. He's about to try again when a shadow passes over him. He looks up in time to see a red-clad figure sliding down the observation window.

Sable!

All pain forgotten, Jaio surges to his feet and grips the rail. Sable reaches the forward edge of the glass, but instead of falling off, she plants her feet on the riveted seam and stops. She then lifts her goggles and looks down at the scene below. Two heartbeats later, she shifts left, adjusts the strap of a slung stuttergun then leans forward.

Dread explodes in Jaio's gut. She's going to jump!

Sable casts a determined look back into the gondola and catches Jaio's eye. Numb as he is, he manages to shake his head. She just lowers her goggles, turns back to the *Dawn* and pushes away.

"No!" Jaio yells.

Sable drops out of sight.

INVINCIBLE DAWN

As Sable plummeted through the air, she gave all her attention to the tangled bunch of torn sail hanging from the broken spar. It was the only thing between her and the hard deck far below. She slammed into the twisted bundle of canvas much too quickly.

Clawing to get a grip on the fabric, she knew immediately, she lacked the strength to overcome her momentum. Nothing but the grappler hooks on her scaler's belt could have stopped her plunge and those she'd left behind in her race to escape *Tigress*. Regret flooded her as she tumbled. Her desperate attempt to save Jaio had failed.

A sudden, bone jarring jolt arrested her fall for the briefest of instants. And in that instant, she made an iron fist around the last trailing scrap of torn sail and wrenched to a stop.

When she recovered her bearings, she found herself looking at the stuttergun. It hung by its strap from a rope-bound spar-splinter. The strap's capture had abated her fall just long enough for instinct to do the rest.

She offered Sister Spider silent thanks and hauled herself up the fabric scrap, hand over hand, to the cracked spar above. She clambered on top and took stock of her position.

Above her, *Daybreak* strained to rise, but could manage no more than an ineffectual wobble. Sable identified the problem right away. The tip of the *Dawn's* broken main mast had, in effect, harpooned the cloudship. The straining top-rope tethered the two vessels together. And, much to Sable's relief, the remnants of the obliterated voicecaster dangled by wires from the impact point. She had wanted to blast it during *Daybreak's* harrowing dive, but her priority had been survival.

Shouts rose from below and Sable's relief vanished. She looked down and saw the deck swarming with Breakborn. Some tended to injured riggers who had been thrown from their high stations. Others climbed.

Sable fought down the fear this triggered and scrambled along the spar to the main mast. Then she too climbed. As she closed in on *Daybreak*, she tried to focus on freeing the cloudship before the Breakborn reached it. That meant cutting the rope. Not a problem. Even the fastest Breakborn climber had no chance of catching up to her. And, at this point, she still enjoyed the advantage of anonymity. Thanks to her outfit, and the fact that she had not fired on them, the crew of the *Dawn* likely considered her an ally. They wouldn't even think to shoot her down until it was too late.

Then she'd just hang on to the cut rope and float away. The thought of Jaio's surprise when she climbed back aboard the cloudship brought a smile to her face. She let it linger even though she knew it to be premature.

Boom!

The startling explosion yanked her attention over to *Frostbite*. At first, she thought the smaller skateship had fired on the *Dawn*, but when its sails unfurled and billowed full, she realized she'd heard the breaking claws retract. This elicited more shouts from the deck below. Most of the Breakborn turned from what they were doing and dashed for the stairs.

At the same time, *Frostbite* began to slide away. Another unbidden smile spread over Sable's face. With renewed determination, she pressed on.

Suddenly, a storm of explosions tore open the sky and the *Dawn* bucked sideways. Sable had all she could do to hold on. When the skateship steadied, she looked over and saw smoke pouring out of *Frostbite's* rear quarter. And worse, the aft port skate dragged across the Ice at the end of its mangled leg.

This caused the tail of the Oromola vessel to sag so badly, it almost bottomed out. Then loud metallic chattering commenced and, as *Frostbite's* middle leg shifted aft, and its aft starboard leg slid to center, the hull rose again. Once righted, *Frostbite* limped away, far more slowly now as the damaged leg banged and bounced across the snow.

Below Sable, *Invincible Dawn's* sails unfurled. At the same time, another braking claw boom resounded and the immense skateship lunged after *Frostbite*.

Overhead, *Daybreak* jolted and groaned as the *Dawn* dragged the cloudship forward. It began a silent lazy spin. Then, after a handful of heartbeats, the engines coughed one then the other. Puffs of black smoke burst from each and they roared to life.

The cloudship's engine-fins cut into the howling propeller wind and spun the floating vessel south, directly away from the *Dawn*. In response, the top-rope tether creaked and popped from the new strain and the giant skateship's advance slowed to a crawl.

"Yes," Sable hissed. She pressed on toward the rope, now intent on leaving it intact for as long as possible. Considering *Frostbite's* damage, it would need the biggest lead she could give it.

A sudden sear of green flame ripped past Sable and struck the hull of *Daybreak*. Thinking they'd somehow identified her as an enemy, she almost panicked. Then the next volley tore into the dangling voicecaster debris and she realized the men below were not shooting at her, but at the rope. And if they hit it…

"Oh, no" she breathed and practically bounded up the mast.

More shots sizzled the air around her. She ignored them and clawed her way aloft. With just an arm's length to go, a volley hit its mark. The rope split in two.

Sable froze. She clung to the mast, staring overhead in horrified dismay as *Daybreak* surged up and away. Beneath her, the *Dawn* leapt forward and a terrible cheer rent the air.

Panic again threatened to consume her. Breathe, said a deep inner voice. Breathe.

Sable closed her eyes and complied. A single calming thought surfaced. They still suppose I'm one of them.

Sable opened her eyes, checked to make sure her goggles were in place and pulled the collar of the airsuit up over her chin as high as she could. Then she started down the mast. If she could maintain her disguise long enough to reach one of the air circulation vents, she could disappear into the *Dawn's* interstitial world. She cast Aleekio a silent thanks for his insistence on showing her all of it, despite the danger of discovery.

At the bottom of the mast, a Breakborn barking orders to the riggers paused and glanced in her direction.

"You, Red!"

She halted, faced him and, in the most confident, controlled way she could manage, offered a sharp nod.

"Report to the Pilot House! Brief Cappen Ladashi on the situation aboard *Daybreak*."

She nodded again and dashed away before he could say anything else.

As she hastened up the stairs, she consulted her mental map of the *Dawn*. Between the deck and the pilot house, she knew of several promising ways into the vent system. She ran for the first.

At the head of the stair, she paused to look out across the snow ahead. *Frostbite* neared the drop-off, but the *Dawn* was closing fast. She glanced overhead, searching for *Daybreak*. She saw nothing but cold, clear sky. What could Jaio and Aleekio hope to do anyway? *Frostbite* only had one chance now.

If she was going to give it to them, she needed to hurry.

DAYBREAK

By time Jaio and Aleekio arrest *Daybreak's*
breakneck climb and swing the cloudship around,
both *Frostbite* and the *Dawn* are far away, racing
down the glacial ramp toward the Anthemar
Plain. *Frostbite's* only hope is to reach the Plain
before the *Dawn* catches up. With skates planed,
the Oromola skateship won't have to stop, but the
Dawn, still running on edges, will. However, Jaio
doesn't need to watch long to see the gap between
them closing too fast.

Then the disadvantage of planed skates and
one leg dragging becomes all too apparent. On
the glacier, the edge-running *Dawn* can move far
more quickly. Unless something changes, the
eight-legged monster will overtake *Frostbite* with
nearly half the glacier to spare. And Jaio can think
of nothing else he and Aleekio might do to slow
the pursuing skateship down.

To make matters worse, he's all too aware of
Eukon Thorne's gaze upon him. Jaio tries not to

pay the old man any attention, but every inadvertent glance is met with a hot unblinking stare.

"Spider's going too fast," says Aleekio.

"I know,"

"We could bash 'em again."

Jaio has considered it, and rejected the idea. "We were lucky the first time. They'll be ready for us now."

"We could dump stuff on 'em."

"No." Jaio is about to shove the thought from his mind when a slight modification causes him to perk up. "Wait! What kind of stuff do we have available? It's got to be big and heavy."

"We've used up two float-gas tanks, or three. They're big and heavy. Kind of like the nukebomb. From way high, they'd make a big hole in that nasty spider."

"We could never aim it from way high. But what if we dumped the tanks in front of the spider."

A mischievous smile spreads over Aleekio's face. "Trip the big bug!"

"Trip the big bug." Jaio looks over at Thorne on purpose now. He's disappointed to see a smile in the old man's eyes. Trying not to feel defeated, he turns his attention back to Aleekio.

"Where are the tanks?" asks Jaio.

"Empties are behind the middle door, that

side." Aleekio releases a pommel just long enough to point to port.

Jaio dashes down the stairs to the door. He spins the hatch wheel and heaves it open. Three enormous cylinders line the inner wall. As soon as he sees them, his idea dies. They are too big and too heavy. Without cranes and pulleys, he has no way to move them.

Then another disconcerting thought sends him dashing back to the pilot house.

"You said two maybe three tanks are empty. I only saw three tanks down there."

"There are three more on the other side, silly. Or we'd go in circles."

Jaio's relief is short lived.

"We'll be out of engine juice way sooner."

"You mean fuel?"

Aleekio nods. "But not for a while. There is plenty left to trip the bug."

"We're not going to be tripping the bug."

Down on the glacier, green flame erupts from the aft port quarter of *Frostbite*. The shot is aimed not at the *Dawn*, but at *Frostbite's* own dragging leg. Sparks fly as the volley strikes metal and a few pieces of debris careen away. Two more shots cut loose before the better part of the leg sheers free and tumbles to the ice. It kicks and crashes its way to a halt directly in the path of the *Dawn's* port legs.

"Whoa," breathes Aleekio. "Looks like we might not have to trip the bug."

Jaio holds his breath as the spider ship races toward the wreckage. He can see the vessel veering to port and finds himself leaning the opposite direction as if the force of his will might slow their turn. At the last moment, the *Dawn* straddles *Frostbite's* shed limb. It passes beneath the skateship and emerges untouched from behind.

"Dammit," says Aleekio, drawing surprised looks from both Jaio and Sable.

Back on the glacier, the gap continues to narrow, though now more slowly. Even so, the *Dawn* has more than enough distance to reach *Frostbite* and bring the chase to an end.

Then, without warning, the great eight-legged vessel pitches forward. The front legs fold to compensate until they are bent elbows high. Between them, the forehull strikes the snow again and again, sending up crystalline splashes like a skipping stone bouncing across the surface of a pond. The skates at the ends of the rear legs lift off the snow. On deck, most of the crew is sliding forward and panicked riggers are hoisting as fast as they can to roll in the sails.

Then the front port leg gives out and it's over. The *Dawn* noses in. Impact unleashes a swelling thunderhead of exploding snow. It boils upward, engulfing the hull.   The sails and masts vanish as they twist and tip into the expanding maelstrom. And in less than a breath, *Invincible Dawn* disappears.

What emerges in the aftermath is an unrecognizable fan of debris strewn down the face of the glacier. In the distance far ahead, *Frostbite* speeds away.

"Sable," whispers Jaio.

"She tripped the big bug," says Aleekio.

This time, Thorne collapses to his rear without making a sound. He simply stares out the glass at the wreckage.

"How?" asks Jaio. "How did she trip the big bug?"

"Took my sneaky way into the braking chamber. Pulled the lever."

Of course, the emergency brake release. Jaio remembers his long hours spent at the ready to pull *Frostbite's*. But to pull it going full sail with a tailwind on a steep slope…

"Take us down there," says Jaio, without need.

Aleekio is already shoving the wheel column forward. "Vent!" he shouts.

Jaio jumps to the control console and pulls back on the lever.

Having learned from their plunge toward the *Dawn*, both Jaio and Aleekio begin the leveling process sooner than before. As they draw near, the extent of the damage becomes more apparent. Most of the debris in the fan is composed of smaller loose objects like storage crates, tools, coils of rope and bodies, inhumanly contorted and unmoving. Jaio glances over at Aleekio, wondering what the boy sees.

Aleekio appears not to register some of the shapes on the snow as members of his Breakborn family. His focus seems to be fixed on flying.

Jaio looks back out the window, this time at the *Dawn's* main hull. Much to his relief, it looks mostly intact, the nose having held together as it burrowed into the glacier, shoving up a great berm of snow and shattered ice.

"Land just in front of the berm," says Jaio.

Aleekio nods and guides the cloudship down. "Engines off," he says.

Jaio twists the ignition knobs to the vertical position. A pair of loud smoky pops belch from the motors and they fall silent.

Aleekio releases the wheel and steps up to the console beside Jaio.

"Shouldn't one of us be steering?" asks Jaio.

"We need engines for that." He opens a small panel on the left side of the console and a grabs the lever underneath.

The cloudship shudders upon gently impacting the snow then begins to rise again.

Aleekio pushes the button at the end of the

lever. A sharp bang resounds and *Daybreak's* slow ascent abruptly stops.

"Push the button again and up we go," says Aleekio. "I'll wait for you to come back."

Jaio nods and dashes for the stairs. Muffled shouts of anger bleed through one of the hallway hatches he passes on his way down the corridor to the rear entry hatch.

Opening the hatch assails him with a blast of frigid air. He pulls up his hood, hops down to the snow and sets out for the wreck of the *Dawn*. So cold is the air, the light of the full sun fails to even soften the surface layer. Jaio is able to move quickly.

He doesn't slow until her reaches the berm. Hand over hand he clambers up the hill of shattered ice and snow to the summit. The view of the other side stops him in his tracks.

Breakborn are emerging from the wreck, crawling out gun ports, helping each other through gaps rent between panels of ancient railroad car skin wrested apart by the force of impact. Jaio's eyes dart from movement to movement, look for a red airsuit.

If Sable is out, she'll be somewhere near the nose of the *Dawn*. But she would have been at the very bottom of the ship and very likely still is.

Jaio starts down the far side of the berm. He veers to avoid getting too close to any of the

Breakborn and searches for a way inside. As he nears, the *Dawn's* upper decks loom above. The angle is so steep he can look straight up along the plane of the deck at the face of the Pilot's tower. He wonders if Ladashi is still in there.

"Jaio!" calls a voice from his left.

He looks over and sees half a face and a red-clad arm poking out through a partially-buried forward gunport.

"Sable!"

By the time he reaches her, she's clawing at the snow, trying to open the gap enough to allow her to squeeze through. He drops to his knees and starts digging too. "Are you all right?" he asks as he flings snow aside.

"For the most part," she says, sounding rattled. He hears her sniff.

"What's wrong? Are you hurt?"

"I just wanted to stop them," she says. "But not like this."

"I know," he says. "But you didn't have a choice. You saved *Frostbite*!"

"So many dead down there," she goes on as if she doesn't hear him.

"I'm sorry," he says and focuses his attention on freeing her.

Their combined efforts soon clear the port. He helps pull her out and, still on their knees, they lunge into a fierce embrace. They hold each other too long, but he can't make himself break loose. And apparently, neither can she.

"Red!" shouts a voice from the top deck rail. Jaio glances up through the shadow of his hood to see a menacing Breakborn peering down at them. "Wait there, I'll bring help!" The Breakborn caller disappears from sight.

"We have to hurry," says Sable.

She and Jaio leap to their feet and run for the berm. Some five paces from the summit, the Breakborn calls again. "Wait, where are you going?"

Jaio sees Sable pause and give a wide-armed wave in the direction of *Daybreak*.

"Tell him we're bringing more help," she says under her breath.

Jaio realizes her ruse and nods. Using the deepest voice he can, he conveys the message and hopes the Breakborn thinks she is the one calling out.

The Breakborn nods. "Understood! Hurry!" Then he turns and heads back into the chaos. Sable aims for the airship and takes off again with Jaio right beside her.

They sprint through the strewn debris and past several lifeless riggers who were catapulted well beyond the berm. Each new macabre sight causes Sable's pace to falter, but she manages to press on. Finally, they reach *Daybreak* and clamber inside.

Jaio slams the hatch behind them and spins the locking wheel.

Side by side, he and Sable start for the stairs. Half way there, she reaches over and takes his hand. "Thank you," she says. "For coming after me."

"I would never leave you behind," he says.

Her grateful smile transforms into a look of determination. "Let's make this count for something," she says, her voice heavy with emotion.

"To Anchoresk," says Jaio.

"To Anchoresk."

Hand in hand, they mount the stairs. The sight at the top causes them both to freeze. Aleekio is standing in front of the wheel, a pace from Thorne, looking out the window at a body the slow rotation of the tethered cloudship has brought into view. Jaio can hear the boy crying.

"Aleekio," he says. "Are you o—"

The boy whirls around and races with arms outstretched toward Jaio. Jaio crouches and absorbs the impact of a grief-stricken hug. Head on Jaio's shoulder, Aleekio sobs and shudders. Jaio makes no move to stop him despite the urgency of the situation.

Finally, Aleekio breaks away and spins Sable's direction. He now wears a wet, red mask of rage. "Your fault!" he shouts. Jaio lunges to his feet to stop the boy's apparent forthcoming assault on Sable, but Aleekio keeps spinning and levels an accusing finger on Thorne. "Your fault!"

Thorne simply watches, his expression as blank and battered as those worn by the Mountain of Faces.

Aleekio storms to the control console, grabs the lever and pushes the button. With a boom, the grappling cable releases and *Daybreak* lunges skyward.

Then Aleekio flips the two ignition switches in rapid succession. The engines bang and sputter to life. He swivels the velocity dial to full speed. The accompanying roar rises to fill the gondola. Aleekio stalks to the wheel. Steering restored, he aims the cloudship north.

"To Anchoresk," he says.

PART 5

CONCORA's FLAME

44

THE ADMINITHEDRAL

Jaspen stood with Kem and Rawl in the forbidden Adminithedral tower at the heart of Anchoresk. They watched Jaspen's father, Dictorian Consul Dalsen Ario, hasten away to arrange a meeting with his archenemy, Lord Salazriole Maxamant. The armies of the one-eyed Liege and his allies surrounded the Catalogian Monastery, the final obstacle between Maxamant and his desired goal of imperial ascension.

Despite the gravity of the situation, the savory scent of hot meat, garlic, and onion drove all thoughts of impending peril to the far periphery of Jaspen's mind. As soon as the chamber door shut behind her father, she, Kem and Rawl practically pounced on the covered platter of food sitting on the cart beside the small table near the center of the room. When Rawl lifted the shiny silver dome, the uncapped aroma drove the final vestiges of peril somewhere beyond the periphery.

"Oh," moaned Rawl. "I should 'a taken up the robe."

"Trust me, we don't all eat like this," said Kem.

"Then I'd have aimed for Dictorian. Or better yet, head chef."

They chuckled and Jaspen divided the food. Even though she took only a third, it yielded a larger meal than any she had eaten in weeks. And oh, what a meal: tender venison strips topped with steamed vegetables of all colors and generously doused with some kind of garlic, rosemary, mushroom sauce. She hadn't encountered anything like it since Madam Balisandra's. And then, only in passing, when one of the other girls had walked by while making a delivery to the rare bathhouse guest who could afford such an indulgence.

To have this feast for herself felt somehow wrong. But that didn't stop her from wanting to inhale it. She had to force herself to slow down and savor every bite. Kem and Rawl showed no such restraint.

When they were all finished and had washed it down with mouthfuls of the clear, cool, slightly lemony water from the neighboring carafe, Jaspen took stock of the chamber for the first time.

"What is the place, Kem?" she asked.

"I'm actually not sure. What goes on in here is one of the Order's most closely guarded secrets.

Typically, only the Dictorian, the Tributans, and the Deaf Hands are allowed entry."

"Deaf Hands?" asked Jaspen.

"Monks without hearing who operate that apparatus." Kemren turned and gestured up to a great arched track with an enormous telescoptic magnifier suspended underneath. "During my escape," Kem went on. "I saw orb fragments in a box on the desk." He spun back around and indicated the table beside the cart where the empty platter and carafe now rested. "And see those metal fingers at the top of that alter over there," he pointed toward a modest pedestal standing in the center of a blackened stone alcove at the front of the chamber. "I think they hold the orb fragments up into sunlight magnified by the lenses attached to the arch."

"Maybe," said Jaspen, "concentrating the light is the only way to make broken orbs talk."

Kemren nodded. "That was my thought as well."

"Like starting a fire by holding a piece of clear, curved ice up to the sun?" asked Rawl.

"Exactly."

"They've pulled a lot of ancient wisdom from the flames," said Rawl.

"Wisdom and a great deal more," said Kem with a glance up at the tower. "Including everything else they've built using the knowledge of the past, including the entire social order of Anthemar."

Jaspen strode over to the alter to look more closely at the insect-like orb-support device. Out of curiosity, she removed Major Anchor's orb from her parka pocket to see if it would fit. The orb immediately began to hiss as exposure to the bright sunlight initiated replay. Jaspen held the orb up to the empty space between the metal fingertips just long enough to see that it fit perfectly then shoved it back into her pocket.

"Maybe there are some orb fragments around here somewhere," said Rawl. He broke away and began exploring the chamber.

Jaspen considered going with him, but the opportunity to be almost alone with Kem won out. "Be careful," she said and turned toward Kem. No surprise, he already stood facing her, his teeth framed in a wide smile.

"We made it," he said.

"Thank you, Kem. For—"

"It took all of us, helping each other," he said. "And too many sacrifices made by some."

"You knew, didn't you?" she asked. "About Benethan."

His smile faded and he offered an apologetic nod. "I'm sorry I didn't tell you."

"Actually," she said. "I'm glad you didn't. If not for all this time together and seeing everything he has done for us, I would not have been able to forgive him."

"You forgive him, then? Even after what he did?"

She nodded. "Because of what he did. How he changed. Who he has become, especially knowing who he was." She paused and took a steadying breath. "I'm not much for praying, Kem. But I pray we see him again so I can tell him."

Kem simply stared into her eyes for a moment. "You're incredible," he said and drew her into a hug.

"Hey, lovebirds," said Rawl from the shadows of an overhang along the back wall beneath the magnifier arch. "There's some kind of covered case back here. Looks about the right size for orb storage."

Jaspen and Kem hastened over Rawl. He'd found a shallow rectangular black box measuring roughly an arm by an arm. A roll-top cover hid the contents.

The case itself rested at about waist height on a sturdy table with thick wooden legs and a smooth stone top. Using his fingertips, Rawl gently tried to coax the roll-top cover to unroll. It didn't budge.

Jaspen and Kem searched for a release mechanism. In the dim light beneath the overhang, finding the button on the lower right corner took a few moments.

"Here," said Jaspen and pressed it. The box issued a click and suddenly, the cover began to unroll beneath Rawl's fingers. A clear glass top reflected their faces and the overhang ceiling beyond.

Beneath the glass they, at first, saw only black emptiness. No orbs. Nothing.

Then a pale triangle of elevated yellow-brown parchment appeared in the lower left corner. Other floating fragments emerged after that until the case was completely open, revealing a rectangular arrangement of pieces that had once been a single page.

"What is it?" asked Rawl.

"Some kind of ancient document," said Kem.

Jaspen leaned closer. Faint markings stained the central pieces, and the lower left triangle, but only the triangle maintained enough clarity for anything to be made out.

She focused on the first line of ink. Drawing on the lessons in reading and writing administered by her father during her childhood proved challenging to say the least.

Letter by letter, she sounded out the blocky, mechanical script in her mind then read the line our loud, "By Order of…" followed by blank space.

The neat, handwritten script below that had been underlined, though it suffered the blurring of several water stains. Jaspen struggled to decipher the few discernible letters

"A-n-c-h-o-r." Then came an illegible blot followed by the letters, "e-s." Another blot filled the next space after which a final partial letter appeared. "k." A large blot erased anything that might have come next.

"A.n.c.h.o.r.e.s.k," Kemren spelled out.

"Anchoresk," said Jaspen.

In the face of this startling revelation, she almost missed the faint blocky words visible beneath the handwritten segment.

"Name: Last   First   Middle Initial   Rank." She read this out loud.

And underneath that appeared a faint illegible scroll of ink on a line above the word: Signature.

"I'd wager the Rank was Major," said Rawl.

Jaspen and Kem both fixed him with a quizzical look.

"<u>Anchor</u>. Pr<u>es</u>ton <u>K</u>eith Major," he said as if the clues had been obvious.

"How did you figure that out? You can't even read," said Kem.

"I can listen. And I've been doing it for a few more years than you have, pup."

"You remember his whole name?" asked Jaspen.

"Comes with not relying on ink and parchment to store your memories for you. It's all gotta be up here." He tapped his head. "Believe it or not, there is a downside to all that scribbling. Makes your mind mushy."

"Apparently so," said Kem.

"If you're right," said Jaspen.

"Oh, I'm right," said Rawl, with only a hint of self-satisfaction.

"This might have been the order he signed for the orbs to be taken to…" she can't remember the destination and, against her better judgment, looks over to Rawl.

He smiles. "Texassippi."

"But this is as far as they made it," said Kem.

"So, all the orbs are here somewhere," said Jaspen.

"And apparently, they're all broken," said Rawl.

From behind them, the chamber door opened and closed. Then Jaspen's father strode around the alcove into sight. When he saw them huddled at the back of the chamber, his pace quickened.

"Close the Naming cabinet," he said. "You must hurry."

"Wait," said Jaspen.

"There is no time." He spread his arms and tried to herd them toward the floor hatch. "Head back down the tunnel. Someone will be waiting for you. Go with—"

"Wait," said Jaspen again. She planted her feet and pointed to the ancient writing. "Was this found with a lot of broken orbs?"

Her father froze. "How do you know that? In fact, how do you know about the orbs at all?"

Jaspen reached into her parka pocket and withdrew Anchor's orb. In the shadow beneath the overhang, it remained silent.   She held it up in her open palm.

Her father's eyes grew wide and darted from the orb, to her face then back to the orb. "Intact?" he asked.

"Yes, just hold it in the sunshine."

He reached up gingerly and lifted it from her palm with both hands as if it were the most fragile of bird's eggs.

"Where did you get this?"

"Beneath the Cliff of Faces. It was on a table, inside the command tent with a body," said Jaspen, hoping this was enough detail for him to make sense of it. "You need to listen."

The insistent tone of her final statement seemed to snap her father from his daze. "There's no time. You have to go." He slid the orb into his pocket.

"Hearing it won't take long. You'll have more than enough time while we're getting ready."

Her father paused. "You're right. Once you're

on your way, I'll listen. Now, go. Quickly!" He tried to urge them on again, but Jaspen stepped into his open arms and gives him a long, hard hug.

She felt his limbs close around her. "You are right, again," he said. "If the urgency is too great for this, then it's too late for everything."

Even so, he didn't let the hug last as long as Jaspen would have liked. When he stepped away, he turned and embraced Kem next. Then, much to everyone's surprise, most of all Rawl's, he pulled the old tiger hunter into a hug as well. For the first time Jaspen could recall, Rawl seemed truly at a loss.

"Take care of each other," said Jaspen's father as he released Rawl, hurried over to the hatch, knelt and lifted it open.

Jaspen, Kem, and Rawl headed down in the reverse order of their arrival. As soon as they were on the ladder, Jaspen's father started to lower the hatch. Mid-way he paused and peeked in.

"You still have the keys, Kem? Just in case?"

Kemren nodded.

"Good. I'll see you outside soon."

Jaspen's father closed the hatch.

THE ADMINITHEDRAL

Dalsen Ario stood from locking and covering the emergency escape hatch then stepped to the center of the Dictation Chamber. He took a deep breath, pulled the orb from his pocket and held it up into the mid-morning sunshine. It hissed for a few moments then issued a metallic crash.

Finally, without need of magnifiers or hours of careful positioning in the holder, it spoke.

"Dammit," it said.

And Dalsen Ario lost himself in the story.

By the time Major Anchor's narrative ended, Dalsen Ario's world had been turned upside down. If Sigmos Bomechor had been there with him, Ario had no doubt the highest ranking Dagger would have insisted he smash the orb to bits. Not this time.

Ario tucked the orb inside his robe. When the time was right, everybody would hear it in the light of the sun. First, however, he needed to make the Tributans and Lieges of the four allied Protectorates understand the danger posed by Thorne.

Unless Ario could convince them to listen to the message Jaspen and her companions had brought from the Ice, the snow would again stain red.

Despite the challenge, in his heart, Ario felt a spark of hope. Thanks to Jaspen's warning about Thorne, the bloodless unification of Anthemar might just be possible. If nothing else, perhaps the Liege-lords could be persuaded to leave without a fight. Even if their departure only meant the postponement of reckoning day, it gave more time for another way to be found.

Until that day came, Ario reminded himself, the possibility still existed that it never would. He promised to himself, to Jaspen, to Jaio, to everyone else in Anthemar, that he would do all he could to make sure it never did. Even at the cost of the Order itself.

Dalsen Ario strode to the chamber door and heaved it open. The two Iron Robe guards outside spun crisply to face him and snapped to attention.

"Call the Tributans and the Lieges. Have them meet me here at once."

"Here, Dictorian?"

"Yes. Here." *If this breach of protocol proves too much*, he thought to himself, *then we are doomed*.

"Yes, Dictorian," they said in unison and one of them dashed away.

Ario turned and closed himself back inside the Dictation Chamber. He began to formulate an address as he strode to his table, but quickly gave up. There were simply too many variables, too many unknowns.

Only one thing seemed certain. Tomorrow would bring not just a new day, but a new age.

Ario suffered no illusions. The long precedent of history strongly favored the arrival of a dark age. And most dispiriting of all, despite vehement assertions to the contrary, the Order had been hastening toward the darkness all along, in its singular effort to restore, and then further advance, the historical reality responsible for the unraveling of the world.

The people of Anthemar, he now understood, would never do more than live by scavenging the leavings of a past that could not be repeated. There would be no furtherance. Yet here he stood, trapped in an unfinished, unfinishable, tower of ancient glass, leading the attempt, having long ago abandoned any other choice.

In Ario's mind, he heard a voice from outside history; her voice, speaking of other human potentials, potentials with an even deeper precedent than blood, violence and conquest. She could cast a spell of hope with such words, though in the face of the world he lived in day by day, their effect all too soon wore off.

How he longed to hear her speak them again. Or better yet, to live day by day without need of them.

Close to her, close to Jaspen and his son.

Family.

DAYBREAK

Keep us low, Aleekio," says Jaio. He and Sable
stand behind and to either side of the boy,
watching *Frostbite* through the window. The now-
five-legged skateship has found its stride. Fans of
snow curl from its planed skates as it races north
toward Anchoresk. Jaio's concern is the
intervening fleet.

By now, the other six vessels are very likely in
position, waiting like owls in a tree, for Thorne's
order to pounce on the unsuspecting armies of
Anthemar. *Frostbite* will need to pass the fleet
without getting blown to pieces in the attempt.
Jaio considers guiding *Frostbite* around the other
skateships, but with the daylight already almost
half-gone, they can't afford the added time.
Besides, by going through, the fleet will very
likely pursue, even without Thorne's order.

"We need to cause a distraction," says Sable, as if reading his thoughts. "So the lookouts will be focused on us long enough for *Frostbite* to go by them." She now wears her own parka.

"I think we can do that," says Jaio. "But we'll need to be careful the Anthemari don't see us. What do you think, Aleekio?"

"No problem, Cappen."

"We should reach them fairly soon," says Sable.

Jaio tries to think of something more they can do. After all, even if they succeed in enticing the fleet to expose itself to the Anthemari before the battle between Maxamant and the Order begins, the Ghosts will simply begin a different battle. And outnumbered though they are, with the might of six skateships at their command, a few hundred Ghosts stand a good chance against the thousands they will face. Either way, a bloodbath is a near certainty.

"We're just rearranging the board," he says.

"What do you mean?" asks Sable.

"Chess," he says. "We're still playing the game."

"Isn't that the idea. Uniting them against us

keeps them from destroying each other. And once the fleet has been seen, you can be certain the grievance with *Frostbite* will be forgotten. We will be united as well."

"Against them." Jaio squeezes his eyes shut for a moment. "But how do all of us unite against the real foe: the Ancients?"

Sable remains silent for a moment then Jaio hears the quiet intake of breath he knows will be released as words.

"Maybe, Jaspen has reached her father," says Sable. "Maybe, he knows we're coming and has convinced both sides to refrain from fighting each other as well as us until your message has been heard."

"Even if that is the case, the Ghosts intend to attack them."

"Then it's up to you, All-clan Orol Jaio, to convince the Ghosts to refrain." Sable steps to the voicecaster console and flips up all the switches.

Jaio just stares at her.

"You've done it before," she points at *Frostbite*. "You can do it again."

Jaio's hand seems to guide itself to the bulge of the orb pressed against his chest. He lifts the pouch into view. "It happened when Aiomida and the crew heard this," he says.

"Then let them hear it. All of them." She nods toward the front window and the fleet beyond.

"But none of them speak Fanetongue."

"That's okay," says Aleekio. "I can say it in Molatongue, Paitongue, Kotatongue, all the clantongues."

Again, surprise turns Jaio's and Sable's attention to the boy. "You've heard the orb?" asks Jaio. "How did you listen without being discovered?"

"Dim light makes quiet words."

"Could you translate it into Ghostongue?" asks Jaio.

"Of course, silly. I don't even need the orb." He clears his throat. "Re-Rrrettt-ttt. R-Tetttt," he says in the interclan trade language, Ghostongue, but with a stutter perfectly matching Jaio's memory of the opening sounds made by the Founding Orb. "Want me to go on?" asks Aleekio.

"No, that's great," says Jaio. But even as Aleekio solves the translation problem, the next challenge surfaces in Jaio's mind. The broadcast will only be heard in the pilot houses, by the people least likely to be moved. Somehow, everyone needs to hear.

In his mind, he goes back to what seems like a different lifetime, to the early days aboard *Frostbite*. There, he finds an idea.

Grabbing hold, he joins Sable at the voicecaster console and flips down all but the ninth switch.

"What are you doing?"

"Everyone needs to hear this, not just the Cappens." He picks up the transmitter and keys it. "Cappen Aiomida, are you there?"

An immediate pop resounds. "Go ahead, Jaio."

"A change of plans," he says. "When you reach the fleet, stop just behind the middle ships and turn on your outside voicecaster."

The next pop is slower in coming. "Explain."

"I'm going to play the Founding Orb through my transmitter. I need you to hold to your transmitter to the speaker and send the sound to the voicecaster on the mast so the whole fleet can hear."

"Understood, Orol." Aiomida's voice has taken on a strength it lacked even a moment earlier.

"Be ready," he says.

"Yes, Orol."

Jaio glances at Sable. She nods and smiles.

"Okay," he spins around to face Aleekio. "As soon as we see the fleet, we'll come at them from the side and buzz them like a bee over daisies. That ought to give *Frostbite* time to get within voicecaster range before being spotted."

No sooner have these words left Jaio's mouth then Aleekio whoops. "Fleet ahead, Cappen Orol!"

"All right." Jaio dashes to the engine dial and turns up the power. The soft rumble that filled the gondola as they shadowed the skateship grows to a roar. Almost immediately, *Daybreak* begins to overtake *Frostbite*.

Aleekio pulls the wheel back enough to lift over the vessel without danger of clipping the masts, then he angles the cloudship back down. In moments, they are skimming the snow. Ahead of them, the six skateships enlarge at an alarming rate.

In the distance beyond the fleet, the top of the glass tower rises into the sky.

"All right, Aleekio, turn us hard away port and

come in low on their side."

The boy spins the wheel initiating a great loop that soon has them approaching the port-most vessel in the fleet. *Winter Leaf.*

"As soon as you buzz the fleet, drop and bank away south. We don't want the Anthemari to see us."

"Aye, Cappen Orol."

Jaio's not sure he likes Aleekio's new honorific, but decides he has more important demands on his attention.

Ahead, the deck of the *Winter Leaf* comes alive as the crew hears the growing engine noise and quickly traces it to its source. Jaio can soon make out the Ghosts in more detail. Some are pointing and they all seem to be casting each other puzzled looks.

Much to his relief the gunports remain closed and nobody appears to be aiming any hand weapons at them. Even now, they're not willing to do anything to kindle the wrath of Thorne, despite how incomprehensible *Daybreak's* behavior must seem.

When the cloudship reaches the point where Jaio thinks he can discern eyes on the faces of the

Ghosts, Aleekio pulls back on the wheel and *Daybreak* races over the tops of the six ships. Down below, crews dash from port rail to starboard to watch the cloudship rumble away.

Jaio runs to the forward rail and looks southwest. *Frostbite* is almost in range. Aleekio banks that way and soon the Oromola skateship has moved to the center of the window. Jaio runs to the control console and cuts the engines to a purr.

"Let's face the fleet, Aleekio," he says. "But stay back. We can transmit from out of weapon's range."

"Aye," says Aleekio. He completes *Daybreak's* turn slowly, following the advance of *Frostbite* as the skateship closes on the fleet. Once they're lined up, Jaio kills the engines and cable grapples them to the snow. *Frostbite* follows suit, releases braking claws and lurches to a halt.

"It's time, Aleekio," he says.

The boy releases the wheel and joins Jaio at the voicecaster console where Sable stands holding the transmitter at the ready. With trembling hands, Jaio removes the Founding Orb and holds it covered in his palms. "Okay, Aleekio, while it plays, you tell the story in Ghostongue. Got it?"

"Got it," says the boy. He pushes up his goggles, too high. It makes him look like a startled grebe. Sable reaches over and centers them. Aleekio doesn't seem to notice.

Jaio nods to Sable. She keys the transmitter and Jaio removes his top hand from the orb.

The story begins. Even through the glass, he can hear it carrying across the snow from *Frostbite's* masthead speakers all the way to the cloudship. Up ahead, the decks of the skateships have fallen completely still. Ghosts just stand at the rails and listen. As do Jaio and Sable. And Thorne.

Jaio glances over at the old man and finds him staring at his son, rapt. In his aged eyes, Jaio almost thinks he sees something akin to pride.

Jaio smiles, looks back out the window and gives all his attention to that long ago day from the time before the Ice.

Hearing the story unfold with the voice of a child raises gooseflesh on Jaio's skin. He can only hope it is having the same effect on the Ghosts.

Finally, the story ends. Jaio covers the orb, drops it in its pouch and hangs it from his neck.

Sable passes him the transmitter.

"Great job," he whispers to the boy. "You ready to translate for me now?"

"Ready," says Aleekio.

Jaio sits on the stool and Aleekio stands beside him. Their heads are at almost the same level. Jaio holds the transmitter to his mouth and Aleekio leans close. No time to think now. Jaio presses the button.

"Fellow Ghosts," he begins. "This is Orol Jaio."

Aleekio repeats Jaio's greeting in Ghostongue.

On the skateships, a shimmer of movement ripples across the decks. Then stillness returns. They appear to be ready to hear what he has to say.

But will they listen.

ANCHORESK

The bitter Snowsea wind bit Jaspen's cheeks. Dressed now in a ragged, smelly parka with a stained Kestian shoulder band, she stood at the monastery gate with Kem, Rawl, and a retinue of Iron Robes, including their rescuer from the catacombs. Ahead of them, the two armored carriages blocking the entrance gate hissed steam and belched smoke at the front of an expanse of bare ground laboriously cleared of snow. The ominous machines were warming up so they could make a show of the grand exit, when the time came for she, Kem, and Rawl to walk out with her father for the meeting with Lord Salazriole Maxamant at his palatial command tent far to the south of the Squells.

As Jaspen and her companions waited for her father to arrive, she glanced around at the grim faces of the Protectorate musketeers. They lined the defensive walls and, behind her, stood in vast columns spread all across the broad central plaza awaiting the order to march out onto the field of battle. Hundreds of colorful banners crackled and flapped among them, displaying the insignia of the four Protectorates to have joined with the Order to put down Maxamant's bid for Empire.

Within the sea of musketeers, she also saw smaller contingents of fighting men armed with stutterguns. These, Kemren had told her, were the last resort, not to be used until all the powder-and-shot troops were gone.

The calculated disregard for so many lives left her cold inside. Colder than the buffeting gusts of wind. Something about the way some of the gusts seemed to whisper caught her ear. She turned south and squinted into the frigid onslaught.

Being from Brink, Jaspen knew many of the wind's varied voices, some almost human, but never before had they sounded this human.

She leaned toward Kem. "You hear that?"

"Hear what?"

"The wind. It sounds like voices."

Kemren lowered his hood and listened. His ears turned red in the cold air as a few wordless gusts washed through. Finally, he shook his head and lifted his hood.

Movement to the east drew Jaspen's attention from the far-off wind, back to the immediate. She and her companions turned to face her father who strode toward them within a circle of Iron Robe guards. The warrior monks all brandished large stutterguns she'd only seen in one other place; the Cliff of Faces.

"Remember," muttered Rawl. "The Dictorian doesn't know us. And we don't know him."

The circle of guards reached them and opened. Jaspen, Kem, and Rawl knelt and bowed their heads as they'd been instructed.

"Rise," said Jaspen's father. His tone and mannerisms made him seem a different person from the one they'd met earlier.

They straightened to face him. Slightly back and to his right stood the rescuer monk. He wore a pack from which multiple long handles protruded, each a different shape and painted a different, bright color. The monk nodded a solemn greeting.

Jaspen's father smiled at her and her companions, looking in turn at each of their faces, Jaspen's last and longest. "First, I thank you for the news you have brought from the Snowsea, and I mourn the sacrifice your team made to deliver it. Wolfe's Pride will be remembered as heroes."

"Thank you, Dictorian," said Jaspen.

"You have been told why I summoned you?" he asked.

"We have," said Jaspen.

"What is your answer then? Will you join me

to deliver your message to Lord Maxamant?"

"We would consider it an honor, Dictorian," said Jaspen.

"Very good." He glanced over his shoulder at the rescuer monk. "This is Brother Shasten. He will accompany us to Maxamant's camp. When a decision is reached, Shasten will relay instructions to our allies with the flags he carries. Your job is to make sure the red one stays where it is."

"Understood, Dictorian," said Jaspen.

"Good." Jaspen's father turned to Brother Shasten. "We are ready."

A sudden shout arose from outside, beyond the steam carriages. "Hold! Hold!"

Troops on the wall tracked an as yet unseen figure whose fast footfalls on the snow could be heard approaching the entrance gate.

"Hold," said the runner again as he appeared in the gap between the war machines.

"Brother Kovo," said Jaspen's father.

"I bring a message from Lord Maxamant!" he wheezed. "He bowed and held up a rolled parchment sealed with red wax and bound in a purple ribbon.

Jaspen's father took and with a furrowed brow, opened it. His jaw tightened as he read, then he crumpled it and threw it to the ground.

"What is it?" asked Jaspen then quickly added, "Dictorian."

"Maxamant has changed the terms. Only myself and one other are to go."

At this, several of the Iron Robes rose up in protest, but Jaspen's father merely lifted a hand for silence. "Give me the flags, Brother," he said to Shasten. With obvious reluctance, the subordinate monk complied.

Kem took a step closer to Jaspen's father and opened his mouth.

"I'll go," blurted Jaspen.

Kem spun on her. "No, it's too dangerous!"

"For you no less than me," she said. Then, barely above a whisper, she added, "I can't watch both of you walk away from me."

Kem appeared to be considering a response.

"I can't," she repeated.

Kem lowered his head and nodded. "I'll be waiting here for you when you get back," he said.

How she wanted to embrace him one last time. But for the sake of their ruse, she refrained. "See you soon, Kem."

He clenched his jaw as tears threatened and gave her a nod.

Jaspen's father slung the flag pouch over his shoulder. "Watch for the signal."

Brother Shasten nodded and turned his attention to the commanders of the steam carriages. "Make way for the Dictorian," he yelled.

"Aye, Brother," shouted both commanders. They leaned down and conveyed the order into their respective vehicles. In response, the machines released jets of hot vapor and lurched backwards, their pistons hissing and their massive metal-rimmed wheels crunching over the frozen earth. Black smoke boiled into the sky from their stacks as they parted to either side of Jaspen and her companions.

The view through the gate froze Jaspen with terror. Out beyond the abandoned shanties of the Squells, the crop fields were filled not with row upon row of wheat or corn, but of men. Thousands of men.

Arranged in lines and blocks, they spread around Anchoresk in both directions as far as Jaspen could see. Countless banners sprouted among them, flying the colors of the five enemy Protectorates.

And on a hill in the midst of the largest mass, stood a great tent. An immense purple and red banner wafted in the south wind.

"Let's go," said Jaspen's father.

Jaspen couldn't move. Not until Kem reached over and gently touched her shoulder, did she find the will to shift her leaden feet. She stepped up beside her father and together they strode out the gate and down the gentle hill descending into the Squells.

"Benethan?" she asked as soon as she felt sure everyone else was out of earshot.

"He lost his arm below the elbow, but he'll live."

This news brought Jaspen both relief and sorrow. She could not imagine such a sacrifice despite the similarity of their circumstance. Having been born without a second hand, she had no personal contrast with which to compare the loss.

Benethan's last words to her replayed in her mind: "I hope I have been a better monk than the first one you met, Jaspen Stillwind."

She glanced at her father. "He knew me as Jaspen Stillwind. Why? And how is it, even thinking the name makes me want to run for my life?"

Her father's gait visibly faltered and his wide eyes spun to meet her gaze. "Benethan was the one Noyova sent to..." His voice failed.

She nodded and told her father Benethan's tale.

"So," he said at the end. "Your sleeping mind heard the warning I recited those many childhood nights when I sat at your bedside rubbing your back, whispering of dangers you might one day need to flee."

She nodded. "But why Stillwind?"

"Unlike water, the wind can never be still, so

the odds of an inadvertent utterance seemed remote. I then injected the word into the rumor of your existence as a last desperate safeguard against the day a hunter finally came calling for you."

Jaspen opened her mouth to thank him for all he'd done to keep her safe, but a fanfare of horns from behind cut through the air before she could speak. The high, long notes seemed to awaken thunder. Unlike the periodic rumblings made by storms however, this thunder rolled steady and unwavering.

Jaspen only needed a moment to identify the source. Thousands of marching feet.

Through not only the west gate behind her, but from various openings all around the periphery of Anchoresk's log wall, columns of musketeers poured out like liquid from a bucket with many leaks.

She leaned closer to her father. "I thought we were trying to stop the battle," she hissed.

"We are," he replied. "Maxamant needs to see the might he faces. He needs to recognize for himself the illusion of his superiority. Your words will fall on deaf ears if he does not first grasp this reality."

Jaspen didn't like it, but had to admit it made sense.

"By the time we reach his pavilion," he went

on. "Our forces should be in place."

A movement to Jaspen's right drew her eyes into the adjacent hovels. There she saw a barefoot figure in filthy furs watching them. His mud-caked black hair jutted out in random directions and his beard hung in sticky strings from his chin. The moment he realized he'd been seen, he ducked and, inexplicably, disappeared. Jaspen blinked hard and looked again. The man was gone.

"We couldn't coax them all inside," said her father who must have seen the man before he vanished. "Some preferred to take their chances out here."

More horn blasts sounded from behind and Jaspen's attention turned to the wall where the last of the columns were dribbling through the openings. Into each gap on the heels of the last of the soldier lurched a pair of steam carriages. Massive cannon barrels jutted from their noses.

Jaspen looked south, to the rise with the tent. It still seemed very far away.

"Shouldn't we be going that way?" she asked with a nod toward the extravagant structure.

"Once we're through the Squells, we'll turn. Walking will be easier in the open."

Jaspen glanced at the four flag-handles rising above her father's shoulder. Each was a different shape: hexagonal, square, triangular and round.

"What signals can we send?" she asked.

"The most important is the round handle. The green flag at the end will tell our allies to stand down."

"What are the others?"

"The hexagonal handle will tell the reserve force to move into position."

"The square one?"

"That one signals for breakout. And the triangular handle means fight."

"What about a flag for surrender?" she asked.

"I only brought the ones we might use."

They continued on in silence. On either side of Jaspen and her father, the empty shanties came and went. Each dark entrance prompted Jaspen to wonder if the disappearing man or other hiding eyes peeked out from inside. More than once she mistook the movement of a loose door flap or torn curtain for another wretch scuttling out of sight.

Finally, they neared the edge of the Squells. Here, the shanties more resembled jumbled piles of debris than shelters. She could not imagine calling one of them home.

Jaspen and her father rounded the last forlorn lodge and found themselves facing the full spectacle of Maxamantan might. Not a hundred paces away, the first double row of musketeers stood at the ready behind makeshift barricades made of sharpened poles. Bayonets glinted at the ends of the soldier's shouldered weapons.

Without pause, Jaspen's father strode out into the open. A shout went up followed by the clatter of weapons being raised. In half a heartbeat, Jaspen found herself looking down at least a hundred leveled barrels.

Jaspen's father came to an abrupt halt.

Did these men not get the word? she wondered.

From behind the musketeers, in the direction of the tent, a grumble grew. A rising column of black smoke jetted into the sky from some enormous vehicle headed their way.

After a few moments, the musketeers shouldered their weapons again. Several men hastened to open a gap in the barricades then the line of soldiers parted. Through the opening, a great eruption of snow approached. The column split as it curled left and right in two roiling arcs.

The distance quickly closed. The nearer the vehicle came, the more Jaspen wanted to turn and flee. But her father held his ground. So, she did too.

At less than ten paces, the eruption abruptly ceased and the advancing menace halted. Jaspen watched with breathless trepidation as the last of the upthrust snow settled.

There before them sat a giant steamtank, its entire surface painted in bold tiger stripes. Mounted to the front was an immense iron wedge forged in the shape of an open-winged condor. A small glass dome, barely larger than the head of the man who looked out through it, bulged from the forward right quarter of the vehicle. Inside the dome, the head nodded. A metallic scrape accompanied the descent of the dome into the hull. Its disappearance concluded with a sharp clank.

After that, nothing happened.

"He's just trying to unnerve us," said Jaspen's father.

"It's working," said Jaspen.

"I know, but try to pretend it isn't."

This made her smile, something she thought she might never do again.

Finally, as smoke continued to roll from the soot-blackened stack, the sounds of scraping metal and chattering gears emanated from the tiger-crawler. Movement on top drew Jaspen's eyes upward again.

A shimmering kineticloth half-circle slightly wider than a person slowly rose into view out of the center of the hull. Inside the half-circle on the left, the shaved head of a boy appeared. Around his neck, he wore a heavy iron collar trailing a chain of thick links. A wide leather shoulder strap crossed over the front of his moth-eaten wool tunic. The strap held up a slender back-pouch from which a single, triangular wooden handle protruded.

As the kineticloth backdrop continued to rise, a seated old man came into view to the right of the youth. The old man wore a golden eye-patch and a fat wolf-fur hat with a golden top-tassel. A full length coat of overlapping, gold-trimmed, silver panels covered his body from head to mid-shin. Similar boots shod his feet.

In his bejeweled left hand, he gripped a long scepter capped with a black obsidian sphere.

An orb!

It looked complete, but even in the bright light of the mid-day sun, it emitted no sound. *Blank? Or maybe it's damaged on the inside?*

Jaspen had no way to know and forced her attention back to the unfolding revelation of the old man. He sat in an elaborately carved wooden chair. Actually, given its scale and gaudy embellishments, she supposed it to be his throne. Yet despite its lavish decorations, its most obvious feature was the fist-sized lock fastening the boy's chain to the lower leg.

Jaspen's eyes followed the chain back to the boy. He looked to be nine or ten years of age. And despite wearing only a thin threadbare tunic, tattered, knee-length pants and rawhide sandals sprouting clumps of straw, the captive did not shiver. He stared ahead with dull eyes and an expressionless face. Seeing him made Jaspen's heart ache and her blood simmer.

The old man's elevating platform banged to a stop. Only then, did Jaspen notice its final feature, a chest-high wall made of some thick, clear material. It completed the old man's circle of protection. Only the upper third and the top remained open.

"Greetings, Lord Maxamant," said Jaspen's father. He even offered a bow. "Thank you for agreeing to this meeting."

"How could I pass up the opportunity to accept the surrender of the Order from the Dictorian himself?"

"As should be quite obvious, I have no intention of surrendering."

"Then we're done here." He leaned slightly to his right and glanced up at the chained boy. "Signal—"

"Lord Maxamant," said Jaspen's father. "We know about your discovery of the mountain cache."

Maxamant returned his one-eyed gaze to Jaspen's father. A self-satisfied smile grew on his face. "Then you know you can't win."

"Preventing a battle often yields a greater victory than winning it." Jaspen's father reached over his shoulder toward the flag handles.

Maxamant responded by grabbing up a stuttergun from his lap.

The old man pointed the weapon at Jaspen's father. "Stop!"

Jaspen's father just smiled, felt each of the handles and grabbed hold of the hexagonal one. He pulled out a blue and white striped flag and waved it over his head.

Maxamant thrust the stuttergun forward and the barrel banged against the clear barrier.

"Plexishielding works both ways," said Jaspen's father.

Maxamant started to stand so he could aim the gun over the top, but then something in the distance caught his eye. He dropped back into his crimson cushion, leaned his scepter against its thick wooden leg and rummaged inside his plated coat.

He pulled out a golden telescoptic tube, clicked it open and held it to his eye. As he panned the Catalogian stronghold, his movements became more jerky. "What is this?" he hissed.

Jaspen wanted to turn and look as well, but thought better of it. Besides, she had a good idea of what she would see; hundreds, if not thousands, more men pouring out through the wall, all of them armed with the big stutterguns from the Cliff of Faces.

"We found a generous cache of our own," said Jaspen's father. He returned the flag to the pouch.

"This can't be," whispered Maxamant.

"I assure you, it is. And I choose to reveal my hand now in the hope that you will reconsider your attack. It will not bring you victory. The only outcome will be terrible suffering on both sides."

"This is a trick!" yelled Maxamant. "A bluff! Those weapons are carved of wood! They are painted black! If you had found a real cache, my informants would have known. I would have known."

"Are you willing to risk being wrong about that?" asked Jaspen's father.

Maxamant's good eye leveled on him and narrowed. "What if I am?"

"It very likely won't matter." Jaspen felt her father's gaze turn to her. "This is Jaspen, a member of the Kestian Ice Watch team, Wolfe's Pride. She just returned from the Snowsea with a message you need to hear. A message regarding an old acquaintance of yours, Eukon Thorne."

Maxamant's eye widened and shot to Jaspen. "Thorne is dead!" he barked.

The stab of his singularly piercing stare froze her words in her throat. All she could do was shake her head.

Maxamant's gaze tore away and returned to her father. "Is this the best you can do, Ario? Using a pretty girl to distract me with some yarn about old traitors come back from the dead?"

"He's not dead," Jaspen heard herself say.

Maxamant again leaned right and glanced up at the young slave.

"He has a nukebomb and is coming here to use it on everyone," said Jaspen.

The old man chuckled and swiveled to face her. "Really?" he sneered. "Now the dead traitor has a fictitious weapon. This is a story I must hear."

Jaspen pressed on before he could change his mind. "Thorne revealed the mountain cache to you," she said.

"My men killed the band of Thracks they tracked to the site. Are you telling me, Thorne is in league with Thracks and that these Thracks let themselves be slaughtered for him?"

"Yes, to allay any suspicion."

"Convenient. And beyond far-fetched, but let us pretend you speak the truth. It still doesn't provide a reason."

"So you would move against the Order. Thorne knew alliances would form and all forces would converge here. Once they did, his weapon would be able to finish everyone off."

"So, why then are we not all finished off?" asked Maxamant. "We've been here more than long enough for a dead traitor to annihilate us with his fictitious weapon."

Jaspen's heart quickened as she watched his

stuttergun come up again.

"I expected more of you, Ario," said Maxamant. "To think I'd fall for so feeble a tale. It's almost insulting." He leaned into his scepter, lifted the gun and started to stand.

At that moment, a horn sounded from Anchoresk. It sent a quick series of notes out into the icy air. Several more horns followed in quick succession, playing the same notes.

Then from the rear of Maxamant's lines, another round of horn calls resounded, different from the first, but identical to each other.

Maxamant sat back down in his throne, dropped the gun in his lap and grabbed a lever on the armrest. He gave it a shove to his right and the platform began to rotate southward with a chatter.

Jaspen's father cast her a puzzled look and hastened to the top of the snowmound shoved up by the condor-wedge. She clambered up to stand beside him.

At first, she saw only the tent on the hill. Then, just to the right, a set of sails rose into view. On either side this set, another set appeared and another, until a total of seven sets could be seen. They quickly grew larger and more distinct. Jaspen didn't need to see any more to know what was coming. Or why.

The brief elation she felt at her first thought—

that Jaio had stopped Thorne from using the nukebomb—evaporated in the face of her second thought. Thorne had found another way.

"Thorne *is* alive," whispered Maxamant. "And he actually built them."

"What are those?" asked Jaspen's father.

"Skateships," said Jaspen.

Maxamant leaned back in his throne. "And if you were telling the truth about Thorne," he said. "Then you were probably telling the truth about his associations. Those ships are manned by Thracks! Bows and spears! Did they ever pick the wrong day to test us!"

"They have more than bows and spears," said Jaspen. "And not just stutterguns, but hyperpulse cannons. Everything you have and more."

"Why didn't you tell me of these terrors?" asked her father.

"I never thought they'd be a threat. They run on giant blades. They're not supposed to be able to leave the Ice. But I guess with all this snow..."

Maxamant peered through his telescoptic. "My outer lines are already turning to meet them."

Jaspen looked back out toward the incoming skateships. She could now see them clearly from mast tip to skate. She recognized the leader. *Frostbite.*

The Oromola vessel headed straight for

Anchoresk. Surely, Thorne had replaced Cappen Aiomida with one of his lackeys.

When *Frostbite* seemed about to overrun the farthest defensive musketeer lines it executed an abrupt turn accompanied by the bundling of the sails. Then a sharp boom echoed across the field and *Frostbite* jolted to a halt.

One by one, the other skateships peeled away and began to encircle the combined armies of Anthemar. At even intervals, the skateships folded sails and engaged breaking claws. Soon, Anchoresk and the forces around it found themselves surrounded.

All the cannonports on every skateship then slid open at once.

In response, both the Catalogian and Maxamantan troops hurried to adjust their positions. Musketeers formed new lines. Steamtanks rotated 180 degrees in the surrounding circles of bare ground that had been cleared by their crews.

As Jaspen watched the scene unfold, a foreboding grew in the pit of her gut. Numerous as they were, the Anthemari had no idea what Thorne's monstrous vehicles were about to do to them.

A faint hum to the south drew Jaspen's gaze away from the skateships. Far off, in the sky, a pair of floating cylinders drew nearer. The top cylinder shone smooth and silver and dwarfed the darker, blockier cylinder suspended beneath. As the cylinders grew larger, the hum built to a rumble and features sharpened. Jaspen made out windows in the lower cylinder. Two pods, one on each side, issued streamers of smoke. Engines. They drove fast spinning blades. Horizontal and vertical fins preceded and trailed behind each engine and at the tail of the top cylinder like fish fins.

Jaspen had no doubt every pair of eyes on the field below now took in the sight of this incomprehensible flying machine. It soared toward *Frostbite*. When it was almost above the skateship, the roar of the engines quieted. The blades shuddered to a stop then reversed direction. They spun lazy circles, bringing the floating vessel to a halt directly above *Frostbite* and holding it there.

The sudden total stillness all around brought Jaspen back to the ground.

"We need to get down," she said. "Find cover."

Her father nodded and the two of them started to descend from the snowmound.

But instead of cannonfire, Jaspen heard a lectric pop followed by a loud, sourceless hiss. It seemed to come from everywhere.

"People of Anthemar," said a slightly scratchy

voice she nonetheless instantly recognized.

"Jaio!" She whirled around and raced back to the top of the mound. Her father joined her a moment later.

"Are you certain?" he asked.

"Yes, somehow he stopped—"

"People of Anthemar," Jaio repeated. "Today, each one of us faces a choice. And it is this: will today mark a new beginning for all? Or will today mark our long slow ending, an ending destined to go on and on until a final vengeful thrust marks its absolute conclusion?

"Each of you, in this moment, has the ability to bring either option into being. The first choice, however, requires unanimous agreement. We must all decide to make the beginning happen together.

"It is the harder choice. The inclusive choice. The cooperative choice. The trusting choice.

"The easier choice is the second. The exclusive choice. The coercive choice. The deceiving choice.

"Once any one of you makes the second choice for yourself, you become a thief, for you have stolen it from the rest of us. Yes, this makes you powerful as an emperor, but it is a power rooted in weakness.

"The Ancients relied on this kind of power. It drove their every action including the invention and construction of the weapons we now point at one another. It drove them to amass those weapons in preparation for a battle they never fought because the Ice defeated them first.

"But did you know, their own weakness caused the victorious Ice to cover the land? Yes, the Ancients could not find the strength to change themselves even when they became aware of how their actions were causing their world to unravel. Not until it finally froze did the survivors overcome this weakness and find their strength. But the invitation to weakness remained hidden in the Ice.

"And we found it once the Ice began melting over a thousand years ago. Ever since then, we have been trying to pick up where the Ancients left off. Trying with all our might to revitalize and carry their weakness forward.

"In this effort, we have fought over their leavings. We have striven to emulate their ways. We have tried to dream their dreams.

"Only now has it become possible to see where our efforts have led. Here, to this field where we are about to do one last thing for them: fight their last battle.

"There can be no victory. The caches are all but emptied. Everything we expend and destroy this day will go unreplaced. And the survivors will fight like dogs for whatever remains until the very last scrap is gone.

"The only way to keep this from happening is to accept the new truths of the world we now live in and make for ourselves the choice the Ice made for the Ancients.

"I implore you, leave this fight unfought. Come together to find a different way forward. Let the legacy of the Ancients finally die so that a new legacy, our legacy, might be born."

Jaio's words ended with another lectric pop. A moment later, the cannonports on all the skateships slid closed.

"Idealistic fool," said Maxamant. "I won't even need to give the signal to attack for his delusion to end. The silence will end it. You can already feel the tension building. The distrust. The fear. In a matter of moments, someone will break."

No they won't, thought Jaspen. She slipped behind her father and, as quickly as she could, reached up and yanked the round handle free from the pouch on his back. She thrust the green flag high above her head and waved it in a wide arc, back and forth.

The swift and lethal retaliation she expected from Maxamant didn't happen. Instead, he laughed. His sharp cackle lacked all mirth. "Another idealistic fool!" he proclaimed.

"You can't win," said Jaspen's father. "You face enemies on two fronts."

"I cannot lose, for I am Caesar. And this is my Alesia!"

Jaspen ignored him and just kept waving.

48

ANCHORESK

Sanderzal LeTrenk reached up to adjust the red scarf now wrapped around his head. Beside him stood his Liege-lady, Treyannon Kest and on her other side stood Warwick Gant, her Catalogian advisor. The diminutive monk held a telescoptic to his eye. Even without it, their vantage on the gentle slope at the base of the Catalogian wall, offered an excellent view of the armies arrayed across the field below.

Lined up in double-row formation directly ahead of them, and facing the forces of the Maxamantan alliance, as well as the encircling skateships, Sand's Red Strand riders stood shoulder to shoulder, rifles at the ready. The ends of their signature crimson scarves wafted at their backs as they awaited orders. All they needed were their horses, but the snow had removed cavalry from play. Unlike footmen, thousand pound animals with sharp hooves would punch right through the snowcrust.

"Signal flag!" blurted Gant. "Signal flag!"

"What is the signal?" asked Lady Kest, the aged leader of the Kestian Protectorate.

"Oh, yes, of course. Green," said Gant. "Green. Stand down."

Sand glanced at Lady Kest. "Orders, my lady?" he asked.

She held up her hand to Gant. "The glass, please," she said.

Gant placed the telescoptic in her open palm. She raised the magnifier to her eye and scanned the field.

"Nobody is responding."

"Nobody wants to be first," said Sand.

"Myself among them," she said.

"Please, my lady. Jaio speaks the truth."

"First Anchor, the Ancient major and now Jaio, the boy Thrack." She lowered the telescoptic and slapped it back into Gant's awaiting hand.

"As I told you, my lady," said Sand. "His people sent him here to end the long conflict between our peoples. And that is what he's trying to do. We have to help him."

"No, we don't have to help him," said Lady Kest. "We choose to help him." A mischievous grin upturned her withered lips. She nodded. "Let's see if anyone dares to be second."

"But, my lady!" Gant protested. "We—"

She silenced him with a sharply raised hand.

"Thank you, my lady," said Sand. He ran to the front of the Red Strand lines.

"Riders of the Strand," he called out. "By order of our Liege, Lady Kest, stand down! Again, I say, stand down!" He laid his long-gun on the snow, unbuckled his sword belt and let his command saber drop.

Aside from receiving a few quick sidelong glances of uncertainty, his men complied. They unshouldered their weapons and put them down.

One by one, Sand ran to the commanders of the Kestian regulars to convey the orders. Soon, the entire force from the Protectorate of Kest stood without weapons. On the opposing line less than a hundred paces away, men from an Adruc infantry battalion shifted uneasily.

"Look!" said Gant. He pointed toward the combined forces of Kiddyon and Vantling who faced the far larger armies of Coretgras and Prees. The Kiddyon and Vantling troops were laying down their arms.

Given Lord Froynen's daunting task of confronting the Maxamantans and the Cortegrans, his slow response came as no surprise. However, eventually, he too gave the order, leaving only the Catalogians to heed the green.

It began with the Iron Robes. Then the cannons of the steam carriages dipped until the ends of their barrels nearly touched the snow. Finally, the Daggers laid down their weapons.

All telescoptics then turned to the solitary figure waving the green flag.

The Maxamantan alliance awaited their Lord's response.

But nothing happened.

Sand scanned at the Strand. Some of his men had already started casting glances down at their guns. Unless the second green flag flew soon, all would be lost.

A sudden clatter of movement from the Adruc lines sent Sand's hand for his saber. Of course, his grip closed on empty air.

Fists clenched, he whipped around expecting to face a bayonet charge bare-handed. Instead, he found himself looking at another force in the process of unshouldering weapons and laying them down. The forward row of kneeling musketeers then stood and turned toward their allies.

Sand could hardly believe his eyes. The armies of Cortegras, Prees and Satcha all followed Adrucat's lead.

Finally, Maxamant's army stood alone.

ANCHORESK

Jaspen had never seen a person undergo so profound a transformation so quickly. At first, Lord Salazriole Maxamant's face had held an amused look as the Catalogian allies and then the monks disarmed. But the moment Lady Adrucat's men had joined them in standing down, Maxamant's amusement had vanished.

In its place, a red fury had risen to flush his skin. When at last, his final ally forsook him, he sat paralyzed by rage.

Jaspen kept waving the flag.

"Everyone else has chosen, Lord Maxamant," said Jaspen's father. "The will of Anthemar is clear. We want a new beginning."

"Then," said Maxamant in a barely audible growl. "You shall have it. The beginning of my Empire." He stood with slow deliberate intent, making a show of hefting the stuttergun.

Jaspen turned to look one last time upon her

father and found him looking at her, his face a mirror of the sorrow she felt. So brief was their reunion, to have it end now, like this, seemed the cruelest fate.

Overhead, she barely registered the dark flashes whooshing through the air. The single clack and accompanying staccato of soft thuds seemed distant and unreal. Her eyes followed the sounds and came first to rest on a short black shaft imbedded in the clear shielding. She then noticed five more shafts protruded from Maxamant's chest.

A distant, maniacal tongue-trill of triumph resounded for deep within the Squells as Maxamant's hand fell to his side. The gun slipped free and his head fell to his chest. His wide eye stared at the five sections of the splinterbolt jutting from the middle of growing red stains unevenly dispersed over his torso. He slumped back into his throne.

"Lord Maxamant!" came a dismayed shout from one of the nearest hovels.

Jaspen spun to see two of the moundlike shelters burst open. From each, three men leapt up. They held stutterguns and wore long silver coats of scalloped armor plates like Maxamant's only purple-trimmed instead of gold.

As the men kicked debris aside in their efforts to wade out of the wreckage toward their stricken lord, two figures clad in white fur parkas rose up behind them, one for each trio. The two white figures both held long staffs. And they knew how to use them.

Jaspen tried without success to follow the movements of the mysterious white warriors as, staffs whirling, they pounced on the Maxamantan soldiers. First, six unfired stutterguns went flying through the air. Then six armored men folded in rapid succession and collapsed back into the pile of sticks from which they had emerged. Finally, the two white warriors stood over the inert bodies, quick eyes casting around for more foes.

Into the aftermath stepped a third figure, hooded and dressed in the same white furs. This one, a woman, held no staff. She strode straight toward the tiger-striped steamtank.

The two white warriors took up positions on either side, alert as cats. They crouched low as they neared.

"Quickly," called the hooded woman, her eyes on the slave boy. "Raise the other green flag."

Jaspen looked up to the slave-boy who stood in wide eyed shock behind the seated corpse of his master.

Again, Jaspen saw only a single, triangular handle in the pouch on the boy's back. She turned to the woman.

"He only has red," she said as the trio ducked

past her and pressed themselves into the curve of the condor-wedge.

"Wait," said the boy, his heavily-accented voice weak, but clear. He unslung the flag-pouch, gripped it tightly in one hand and shoved his other hand inside, past the triangular handle. Jaspen heard a rip. Then he pulled out a knotty stick. From the end hung a flag composed of many cloth fragments of various greenish shades all stitched together to form a more-or-less rectangular whole.

The boy held the makeshift flag high above his head and waved it in great sweeping arcs. Tears ran from his eyes and a broad smile filled his face.

A laugh burst from Jaspen and she took up waving her flag with renewed vigor.

"They're standing down!" said Jaspen's father. "Maxamant's army is standing down!"

The hooded woman let out a relieved sigh. "Oan, Pren," she said. "Seal the creeper. And free the boy."

The two white warriors skirted the condor-wedge, one in either direction. Once in position, they nodded to each other and clambered up their respective snowmounds. At the top, they slipped over to the other side.

The woman, Pren, disappeared from view, but the man jumped, or more accurately, seemed to float up onto the top of the tiger-crawler. He landed without a sound and ducked over to the throne platform where the now-shivering boy nonetheless continued to wave his flag.

The white warrior found a release latch on the inside of the clear shield, reached over and opened the front half. Once inside, he searched the old man's plate-coat and, from the first pocket he tried, produced a set of keys. He knelt by the throne leg and started testing the keys one at a time to find the fit.

"I'm Oan," the warrior said to the boy. "What is your name?"

"Ttt-Tandut," said the boy.

Mesoric, thought Jaspen. "What clan?" she asked.

"Blue Cccc-Camel," said the boy, his voice rising with sudden pride. In a rush, he dropped the flag, reached past Oan and snatched up Maxamant's scepter. Eyes blazing, he raised it high.

Oan whirled to block, but the boy brought it down not on him, but on the iron roof of the tiger-crawler. The orb exploded into thousands of pieces.

Tandut then lifted his chin and let out a tongue-trill like the one Jaspen had heard in the Squells. When he finished, he flashed a victorious grin from face to startled face. "We have been avenged," he said, and threw down the scepter.

A moment later, shouting and banging commenced from inside the crawler.

Pren peered over the top of the condor-wedge. "All hatches sealed," she said. "And apparently not a moment too soon."

A click and scrape from the top of the crawler preceded the reappearance of the glass dome. The wide-eyed face within cast frantic looks around, taking in the scene. The revelation of the six fallen soldiers at the edge of the Squells prompted a hasty turn toward the throne.

"We need to get out of here!" said Jaspen's father.

When the Maxamantan's gaze fell upon the lifeless body of his master, he froze.

Jaspen's breath caught. She and the rest of her companions stared at the stunned driver. When he finally moved again and his face came into view, Jaspen could not believe her eyes. He was smiling. "Go!" he called to them, though his shout could barely be heard through the dome. "Go!"

Jaspen and her companions did not need to be told again.

Oan bundled up the boy's chain and handed it to him. As Tandut cradled the heavy mass of links and squeezed past the white warrior, Oan snatched Maxamant's fur hat and put it on the boy's head. It fit surprisingly well. The boy touched it and grinned up at Oan. The warrior winked and hustled the boy forward. Together they clambered down off the crawler.

Ahead of them, Pren bounded over the condor-wedge eliciting an amazed gasp from Tandut. She turned and reached up to grab him as Oan lifted him over. When Tandut stood out of the way, Oan cleared the condor-wedge in a single leap.

Behind him, the crawler emitted the same mechanical chatter that had announced Maxamant's emergence from within. Now, it signaled his descent, back into the tiger-striped behemoth. In the distance to the rear of the crawler, the sound of many running boots carried over the snow.

"Back to Anchoresk," shouted Jaspen's father. The six of them took off.

50

DAYBREAK

All the armies have put down their weapons,"
says Sable from where she stands at the front
gondola rail peering down over the snowy field
through *Daybreak's* telescoptic viewer.

Jaio sits at the voicecaster, not quite believing
her words.

"We did it," he says.

"Every one of us," says Sable. "But we can't
celebrate yet. The leaders must meet."

"Where?" says Jaio. "Any camp we choose
will cause the others to think we're playing
favorites."

"Somewhere neutral then," says Sable. She
raises the telescoptic and pans the landscape.
"There's a dark stone hill in the northwest. The
summit looks to be snow free. And none of the
skateships are close.

"There's nothing clos—"

"Wait!" shouts Sable "Oh, no! Jaio, we have a

problem!"

Jaio leaps up from the voicecaster stool and dashes to the front rail. Sable steps aside. Through the lenses he sees a group of Maxamantan musketeers charging for Jaspen and her five companions.

"The hill it is," he says and races back to the voicecaster. He picks up the transmitter and keys it.

"The choice has been made," he says. Again, he finds the delayed return of his own voice from the skateships unnerving. The eerie echo effect it produces is made all the more haunting by the intervening panes of glass. He wonders what he sounds like to everyone on the ground. No time for that.

"Our new beginning is here. I shall land at our meeting place to await the arrival of your delegations." He releases the button and turns to Aleekio who sits on the control console stool, swinging his legs. "Full forward, Aleekio!"

"Yes!" The boy flicks a switch to change the direction of blade rotation. He waits for the engines to go quiet and then resume their murmur before he twists the power dial to full and hops to the wheel. The now-familiar roar fills the gondola.

"Which way, Cappen!" shouts Aleekio.

"Northwest, to that hill." Jaio points out the window.

"Aye, Cappen" Aleekio spins the wheel.

As they set off, Sable steps back from the telescoptic. "I think Thorne has seen enough," she says. "Lock-up?"

Jaio glances over to the old man bound to the rail. He stands with his head down, apparently lost in some thought, or just contemplating the floor-grate.

Jaio nods, even though the scene on the snow below still looks too much like a chess match waiting to be played.

"About time." Sable draws her dagger and steps over to the old man.

THE SQUELLS

Jaspen barely heard Jaio's voicecaster call as she ran into the Squells with her five companions. She risked a glance back just in time to see several dozen musketeers in Maxamantan uniforms surge into view on either side of the tiger-crawler. *Shouldn't have looked. Bad idea.*

Beside her, she heard Tandut panting. Between his chains and his small legs, he could not hope to keep this pace for long.

"Tandut," she called as she stopped and knelt. "Climb on!"

Tandut veered over and threw an arm around her neck. Jaspen heaved the boy up onto her back and made a seat with both arms behind her. Once he was no longer choking her, she ran. Now she wondered how long she could last.

Behind them, the steamcrawler began to chug. When the squeak and clatter of tracks commenced, she knew the crawler was on the move. She also knew she and her companions were done for.

Then, despite her previous experience, she glanced back again and saw the ominous vehicle growing smaller, accompanied by the footmen.

"Wait," she gasped. "They're falling back."

The rest of the group heaved to a halt and spun to watch this most incomprehensible sight.

Then a growing roar drew their attention upward. The flying vessel fast approached. In almost no time, it soared overhead and continued on toward the distant hill Jaio had indicated in his call.

"No time to marvel," said the hooded woman. "Follow that ship."

Jaspen hitched Tandut higher on her back and set off again with her companions.

They hadn't taken more than a few steps when her left foot broke through the crust. She sank in almost to her knee and nearly dropped Tandut.

The boy climbed off and she worked to extract himself. "We'd better hurry, or this journey is going to get a lot harder and a lot slower."

As they waited for Jaspen to regain her footing, the boy shivered and clutched his knot of chain. Oan removed his staff and pack and pulled off his parka. He then lifted the fur hat off Tandut's head and slid the parka over the boy's small body. The Oan-sized garment practically enveloped Tandut. "We'll take turns," said Oan and placed the hat back on the boy's head.

The group then pushed on, headed northwest. In the far distance, they watched the flying ship descend to the summit of the dark, rocky hill, settle and go quiet. Closer at hand, the early afternoon sun was making slick mush of the upper layer of the snow crust. The threat of having to peghole all the way to the hill inspired a brisk pace.

They soon settled into a kind of rhythm and Jaspen's attention turned to their mysterious, white-clad companions; the hooded woman in particular. Jaspen glanced toward the woman just as she reached up with her right mitten to adjust her hood. The mitten had no thumb.

Jaspen froze, which caused everyone else to turn her way and stop as well.

Jaspen stared at the woman. "Who are you?" she asked.

The woman peered back through the shadow of her hood. Only the whites of the woman's wide eyes could be seen within its depths. They aimed from Jaspen to her half-raised mitten then back to Jaspen.

Finally, the woman raised her left hand and pulled off the right mitten.

Jaspen stared at the woman's stump waiting for her mind to accept what her heart already knew.

"Quoia?" whispered Jaspen's father.

"I'm here, Dalsen," said the woman as she tugged the mitten back on then pulled back her hood.

Despite the startling celestial tattoos, the tear-streaked, smiling face before Jaspen could easily have been a reflection in a pool of still water. Yes, lines of gray streaked the woman's sandy hair and more lines creased her skin, but otherwise, the two of them looked the same.

The woman's legs seemed to give out and she dropped to her knees. "Jaspen," she said. "My daughter."

"Mother?"

The woman nodded.

Jaspen's mind could only dredge up one thing to say. "Why did you leave me?"

"Oh, Jaspen." She looked into Jaspen's eyes for a moment then glanced at Jaspen's father. "Dalsen. Forgive me. I had to." Her eyes shifted back to Jaspen. "So this day might come, I had to."

"What do you mean?" asked Jaspen's father. "You were safe. Nobody suspected. You didn't have to just disappear."

"I did, Dalsen. Or I would never have been able to go. Seeing your face would have broken my resolve."

"How did your leaving me and my father lead

to this day?" asked Jaspen.

Jaspen's mother rose to her feet. "To answer that, I need to tell you how I first came to Anthemar many rounds ago. But before I do, we must keep moving." She began walking.

Jaspen and the others set off with her. Jaspen wanted this reunion with her mother to feel like the reunion with her father, but in the absence of a prior relationship to rekindle, it felt more like trying to light a fire with no fuel.

"You were a captured Ghost," said Jaspen's father. "And I freed you, hid you, protected you. Loved you." His voice threatened to break.

"All true," said Jaspen's mother. "Except for the means of my capture. I let it happen."

"You…" Jaspen's father began. His voice then failed.

"Why?" asked Jaspen.

"To find a way to infiltrate Anthemar and learn if coexistence with the clans might be possible." She took a hesitant step toward Jaspen's father. "You convinced me it was, Dalsen. And as soon as I learned I carried another child, I knew my time to leave had come."

"You didn't even tell me," said Jaspen's father.

"Please, understand, Dalsen. I couldn't add anymore pain to that choice or I wouldn't have been able to make it. But the Plain and the Steppe both needed a child; siblings, to bind the two

peoples in blood. The girl stayed here with you."
She cast a hopeful look at Jaspen. "My mother,
Taika, took the boy to the Steppe. I would have
taken him myself, but my Ghost tattoos made my
return impossible. So, I had to let him go." Her
mouth turned down as the effort to hold back
tears grew harder.

"You don't wear the skull," said Jaspen.

"It's still there, hidden now in the night."

"Then why didn't you come back here?" asked
Jaspen's father. "For your daughter. For me. I
could have kept you safe as I already had for
years."

"No, Dalsen. We were only safe so long as you
lived in the outermost shadows as a lowly monk.
Once you became a Tributan, you stepped forever
into the light. An illicit lover with a skull tattoo
could not long have remained a secret."

Jaspen saw the anguish of this truth carve itself
into her father's face. She couldn't bear it.

"After you gave up your son, then what did
you do?" she asked in an attempt return to the
story.

"I wandered," said her mother. "In what
remained of my mind, I thought my route aimless,
but eventually I found myself in lands of the
Numola who dwell in the Cindermist Mountains,
far in the southeast, between the Steppe and the
Midewin Valley. The Numola are distant kin of

my people, the Oromola. Thanks to this kinship, they accepted me as one of their own, under one condition. I somehow had to erase the mark of the Ghost. This," she gestured to her night-inked face, "was my solution."

"So how did you end up coming back here?" asked Jaspen.

"The Numola belong to group called the Keepers Council. This Council is very old. It exists to keep watch over the lingering dangers left by the Ancients and to warn others away. Where possible, we help dismantle those dangers. And in places such as Anthemar where relic technologies and ideas have been culturally incorporated, we help phase them out in favor of indigenous alternatives.

"We also invite every culture we encounter to join the Council and establish a Hall where select relics are kept and new generations of Keepers are trained. But only for as long as necessary. The Keepers ultimate aim is to eventually empty and dismantle their own Halls and become extinct for lack of purpose. Unfortunately, thanks to the Ancient's utter disregard for the lasting consequences of their actions, that day is still a long way off.

"As for how the Council led me back here, when I learned of it, I saw an opportunity to return to Anthemar as a Mediant."

"What is a Mediant?" asked Jaspen.

"A Mediant is kind of Keeper who travels far afield to help free the people who are caught in the thrall of the Ancients and thus bound to a borrowed legacy instead of their own."

"How many people besides the Numola have been freed?" asked Jaspen.

"Many, but none so tightly bound as the people of Anthemar."

"What do you mean?"

"The Ice offered Anthemar enticements of power unknown anywhere else we've yet traveled."

"The relic weapons," said Jaspen's father.

Jaspen's mother nodded. "Giving them up will be very hard for you, I fear. They have insinuated themselves into every aspect of your lives. But I have come to help you unravel from their coils."

"How?"

"In truth, I am not sure. Each instance of unraveling is unique in its expression. But what they all share is a common conviction to leave the ways and works of the long-dead past behind. From that conviction, the 'how' unfolds as it will, like meltwater first carving the snowchannel it will follow from then on. You can't know the route the water will take before it starts flowing.

Jaspen's mother pointed her stump toward the

hill. "Whoever's in that skyship. He just released the water."

Jaspen considered letting the answer be a surprise. But then decided against it. "His name is Jaio."

Jaspen's mother stumbled and almost went down. She righted herself and looked over at Jaspen, disbelief in her tearing eyes. "Jaio?"

Jaspen nodded. Best to just put it all out there. "He's the Ghost Orol of the clans. Taika sent him."

52

THE NAMELESS HILL

Jaio, Sable, and Aleekio climb down out of the cloudship on the far side of the broad hilltop. Though larger and higher than the Sacred Hill of the Steppe, the gentle summit of dark, almost black, stone reminds Jaio of the place where he passed his fateful solitude. That night of the Kestrel Moon seems so long ago and so far away, another lifetime, another world.

Remnant pockets of snow dot the rock-strewn ground where new green shoots struggle to right themselves after being flattened by the early summer blizzard. The Ice may be melting, Jaio thinks, but it is still the real power in this land, capable of casting down a frigid reminder at any time of year.

Jaio breathes in the familiar scent of sage and looks southeast. Somewhere nearby, a rasper finch grinds out its monotonous call. Jaio never thought he'd find so much joy in that sound. But after all his weeks in the birdless realm of the Ice, it strikes him as pure music. He offers silent thanks to the drab little rasper.

Far off in the northwest, on the plain below the hill, a trio of animals struggles to open the gap between themselves and the cloudship. The depressions where they bedded during the storm now appear as three oblong shadows with a single-file furrow-line moving away. The play of light, distance, and snow gives the large quadrupeds a bluish cast. Jaio's mind automatically tries to identify them. They don't move like rhinos or pakas or anything else he recognizes and when one turns slightly to glance toward the hill, he sees a pair of humps on its back.

"Camels," says Sable, providing an answer to his unasked question.

"I've never seen camels," says Jaio.

"Me neither," says Aleekio.

"They are from much farther north," says Sable, her words quiet and weighted with sudden emotion.

"Well, they're here now, like us," says Aleekio.

Jaio offers his hand to Sable. "And they're *with* us," he says.

She takes his hand and looks over at him, the smile in her eyes at once both sad and grateful. "Yes, they're with us."

"But they did come a bit early," Aleekio adds.

"This snow will melt fast," says Jaio. "And from now on, winter will no longer be able keep pace with the Thaw. The same goes for the winter in our hearts. It must thaw as well lest we lose our place in the world." He turns away from the camels and focuses his attention in the opposite direction.

In the distance, the Adminithedral tower looms. He and his companions start to head that direction. Before they've taken three steps, Aleekio reaches up and grabs Sable's other hand. She glances at Jaio. Her smile has lost a little more of its sadness.

Side by side, they head east. Low scrub scrapes across their shins and dry, yellow, year-old seed pods rattle as the trio makes their way toward the rimrock on the other side of the hilltop.

At the subtle peak of the hill, they come upon a ring of soot-stained stones with a few long-cold coals inside. Smudges of pale green and yellow lichen grow over the remains. The sight gives Jaio an idea.

"We need to build a welcoming fire," he says, releases Sable's hand, and starts gathering stones and arranging them into a new ring next to the old one.

"Why not use that ring?" asks Sable.

"There's already a fire in that one," he says.

Sable and Aleekio give him puzzled looks.

"I have a plan," he says. "Do you see any fuel?"

"No problem," says Aleekio. He lets go of Sable, whirls, and dashed back toward *Daybreak*.

Sable shrugs and follows, leaving Jaio alone to build the ring.

The delight Jaio finds in the simple task of gathering and arranging stones surprises him. This too he has missed more than he would have imagined. Doing it again feels somehow like coming home. He takes a long slow breath. The fears and uncertainties in his mind surrender to the quiet, effortless pull and push of air in his lungs. And for an all-too-brief moment, Jaio is in the moment.

Aleekio hops down out of the cloudship carrying a single stick in each hand. He holds them up proudly. "Firewood!" he shouts.

Behind the boy, Sable appears with an armful. "There's quite a bit more," she says.

Aleekio and Sable drop their respective loads nearby and join Jaio as he lays the last of the stones down, completing the ring. As grateful as he is to have them near, his delight melts away in their presence. His mind wastes no time rushing in to fill the vacancy with what ifs and worry; the meeting might fail; he might lose them; he might lose everyone who means anything to him.

Sable casts Jaio a concerned look. "Are you all right?" she asks.

"Uh, yes. Let's go see what's happening in the valley." He starts off in the direction of the soaring glass tower.

Soon, the wide valley comes into view below. The defined patterns of the different armies have grown amorphous. Several are mingling. Jaio decides to take that as a good sign.

The surrounding skateships bustle with activity. Small knots of Ghosts from each move toward one another; the delegations coming together to make the ascent to the hilltop. Parties from the Protectorate camps do the same. Another group from Anchoresk trails some distance behind the nearest group of six: Jaspen, and her five unknown companions. They are only a few hundred paces away, but moving slowly against the softening snow.

"Stay here to greet them," says Jaio. "I need to go start the fire." Without waiting for a reply, Jaio hastens back toward the fire ring.

53

THE NAMELESS HILL

Masisda!" came a shout from the snow slope below the rimrock perch where Sable and Aleekio awaited the arrival of Jaspen and her companions. Hearing the Mesoric term for a daughter born of a mother's sister came as a shock to Sable. She scanned the five climbers and found the smallest one waving. The oversized sleeve of the figure's white fur parka flopped back and forth. Sable recognized the face beneath the rim of the gold-tasseled fur hat.

"Tandut!" A swell of emotion rose from deep within Sable's core. If her cousin lived, perhaps other members of the Blue Camel clan did as well.

"Masisda, Tawen!" the boy called again. He stopped waving and resumed climbing with renewed energy.

No surprise, Tandut made it to the rim first. He thrust his arm out of the parka sleeve and reached up to grab Sable's outstretched hand. She helped haul him up to the top of the hill and almost fell over backwards when he lunged into a tight hug. A bundle of chain crashed to the ground at his feet. Sable then felt the cold hard metal of the collar shackled around Tandut's neck. Her fault.

She couldn't keep the tears from flowing as she held him close.

"One-eye said I was the last Camel," he whispered and gave a wet sniff. "But he lied. Masisda Tawen and Masisso Gendut both live!"

Tawen jolted with a start and freed herself from the hug to look into Tandut's eyes. Despite his youth, they stood face to face. "How do you know Gendut lives?" she asked. "Did you see him?"

"No, he was far away. But he gave his victory cry after he avenged us, Masisda!"

"How? How did he avenge us?"

"He killed One-eye," said Tandut.

Sable's fear transformed into something she couldn't quite identify; a discomfiting mix of profound relief and terrible guilt. Gendut had not revealed the reason for Maxamant's destruction of her clan. So, Tandut had no idea she was the cause of his enslavement. "I'm sorry," she breathed.

"Sorry? For what?"

Sable considered telling him the truth, but this

did not seem the time. "I'm sorry you didn't see Gendut," she said.

"I called back. He'll find us."

Sable strongly doubted she or Tandut would ever see Gendut again. His crime surpassed hers in the eyes of the Clan. To kill a brother and two of Tandut's elder siblings for horses would almost certainly insure his absence. Sable decided she would keep this truth to herself as well. Tandut needed family more than truth.

"We found each other, Masisso," she said.

Tandut hugged her again.

To their left, Jaspen and the rest of her party clambered up through a nearby cleft in the rimrock. Sable and Tandut broke apart. Tandut gathered up the chain and turned with Sable to head toward the others. As they walked, Aleekio tapped Tandut on the shoulder and stuck out a hand.

"I'm Aleekio," he said.

Tandut cast an uncertain glance at Sable.

Aleekio continued to hold out a hand and adjusted his goggles with the other.

Sable smiled. "Sorry," she said. "In all the excitement, I forgot introductions." She nodded to the begoggled boy. "Aleekio is my good friend. And I think he'll be able to help get you out of that collar."

"No problem," said Aleekio.

Tandut considered Aleekio's extended hand for a moment then reached out and took hold. "I'm Tandut," he said. "Tawen's Masisso."

Aleekio's brow furrowed. "Tawen? Masisso?" He released Tandut's hand.

"Tawen is my clan name and Masisso means the son of my mother's sister."

Aleekio's furrows deepened.

"Tandut is my cousin."

Aleekio's eyes widened with understanding. He smiled at Tandut. "Let's go bust that collar," he said. Before Tandut could reply, Aleekio grabbed his hand again and dragged him away toward *Daybreak*.

Sable turned her attention back to Jaspen and her companions. One of the men wore only a woolen tunic over his torso. His nose, cheeks and ears glowed red in the chill air.

"Aleekio," Sable called out. "Will you help Tandut into an airsuit too? I think Jaspen's friend needs his parka back."

"We're on it," said Aleekio.

Sable smiled and prepared to greet Jaspen and the four newcomers.

THE NAMELESS HILL

On his way to the fire ring, Jaio veers to pluck the straightest, stoutest seed pod stem he can find. IT takes him a few moments as most have been bowed and broken by the snow. Then he finds a pair of cobbles, one hard quartzite, the other, a softer basalt. Finally, he seeks out a large, dead sage plant. The main stem is nearly as thick as his wrist, and elevated above the ground where it has had time to dry out.

With a few deft blows of Quartzite against basalt, Jaio fashions a chopper. He uses the sharp edge he's just made to cut out the thickest segment of the sage stem. Standing it on end, he then uses the chopper to split it into thirds. The middle section will work perfectly as a platform.

He pockets the platform, the hammer and the chopper and gathers clumps of brittle branches and old dry leaves as he closes the final distance to the fire ring. There, he kneels, piles the kindling in the center of the ring and lays the long branch aside. Removing the chopper and platform from his pocket, he carves the spindle notch, places it under his foot on a patch of dry stone, picks up the straight branch and nests the fat end in the notch.

Branch pressed between open palms, he starts to spin. Back and forth the spindle whirls and soon smoke begins to billow forth. He spins until a thick streamer is rising up into the air. Finally, he stops.

The smoke continues to swirl away. He moves the notched platform to the side. The little coal left behind breathes and glows for a few moments while he prepares the kindling nest. Once finished, he lifts the coal into the nest with a piece of sage bark then adds a few gentle breaths of his own.

A flame jumps up from the smoke. Hot fingers reach out to snatch the surrounding twigs and leaves. Jaio quickly adds larger pieces until he has a small blaze crackling at the heart of the ring.

He gathers a few of the stout branches from the bundle brought by Sable and lays them on. Soon, the flames are leaping, snapping, sending a column of rippling heat and fast flowing smoke into the sky. Jaio just stands and stares.

"Jaio," says a familiar voice from behind.

He turns and there before him stands Jaspen at

the front of a most unusual group of people; a woman in white furs with the night sky and a kestrel moon tattooed on her face, a tall man with a graying beard wearing a Catalogian robe, a slight woman also in white with a long staff fastened to her back, and a young man in parka pants and a woolen tunic also with a long staff protruding above his shoulder. To the side of the newcomers stands Sable.

Jaspen and the strangers are all looking at Jaio with very odd expressions on their faces. All at once, he sees anticipation, excitement, anxiety, uncertainty, and a whole host of lesser expressions he can't quite identify. The only thing for certain is, the bewildering combination mutes his enthusiasm for this reunion with his one-handed companion.

"Jaspen?"

"Jaio," says Jaspen in a way that often precedes bad news and he realizes none of the other members of the Pride are with her.

"Kem, Sand, Rawl, Benethan?" he blurts, feeling his heart-rate increase.

"Benethan is hurt, but alive and the rest are okay," she says. "Everything is okay."

"Then what?" Hearing her words has not helped to calm his heart.

"There's no way to do this gently," says Jaspen.

"Do what?" Sweat erupts on his brow.

Jaspen turns to the newcomers and points her stump at the tall Catalogian. "This is my father, Dictorian Consul, Dalsen Ario."

This comes as no surprise, but Jaio can tell, Jaspen is not finished.

The man offers Jaio an unreadable nod and glances at the woman with the moon tattoo. Jaspen turns to her next.

"And this is my mother. Annequoia Moon."

Jaspen's mother? This is a surprise. But what does it have to do with him?

Jaspen's introductions end there and she looks back at him. Why doesn't she finish?

The answer comes slowly, rising from the memory of his brief time at Vanquisher's Break when Aleekio's mother, Mayrel, told him the name of his mother.

Annequoia.

Jaio's eyes widen with sudden understanding.

His legs start to give out and Jaspen leaps to his side to help steady him. "I bet you never thought you had a sister," she says.

55

THE NAMELESS HILL

As the introductions and stories unfolded around the fire, Jaspen kept a close eye on her brother in case his legs gave out again. However, aside from his initial shock, Jaio seemed to be soaking up the new information with enthusiasm. How was it, she wondered, that he could welcome the sudden appearance of parents he never knew, but she felt only resentment for Annequoia?

"Jaio!" came a gruff shout from the southeast. "You silver-tongued magician!"

Everyone turned that way. Headed toward them were Rawl and Kem accompanied by Shasten and a contingent of Iron Robes, many of whom were helping the most aged of a dozen monks, each with silver shoulder sashes.

Jaspen's father broke from the circle around the fire and hastened toward them. "Tributans!" he called out. "Welcome!"

Jaspen's father joined them and walked with

them to the fire where space was made. Iron Robes produced stools for the Tributans who seemed eager to get off their feet.

Everyone settled and introductions commenced, with careful avoidance of the subject of familial ties. When attention turned to Jaio and they learned that his had been the voice from above, more than one of the monks shifted uneasily.

"Brother Ario," said one of the younger Tributans. "Do you really expect us to believe a Thrack boy capable of such persuasive articulation? Or that he possesses so keen a knowledge of the Ancients?"

"When the rest of the delegations arrive, you shall have the opportunity to judge for yourself, Brother Bomechor."

The imposing man huffed, crunched up his face and turned his gaze to the fire.

After that, a few hushed conversations occurred at sporadic intervals, but for the most part, all parties gave their attention to the flames. Aleekio and Tandut, who was now unshackled and wearing a red airsuit, made sure the fire stayed well-stoked. Jaspen couldn't imagine what might have happened had there not been this bright point of focus.

The leaders of the Protectorates arrived next. Sand smiled and nodded from his place beside his

Liege-lady who strode toward the fire with surprising vigor given her obvious age. Jaspen also recognized the Maxamantan representative. The driver of the tiger-crawler.

"Who is that?" she asked her father with a gesture to their unexpected ally.

"Ennard Maxamant; Salazriole's nephew and heir. He appears to be open to a different future than the one envisioned by his late uncle."

The imposing man glanced Jaspen's way and offered a quick, conspiratorial nod.

Again, the circle opened to admit the new arrivals. As they took up places around the fire, tensions remained surprisingly low. Lieges and Tributans quickly struck up conversations that sounded almost casual.

That all changed when the Ghosts arrived. The large troop of Cappens trailed by key members of their crews, all tight-jawed and looking out through their skeletal masks of ink, raised the temperature around the fire well above the heat put out by the flames.

Jaspen spotted Cappen Aiomida, Lash, Segray, Bengus, Syree, Kahala, Brye, Keethu, Teeg, and Galees as well as a few others she recognized from her time with the Oromola Guardians. She glanced at Jaio to see if he too had spotted them. But he hadn't even looked up from the fire.

When the first of the Ghosts reached the circle,

it remained closed. Jaspen was about to nudge Kem and Rawl to make room when her father stepped aside, nodding to the Tributans to shift. Much muttering ensued as the monks struggled to their feet and tightened the spacing of their stools.

Aiomida, Leegon, the other five skateship Cappens as well as Segray stepped into the gap. The rest gathered behind. No sooner had they settled than Aleekio and Tandut squeezed through the crowd carrying more branches.

Jaio turned his attention from the fire and looked their way. "No more wood," he said.

The two boy's shoulders slumped. They nodded, dropped their branches in the adjacent pile and plopped down on their rears in front of the flames.

All eyes turned to Jaio. He gazed without expression from face to face all the way around the circle. He didn't even pause when his eyes fell on those he knew. Except for Jaspen and, last of all, the person next to him. Sable.

Then he looked back into the flames. Already, their reach had diminished. At Jaspen's back, she could feel the cold pressing in, driving the heat toward its source.

Still, Jaio waited.

A few looks of uncertainty passed between members of the circle. But nobody broke the silence.

It held until the last struggling finger of flame let out a soft pop and transformed into a line of smoke.

"Here we are," said Jaio as he looked up. "Gathered like storm clouds around the embers of the past."

Jaspen could hear Segray quietly translating for the Ghosts.

"For a thousand years, we have been laying on fresh tinder." Jaio nodded to Aleekio and Tandut and mouthed, "Now, more wood." The boys beamed, leapt to their feet and laid several branches on the coals. They then stepped back and stared at the sticks, entranced, waiting.

The wood quickly began to smoke.

Jaio stepped up between the boys and knelt.

"Our storm could have brought the winds of battle." He blew into the embers. Orange radiance swelled and heat surged out. The smoking sticks began to pop.

"But instead, we chose to meet here, to bring rain." He reached into his parka and pulled out a waterskin. He uncapped it and poured the contents over the sticks. They puffed and hissed, sending up hot bursts of steam as the water ran down into the embers.

Jaio's waterskin ran dry and the steam abated. Peripheral coals still glowed and smoke threads wove through the blackened sticks into the sky.

"But our work is not done." He leaned close to the coals again and inhaled deeply.

"No, don't!" shouted Aleekio.

Jaio smiled and straightened. "The embers are still hot. What we decide today will determine if they will continue to cool down or re-ignite. It is the most dangerous moment. We cannot risk even the slightest breeze." He wafted a hand once over the smoking coals, unleashing numerous momentary flashes of radiance. Near the center, a solitary flicker of flame made a brief appearance then guttered.

He stood. "The question is how do we keep the winds from rising again?" He lifted the waterskin and held it upside down. A single drop fell from the lip. "We have to do better than count on the rain. It might not come. The only lasting choice is to let the embers die.

"I don't know how we'll do that. None of us do. We have all lived for a thousand years by fanning the embers. We have come to see the embers as essential to life itself. So total is this view, we completely overlook any evidence suggesting otherwise. Even when it is right before our eyes."

Jaio stepped to the neighboring fire ring and knelt. "Look closely at the coals in this old circle. They are not cold. They burn green, with life. Yet, lay on as much wood as you like. Blow as hard as you want. No conflagration will erupt. No flames will scald you. No rain will be needed to put the fire out. In fact, rain only feeds it.

"The challenge we all face together today is to relearn how to live from these coals. I say relearn, because living from the fire in this ring is our deepest tradition. We've just forgotten what our ancestors knew for millennia before we came to live off the flames of the Ancients.

"We can recover true prosperity when we once again honor the one imperative that doesn't change: we must always live by the fire in this circle." Jaio pointed into the lichen covered fire ring at his feet. "Without exception."

Leegon growled a single clipped word in his own language.

"Impossible," Segray translated.

"No," said Jaio. "I just learned that it has been done many times." He turned to his and Jaspen's mother and bade her forward. Annequioa Moon stepped up beside him.

Jaio introduced her and stepped back. Jaspen and Jaio's mother then told a highly edited version of her story including the consise description of the Keepers Council that Jaspen had heard earlier. The Mediant's account ended with an invitation to join the Council and an offer of help to all gathered parties in stepping out of the smoking embers and into the ring of green fire.

Leegon remained silent and Jaspen glanced his way. To her surprise, she saw no sign of the Ghost Cappen.

56

THE NAMELESS HILL

A series of loud bangs from the west sends a
startled jolt through the whole assembly. More
than one hand shoots inside a parka or robe as all
heads turn toward the noise.

Jaio whirls in time to see puffs of black smoke
rising from the engines of *Daybreak*. Leegon leans
out the rear hatch brandishing a stuttergun. He
cuts loose a burst into the air.

"This is the only green fire I believe in," he
yells. "Best of luck with yours! See you when we
come back!"

Jaio glances toward the front of the gondola
and through the glass he sees Thorne standing at
the wheel. The old man turns and looks out the
window. His eyes find Jaio's and narrow. He
looks away and his mouth moves as he gives some
soundless command. The anchor cable
disconnects with a pop and the cloudship races
upward.

Thorne turns the vessel southeast, in the rough direction of Vanquisher's Break.

All around circle, Jaio sees more than one ancient weapon pointed skyward.

"Put them away," he yells. "We're done with the Ancients."

"But you heard his threat!" shouts Lash.

Jaio is at a loss to respond. They need time to work out how to defend against such threats without reverting to their old habits.

Lash is taking aim along with several Iron Robes as well as a number of the guards who accompanied their Liege-lords, including Sand who has his long-gun trained on the cloudship, red dot reflecting off its shiny skin. Suddenly, one of *Daybreak's* engines gives a sharp, smoky cough. This is followed in close succession by coughs from the other engine. Then, within a pair of long breaths, both motors die. The propellers jolt to a stop and the cloudship begins to veer from southeast to southwest as it climbs higher and higher. Unless they set down on the Plain, the only thing ahead of them is the Ice.

"Engine juice gone," says Aleekio.

"Nothing but a big tuft of thistledown now," chuckles Rawl.

Lash lets out a single snort of contemptuous air and looks at Jaio. "So, you do not have all the answers," he says in rough Anthemari. "Good."

Jaio expects the tall Ghost to return the stuttergun to its hiding place in his parka. Instead, Lash steps up to the old, overgrown fire ring. He leans down and lays his weapon amid the lichen encrusted coals inside. "Together," he glances around the gathered circle, "I'm sure we'll come up with another way," he says.

This appears to serve as the cue for the others holding stutterguns to follow suit. Jaio recognizes the challenge in Lash's words. The burden of the unknown future grows as the pile of weapons in the old fire ring grows. Jaio is so lost in thought, he almost doesn't notice Aleekio shuffle up next to him.

"Looks like Daddy's not going home," says Aleekio.

Jaio kneels down so they are face to face. "Looks like."

"Mommy will be sad. I miss Mommy."

"Speaking of Mommy, does she know where you are?"

"Of course not, silly. I was hiding when Janpesh broke into the cave. I heard him tell his Ghosts not to hurt anyone, so I knew Mommy would be okay."

"Janpesh is in control of the Break?"

Aleekio shrugs. "Probably. I snuck onto the spider ship and we left before he reached us. I don't think Daddy even knows what Janpesh did.

But now I want to go home."

"When this is all over," says Jaio. "I plan on heading back to the Steppe with word of what we've done here. The Break is on the way. I'll make sure you get back home, Breakborn Brother." He gave Aleekio's shoulder a firm squeeze. "But at the moment, I need to keep talking with all of these people. Maybe, you and Tandut can find more wood. Now that my demonstration is over, the fire needs a boost."

"All right!" Aleekio hops down and runs to collect his Mesoric friend. Jaio marvels at how easily they found their friendship. The divide between Breakborn and Mesoric played no part. They both still dwelled in the common country of childhood.

The final stuttergun clatters into the pile and everyone returns to their place.

"The subject with which to begin these proceedings appears to have been decided," says the abrasive Tributan, Bomechor. "Self defense; supposing we equal the field among ourselves, how do we do so without increasing our vulnerability to outside threats?"

Jaio's mother steps forward. "The threats to Anthemar are minimal," she says. "The truth is you have been a far greater danger to your neighbors than they have been or ever will be to you. Nobody else has found but a tiny fraction of the relics you have unearthed along your border with the Ice. And most of these other peoples have already joined the Keeper's Council. In this atmosphere, the banded staff and the training to use it provide all the protection they need."

"A staff?" Bomechor scoffs.

The two Escorts step up next to Jaio's mother. "May we?" asks Oan. Jaio's mother nods.

"Allow me," says Pren. She unclasps her staff and holds it before her. Jaio sees it clearly for the first time. A dark, fine-grained hard wood makes up most of its length, but at both ends and in the middle he sees an encircling, fist-wide band of dull, silver metal.

"I challenge anyone among you to attack me in close combat," she says.

One of the guards standing at the shoulder of Lord Satcha smirks and steps into the opening. He wears a command saber at his hip. But he leaves it there and raises his fists. "Wouldn't want to risk cutting you," he says.

"Suit yourself." Pren hefts her staff and settles into a semi-crouch. There, she waits.

The guard surges forward and swings. Pren barely moves to counter, and rather than deflect his blow, she seems to catch it and turn it. His own momentum spins him almost completely around and he nearly falls over.

He whips back to face her and lunges forward

with his whole body as if to crush her beneath his huge frame. She simply sidesteps, slides her staff in so his belly catches it and spins it around behind him where its arc concludes in a well planted blow on his rear. He plows face first into the ground.

He surges to his feet, blood on his lips and fury in his eyes. He draws his sword. With lethal intent, he surges forward and swings. The falling blade clangs against a metal band and carries through into the dirt while the other end of the staff loops around and comes down hard on the man's head. He drops and stays down, groaning and groping for his skull. Two comrades help him back into the circle of onlookers.

"My turn!" shouts another guard, this one standing behind Ennard Maxamant. The guard comes out with blades in each hand, saber and dagger.

The two weapons offer no advantage. He falls just as fast as the Satchan. The third aggressor fares no better. Nor does the fourth, fifth or sixth.

Into the hesitation that now prevails, Brother Shasten steps forward. The Iron Robe picks up a stout stick from the wood pile, gives it a couple spins to test the balance and faces off. His advance is lightening fast. Even so, Pren hardly moves to intercept and the next thing Jaspen sees is the monk stumbling to regain his footing.

After that, his next approaches are more cautious, but he is unable to bypass the deflections of her staff.

Their dance goes on for some time. Finally, sweating and panting, the monk yields. Pren nods a respectful acceptance of his surrender. Her breathing does not seem to have increased in the slightest.

Pren waits for the next challenger. For several long breaths nothing happens, then much to Jaio's dismay, Jaspen steps forward.

He catches her eye and shakes his head. She simply turns her attention to her opponent.

Pren faces her and nods. Numerous spectators groan in anticipation of the impending route. Jaspen settles into a slight crouch, her one good hand raised to block whatever Pren might throw at her. In response, Pren settles again into her ready stance.

And there they stand, and stand. Neither moves. Finally, Jaspen eases out of her stance and straightens.

"Well done," says Pren. "You win."

"What!" bellows the Satchan guard who is holding a rag to his swollen lip.

"Metaflexion is a defensive art," says Pren. "With it you use the energy of your opponent against your opponent. If the opponent applies no energy, then there is no conflict. This is how

Keepers help keep the peace."

"It is very effective," says Jaio's mother. "And metaflexion is only one aspect, the physical aspect, of a much broader philosophy called the Rounding Way. With the Way, we Keepers approach all aspects of life using the same principles Pren just demonstrated with the staff. We would be happy to teach anyone who has an interest in learning."

Brother Shasten raises a hand. "Please, consider me your first pupil."

More Iron Robes as well as Protectorate Guards and Oroken Ghosts express their eagerness for instruction. Jaspen steps back into the circle.

Jaio glances over at Tributan Bomechor. The imposing man offers what looks like a conciliatory nod, but at the same time folds his arms. "Perhaps, in matters carnal, the people of Anthemar and the Th... Oroken might be able to come to some agreement, but in matters of spirit and soul, there can be none. Our differences are beyond reconciliation."

Jaio feels the Founding Orb hanging at his chest. The moment he has dreaded has come, and much sooner than he imagined it would.

"Our two peoples might seem of different hearts, Tributan," says Jaio. "But the differences do not go that deep."

"Nonsense! You are heathen savages! Painting skulls on your faces! Perpetrating merciless massacres! Engaging in senseless destruction at every turn!

"I will not spar with you on these matters except to say that everything you speak of, and equal assertions I might offer, must be left in the past. We must choose to find our way forward from here in kinship." These last words Jaio adds as bait. And Bomechor bites.

"But we share no kinship."

Jaio reaches into his parka and pulls out the pouch with the orb.

"What is this?" hisses Bomechor.

"It is the most sacred object of my people. We call it the Founding Orb. The story it tells informs every aspect of our lives. And it also reveals the common origin shared by the people of Anthemar and the people of the Steppe."

Bomechor surges to his feet. "Blasphemy!"

"Sit down, Brother," orders Jaio's father. "We will listen."

Bomechor casts frantic looks at the other Tributans searching for support. They merely watch him with hard faces. Many are clearly displeased, but not enough to overcome their curiosity.

Bomechor drops back onto his stool.

Jaio waits for quiet, then lifts the orb out of the

pouch and places it on an open palm held up into the radiant light of the sun.

"Te-Tttesss-esst. T-Testtt," says the orb. More than a few dismayed gasps resound from the Anthemari portions of the crowd. The Ghosts merely wait in obvious anticipation to once again hear the story of Doctor Bel and Hernán.

And so, the ancient event unfolds on another hilltop in a land on the opposite side of the Ice from where Jaio first heard the heartbeat of his people.

Periodic pauses interrupt the narrative so he can offer explanations of the sounds they are hearing. But even so, the recording seems to take no time to reach its conclusion. Jaio covers the orb and tucks it away.

Around him, many blank eyes reveal gazes turned inward, lost in deep introspection. Finally, Bomechor huffs.

"So, this Belara Oroken created the orbs we both use for guidance," he says. "They are not the same orbs. We are not the same people."

"Both the Anthemari and the Oroken derive their meaning and identity from the voices of the past," says Jaio. "That in itself is the common thread. You may have striven for a millennium to piece together a coherent story from the sea of information drawn from many orb fragments. And our striving may have ended long ago when we found coherence in a single intact orb. But a thousand years of divergence does not change the fact that we are all children of the orbs. The time has come to grow up. Together."

"A thousand-year divergence cannot be undone," says Bomechor.

Jaio's father steps forward. "Perhaps it can, Brother Bomechor," he says.

"The message in that single orb is clear: for all we have learned in a thousand years, from hundreds of fragments, the result has not been enough. Our guiding text, the *Companta*, remains incomplete. The Adminithedral remains incomplete. And we, the people of Anthemar, remain incomplete. The opportunity before us here today is nothing less than completion. Through the recognition of our kinship with our Oroken neighbors."

Bomechor's jaw muscles clench, but he holds his tongue.

Jaio's father reaches into his parka pocket and withdraws a black satin pouch nearly the same dimensions as the leather pouch containing Founding Orb.

Jaio glances at Jaspen. *She did it*, he thinks. Somehow, she delivered Anchor's Orb to their father.

"This is another complete orb," he says with a nod to the bag. Then he turns to Jaspen. "A brave

Kestian Ice Watch team, Wolfe's Pride, found it in a cache and at great sacrifice delivered it to me." He offers Jaspen a thankful bow then turns back to the assembled delegates.

"It is the first complete orb any Dictorian has ever held. And in it, the foundation of our order is laid bare. In the spirit of open *convergence*, I offer it to you." He upturns the sack and lets the orb drop into his open palm. In the early afternoon sunlight, the familiar hiss commences.

Jaio glances at Bomechor. The Tributan's seething anger has given way to wide-eyed shock. He, like everyone else but Jaio, has their eyes riveted on the small glassy sphere in Jaio's father's hand.

And into the uncertain silence, Major Anchor says what he has to say.

When the playback finally ends, Jaio's father bags the orb and returns it to his pocket. He lets the crackle of the fire do the speaking for a few moments before adding his own voice.

"The center of the Catalogian world—Anchoresk—is named for Major Anchor. And it stands there," he points at the glass tower, "because that is as far as Anchor's soldiers made it in their efforts to carry out his order and take the orbs to a safe place very far from here. As fate or coincidence would have it, the ending of their journey occurred in the exact place where the long ending of the Ancients began. Older remains discovered during the construction of the Adminithedral told the story."

"A story you are forbidden to share," growls Bomechor.

"*Was* forbidden to share," says his wizened neighbor, a Tributan who looks to be nearly as old as the Ice. "We are all operating under new rules now, Bomechor." The aged monks returns his attention to Jaio's father. "Please, Brother Ario. Continue."

Jaio's father offers the monk a grateful nod. "Some two centuries prior to burial beneath the Ice, an invading army from a nation called Yuësay descended on a sleeping camp of a people known as the Kotasoo.

This name elicits a collective gasp among a handful of Ghosts standing near Aiomida and her crew.

"The ensuing massacre," Jaspen's father goes on, "signaled the end of a long resistance to the invaders once fought all across this land.

"Afterward, citizens of Yuësay poured into the now-uncontested territory unaware of the significance of this act, not just here, but all across the round world; the defeat of the Kotasoo marked the moment when the world as a whole ceased opening before the Ancients and began closing in on them, at an ever more rapid rate.

"In fact, the rate of closure exactly matched the rate of the Ancient's spread for the simple reason that the latter caused the former. Yet, the Ancients were so blinded by their success at spreading, they failed to recognize the contraction it actually represented and where it would inevitably lead; to an inescapable end.

"In the same way the defeat of the Kotasoo symbolizes the beginning of that end, the arrival of that end itself is symbolized by the defeat of Anchor's troops, whether as a result of exhausted fuel or enemy attack or some other obstacle that stranded them here so far from their desired destination.

"Yet, even then, those soldiers did not grasp the magnitude of the change before them. They chose to destroy the orbs rather than risk losing them to their enemy unaware that the real foe they faced, a foe of their own making, cared not at all about orbs, or secrets, or even national identities. The world itself just wanted the abuse at the hands of the Ancients to end. A century-long fever didn't do it, so the world sent the Ice.

"It arrived here shortly after Anchor's troops and covered the remains of their cargo for thousands of years. When the Ice finally receded a millennium ago, the founders of the Order discovered these remains. They learned of the words hidden in the orb fragments and how to focus the sun so they could draw those words out. They built the first Monastery on the site and set about penning the first chapters of the *Companta*.

"The time has come to close the book and I can think of no better story than the story on this orb to serve as the last chapter."

A number of the Tributans mutter and shake their heads. A larger number offer hesitant nods. But the wizened elder beams and claps his hands to his knees.

"Well compiled, Brother Ario," he says. "I second your proposal."

Bomechor turns to glare at the old monk. "It was not a proposal, Brother Cordenelle."

"Then I propose we make it one," says Cordenelle.

"This is not a council of deliberation," says Bomechor.

"What is a bent protocol when so many others with far longer precedent have already been utterly broken this day?" asks Cordenelle. He glances to the other Tributans on both sides of him. "Besides, we all appear to be present."

"But—" Bomechor begins.

"I second," says another Tributan Jaio does not recognize.

Cordenelle's head bobs in a satisfied nod. "See how easy that was. Now, given that Brother Ario cannot preside over his own proposal nomination, that duty falls to you, Brother Bomechor. So, if you please, call for the vote."

Bomechor clenches his jaw and says nothing.

"Very well," says Cordenelle. "I suppose, if I can bend a protocol, so can you. We shall let the matter rest for now."

The circle falls silent.

Jaio's father raises a hand for attention. "I have one other story to share, from an orb fragment with a recording made shortly after the events contained on the Founding Orb."

Sigmos Bomechor stiffens, but he says nothing.

Jaio's father goes on to tell the tale of Doctor Oroken's meeting with the minister and of Hernán Lopez's successful delivery of the message to the other genetic repositories. Jaio wonders what would have become of the world had the animals not been set free and offers the ancient conspirators a silent thanks for their act of moral revolt.

At the conclusion of the tale, Jaio's father proceeds to answer the many questions it has raised. Silence then returns. It lingers for many breaths as the significance of that long ago event sinks in around the circle. The minister's proclamation of the animal release as pointless could not have been more wrong.

Finally, the Kestian Liege, Lady Kest, leans forward on her stool. "Forgive me, Dictorian," she says. "This is all so much to take in, and I may have misheard, but the recordings on the orbs and your concise oration of Anchoresk's sorrowful history suggest that the Ancients recognized the consequences of their actions well before the Ice ended their line. Yet, even as the unmelting snow began to fall, the heroics of Doctor Bel and Hernán were seen as criminal.

"If not for them, the authorities—our counterparts in their time," she casts an intense, almost accusatory, gaze around the circle, "would have erased all other forms of life from this land and forsaken us, their descendants, to an utterly impoverished world."

Rawl clears his throat. "Take it from this old tiger hunter," he says. "We're following the same path, albeit a bit slower. I know because getting old didn't turn me from snowtip's tracks. I quit the hunt for lack of tracks; too much success, you might say. I didn't want to admit it, but the signs, or should I say, the lack of signs, were clear. And it wasn't just the tigers, but wolves, lions, bears, rhinos, woolephants—I've been around long enough to watch all of them go from common to rare. If we're not careful, they'll go from rare to gone."

Lady Kest offers Rawl an affirming nod. "My huntsmen have made similar observations," she says. "The difference is the Ancients were planning a deliberate eradication. For what? A few extra meals before the end? How is it, in the face of such obvious and costly futility that they did not do what we are doing now?"

"We will never know, Lady Kest," says Jaio's father. "But bear in mind, the influence of the relic technology on their lives and on their world eclipsed its influence on ours. The Order's greatest achievements merely serve to remind us of how much more we'd need to learn to even scratch the surface of what they knew. The impending reality of losing nearly all of these achievements may have produced an equally potent sense of denial."

Jaio raises a hand to interject. "Specifically," he says, "they denied the truth of fire itself: to burn hot is to burn fast. And they burned very hot."

"On top that," his father continues, "the Ancient's exceeded us in numbers the way the waters in a lake exceed the runoff in a puddle. Unimaginable as it is now, their society spanned the entire world.

"This last fact alone meant they could not have all come together in one place to hear a message such as Jaio's even if they'd wanted to. There were simply too many of them spread over too vast an area and too ensnared in a trap they mistook for freedom."

"Actually, Dal...Dictorian," says the Jaspen's

mother. "In the Ancient's final decades, the vast majority of them did spend most of their time together in one place, a last refuge called Veyar, said to have been untouched by the troubles that otherwise plagued their world. A single message could have reached them all and they could have come together there as we have here, but for reasons not yet known, they didn't. Instead, they used Veyar as a place of escape while their world crumbled around them. And ultimately, Veyar itself succumbed."

"Where was this Veyar?" asks Lady Kest. "Surely, a place capable of containing so many people at once must have been huge. There have to be ruins. Marks of some kind."

"The Keepers have sought to determine Veyar's location for generations. But so far, of the few cultures known to the Keepers who have references to Veyar, none of those references contain directions."

"Perhaps, Veyar is mythical and did not actually exist," says Lady Kest.

Tandut leaps to his feet from where he sits before the fire. "V'yar does exist," he shouts.

This catches everyone's attention and they all look over at the tense Mesoric boy.

"Before One-eye came," says the boy. "The elders told stories. They called V'yar a paradise where people have many lives. I'm going to find it. I'm going to find V'yar."

"I hope you do," says Jaio's mother.

"I will," says Tandut. He then seems to notice all the eyes on him and quickly sits down.

"But for now," Jaio's mother continues. "We cannot let anything distract us from the task at hand: bringing a new beginning to this place in this time."

Jaio steps into the opening created by these words before his mind can think better of it. The next part of the new beginning fills him with misgivings. But he recognizes the necessity. The foe who has fought for them across the span of a thousand years must be laid fully to rest.

He turns to face his father. "Dictorian Ario," he says. "This I return to you." Jaio reaches into his pocket and pulls out the *Companta*.

Several Tributans gasp and they all look at one another. "The stolen volume," one whispers.

"Taken long ago and brought home," says Jaio's father. He reaches into his own pocket and pulls out the satin bag with Anchor's orb. He offers it to Jaio, but Jaio redirects him to give it to Jaspen.

57

THE NAMELESS HILL

The sudden shift of attention Jaspen's way caused a jolt of nervousness to erupt in her stomach. She looked at Jaio with questioning eyes.

Jaio nodded. "You brought the orb here. I ask you to be its keeper one last time."

Jaspen stepped forward to stand beside her father and nodded. Jaio placed the orb in her hand and left her holding it. He then took into his own hands the leather pouch with the Founding Orb. He stepped to the crackling fire and held it up over the flames. "The guidance of this orb has helped lead us all to the brink. Under its influence, my people committed countless young clan members to the symbolic death of the Ghost and sent them to the Ice to finish out their existence defending their loved ones on the Steppe by any means possible, under penalty of death. In this existence, they took up the weapons of the Ancients and used other relic materials to built monstrous vehicles intended to keep the people of Anthemar at bay. And so we became servants of the Ancients. On behalf of the Oroken, our service to the foe we long thought to be a friend now ends."

Jaspen almost cried out as Jaio's hands came down, lowering the orb toward the fire and its destruction. This, she realized, is what he wanted her and her father to do with the artifacts they held. She didn't think she could.

But then he stepped away and repositioned in front of the fire-ring filled with discarded weapons. He knelt and gently laid the orb pouch on top of the pile then turned to Jaspen's father. The Catalogian Dictorian stepped up beside his son and knelt. He held the *Companta* out before him. "On behalf of the Catalogian Order, our service to the foe we long thought to be a friend now ends." He set the worn, leatherbound volume down beside the orb.

Finally, Jaspen understood the immense duty her brother had just assigned to her. She glanced around the circle at all the different faces of the Anthemari Protectorates. Surely, they would never allow her, a bathhouse dung-gatherer turned Thawrunner on an Ice Watch team in the service of the weakest house, to act as their representative. But as she stepped up beside her father and knelt, nobody tried to stop her.

"On behalf of the Protectorates of Anthemar, our service to the foe we long thought to be a friend now ends," she said and placed Anchor's Orb beside the *Companta* and the Founding Orb, forming a triangle.

Together, Jaio, Jaspen, and their father stood up. Without thinking, Jaspen reached beside her and grasped her father's hand. He then offered his other hand to Jaio. The Ghost Orol took it and the three of them raised their clasped hands high.

"To a new beginning," she shouted.

"A new beginning!" the call went up all around the circle.

Jaspen glanced to her mother who stood with palms clapped together before her tearful, smiling face. Jaspen reached out her stump in invitation. Her mother let out a half-sob and hurried forward to take hold. Their limbs joined and thrust high into the air.

"A new beginning!"

58

THE NAMELESS HILL

The reverie has barely died down before Jaio hears Rawl clear his throat. "This is all well and good," grumbles the old tiger hunter. "But what in snow's name are we supposed to do with this heap of discards?" He jabs a finger at the pile of relics inside the overgrown fire ring. "And for that matter," he turns and jabs again toward Anchoresk and the encircling Ghost fleet, "all those heaps over there?"

"One thing's for sure," says Bengus from the other side of the circle. "The skateships aren't going anywhere. Once they stopped movin', the skates absorbed enough'a the sun's warmth to melt the snow beneath 'em. They're skatin' on rock now."

Jaio glances toward his mother. "Sounds to me like we need the advice of a Keeper," he says.

His mother steps forward. "We start by neutralizing the dangers in this heap," she says.

"Then we head down to begin dealing with the dangers in the valley below.

"Oan, Pren," she says. "Please, collect the orbs and the book and help disarm the weapons."

"Yes, Mediant," they reply as one and move to the pile. Pren pockets the ancient spheres of glass and the text created from what the fragments of other such spheres once contained then she and her partner turn their attention to the guns. Several members of the various delegations join them, all keeping a watchful eye on one another.

"Sometimes," says Oan to the assembled group, "Before you can discard the master's tools, you have to use them to dismantle the master's house." He pulls something from his pocket. His body is in the way so Jaio can't see what it is. "The Ancients called this a screwdriver." He plucks a stuttergun off the pile, deftly relieves it of its ammunition and then sets to work on it with the tool.

Meanwhile, the rest of the delegation parties ready themselves for the descent from the hill and the long hard work ahead.

Jaio's mother turns her attention to him.

"Gilinath would be so proud of you," she says.

"You know my mentor?"

"I knew him. He cared for me when I was a child and my mother was away. Which was most of the time."

"What about your father?" asks Jaio.

"He died hunting pakas when I was very small. In truth, Gilinath was more of a father to me than my blood father. And I remember Gilinath's many lessons; how he found just the one he sought waiting for him in the land. Your use of the fire rings earlier...It reminded me of his method."

"I never imagined I'd have the chance to see him again," says Jaio. "But I think now, we Ghosts can finally go home."

She nods and looks like she wants to say more, but apparently can't find the words. Finally, a tearful smile grows on her face. She reaches into her white fur parka and pulls out what looks like a pale slender stick. Only on second glance does Jaio see the holes bored at even intervals along its length. It looks just like his flute. His eyes widen with surprise.

"This one is from the condor's other wing," she says.

The burst of excitement accompanying this revelation lasts only a moment before turning bittersweet. Jaio extracts the pieces of his flute from his pocket. "I fell on mine."

"No matter, this one is for you too." She offers the flute to him.

"No, it's yours. I—"

"Jaio," she interrupts and holds up her stump.

"I made it not to play, but to hold close to my heart until I could give it to you when next we met. Which is now."

Jaio feels the emotion surge forth and dampen his eyes. He takes the flute. His fingers seem to find the holes on their own and he lifts it to his lips.

He plays the first tune that comes to mind: the dawn song of a cliff wren.

Jaio's father looks over. His nod is slight, but in it, Jaio sees boundless love. Then, without changing expression, Jaio's father turns his attention to Jaio's mother. A quiet laugh escapes her lips. Jaio is sure she sees it to. "I need to go help," she says.

Jaio nods as she turns to walk away. "Thank you." He lifts the flute again and fills the air once more with the call from the dawn-time of a day at the dawn-time of a year. Now, it heralds the dawn-time of an age. How will that age unfold?

Sable steps up beside him. "That's beautiful," she says.

Jaio stops playing, pockets the flute and turns to face her. Words of gratitude and admiration rise in his mind, but when his eyes meet hers, he realizes, this time he needs no words. She already knows.

As if reading his heart, she nods. They wrap their arms around each other and draw close into a long embrace.

THE NAMELESS HILL

No sooner has Jaspen climbed down into the rimrock cleft ahead of Jaio, leaving him alone on the hilltop, then he catches a movement to his right. He whips his gaze that way and finds a lone, gray wolf loping toward him. The moment their eyes meet, the wolf stops.

Time stops as well. Unblinking, unmoving, they hold each other's gaze. Not even the crunch of stones to Jaio's left has the power to break their link. His attention remains fixed on the wolf until several louder crunches carry his way.

He tears his eyes away and slowly rotates his head to peer the opposite direction, toward the sound.

A yellow-eyed tiger comes to a halt not five paces distant.

Wolf forgotten, Jaio tries to calm his pounding heart as he and the tiger face one another.

A sharp yip restores his memory and he spins

his head back toward the wolf. He sees no sign of the large gray animal and doesn't take the time to look further. The tiger again becomes the priority even though he already knows what he'll see.

Nothing.

Breathing hard, Jaio turns and scans the entire summit. All hints of both tiger and wolf are gone.

A rasper finch flits into the heart of a stunted sage bush in front of him. Jaio notices a tuft of brilliant yellow feathers at the crown of the bird's head. The finches of the Steppe have only a narrow streak of white.

The bird lets out a single hoarse call then trills the refrain from the song he played earlier; the perfect imitation of his imitation of a wren.

Jaio pulls out the flute and again puts it to his lips. This time he plays the music of a winter warbler.

The finch rasps again, but instead of repeating the warbler song, it sings a melody Jaio recognizes but, at first, can't place. Only when the finch sings it a second time does he remember where he heard it. The Founding orb. It is the call of a species long gone, its voice come back to fill the air once more.

When the finch calls a third time, it is not the ancient bird song, but a mix of the wren call with the ancient call to create a completely unique melody. Over and over, the finch repeats this new call. Jaio swears the call is louder and is filled with a joyfulness not present in the imitations.

And finally he understands. The rasper is a master at helping fill holes in a world with many holes to fill.

Thus, the world heals.

Jaio's mind replays the events of the day. Maybe, he thinks, we can do it too.

The idea makes him smile.

"Jaio," calls Jaspen. "Are you coming?"

The finch sings the new song again then flits past him over the rim, out of sight.

"On my way." He pockets his flute and follows his sister down from the summit of the Nameless Hill, the place where the Keepers Age began.

ACKNOWLEDGMENTS

I am grateful to the Wordos writing critique group of Eugene; to the Lone Goose writer's workshop, with particular thanks to Gary Gripp, Nedra and Rick Sterry, Sarah Burant, Nowell King, and José Campion-McCarthy; to Rick Reese for helping with the technical aspects of readying the manuscript for publication; and, once again, to Gila and Galen for their invaluable input and support.

ABOUT THE AUTHOR

Tim Fox lives with his family in the western Oregon Cascades. Some of his other fiction and non-fiction writings have been published in the anthologies *Walking on Lava, Forest Under Story*, and in "Dark Mountain" Issues 4, 5, 9, and 11, "Orion" magazine, "Green Spirit" magazine, and on the "Yes!" magazine, and "Mother Pelican Journal" websites. *Legacy of the Orbs* concludes his AFTERLANDS CONVERGENCE trilogy.

Made in the USA
Columbia, SC
10 April 2019